W9-ADC-170

STARLIGHT NIGHTS

FORGE BOOKS BY STACEY KADE

738 Days

Starlight Nights

STARLIGHT NIGHTS

STACEY KADE

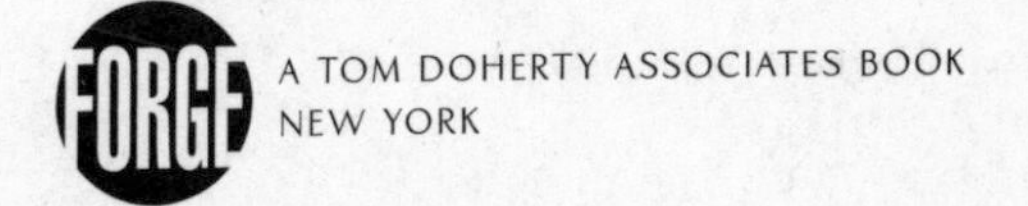

A TOM DOHERTY ASSOCIATES BOOK
NEW YORK

This is a work of fiction. All of the characters, organizations, and events portrayed in this novel are either products of the author's imagination or are used fictitiously.

STARLIGHT NIGHTS

A Forge Book
Published by Tom Doherty Associates
175 Fifth Avenue
New York, NY 10010

www.tor-forge.com

Forge® is a registered trademark of Macmillan Publishing Group, LLC.

Library of Congress Cataloging-in-Publication Data

Names: Kade, Stacey, author.
Title: Starlight nights / Stacey Kade.
Description: First edition. | New York : Forge, 2018. | "A Tom Doherty Associates Book."
Identifiers: LCCN 2017039440 (print) | LCCN 2017045111 (ebook) | ISBN 9781466874145 (ebook) | ISBN 9780765380425 (hardcover) | ISBN 9780765380432 (trade pbk.)
Classification: LCC PS3611.A29 (ebook) | LCC PS3611.A29 S73 2018 (print) | DDC 813/.6—dc23
LC record available at https://lccn.loc.gov/2017039440

Our books may be purchased in bulk for promotional, educational, or business use. Please contact your local bookseller or the Macmillan Corporate and Premium Sales Department at 1-800-221-7945, extension 5442, or by email at MacmillanSpecialMarkets@macmillan.com.

First Edition: January 2018

Printed in the United States of America.

0 9 8 7 6 5 4 3 2 1

One of the hardest lessons in life is learning that just because someone loves you (or says they do) doesn't mean they know what's best for you. Standing up for yourself and taking the risk of finding your own path is sometimes as terrifying as it is exhilarating. Stay strong. This book is for you.

STARLIGHT NIGHTS

PROLOGUE CALISTA

SEVEN YEARS AGO

I'm losing the room.

There's a distinct sensation that accompanies blowing an audition. It feels like something from one of those game shows where the floor starts to drop out from beneath you and you're scrambling to stay on your feet and in the room.

My eyes are firmly shut, but it doesn't matter. After more than ten years in this industry, I can practically feel the linoleum tipping beneath me. In reality, the signs are more subtle: the slight throat clearing, the rustle of fabric as people shift in their seats, the loud clicking as someone texts or responds to an email on their phone. But I can feel their gazes sliding away from me like I'm a particularly gruesome accident on the 405. I'm slowly becoming invisible to them even as I stand at the front of the room.

Breathe. Find the moment. I can easily imagine my mother's exasperated voice in my head, but it's tinged with panic—hers and mine.

It doesn't help that I have a big blond guy attached to my mouth, and I'm as stiff as a wind-dried towel. He was a stranger as of five minutes ago, and he's ten years older than me, twenty-six to my sixteen.

The guy—Tyler, I think—seems to sense the imminent failure, too, because he grips me harder, his fingers digging into my waist, his wet mouth pressing tighter against mine.

I go rigid, and my eyes snap open, giving me a close-up view of his sharply angled cheekbone and one perfectly groomed sideburn.

Beyond that, Eric Stone is watching, smirking.

The son of one of the most famous television producers of all time will be playing my—Skye's—brother, Byron. He's sprawled in a chair, waiting to read with me—assuming I even get that far. And judging by his expression, it's pretty clear he doesn't think that's going to happen.

"Okay, that's great," Drea, the casting director, says with a forced smile in her voice.

Tyler releases me and steps back. It takes every ounce of my willpower not to reach up and wipe my mouth off with the back of my sleeve.

Willpower and the presence of my mom, Lori, near the door, glaring at me in that way she has. It's like target-focused laser beams from the eyes. Her forehead is completely smooth, her mouth curved upward in a slight smile. No one would know how pissed she is—no one except me. Which is exactly the point.

"Okay," Drea says. "That was great, Tyler. Thank you. And Calista—"

"Oh, can we just have a minute?" Lori asks, stepping forward and beaming a smile at Alex, the showrunner. My mom is young and pretty—even for a Hollywood mom—and she knows how to use it. "I think Calista's just a little nervous. She'll do better the next time."

Alex sighs. "Eric. You want to read with her?" he asks, sounding bored and tired, scrubbing his hands over his face as Tyler leaves the room.

My heart sinks.

Lori slips quickly to the front of the room to stand before me, under the pretense of fixing my hair while Drea and Alex whisper with the two unnamed studio execs at the back of the room.

"Look at me, Calista," she says through her perfect white teeth. Caps, all of them. "We need this. You know we need this."

The rent is due.

We need to eat next month.

THIS is your chance at stardom. Sometimes you only get one.

I've heard it all from her over the years.

It's too late, I want to shout. But I just nod, my throat tight.

Then she continues in a louder voice. "I just think you're maybe tensing up too much during the kiss."

Right.

"Remember, passion! And you need to watch his angles and yours, make sure you're not blocking him, but try to make it look natural," she says, as if this is the easiest thing in the world.

She demonstrates then, draping her arm around the neck of an invisible man, tilting her head at an angle, and thrusting her chest in his direction.

"Now you try it." She grabs my hand and lifts it up, curving my hand into place on his "neck."

I feel queasy. I can't do this.

"No," Eric says.

I jolt, jerking my hand away from my mother's.

Behind her, Eric unfolds himself from his chair and strolls toward us, hands shoved in his pockets.

Oh, God. In person, he's more handsome, if that's possible, in a black T-shirt and expensive jeans that are deliberately worn and faded. Tall, with tousled dark curls, tan skin with a smattering of freckles across the bridge of his nose and the tops of his cheeks. I don't know how old he is. He looks closer to my age than Tyler, but still older than me. Adult. Male.

"Excuse me?" Lori says, her smile tightening into more of a snarl.

"That's bad advice," he says. "For her." He nods at me.

"Thank you for your concern," she says. "But I'm not sure your expertise is needed here. She needs more than the right last name to land this."

"Mom," I say sharply.

Eric stiffens, ever so slightly, but shrugs and steps back, his mouth twisting wryly. "Whatever."

Lori rolls her eyes, not discreetly, and then returns her attention to me. "Now, as I was saying—"

"Am I shiny?" I whisper at her. "I feel shiny."

Her eyes focus immediately on my face. "One minute, baby. I'll be right back with the powder."

She heads for her bag near the door.

As soon as she moves away, I edge in Eric's direction.

His gaze flicks toward me.

"I'm sorry. I don't know why she . . ." I shake my head. She worships the ground Rawley Stone, Eric's father, walks on, but for some reason, Eric is not in that same category. He's the mud beneath said holy ground and therefore beneath her attention.

"I saw you in *Seven Sins*," I add. "It was good." Demons representing the seven deadly sins possess teens with the intent of corrupting the last pure soul in town. Eric played Lust. And, uh, yeah, if I'd been the last pure soul, the hope for all mankind would have been lost.

He snorts. "No, it wasn't."

"Okay, it wasn't, but you were," I say, flushing. Then I glance back over my shoulder to see Lori still digging in her huge bag. "What's your advice? I . . . need this."

"Do you?" he asks.

I open my mouth to answer.

"Or does your mom?" he asks, his voice hardening.

"Is there a difference?" I ask helplessly. It's gotten better since my mom married Wade, my stepdad, but my career is still the primary source of income for all of us.

"Calista, I have your powder," Lori says, glaring at Eric as she returns, stepping between us as if he isn't even there.

He raises an eyebrow at her, his jaw tight, and I'm expecting him to turn and walk away. Instead, he steps around her and takes my wrist. "Excuse us," he says with a smirk that dares her to protest, as he tugs me away.

"Calista!"

"One second, Mo . . . Lori." She doesn't like it when I call her Mom in front of industry people.

He leads me to the opposite corner of the room. When I glance over my shoulder, my mother is staring, her mouth agape.

His dark-eyed gaze fixes on me as if I'm the only person in the room, and the attention makes my knees go wobbly. "This your first time?" he asks.

I blink at him. "Auditioning? Uh, no, I mean, I've been—"

"With a kissing scene," he clarifies. Then he cocks his head to the side. "Or your first kiss, in general?"

Whatever he sees in my expression—mute horror, perhaps at being discovered as the only sixteen-year-old who hasn't been kissed other than a peck on the mouth for a scene when I was twelve—must confirm his suspicion because then he nods. "Thought so."

Betrayal and humiliation wash over me in a fiery wave, and I pull my hand free of his. "I don't need you to make fun—"

"I'm not," he says. "I'm trying to understand. It makes sense." His tone goes flat with distaste, his focus shifting to someone behind me. My mom, most likely.

I face Eric. "Is it . . . it's that obvious? I mean, the haven't-been-kissed . . . thing," I stutter out.

He ignores me. "Forget her bullshit. It's not about the camera angles. You can tweak that stuff later. You have to make them," he jerks his head in the direction of Drea, Alex and the execs, "feel something. That's the most important part."

I nod. I know this already; the problem is, I don't know how to *do* that.

"You're trying to show them passion, but that's not it," he says.

"It says 'passionately' right on the page in the—"

"Fear. You should try fear."

I narrow my eyes at him. I've heard of actors sabotaging one another with deliberately shitty suggestions, but that's usually when they're competing for the same part.

He makes an impatient noise. "Not like 'there's a shark in the water and it's coming this way.' Fear of losing, fear of being hurt. Anytime you feel that much, it's a risk. And Skye knows it can't work between her and Brody. He's immortal and her guardian angel. There's no happily-ever-after for these two."

I want to protest—love conquers all (or ratings do, and if viewers want Skye and Brody together, the writers will find a way)—but Eric's right. From Skye's perspective, any kind of future together would seem impossible. Forbidden, even.

"But then there's also the risk that you won't feel that way again, with anyone else, for the rest of your life. Is it better to take the chance and know there will be pain, or to miss out on something life-changing? To live a small, safe life so you don't get hurt? It's a choice, but there's fear on both sides. Make them see that, make them *feel* it," he says fiercely.

I blink up at him.

"Got it?" he asks, straightening up slightly, seeming to recover himself.

I don't have words, or I can't speak them over the lump in my throat, so I bob my head at him.

"We're ready," Eric calls to the others. Then he leads me back in front of the chairs, waiting with barely disguised impatience for my mother to step out of the way.

"We're going to run the Brody/Skye scene instead," he says to Alex, calmly and with such confidence you'd think he was the one in charge.

I freeze, waiting for the protest. Eric is already cast as Skye's brother. What Eric's proposing makes no sense . . . except to help me redeem myself.

But Alex just waves his hand in a gesture of acceptance. Clearly he's already made up his mind about me, so it doesn't matter what scene we do. "All right, let's go," Alex says as soon as we're in position.

"It's too dangerous, Skye. I won't let you," Eric-as-Brody says quietly, but his fear and anger are simmering just beneath the surface. It's a more subtle performance, unlike Tyler's—he insisted on yelling the lines because he was ANGRY.

I fold my arms across my chest, cocking an eyebrow at him. "Funny, I thought your boss was kind of big on the whole 'free will' thing." But it's a front, bravado. I want him to stop me—because it means he cares—as much as I need him to let me go. I squeeze my arms tight around myself, indicating that vulnerability and that desire—oh, God, that desire—for him to touch me, to pull me close. To keep me with him.

"You're too important to the world," Brody says, but he can't meet my eyes, his gaze focused on the ground.

"Maybe I don't care about the world," I say, a tremor in my voice.

The muscles in the back of his jaw jump. He knows exactly what Skye is doing.

"You're too important to me," he says finally. "Is that what you want to hear?"

I edge closer. "Only if it's true," I whisper, my chest aching with longing. I want him. But I want him to want me, too. Not as Skye Danvers, future savior of the world, but as Skye Danvers, a girl in love with someone she can't have. Someone she'll never have.

He looks up at me then, and all that pain and frustration is mixed with love and desire, a roiling sea of torment in his gaze.

I close the distance between us, rising on my tiptoes to wrap my arms around his neck.

He shakes his head, those soft curls brushing my cheek. "I can't." His struggle within himself, between right and wrong, duty and destiny, love and honor, is plain on his face, but his arms slide around me, steadying me.

The scene calls for him to lean down and kiss me anyway. But following the emotion of the scene, the current of energy that is making this moment hum, I make a change.

I am Skye, deciding which kind of fear I can live with.

"I can," I say. I tip my head to the side and lean in.

Eric's breath flutters against my cheek, and I feel the jolt of surprise run through him the second our lips touch. After a second, his hands tighten on my waist, then his mouth moves over mine, taking the lead, and it feels good to surrender control.

My eyes automatically shut, and my hands slide up past the warm skin at the back of his neck to tangle in his hair. When his tongue touches mine, so briefly I might have imagined it, it sets off a spark of heat low in my belly.

I press myself against him until there's no room between us. *This.* This is what it's supposed to feel like.

"Wow."

"Holy shit."

Those two muttered exclamations are enough to break the moment.

My head spinning, I lower myself from my tiptoes. Eric pulls away slightly, not enough that it feels like a rejection exactly. But a definite ending.

"Good enough?" he asks the room, as if nothing has happened.

Blushing, I remove myself from him, taking a step back. I feel the loss of his closeness immediately, and it strikes with unexpected fierceness. *What is wrong with me?* He was acting. It was just a scene.

"Drea, we need to see some more Brodys," Alex says, sounding stunned. "Do a fresh call. Because I think we've found our Skye."

His words electrify me. I'm hired? I got the job? As in, potentially steady work that could last months or even years without the stress of auditioning?

The thought makes me dizzy.

As if in answer to my silent questions, the room bursts into spontaneous applause, none louder or more enthusiastic than that from my mother. But she stays back in her corner. I'm pretty sure Eric's responsible for that, too.

"Thank you," I say to Eric, hearing the wonder in my voice. It's hard not to reach out, to touch his arm or squeeze his hand.

He shakes his head. "Don't thank me. That was all you."

"No, I—"

"Welcome to *Starlight,* kid," he says with a smile. Then, with his hands stuffed in his pockets again, he ambles back toward his chair. The only sign of our interaction is a faint flush in his cheeks.

I'd never understood why people called it "falling" in love. You either love someone or you don't, like an on/off switch. End of story.

But in that second, I get it. Because suddenly it's not the floor tilting anymore, it's my whole world. And I'm sliding helplessly toward feelings that are way bigger than I am.

1 CALISTA BECKETT

"Come on, Tamara, it's supposed to be the biggest party on campus this semester," Ginny says, her voice muffled through the twisted layers of scarf.

A step behind Ginny and Tamara, I brace myself, my stomach clenching in anticipation. It's coming. I can feel it, the impending awkwardness rising like a monster out of the ocean in one of those old cheesy horror movies.

Not that there's anything resembling an ocean anywhere near here.

Tamara shakes her head. "This is the one with all the black lights, right? Where they hand out T-shirts and highlighters?" she asks, sounding skeptical.

Good, maybe she'll be able to redirect the conversation.

I tuck my freezing hands deeper into my coat pockets. I can never seem to get warm here. Then again, that might be because the temperature has actually fallen below zero—what *is* that? How can it be a temperature that doesn't even exist on a thermometer?—and we're shuffling to our dorms on a small cleared path between three-foot-tall drifts of snow. The Midwest in winter. Forget flames and perpetual sweatiness and thirst—hell is your nose being so cold you can't tell if it's leaking a river of snot again. So sexy.

I sniffle, just in case.

Plus, the cold makes the perpetual dull ache in my arm sharpen to a knifepoint, which scares me, even now. *You can make it go away,* the perpetual refrain in my head whispers. *It won't be like last time.*

I ignore it and refocus my attention on the conversation.

"Yep, that's the one." Ginny bobs her head eagerly. "Tonight. At the Beta house."

"I don't know. It sounds like an opportunity for strangers to touch you under the pretext of 'writing' something," Tamara says.

Ginny laughs, and the sound is clear and crisp in the cold air. "Exactly."

The silence holds for a moment too long.

And here it comes . . .

Ginny turns partially. "You should, um, come, too, Calista."

The invitation is weak, flat, like a child's depiction of a sun in the corner of a drawing instead of the real thing. But it's progress.

I make myself smile. "Sounds great!"

Ooooh, too chirpy. I flinch inwardly. They're going to think I'm being sarcastic. Calista Beckett, former TV star, a *Maxim* It Girl four years ago, too cool for a college fraternity party.

And from sudden tension in the air, and the way Ginny and Tamara are studiously avoiding looking at each other or me, I'm right. I've already got so much working against me, I have to try to fix it.

"So, if they give you a shirt to wear, what do you wear down to the house?" I attempt to sound genuinely enthusiastic. Which is hard, because I'm not. But I should be, as this is my life now. Calista, the regular person. And I *want* to care.

At twenty-three, I'm the oldest freshman at Blake College—one of the oldest students on campus, actually—and I've got three and a half more years here. I need to blend in and make this work. Because beyond this, no matter what my mother is hoping, I have countless years of Calista, average citizen and possible bookkeeper (or maybe accountant), and I need to find a way to make friends and enjoy my new life.

You'd think that being connected to a former hit show like *Starlight* would help here, but it's the exact opposite. The guys are only interested in the stuff I'm rumored to have done (and with who). The truth would make them keel over . . . with boredom. I was a working child actor with my mom as my manager for the first eighteen years of my life. Please. Prisoners have more freedom than I did.

And my "bad girl" phase was very dramatic, yes, but ultimately had more to do with naïveté and stupid choices than raunchy sex with anything that moved.

The girls, from what I've overheard from whispers in the bathroom—really, ladies, remember to check the stalls first—are less than thrilled to be competing with me, whether it's for hot water in the morning or for the attention of the handful of guys on this tiny campus who aren't complete assholes.

But the truth is, it's not a competition. I'm just trying to fit in.

"I think most people wear a cami or tank top under their coat," Ginny says to me quietly, her enthusiasm for the party dimmed. Or maybe it's just her enthusiasm for me coming along.

Crap. I bite my lip, then immediately regret it when the cold sizzles up the nerve endings in my teeth.

After most of a semester, Ginny and Tamara are, sadly, the closest things I have to friends at Blake; our bond is based mostly on shared proximity and the fact that we have freshman core classes together. I'm really terrible at this—making friends. I never went to a real school. Years of homeschooling followed by on-set tutoring have made me absolutely wretched at relating to my peers. I didn't suffer through gym, work on group projects, or go to prom or on group dates to the mall—I was working.

"Maybe we'll see you tonight, then," Ginny says with a vague nod and smile, as she and Tamara take the split in the sidewalk toward their room in Henderson Hall.

Tamara waves, then the two of them continue on, heads together, talking quietly.

Damnit. Even I—without the aid of regular school and the shared experiences of it—recognize a polite blow-off.

Tears of exhaustion sting my eyes, but I blink rapidly to keep them from falling. I don't want them to freeze to my face.

Tucking my head down, I tromp the rest of the way to Ryland Hall, my dorm.

There's always next weekend. Well, after break. We're off for two weeks for Thanksgiving, starting on Saturday. I'm not going anywhere, but maybe when everyone else comes back and sees that I'm still here, something will have shifted. Maybe then I'll belong, and it'll be better.

I'm halfway up the steps to the main entrance before I notice the guy leaning lazily against the brick wall to the right, an unlit cigarette between his bare fingers.

He most definitely does not belong here in Blake, Indiana.

Eric.

The sight of him hits just as hard as always, stealing my breath.

He's wearing faded jeans and a dark blue peacoat, heavy and warm-looking. It makes his shoulders look even broader and sets off his dark eyes and dark curly hair, which is currently being tousled by the wind. His mother, an Australian model who was married to his father for about five seconds in the nineties, is half-English and half-Filipino. Eric looks like her and is 100-percent gorgeous. Straight nose, to-die-for cheekbones and a dimple in his chin. Seriously.

"Hey, kid." He pushes off the wall to stand up straight.

"You can't smoke here." I jerk my chin toward the NO SMOKING sign on the wall next to him.

I'm twenty-three, three years older than he was when we first met. But to Eric, I would always be sixteen.

He glances at the wall. "I'm not smoking," he says. "I quit. I'm just holding it. That would be a different sign entirely." He tucks the cigarette into his coat pocket and smiles tentatively at me. And my stupid heart, which should know better, works itself into a frenzy in my chest.

I make myself walk past him to the door, holding my breath because I'm afraid that if I catch that unique combination of scents that is Eric—new clothing, expensive cologne and just *him*—I'll bury my face in his collar, against his skin, and demand to know why he couldn't just love me back.

Oh, God.

My hands tremble as I hold my ID against the security square thing and yank open the door.

"Hey, come on, Callie, I just want to talk." He follows me inside, sounding unhurried and unconcerned.

Classic Eric. Nothing bothers him. Certainly not me. No, that would require caring.

I move faster, with every intention of getting to the elevator and to my room before he can catch up.

But as soon as I pass the visitor check-in area, I'm caught. Just not by Eric.

"Skye!" Beth blurts, standing up from her post behind the desk as soon as she sees me.

I pause and turn toward the desk, trying to force my features into something resembling pleasantness. "Hi, Beth."

Beth is one of my floormates and very nice, one of the few people on campus to always greet me enthusiastically. But she's not really helping with my transition to normal life. She keeps accidentally calling me Skye, my *Starlight* character's name. And she has a giant poster of Season Two, featuring my huge face, dominating the wall of her room. Eric and Chase are in the background, one over each shoulder, like a devil and an angel. How appropriate.

Beth blushes. "Sorry, I meant Calista." She offers me a shy

apologetic smile. "I was just excited. Someone said that there's a guy outside who looks like . . ." Her gaze catches on Eric behind me, and her mouth falls open.

"Skyron," she whispers.

I squeeze my eyes shut. I should have known. The most devoted *Starlight* fans are usually also Skyron believers. Byron, Eric's character, was Skye's *brother* on the show. But a large—and vocal—contingent of fans saw something different. Particularly when the storyline about Skye being adopted came up at the end of Season One. Hence, Skyron: Skye/Byron.

But it wasn't just fans' overactive imaginations. Our directors were always yelling at us: *Goddamnit, Callie, he's supposed to be your brother. Stop smoldering at him. Eric, brothers don't touch sisters that frequently. We're not making* Flowers in the Attic, *people.*

The ever illusive "chemistry." Eric and I had it. But, as it turned out, that's all we had, no matter how desperately I once wished for more.

"Skyron," Eric repeats with a smile in his voice. He was always good with the fans, better than Chase and me. The attention made Chase uncomfortable, and I never knew what to say.

But Eric was born for it.

He brushes past me, in a way that has to be deliberate, and it sends electricity through my veins.

"You're a Starlighter?" Eric asks.

I open my eyes in time to see Beth, her cheeks hectic with color, nod.

"It's nice to meet you. We couldn't have done it without you guys," he says, holding his hand out for her to shake.

Beth, in turn, is staring at his hand, as if touching him and having him touch her in return will be a life-altering experience, one she wants so much it scares her a little.

I wish I could say I didn't understand that feeling.

She takes his hand and shakes it, a nervous giggle escaping at the same time. "What are you doing here?" she breathes.

"Just leaving," I say for Eric.

But he speaks over me. "Came to talk to Skye. Like a good big brother should." He winks at Beth, and she gasps.

I groan inwardly. So much for building a normal life here; Eric is taking that down, brick by brick. And I don't have that many bricks to begin with.

"Is it okay if I . . ." Beth holds up her phone. "Just one picture . . ."

I'm stepping forward with my hand out to take the phone and snap the picture of the two of them for her, anything to get this over with and Eric on his way, when she pulls back.

"Oh, no," she says. "Of you two together." She beams at us.

"No," I say immediately. It'll hit the Skyron blogs—there are still a surprising number of them, thanks to the show's new life streaming online—and then once it's on social media, it won't be long before it spreads to campus.

"Of course," Eric says at the same time, easily, as if nothing about it troubles him. Because it probably doesn't.

I glare at him, but he shrugs, telling me in not-so-many words that I'm taking myself too seriously again. But he doesn't understand what's at stake for me here.

I open my mouth to say no again, but then I catch Beth watching both of us with a hopeful expression, her hand clutched tight around her phone. Nice Beth who waves me over in the cafeteria and makes everyone shove down a seat so I won't eat alone. I can't be the bitch who crushes her dream.

"Okay," I say, swallowing a sigh.

Eric steps up next to me, sliding his arm around my waist and pulling me tight against his side. Air whooshes from my puffy down-filled coat as a result, and that should be enough to break the moment, but it's not.

His grip on my hip is firm and familiar enough, even through multiple layers, that for a moment it makes me want to cry for everything that's been lost. Though, is it truly lost if I never had it to begin with?

But then Eric turns his face toward mine and his nose, still a little cold from outside, nudges my cheek. "Smile, kid," he murmurs.

My breath catches, and I'm stuck between the messy clutch of lust and longing and pure, unadulterated fury.

As soon as Beth's phone makes the artificial shutter-click noise, I yank away from him, though his hand trails along my waist like he's reluctant to let go. But I'm not falling for that again.

"Can we talk for a second?" I ask Eric, through clenched teeth in an expression that might resemble a demented smile if one squints. "Just over there." I jerk my head toward the empty lounge area just past the check-in desk. I'm not letting him in my room. He's not a danger to my body as much as to my peace of mind, which is precarious enough as it is, thanks.

Eric bobs his head agreeably and holds his arm out in a lead-the-way gesture.

Beth claps her hands in delight.

It takes every bit of effort I have to walk instead of stomp the twenty feet past the desk and around the couches to the center of the lounge. I spin to face him as soon as I'm there.

Eric strolls after me leisurely, his hands stuffed deep in his coat pockets.

"Why are you here?" I demand when he finally reaches me.

"I told you, I came to talk to you." He towers over me, his dark-eyed gaze searching my face as if he's cataloguing the differences since we were last in the same room. There are plenty. Young and famous in Hollywood is a perishable commodity. I'm neither one anymore. I hate thinking about the new flaws he's seeing—I'm not even wearing basic makeup, which means I'm pale and colorless, and my blond hair is stuffed under a knit hat.

I fold my arms over my chest like I need to protect myself. Like that will work. "About something that couldn't be handled with a text?" I ask. The last time I had contact with Eric—You ok?—I was lying in a hospital bed, recovering from the first surgery on my arm. Three years ago.

To his credit, Eric flinches and drops his gaze to the ground somewhere near his feet. "I am . . . sorry about that. I just wasn't sure you'd want to see me. After." He clears his throat and raises his eyes to mine.

After the car accident that shattered my arm, which wasn't even the worst thing that happened that night?

"Yeah," is all I say. "It's fine. It was a lifetime ago. I don't even really remember anymore." My cheeks turn to flame with the lie.

His brows draw together. "Callie," he says, shaking his head. And I'm not sure if the softness in his voice is sympathy for what happened or pity because I'm pretending not to remember.

Either way, it's humiliating.

Suddenly, I'm tired of this conversation, of him, of this whole tangled history between us that has done nothing but hurt me.

"What do you want?" I ask sharply.

He takes a deep breath and scrubs his hands over his face. If I didn't know better, I would say he was nervous.

But Eric Stone, son of the famous producer Rawley Stone, doesn't get nervous. That would involve giving a shit about someone or something other than his next good time.

"I started my own company," he admits in a rush of words.

"Your own . . . production company?" Honestly, knowing Eric, it could have just as easily been a falafel import/export business, if that amused him. His father could line the ocean floor with money and still have some left over.

Eric nods, looking uncertain, a smile pulling at his mouth. "Yeah."

"Okay," I say slowly. "But I thought you said you never wanted to do that." I've forgotten how many deep 2 or 3 A.M. conversations we had between takes or while we waited for the crew to set up a shot. But I knew once, to the exact number. At sixteen and seventeen, I thought it was proof of something.

Now I know better. At that time of night—or morning—everyone is tired, and the cover of darkness makes you feel closer to those you're with, like it's safe to be vulnerable.

It isn't.

Eric's expression tightens. "I don't want to be my father. But this is different. We're starting off small. A web series." Enthusiasm warms his voice.

"Congratulations," I say, trying to ignore the faint grind of envy coming from somewhere deep within me. A long time ago, I used to love what I did. Telling stories, helping transport people out of this world and into another one that hundreds of us worked together to create.

"I got it," he says, watching me expectantly. "Bought the rights."

I stare at him blankly. "Bought the rights to . . ." Then it clicks, and my heart sinks. "*Fly Girl.* Are you serious?"

I've read that book a dozen times. It's old, but it's still my favorite. I was sixteen when I found it—the antithesis of every superhero story blowing up the screen at the time. It's about a girl born with superpowers. She resents the gift and the accompanying responsibility until she loses her abilities. Then she has to figure out her new purpose in life and who loves her for who she is versus what she could (once) do.

There are no big fight scenes, no big set pieces. It broke no best-selling records, and hardly anyone else has heard of it. But it was the first book I ever read that made me feel less alone. It was like someone had taken my soul and captured it in paper and ink. I wanted to climb inside that book and stay there. I even made Eric read it, back when we were friends. Once, during a particularly long night on set, I went through my copy of the book and marked it up with the lines and scenes I would translate to screen.

"Yep." Eric grins at me.

I want to throw up.

Am I being punished for something I don't know about? Because it sure feels like it. My nightmare scenario: my former crush showing up three years after he demolished my hopes and my self-confidence to tell me that he's bought the rights to a project I used to dream about taking on myself.

I force myself to smile. "That's fantastic." And it is. That book deserves the attention, and the additional readers, that a different medium will bring to it. Assuming Eric can keep up this new responsible-citizen act, anyway. I always thought he was capable, brilliant even, just not interested. Apparently I was wrong. "Really, congratulations!"

His mouth quirks in a knowing smile, as if he can see right through my fakeness. "I want you to play Evie," he says gently, as if breaking bad news to me.

My mouth falls open, and in spite of my best efforts, I feel interest unfurling in me, like a petal loosening on a tightly wrapped bud.

But I shake my head. "No, no way."

"It's two weeks' worth of work for the first six episodes. I know you have a break coming up and—"

"I'm done. I'm retired."

His mouth twists in disgust as he looks around the lounge, taking in the dinged-up walls and the faded furniture painted in the dull gray light of a winter afternoon. "No, you're hiding."

I ignore the automatic stab of fear that he might be right. Eric does that, makes me doubt myself. All the more reason to stay away. "This is my life now," I say through gritted teeth. "Find someone else."

"No," he says. "You're perfect for Evie, and you know it. Plus . . ." He glances back at the desk where Beth is pretending not to watch us.

Then it makes sense. "Plus, you're going to capitalize on an existing fan base," I say faintly. Of course. Especially if he's playing the role of Cory, the love interest/villain. The Skyron legion will turn out in droves for that.

So it has way less to do with me being perfect for the role and more to do with funneling Skyron fans to the new series.

Hurt throbs in my chest for exactly three seconds before I shut it down. This is exactly why I left acting and want to stay gone. Too many people presenting false faces to the world.

"Go home, Eric. Leave me alone. This is my life now." I push past him, leaving the lounge.

"Not according to your mother," he calls after me.

I laugh and keep walking. "Like you agree with anything my mother says." Half the time—or more—I'm not sure I do either. My mom dreamed of becoming a movie star—not an actress, a star. And when I was born, that became her dream for me. Whether or not that was a realistic goal.

After everything that happened—the show being canceled, the accident, my drug arrest—she enacted her version of the "Natalie Portman/Emma Watson plan." (Never mind the fact that they're both A-List movie stars who didn't *need* an image revamp, just some distance from their most famous roles.)

According to Lori, I wasn't getting jobs because I was overexposed (thanks to all my legal trouble) and pigeonholed as "Skye." Going to college would show my newfound maturity and stability. And going to college somewhere absolutely no one gave a crap about, a place no paps would follow, would ensure that I would have a chance to make a "grand reentrance." So tiny little Blake college, in my mother's home state of Indiana, would become both my hideout and the stage for my eventual reemergence from the ashes.

Officially, I'm taking a hiatus from my acting career to focus on my education. In reality, my mom's hoping the time and distance will help people see me differently, as someone other than *Starlight* Skye or the troubled actress ordered back into her parent's custody. And then the good parts will start rolling in again.

"Lori is going to need money," Eric says. "And soon. It's been, what, almost four years since you last pulled a salary?"

I freeze.

"You've got residuals, but she's got a husband and three other kids to support. And you're her meal ticket. You know it, and I know it."

Eric hasn't forgotten our late-night conversations either. I spin around to face him. "So what?"

But he seems undisturbed. "So, the next thing you know, she'll be signing you up to audition for a local car dealership commercial or one of those TV movies where you get eaten by an ant-octopus-shark creature in the second act. All for her percentage."

He's right, as much as I'd like to pretend otherwise. But I've been hoping that I can hold her off long enough to graduate from Blake and that, by then, I'll have found another career that I love, and she'll be forced to recognize that Hollywood is not the—

A sickening realization dawns. "Wait, you talked to my mother?" I ask, barely able to force the words out.

For the first time, Eric looks ashamed, his gaze bouncing away from mine, patches of color appearing on his cheeks.

But then he lifts his head and gives me the cocky smile that used to make my heart beat just a little faster. Only this time it's tinged with sadness. "Money talks, and your mom is fluent, kid."

On cue, the phone in my pocket begins to buzz in the rhythm I have set for my mom. Three short, three long, three short. Like SOS. Only I'm not sure who the cry for help is really for.

Tears burn my eyes. "I hate you," I say to Eric, my voice shaking, as I pull the phone out of my pocket.

He takes a deep breath and nods. "I know."

2

ERIC STONE

With a deliberateness so sharp that it cuts, Callie turns her back on me and moves to the far corner of the room, speaking quietly to her mother.

I should have expected it. And I did, sort of.

The pain, though . . . *that* catches me by surprise. I thought we were past that, the way we used to hurt each other, all of our sharp edges and weak spots revealed.

She's never looked at me like that, though. Not even that night.

Callie's face, pale in the sliver of light from the doorway, her hand flying up to cover her mouth in surprise. Her eyes instantly bright with tears.

Fuck.

I shake the mental image away. None of that matters anymore, anyway. We were just stupid kids then. This is business.

Even from ten feet away, I can hear the sharp tones of Lori Beckett coming through the phone, in direct contrast to the soothing—placating—voice of her oldest daughter.

I grimace. Lori Beckett deserves to be dropped on the nearest freighter heading out to sea, preferably one with a hole in the hull. But she is, unfortunately, the key to what I need, the key to Calista.

Always be ready to do whatever it takes. One of the first lessons Rawley imparted when he was in a rare "dad" mode. Or at least, one of the first that stuck.

Even if it means taking a plane and then a rented limo to the middle of fucking nowhere. Blake, Indiana is like the set of another shitty remake of *Children of the Corn*. The sheer number of cornfields I had to pass by to get here was enough to give me visions of bloodied scythes, too much flannel and pale children in those broad-brimmed hats.

Stuffing my hands in my pockets, I take another look around, absorbing the small and worn lobby of the building Calista calls home. It's old and dim thanks to the lack of direct sunlight. Even the furniture looks tired and beat up, like it's inches from giving up. The curtains are sagging off their rods, and the television is an old plasma one with huge gaps of blackened pixels.

Fucking depressing.

Calista doesn't belong here. College is one thing—not my thing, though I could see it being Callie's—but this place? No. There are better schools in better locations. Locations that get more than six minutes of sunshine per day.

Isolating herself here makes no sense. Everyone makes mistakes, especially in Hollywood. And Calista's mistakes weren't entirely hers anyway; they were mine. I messed up—multiple times in one evening—and the fallout from that is what cost her.

Callie's voice rises. "Isn't that my decision?" she demands, and I look over at her.

In spite of her words, her shoulders are slumped. She looks so pale and small and defeated. Side effects of dealing with Lori.

It's hard not to cross the room, yank the phone from Callie's hand, and end the call for her, as I would have years ago, without even thinking twice. Now, though, I know she won't let me, even if she is miserable.

I saw her earlier, trudging with her head down, before she saw me. I don't know what those girls said to her to make her look that way, but it was enough to make me want to go over and drag them back to apologize. Calista is too nice to call them on it, but I'm not.

"Hey."

I turn to see the girl at the desk—Beth, that's her name—leaning forward, fidgeting with the pen on a chain. Then she waves me over, a quick furtive gesture.

Oh, why not. I can use all the allies I can get.

"Hey, Beth," I say, making my way to her desk.

"Hey, hi," she says with a nervous laugh, blushing. "You remembered my name."

"Of course." I smile at her. It's one of the easiest things to do, just to use people's names. Gives them a personal moment and earns you more dedication than the simple gesture deserves, honestly. But people are inherently narcissists, right? Who doesn't love hearing their name, let alone on the lips of someone they admire or find attractive?

Katie hates it when I say stuff like that, says it's manipulative and wrong. I say it's just basic psychology. Also, let's face it, not exactly Boy Scout material over here.

"So . . . I didn't mean to eavesdrop." Beth's cheeks color further, giving away her lie. "But are you and Calista really starting a new show?"

"Yeah," I say, with the by-now-familiar quiver of restrained panic every time I respond with a definitive answer instead of a casual shrug or a mysterious smile. Who knew that actually committing to something you love was so fucking terrifying?

"Oh," Beth says.

I raise my eyebrows.

"No, no," she says hastily. "I mean, I'm excited, Skyron on our screens again. That would be *amazing*." Her face beams pleasure at the idea. But it falters after a second. "It's just that, you know, I've gotten a chance to know Sk—Calista here, and I don't know if, well, will she be coming back here? After, I mean?"

"She will be free to do that if she wants to," I say evenly. Not that she'll want to. This show is going to be a success—it *has* to be—and then she'll have her comeback that she should never have needed in the first place. She'll be praised for her bravery in going indie and web instead of groveling in the dirt for another shitty TV role, and then she'll have the opportunities she wants without her mother breathing down her neck. All those people talking about the *Starlight* Curse—idiots, mostly gossip bloggers, who claim to see a pattern in the troubles our admittedly strife-ridden cast has dealt with in the years since the show ended—will have to shut up. And everyone who has doubted me or whispered about me being useless—or shouted about it, in the case of my father—can go fuck themselves.

"She's been trying really hard," Beth says in a loud whisper with a cautious look toward Calista, pacing in the far corner. "And I think it's finally getting better is all."

I frown at her. "I don't understand."

"If she does another show and comes back here, I think it'll start over again," she says, biting her lip. Her Skyron-anticipating glow has vanished, and her forehead is creased with worry. Genuine worry.

My gut clenches tight. "Beth. What will start over again?" I'm surprised to hear my father's voice—terse, pissed—coming out of my mouth.

She starts to speak, but her gaze darts past me and she clamps her lips shut.

"You gave my mother money," Calista says behind me, rage and weariness competing for dominance.

I turn to face her. The bright spots of color in her cheeks are an ugly red in her unnaturally pale complexion. "Cal, I—"

"I'm trying to get her to realize that my acting career is over, and you gave her money." Rage is definitely winning out; her voice is trembling with it. Her hands are clenched into fists at her sides.

I hold my palms up in surrender. "Just her percentage. And she's not allowed on set unless you directly invite her." Which is a better situation than she ever had on *Starlight.*

"Fuck you, Eric," she says through clenched teeth.

Beth sucks in a breath.

"Do you think that matters?" Callie demands. "Do you think any of that will stop her?"

"Callie," I say. "I'm trying to make up for my mistakes. To fix what I broke."

Her hand automatically flies to her arm, near her shoulder.

I'm the one who flinches, though. "You shouldn't be here," I say in a softer voice. "It's my fault."

"Being here is my choice. *Mine,* Eric. One of the few choices I've ever gotten to make."

"No," I say, my temper finally flaring. "It was your mother's, like always." Lori might be her worst enemy, but Callie's the one who lets her get away with it.

Calista steps back as though I've lunged at her, her throat working hard like she's trying not to cry. Or scream.

"And you're going along with it because . . . honestly, I don't know why." I rake my hands through my hair. "Because you think you did something wrong? Because you're punishing yourself for some reason I don't even understand? So many people have messed up way worse than—"

"Not everything has to make sense to you," she says in a cold voice. "You're not my boss or my boyfriend. Or my friend."

Beth gives a slight squeak of distress.

"I'm trying to help, Calista." And I am. Does it not count if I'm helping both of us at the same time?

She folds her arms across her chest, the nylon of her coat hissing with the motion. "So you're doing me a favor. And it just happens to be at the same time you need something from me."

She was always—and still is—one step ahead of me.

I make a frustrated noise, shaking my head. "Yeah, okay, fine, you got me. I need you." My voice comes out rougher than I mean it to, and emotion flickers in her eyes.

It sends a tiny spiral of panic through me; this conversation is getting way too heavy. I can't . . . I'm not . . .

"You know me. Never one to miss a good opportunity. I help you, you help me," I say with a grin, trying to redirect and charm her into relenting. It used to work that way. "Hard to pass up a two-for-one deal."

As soon as the words leave my mouth, I wish I could yank them back.

She sucks in a sharp breath, then her mouth flattens into a humorless smile. "Yeah, I'm familiar with your fondness for that principle."

Damnit, I knew she remembered that night.

Shifting uncomfortably, I pat my pockets out of habit, feeling for my lighter and the pack of cigarettes I no longer carry. Shit.

"Calista, I've said I'm sorry," I begin.

"No, actually, you haven't. Not for that, not once."

Okay. I grit my teeth. "Callie, I'm sorry for how I handled that night. That was wrong, but it really was for the—"

"If you're really sorry, then call my mother and tell her you've changed your mind," Calista says, tipping her chin up in defiance.

"You don't belong here," I argue.

"That's not up to you," she says. "Call my mom. I'll find a way to pay you back." I can see the flicker of uncertainty in her eyes. She has no idea how much I've paid and if or when she'll be able to pay it back.

But it doesn't matter.

"I can't. I've sunk everything I have into this." I hesitate and step closer. "My name is all over it." If anything in our history has counted as friendship, she should understand why that's a big fucking deal—and a big problem—for me. Eric Stone, Rawley's spoiled, waste-of-space kid. Privileged, irresponsible, product of nepotism, good for nothing unless you need a good drug hook up. I've heard it all. I've *been* it all, at one point or another. But not anymore.

I can't let this go. I'm out on a ledge with nothing but concrete and a lethal landing beneath me. I can't fail at this.

She shakes her head. "Why didn't you just ask me?" She sounds tired, and it kills me.

"Because . . ." I look away from her, staring at the water stain in the ceiling. The truth is ugly, but she deserves it. "I couldn't risk you saying no." Another lesson from super producer/Dad: When you want something, remove all the other options.

She stiffens. She might once have said yes to help me voluntarily, but not anymore.

"Your father must be so proud," she manages. "Finally."

The words slice at me in places deeper than should be possible. But I deserve this for what I've done, now and before. And it may hurt, but it's not going to stop me doing what needs to be done.

She must read that in my expression because after a long moment of silence, she just nods. And that one motion speaks volumes. No more pleading, no more questioning, no more anger. It's just a cold, curt movement, an axe falling on our mutual history.

"What time does the plane leave?" she asks flatly.

"Tomorrow morning, but I thought we could drive to Chicago tonight." I offer my best attempt at a roguish smile, unable to stop myself. I want what I want, but I also want her to still like me. I'm not sure that's possible, though. "They have a Geoffrey's. And I checked. It has that hot chocolate cake that you like. Remember when we were at that dinner for—"

But she's already turning away, heading toward the elevator I glimpsed earlier. "See, that's the problem, Eric, when you blackmail without calling ahead," she says over her shoulder. "I have plans tonight."

"Plans," I repeat.

She spins around to face me, her expression bland. "Yes, plans. I have a life here. I'm going to a party. You'll have to send a car for me in the morning. I'm not leaving tonight."

"Blackout?" Beth asks incredulously. "You're going to Blackout?"

I almost forgot she was here, but the alarm in Beth's voice snaps my attention back around to her. "What's Blackout?"

"It's a party," Beth says hesitantly, but that worried furrow in her forehead is back. "At the Phi Beta Theta house. They put on a black light and everyone writes on your shirt with highlighters."

"A fraternity party?" I snort. "Piss-warm beer and shitty music? Really?"

Calista raises her eyebrows at me. "It's not snorting coke off a stripper's chest, but it passes the time."

I wince. "She wasn't a stripper, not professionally," I protest. But that's weak. Calista has me dead on hypocrisy and she knows it.

Beth gapes at both of us.

"Are you sure this is a good idea?" I ask Callie with a frown. Even if it is only a fraternity party. "You've only been out of rehab for—"

She gives a harsh laugh. "Are you serious right now? Not my boyfriend, not my friend," she repeats, jabbing a finger at me. "Not anymore," she adds as she rounds the corner, out of sight.

"It's not a good idea," Beth whispers to me once Calista's gone. "I mean, my brother says it gets pretty out of control sometimes. And Calista . . . is different." She bites her lip.

Calista doesn't fit in here, if the scene I witnessed outside is any indication, and people might enjoy taking the opportunity to prove that to her.

But Calista's right: I'm not her boyfriend, and I guess I'm not her friend anymore. And I don't need her any more pissed at me than she already is. Money can make her show up (thanks to her mother), but it can't make her give a good performance. And depending on how angry she is and how desperate she is to make a point . . .

I shake my head at Beth. "Not my problem." Plus, as harsh as it sounds, if Calista has a horrible time, it might even work to my advantage. She'll realize being here is a mistake, and she'll *want* to come home tomorrow.

Beth nods after a second, but her mouth is curving down in disappointment and dismay, an expression I'm all too familiar with.

I sigh. Good to know some things don't change, I guess.

"Tell me about Blackout," I say.

3 CALISTA

"Welcome to Blackout!" An entirely too-cheerful guy in Greek letters at the door to Phi Beta Theta shouts over the music to the girls in front of me while I shiver in a tank top beneath my buttoned-up coat.

Going to a party to prove a point is a terrible reason to go to a party. In my limited experience, it either doesn't work (the person in question doesn't even notice you're trying to make a point) or it works too well (see: success followed by world-destroying failure).

Three and a half years ago, I went to a party at Eric's house as glammed up as humanly possible. I wanted to prove that I wasn't sixteen anymore. And that other guys (hopefully) found me hot and would act accordingly, even if Eric wouldn't.

In truth, I wanted to provoke Eric. To push him a little, see what would happen.

And for about fifteen minutes at that party, that was the best idea I've ever had. And then it turned out to be the worst and only continued to spiral downward from there, taking my whole life with it.

And yet, here I am again, making a stupid point.

Only this time, I'm not even sure *who* I'm making the point to. I huff out a frustrated breath, watching it cloud in the air in front of me.

Eric isn't here. The people who are won't care.

It's just that between my mother and Eric, it feels like all of my choices are being taken away.

My chest aches, and tears threaten at the memory of this afternoon. I keep my mascaraed eyes open wide, though I'm pretty sure any moisture would freeze before it had a chance to smudge anything.

I'm here because I want to be. And how are you supposed to have the life you want if you're not willing to fight—or in this case, freeze—for it?

I'm going to be the best damn Blake College student for as long as I can, even if that's less than twelve hours at this point.

Assuming I don't die of exposure first.

"Come on," I mutter. My arm aches, and I'm shuffling my feet to keep them warm. The boots I'm wearing are cute, products of my former life; they're not actually meant to *do* anything, like keep my toes alive. And the guy at the door seems more interested in flirting than letting people in.

But finally, the trio of girls ahead of me steps inside, claiming their oversized white T-shirts and chattering among themselves eagerly.

Then the door guy turns his attention to me. He's adorable in an overgrown-puppy sort of way, with floppy hair and a patch of acne on one cheek. "Hey, welcome to . . ." But then he stops, his eyes going big.

And I recognize what's about to happen immediately. "No," I say quickly. "Please don't. It's really not a big deal."

But he ignores me. "You're that girl," he says in an awed voice, pointing at me. Like I'm some kind of mythical creature, a unicorn in the Forbidden Forest. To be fair, though, it's not like I've ventured out much socially here. "That hot girl from that one show," he adds as clarification, though I'm not sure for who.

Years of my mother's training have me filling in the gap. "*Starlight,*" I mutter.

He snaps his fingers. "Yeah, that's it. And you go here now." Then he turns to shout behind him. "You guys, she's here! That chick!"

How very specific.

And yet it seems to work because suddenly the small entryway to the fraternity house fills with five or six brothers, all wearing the same white shirts. Their names—or nicknames—are marked on the back of their shirts with black electrical tape, which I don't understand.

"Welcome!" The guy at the door says with a wide expansive gesture, and I step inside cautiously, hating the feel of so many gazes on me at once. I'm wearing my puffy coat, but it's as if I can feel them peeling away my clothes, layer by layer.

Okay, this is fun.

"Here's your shirt and your highlighter," another brother says, reaching into the cardboard box behind door guy. His shirt says "Dirk" on the back. Or "Dick." It's hard to tell with the tape letters.

He thrusts the shirt and an orange marker into my hands, even as the door guy glares at him.

"Thanks," I say.

And then there's a long second of anticipatory silence, where I realize they seem to be waiting for me to shed my coat and yank this shirt on. Really?

"Um, a place for my coat?" I prompt uneasily.

"Oh, sure, chapter room is through there," door guy says, pointing toward a doorway on the other side of the hall and then elbowing the brother who gave me the shirt hard enough to make him grunt.

I didn't go to parties in high school. Because I didn't go to high school. And at Hollywood parties, it's a competition to see who can look more bored by the event, the food and even the most famous of attendees.

This level of enthusiasm might be flattering in another situation, but here, by myself, it's feeling a lot more like feeding time at the zoo, and I'm the lone lamb in the tiger pen.

"You can use my room instead if you want," a grinning redhead says to me, sliding forward as if to usher me out of the entryway.

I lean away. "I think I'm good, thanks."

"Let me get you a beer!" someone else says, then vanishes before I can say no.

In the chapter room, an open living-room-like space with a big TV on the wall and several couches that look like they've been rescued from the curb, I find the pile of coats on the corner of the nicest of the couches. Which isn't saying much.

Too aware of the gazes behind me, I pull the shirt inside my coat and pull it on over my tank top, ignoring the audible groan of disappointment from the doorway. It's not like I'm taking anything off, but apparently that doesn't matter. Just the chance to leer at the somewhat exposed skin of a once-famous person in real life is enough.

I used to daydream about going to a regular school, about what I was missing in high school and then in college. If this is it, my daydreams needed a severe downgrade. Or reality needs an upgrade, one of the two.

Stuffing my keys and my phone in my jeans pockets, now hidden beneath the oversized T-shirt, I leave my coat, feeling like I might never see it again.

When I head back toward the doorway—and presumably the actual party going on somewhere—the redheaded brother stops me.

"Wait, I need to sign your shirt." He beams at me before leaning toward my chest with his blue highlighter.

I turn swiftly, and he writes something across my back, just near my cami strap.

I try to twist around to read it, but he grasps my shoulders and propels me forward, past the entryway and into a dark and crowded corridor. "Oh, no way, you can't look. Not until the end of the night. That's cheating."

So . . . people will be able to write whatever they want all over me, and I won't even know what's there until hours later?

Suddenly this seems like a much worse idea than even Ginny or Tamara thought.

Music thumps beneath my feet, indicating the party is in the basement, but getting there proves trickier than I would have thought. Every few feet, someone stops to write on my shirt or to demand that I write on theirs. It's only about the fifth time that someone requests *only* my signature that it finally dawns on me that some or all of these will likely be showing up on e-Bay at some point.

Good luck, guys. I'm not sure what a Calista Beckett signature goes for these days. Might not even be worth the price of the T-shirt, except to the tragedy-mongers. The people who collect all the crap desperate child stars try to sell when their fortunes change—Lindsay's half-used lip gloss, Corey's fingernails, etc.

Once I'm at the stairs, though, my escort has gotten distracted, and I slip ahead on my own.

At the bottom of the steps, black light pours out of a large room, turning everything purplish. When I peer in at the doorway, it's no less freaky inside. The whites of people's eyes and their teeth glow a bizarre lavender. But it also makes all the highlighter scrawls on the T-shirts pop with neon intensity. Now I get it: We're like walking graffiti. Or billboards, only none of us have any idea what we're promoting.

A girl, her head tilted back with laughter, drifts in front of me. "Ask to see me naked!" is scrawled across her back in bright pink.

Fantastic.

To my relief, I recognize Ginny and Tamara huddled in the far corner, talking to each other and a couple of other girls. I'm going to have a good time tonight, damnit.

I carefully cut my way through the small mob of dancers—most people are on the other side of the room, waiting for a turn at the beer pong tables.

"Hey," I greet them.

Ginny looks up from whispering at Tamara. "You came!" She smiles at me, and it seems reasonably genuine.

Relief washes over me.

"How could I resist letting strangers write on me?" I say, rolling my eyes, and then immediately regret the words when I see that their shirts are barely marked.

Ginny and Tamara exchange a glance.

Shit. "Here, let me sign yours," I offer.

"Um, sure," Tamara says.

She faces the wall, giving me her back, and I sign my name in my best autograph-worthy signature. I have no idea if it really has any cache here, but at least the people who've been nice to me will have it if it does.

I'm in the middle of carefully marking a smiley face in the "a" of my name on Ginny's sleeve when one of the girls standing nearby sidles closer.

"So, I have a question for you," she says, shouting to be heard over the music. This girl has tied her T-shirt up to reveal her belly, where several distinctly male signatures are residing.

"This is Sosie," Tamara says, nodding at the girl. "She's on our floor."

"Hi Sosie, I'm Calista," I say, pausing to smile and wave in her direction.

She waves back, but it's a distracted gesture. She's clearly got something else on her mind, and the eagerness gleams from her lavender-tinted eyes.

Instinct has me bracing myself, my stomach going tight with dread.

"Did you really get high and fuck Dylan Bradley at his birthday party two years ago?" Sosie asks, far too loudly.

Okay, definitely not my imagination.

"Sosie!" Ginny scolds.

"What?" the girl asks, folding her arms across her chest. "It's not like it's a secret. It was on the front of a bunch of magazines."

Tabloids, actually. Because Dylan, former Disney star and good-boy galore, was looking to muddy his image a little. But not too much. In truth, yes, I was at his birthday party, and yep, I was on Oxy at that point. Further fueling the speculation was the fact that Dylan and I had gone out on "dates" back in my *Starlight* days, arranged by his PR people and mine. We were friends, probably still would be if I hadn't cut off everyone from before. I didn't blame him for the leak. He might not even have known about it ahead of time, and that was assuming it was even his team. I never knew what stories my mother was feeding the gossip mill, even after I'd fired her.

Sosie turns her attention back to me. "I just want to know what it was like." Her expression softens. "He seems so sweet."

Because drunken or drug-fueled hookups are usually "sweet."

"I don't talk about that part of my life anymore," I say as nicely as I can.

Sosie's forehead creases with a frown. "Why not?" she asks.

"Sosie, cut it out," Tamara says. "She said she doesn't want to talk about it."

"I don't get the big deal," Sosie insists. "If I did that, I'd be proud of it." She looks at us defiantly. "I mean, hello, Dylan Bradley?"

On her other side, another girl tugs at her, trying to pull her onto the dance floor, oblivious to the drama playing out.

But Sosie doesn't move.

She's waiting for her answer, and she's not going away until she gets it.

With a sigh, I cap my highlighter and stand to my full height, which—helped by three inches of boot heels—makes me almost a half a foot taller than the scavenger Sosie. "No, I did not get high and fuck Dylan Bradley at his birthday party two years ago."

Technically, I was already high, and it wasn't his birthday party. It was two friends trying to erase pieces of themselves that wouldn't be so conveniently obliterated. Like still being in love with someone who was obviously an asshole, despite previous evidence indicating otherwise. Or, in Dylan's case, trying very hard not to be in love with your (male) best friend when you have thousands of screaming teenage girls worshiping every move you make and funding every career achievement. Not that either of us were exactly upfront about either of those things before. Only after.

Yeah, it seemed like a good idea at the time. Don't do drugs, kids. It fries your judgment, and you end up seeing a very dear friend naked. Which should never, ever happen.

Sosie's eyes narrow. "But you did sleep with him?"

Damnit. "I'm sorry, but I don't talk about that part of my life anymore," I say again. I try to smile. "I'm trying to make a fresh start here, and I'm sure you can understand—"

She gives an indignant huff. "Bitch." And then stomps off in the opposite direction, after her friends.

I shouldn't be surprised, not at this point, that people sometimes feel that sense of ownership, that they have a right to information that they've read or heard. But I honestly thought it would be different here. At least once they saw that I'm a person and not just an image on a screen or in a magazine. I thought three months would be long enough for that.

An overwhelming sense of despair rises up in me. It's possible, as much as I don't want to admit it, that Eric is right, that I don't belong here and never will. But I don't belong at home, in California, in my former profession, either. Then where do I fit? And how many years and how many failures is it going to take?

"Don't worry about her," Ginny says, patting my arm soothingly. "She's just—" But her words cut off like someone has choked out her air supply, and her eyes go wide, staring at something or someone behind me.

I spin around, but don't see anything out of the ordinary. Certainly not Eric, as was my first assumption, based on her reaction. Actually, based on Beth's reaction earlier. I don't think Tamara and Ginny have ever seen the show, thankfully. The sight of Eric wouldn't mean anything to them.

Or me. I tell myself that, squashing the flare of relief that had gone off inside me at the idea of finding him here, and the accompanying disappointment when he wasn't. It's a little lonelier here than I expected, even with the crowd, even with talking to people I know. But I do not need Eric Stone.

"It's him," Ginny whispers. "He's here." Even in the crazy lighting, I can see that her cheeks are flushed. She's also bouncing on her toes with excitement, her fingers covering her mouth.

"Who?" I ask, mystified. I move to stand next to Ginny, trying to see what she's seeing.

"Oh Lord," Tamara says, rolling her eyes but with a fond smile. "Save us from the manly perfection that is Reese."

"Who's Reese?" I ask. There are several guys in the vicinity of where Ginny is staring. Most of them are obviously brothers, in their white T-shirts with the taped names. But I don't see one in particular that stands out.

"Only the tallest, smartest, hottest, fittest being to ever walk the—" Tamara teases.

"He's in my organic chemistry class," Ginny whispers, glaring at Tamara. "And he's looking over here." Her voice ends in a squeak, and she ducks her head, pretending, apparently, to study her shoes.

Suddenly, Ginny's determination to attend this party makes a lot more sense.

I elbow her gently. "You should go say hello."

She jerks her head up, expression horrified. "I can't do that!"

"You can and you should," I say, tugging at her arm and then pushing her out in front of me. "Trust me. Confidence is attractive. Fake it if you have to, but he'll like it, I promise."

"No, I can't!" But she's not resisting me. She just needs a push, and I'm happy to do that for her. I'm happy to be an actual friend.

Tamara sucks in a breath. "It doesn't matter because Mr. Perfect is heading this way," she says, turning her head toward us and talking through her smile.

Sure enough, one of the band of brothers has broken away and is heading straight for us. He does indeed appear tall and relatively handsome, as far as one can tell in the black light.

"Oh, no." Ginny steps back toward the wall.

"Okay," I say. "Keep breathing. Smile and say hello. That's all. He wouldn't be coming over here if he wasn't interested."

To my surprise and pride, she does as I instruct. She inhales deeply, puts on a wobbly smile, and then steps out to greet him . . .

. . . only to have him walk right past her.

He stops to lean against the wall, bracing his arm over my head.

A quick glance to the side reveals Ginny's stricken expression.

"Hey, I heard you were here," the guy who is apparently Reese says to me.

I slide away from him. "Um, yeah, I'm here with my friends, Tamara and Ginny. I think you know Ginny." I gesture toward her. I don't know if she can hear me, but she attempts a weak smile in response.

Reese glances over his shoulder. "Oh, yeah, hey." Then he turns his attention back to me. "So, this party must suck for you. Do you want to get out of here? Make things more interesting?" He taps his pocket, and I have no idea whether he's carrying or he's referring to sex. Or both. He's enough of a douche, it could be both.

The bright spark of temptation surprises me. Not the sex—please—but the idea that he might have something else I want. College kids, I've found, have access to all kinds of prescriptions. Some that are written for them, others that are swiped out of medicine cabinets at home or at other people's homes.

Not that this is news to anyone but me. I lived under my mother's obsessive control for most of my life. I mean, she used to weigh what I ate. I didn't recognize that as strange for years, not until after I'd joined the cast of *Starlight* and had spent time with other people close to my own age.

Getting high under my mother's supervision would have been as impossible as eating a baker's case of cheesecakes. Then when I finally broke free of her, however temporarily, getting drugs wasn't a problem for me. Not at first, anyway.

And now, for just a fraction of a second, I want the heat of that oblivion again. Alcohol loosens your boundaries and lowers your inhibitions; Oxy—enough of it—makes you wonder why you ever bothered with them in the first place. It feels like you've never had a worry in your whole life. Which sounds pretty good right about now. Not just to dim the perpetual dull ache in my arm, but to ease these gnawing feelings of self-doubt and dread. The sensation that I have no idea what I'm doing. Getting high won't fix that—it never does—but it certainly makes you care less, which was and continues to be part of the allure. Who cares that Eric showed up here just to use me? Who cares that my mom is selling me to the highest bidder? Who cares that I can't make friends here at Blake?

Not me, certainly.

"What do you say?" Reese presses closer.

Once won't hurt anything. It won't be like last time. You can control it, and it'll make you feel better, the addict in me whispers.

Lies.

I swallow hard against the dryness in the back of my throat and shake my head. "Not interested." If I use tonight, I'd have to start over again, and I don't know if I have the strength to do that.

But it's too late. Behind Reese, Ginny turns and runs away. My sobriety is intact, but my friendship with Ginny may not be.

"Excuse me," Tamara mutters, edging around me and glaring at Reese.

"Tamara," I try, but she's already gone, chasing down Ginny.

Damnit. I start to follow her. I have to find Ginny and explain.

But Reese's hand locks around my wrist. "Oh, come on, I know you like to party. Everybody knows that."

His fingers are too tight on my skin, and for a moment, in this dim corner, in a room where the black light already makes it hard to tell what's going on, I'm afraid. Predators in Hollywood operate in daylight with freely proffered drugs, slick smiles, even slicker propositions. Rarely brute force. I'm not sure if anyone will be able to hear me protest if Reese tries to drag me away. But worse than that, I'm not sure if anyone here would care if they did.

But when I open my mouth, it's not my words that come to the surface. Not "help!" or "let go!"

Instead it's a line of Skye's, one I'd memorized years ago.

"Touch me again, and your balls will regret it." The words come out even and flat, sounding almost bored. I worked on the delivery of that one bit of dialogue for a couple of days, running it past Eric, trying to get it just right.

Reese takes a step back, startled.

Guess I got it.

I take advantage of his slackened grip and pull free. "Asshole."

Another brother steps between us, shoving Reese back. "Bro, what the fuck are you doing?"

"Just talking, Carter." He jerks his head at me in disgust, as if this is my fault. Then again, I am the one who threatened testicular damage. "None of your business."

Carter pushes him back, away from me. "Go. Find somewhere else to be."

Reese sneers at him. "Yeah? Good luck." But he finally walks away.

Carter is only a little taller than me and possibly blond, though his hair is a lovely shade of blue at the moment. "Sorry, he's a jerk."

"Yeah," I say, rubbing my wrist, not because it hurts but because

I want to rid myself of the feeling of Reese's fingers on my skin. "I can see that."

Carter gives me a pleading smile. "Please don't judge the rest of us by him."

I shake my head and search the crowd for a glimpse of Tamara or Ginny. "I think I'm just going to find my friends and . . ."

Across the room, a visibly upset Ginny is wiping under her eyes. Oh, crap.

Tamara meets my gaze and jerks her chin in a sharp, negative motion.

"I'm just going to go," I finish instead, a sinking feeling through my middle pulling like it'll turn me inside out. I need to go home. And wallow in my absolute failure. Before I have to get on a plane in the morning—an entirely different kind of failure.

Why did I think this would work *tonight*? It's been awkward and uncomfortable since I arrived on campus. I should have known better.

I wanted to prove something, and I did. I guess I was just hoping that it would work the other way, that it would be like putting a bookmark in my life here. A reason to come back, something to give me the push I'll need to resist my mom. Proof that I'm right to resist.

"Thanks again," I say to Carter, tipping my head toward where Reese had disappeared. I start to turn away. "See you."

"Oh, don't go yet," Carter says, following me but careful not to step in front of me. "I know it's probably been tough the last few months, people always watching you."

I stop, surprised.

He lifts his shoulder. "My dad's the mayor of Blake," he says, making a face.

"You're the mayor's son?" I ask, amused. The town is only a little larger than the college itself. There are two fast-food restaurants, three stop lights and one gas station.

"The one and only." He rolls his eyes. "Like it means anything to anyone outside of this dumb town, but everyone here seems to think it's a big deal. They're always watching, bitching to my dad about what I'm doing or not doing." He sighs.

I relax slightly. "Sounds familiar."

"I actually meant to introduce myself to you earlier, but I didn't want to be one of those guys," Carter says, ruffling his hand through his hair.

"Which guys?"

"The ones acting like idiots because you're beautiful and they're hoping they have a shot." He stops abruptly, squeezing his eyes shut. "Okay, yeah, so now I've joined the league of idiots."

He looks so chagrined with himself that I can't help but laugh.

"Can I at least sign your shirt before you go?" he asks, opening his eyes. "Remind you to come find me after break?" He gives me such a hopeful look, with his purple highlighter in hand, that I can't refuse. Nor am I inclined to tell him that my return after break isn't exactly guaranteed, not anymore.

But this is the only conversation I've had all night—actually, all day—that hasn't ended in disaster, and Carter is kind of cute and seemingly sweet. Very different from the others here. Maybe tonight won't be a complete failure.

"Yeah," I say, smiling at him. "Sure."

4

ERIC

I really gotta hand it to these guys, the Phi Beta Whatevers. It's smart. The black light gives them an excuse to make it dark, the highlighters and shirts provide a reason to have your hands all over the girls and their hands all over you, and then the alcohol lowers inhibitions. Instant party.

Yeah, it's cheap and cheesy as hell, but smart, if you consider their goal is likely to hook up early and often. Hard to create a more conducive environment for that.

And Calista's in the middle of it.

Beth tugs at my coat sleeve, and I bend down to hear her. "Do you still see her?" she asks, biting her lip anxiously.

"She's in the corner across the room, talking to some girls." Two of them are the same girls, I think, that upset her earlier this afternoon, but now, everything looks to be fine. Calista is smiling and signing the shorter one's sleeve.

In other words, she's perfectly fine, completely not in need of a rescue.

She even seems to be having a good time, though whatever a third girl—one with her shirt tied up to just under her breasts—is saying to her at the moment is pissing her off. I can't hear anything over the music, but I know Callie. I especially know what she looks like when she's angry and trying to hide it. Shoulders tight, teeth-baring smile, like if you get too close she might take a chunk out of you. A teacup Yorkie. Small but vicious.

But then the belly-shirt girl stomps off in a huff, and Calista and her two friends are back to talking, their heads tipped together.

Guilt rises anew in me, squeezing like a fist around my heart. She really does seem happy here. Maybe I was wrong. Wrong to call Lori. Wrong to drag her away. Fuck.

I reach for the lone cigarette in my pocket, the familiar feel of it soothing if nothing else. Smoking it would be even better, but I promised Katie.

You promised Katie a lot of things. None of them to do with taking this level of interest in Callie's personal life.

I shift uncomfortably. "Maybe we should get out of here," I say to Beth.

"Are you sure?" she asks, her forehead wrinkled with concern as she stands on her toes, trying to see Calista.

Beth's a good kid. She was really worried about Calista. Enough to lie to get me in here.

Beth told the brothers at the door, in a stuttering but determined voice and with a face so red she looked sunburned, that I was her boyfriend. Her out-of-town boyfriend. And her guest for the party.

"Bethie, that guy is not your boyfriend. You don't even have one," the brother closest to the threshold said with a derisive snort.

Jesus, how small was this campus?

But Beth seemed to take his words to heart, curling into herself, like she wanted to shrink into one of the cracks between the porch floorboards.

The pang of sympathy for her caught me off guard and ignited my temper.

I wrapped my arm around her shaking shoulders and leaned

down to whisper in Beth's ear. "Chin up, Beth. He's an asshole, and we don't listen to assholes."

Then I turned my attention to him. "You owe my girlfriend an apology," I said pleasantly, stepping forward into his space.

Uncertainty flickered across his face, and he backed up immediately.

Check.

"She doesn't . . . you don't . . . I don't know you, bro." Flustered, he folded his arms across his chest, but not before looking for help from behind him.

And mate. They should never have put someone on crowd control who was so easily intimidated.

Then Beth surprised me. "Shut up, Steven. Just let us in," she said, brassy as hell. Her face was still red, but now she was trembling with defiance rather than humiliation.

Good for her.

Steven looked shocked. "Bethie, he's way too old for you."

Ouch. Guess that meant my days of playing a teenager were growing short indeed.

"Bye, Steven," she said firmly, before pushing past him and dragging me along after her.

We found Calista in the basement with her friends shortly after that. She was not hard to find, given that someone had scrawled "SKYE" in huge neon yellow letters between her shoulder blades—and then, beneath that, "bitch" in green—but I insisted that we keep our distance.

Now, twenty minutes later, I'm thinking perhaps it's time to add even more distance. Steven has cruised through the room several times, glaring at me with every pass. And managing him wasn't a problem, but if he decides to get a few more of his compatriots involved, it could be an issue. Bribery and smooth talking only go so far.

"I think Callie's doing all right," I say to Beth. As much as I don't want to admit it.

"And she'll be angry if she finds out that I . . ." I trail off as a guy from the pack in the center of the room makes a beeline for Calista. Should have known. It was only a matter of time.

He says something to her, and she shakes her head. That pattern repeats a couple more times, until the girls she's with take off, leaving her alone with him.

Shit. He leans closer, and I can barely see her behind him now. The back of his shirt says Reese.

Then Calista tries to walk away, and he grabs her wrist.

My fingers crush the cigarette, spilling tobacco inside my pocket.

"Are you going to do something?" Beth squeaks.

It's taking everything I have not to. But I have to wait. Calista will be pissed that I'm here, no matter what. But if I step in when she doesn't need it, that will only make things worse.

A second later, she tips her chin up and says something to him, and whatever it is, it makes him step back.

She pulls free from him with a dirty look.

Yep. Small but vicious. Pride makes a smile pull at the corners of my mouth.

But even as that douche is walking off, another appears. Hands waving and gesturing toward Reese, the one who left, this guy seems to be apologizing. His shirt says Carter.

"She's coming this way," Beth says, tugging at my sleeve.

And she's right, for a moment. But then this guy, Carter, catches up to her and whatever he says makes her stop and look in his direction.

He keeps talking, hands moving wildly, almost taking her eye out—because he's only maybe an inch taller than her. And she smiles at him. A real smile. Not the get-away-from-me kind from earlier.

The clutching sensation in the pit of my stomach catches me off guard, and it takes me a second to identify it. Jealousy. Envy. Whatever.

I don't have a right to either of those emotions. Not anymore. Not that I ever did.

"Come on," I say to Beth. "We should go." Before I have to watch her gaze adoringly up—no, across—at this fucker, and they end up walking past us when he takes her to his shitty room in this fire hazard of a shack.

I shake my head. *Not my business. Not my problem.*

It just feels like it.

"Okay," Beth says reluctantly. But before we can turn away, Calista shifts, presenting her back to Carter, who has his purple highlighter uncapped.

In seconds, he's on his knees behind her, still talk-talk-talking, and Calista is laughing at whatever he's saying.

"Oh, no," Beth says. "Shit."

The profanity from her surprises me, and I glance over, expecting to see Steven and a handful of his buddies bearing down on us.

But she's watching Calista and Carter.

"What?"

She frowns up at me, like she's concerned about my ability to cross the street unsupervised. "Don't you get how this works? Look at what he's doing."

The purple marks stand out easily on her back, amid the greens, yellows, oranges and blues. He appears to have the only purple highlighter in the joint.

And at first, I don't understand her concern. He seems to be marking out other signatures on her back. The fresh ink and the color make it easy to track his movements. Though he doesn't bother crossing out the "bitch" part, which would have been my first move.

But then it clicks. He's only crossing through certain signatures. It's hard to tell his pattern from here, except that the ones that are obviously from girls—flowers, hearts, floppy letters—he doesn't bother with.

And then I get it. It's a system of dibs. The brothers are attempting to stake claims via messages/signatures on the back of her shirt. Probably not just Calista's, but she's the one I care about.

And if I wasn't sure about that, what the short asshole does next makes it very clear.

In the remaining white space at the center of her back, he writes in large letters, visible to anyone at a glance, "MINE. BY 11. CR."

His initials. He's fucking branding her.

And Calista is just letting him because she has no idea what he's writing, what others have written. She thinks he's the nice one; that much is obvious, even from over here.

Calista, of all people, should know better than to fall for charm and a pretty face. But then again, maybe that's exactly the problem. She *still* doesn't know better, even now.

"I think we should . . ." Beth begins, but I'm past listening.

The white-hot fury I'm used to only feeling toward myself or my father is boiling up inside me.

It's an easy thing to close the fifteen feet between us.

Calista turns to face Carter as he stands, so she sees it when I slam into him, knocking him to the ground. She gapes at me for a second before she finds her words. "Eric! What are you doing?" She sounds horrified.

Before I can answer, Carter bounces back up. Not hard to do when it's such a short distance. "Hey bro, you're not welcome here. Get the fuck out."

He shoves back at me with a surprising amount of force.

"Eric. You need to leave," Calista says, baring her teeth. "You don't own me. You don't own every aspect of my—"

"I think you're confusing me with your mother," I say tightly, and she reels away from me, like I've struck her.

"You're trespassing. If you don't get out now, you'll be sorry, man," Carter says, bouncing on his toes, as if this is a boxing ring.

By now people are staring. And I can see his fellow brothers watching from various points in the basement. This could get ugly, and quickly.

I feel a flicker of anticipation.

"I'm sure," I say to Carter. The smirk is, unfortunately, automatic.

Several people, not the least of which my own father, have told me that I have a uniquely punchable face, a quality in my features that makes people want to hit me. "Smug bastard," I believe, is what Calista used to call it.

And apparently, Carter is not immune. Without further warning, he takes a swing and connects.

The pressure explodes against the side of my face, and it feels like my eye is going to pop free.

Oh, yeah. This *feeling.* I know this feeling. I hate this feeling.

The urge to hit back is instant and reflexive, and when my fist connects with his stomach—because who the hell deliberately hits against a cheekbone unless you're trying to show off?—Carter goes down, wheezing.

A furious Calista steps between the downed Carter, with his fast-approaching brothers, and me.

"What is wrong with you?" she shouts, pushing at my shoulder. "Get out!"

"Look at your shirt," I say to Calista, touching the tender skin beneath my eye. Okay, yeah, Carter was right—I am a little sorry now. Fuck. It makes me miss the days when Chase, the third of our *Starlight* trio, was the one hitting and getting hit, and I just had to pay the bar tab.

She throws her hands up in frustration. "I know people are probably saying horrible stuff, but that doesn't mean you can follow me around and go punching—"

"If you'll recall, I didn't start the punching," I say tightly.

Calista rolls her eyes. "Eric—"

"Just look at your damn shirt." My face is throbbing now, and

I'm running out of patience. I twist it around so she can look at it. It stretches out the letters, making them muddled, but his initials are clear enough. As is the "By 11."

"What the hell?" She lifts her arm to try to see it more clearly.

"It's all over your back. These assholes marking you like territory, and then this guy"—I tip my head toward the glaring and gasping Carter, who's being hauled to his feet by his friends—"the king of the assholes, crossing out their initials and putting his, along with a deadline."

Calista goes very still, then she turns to stare at Carter.

"It's just a tradition," Carter says, between coughs. "To see if anyone can . . ." Even Carter is smart enough to stop then. "Nobody makes anybody do anything."

Calista pivots away from him.

"You don't belong here anyway!" one of the brothers shouts, a bigger guy. I'm not sure if he's talking to me or Callie. But he's stepping up, like he wants to start something.

I grin at him. This is definitely going to hurt.

Calista grabs my arm. "We're leaving. Now," she says to me, pulling at me.

"Oh, come on, Calista. It's just a game," Carter says. "And I was protecting you."

Callie raises her hand over her head, giving him the finger. "Protect this."

And because I can't leave anything alone . . . "Guess that means you lose."

"Damnit, Eric!" Calista tugs harder at my arm, and I turn to follow her to the stairs and up. Beth is already ahead of us, and we are . . . not running, but moving quickly through the hall and out the front door.

As soon as we're on the sidewalk and away from the front of the house, Calista stops and faces me. "What were you doing there?"

"I told you—"

"No, I mean how did you know?"

"Beth." I jerk my chin toward where she's paused, a couple of sidewalk squares ahead of us.

Callie turns to see Beth, who gives a sheepish wave and edges closer. "Hi."

"She was worried about you. Thought that maybe some people wouldn't like having you there," I say.

"Not that people wouldn't like *you*," Beth says quickly. "It was more that the party gets kind of out of control sometimes, and with you being you . . ." she trails off, ducking her head.

Being an outsider, being different, is always a crapshoot. Maybe it makes you stand out, maybe it just makes you a target.

Callie's shoulders slump.

It reminds me of the first time we met, in that audition room. She looked so worn down and defeated, and Lori just kept haranguing her. It roused protective instincts in me I didn't even know I had, and it's the same now.

I lean forward, over Callie's defeated posture, deliberately invading her space, to annoy her, to provoke anger instead of sadness. Because angry is better than sad.

But Calista smells like vanilla still, and standing so close to her triggers a thousand memories at once. Sitting in Hair and Makeup, listening to her talk about this book, *Fly Girl*, with unfettered enthusiasm. Stupid card games in hotel rooms during press junkets, movie nights at my father's house, the softness of her skin beneath my mouth . . .

In Season One, Lori worked hard to keep Calista away from Chase and me, the "bad influences." Fair enough. But by Season Two, Lori was pregnant with Calista's youngest sister, and she spent most of that year tired, sick and resting in Callie's trailer. So the reins loosened a little.

It was during the second season that everything changed. For me, at least. We were standing around, waiting for a set up, and

Callie had her nose in that book again. I grabbed it from her, holding it over my head.

"Give it back!" she demanded, eyes snapping with outrage.

I tapped her nose gently with my fingertip. "Nope." She was easy to provoke because she was so damn serious, so adult all the time. Because she had to be.

I took it as a personal challenge to make my "sister" lighten up.

But then instead of lecturing me, as I expected, she narrowed her eyes at me and wrapped her arms and legs around mine, climbing me like a tree to get to her book.

Instinctively, I reached out to grab her to keep her from falling.

Her shirt had ridden up, revealing smooth pale skin over her ribs. My fingers rested there, just an inch below the line of her bra, and suddenly, all I could think about was how close I was to touching her, really touching.

But she was seventeen, and I was twenty-one. Hell no.

"Here," I said curtly, handing her the book.

She looked equal parts surprised and disappointed to have won so easily. But she took the book and slid down reluctantly. "Thanks," she mumbled.

I knew I was in trouble then.

By the start of the third season, Calista was eighteen. She fired Lori—long overdue as far as I was concerned—and then suddenly had freedom to move around on her own. Which was a whole other world of danger and still possibly one of the best years of my life.

I clear my throat. "I have to admit, I think Beth's right. The issue was more that some of them wanted you there a little too much."

Calista stiffens and turns her head to give me an exasperated look. For a second, her mouth is much too close to mine.

And the moment catches, snagging in the mere inches between us as if time has slowed down enough to become material.

I lurch back, and it's gone.

She faces Beth, her hair flying out to brush my face. "Thank you, Beth," she says. "I appreciate it."

Beth nods. "I could have told you. If you'd asked me." The tone of her voice, a gentle scolding.

"I guess I was just hoping that it wouldn't matter. That I could just be me, for a night," Callie says.

"You're still you, but it's always going to matter," Beth points out. "Even if you ignore it, other people won't. Especially around here. You're the most exciting thing to happen to us since they put in that other stoplight."

I laugh. Beth looks startled at first, then pleased.

Callie glances over her shoulder to scowl at me, but the effect of it is diminished by the fact that she's shivering so hard that her shoulder almost collides with her chin. I realize belatedly that she's out here in just that short-sleeved T-shirt from the party.

"Where is your coat?" I demand, shrugging out of mine.

She sighs. "I left it on the couch."

"Here." I step up to wrap my coat around her, and she lets me without argument, which only goes to show exactly how cold she must be.

She tips her head up to look at me while I focus on buttoning her in. "That eye is going to be fantastic," she says softly.

"Definitely going to leave a mark," I agree. I can feel the area between my cheek and eye, hot and swelling already. But it's not the first time and probably not the last.

"You need to put ice on it." Callie reaches up with her fingertips but pulls away before touching my skin.

"I know," I manage, my voice coming out gruff and gravelly. "Hasn't been that long since the last time."

"I suppose I owe you an apology," she says, lowering her hand. "Or a thank you."

"Not your fault," I say, pushing the words out. She's close, too close. And I can't. I just can't.

I back up a step. She's buttoned enough to keep the coat from falling off. That will have to do. "Gotta protect my investment," I say with a careless shrug. "Plus, you kind of have a track record of bad judgment when it comes to nearly sleeping with assholes." The grin pulling at my mouth feels forced, empty.

But it has the desired effect. Her mouth falls open, then a flash of fury mixed with hurt lights her expression. Her jaw tightens until I swear I can hear her teeth grinding. "Good night, Eric." She turns away from me and marches to where Beth is waiting.

Damnit. Even though she has my coat, it's still cold out here, and dark. "Let me give you guys a ride back to the dorm," I call after her. The car—and driver—is waiting around the corner.

But Calista ignores me and keeps walking. Beth gives me a wave and a helpless shrug before following her.

5 CALISTA

Eric's coat smells like him. His cologne, his skin, the scent of new fabric, even the faint hint of tobacco from the shredded cigarette—what was up with that?—that I found in the pocket.

When Beth and I get back to Ryland, I hang his coat on the desk chair, all the way on the other side of the room. It's as far from me as it can be in the tiny single that is mine to call home.

But I'm still too aware of it, even with my back turned. As if there's a string running between it and my shoulder blades. As if the man himself is sitting there, long legs stretched out in front of him, daring me to try to figure him out.

See, this is the problem with Eric. If he were a jerk all the time, I could—and so very happily would—ignore him. But he's smart and funny and fiercely protective of me at the same time, one of the only people to believe in me as something more than a generically pretty face spewing lines at the behest of her mother.

So he'll defend me to the death against my mother, going head-to-head with her. Until he decides to use her against me.

He'll rush in to save me, even taking a hit to do so, but then he makes fun of my former feelings for him?

It's infuriating and impossible to understand.

My phone buzzes on the desk, and a quick look reveals yet another text from my mother, this one questioning my water intake and whether I need to have an emergency facial scheduled. I should have known that the radio silence of the last month or so was too good to last. Now, I have to wonder if Eric had made that part of the deal—no money if she didn't keep quiet.

It makes me feel ill to think about it. My relationship with my mother, bought and sold—or shut off and turned back on—as soon as the check cleared.

I power down my phone, ignoring her barrage of queries, and get ready for bed.

My plan, such as it is, is to present this as a temporary move. The money coming in from this job will just have to last her until I graduate and get a new career. Period. I'm coming back here on the Sunday after Thanksgiving, whether Eric is done with me or not. Though, right now, the thought of returning to Blake is almost as unappealing as leaving tomorrow.

But tomorrow, appealing or not, I go back. The girl in the mirror, wiping off her makeup in the dim overhead light, does not look thrilled at this idea. She's also developing two parallel lines on her forehead—the dreaded "11"—that will have her mother bringing up Botox again and lecturing on the perils of squinting.

Shit. I rub at the lines, but they refuse to vanish.

I don't have a choice about going or taking this job. Eric saw to that, I just don't know why other than out of pure selfishness. But he's the one who argued the loudest for me to fire my mom in the first place.

So which Eric is the real one? I thought I knew once. I thought I was seeing glimpses of the true him beneath the surface, the Eric who kept me company late into the night when we were on set and my mom had long since crashed in my trailer. The Eric who paid attention and brought me a bagel, telling me to eat, because I was dizzy and my stomach was growling thanks to my mom insisting on yet another cleanse. The Eric who encouraged me to take charge of my own life when I was eighteen.

I miss that Eric.

I brush my teeth and wipe my mouth. The girl in the mirror is now flushed and agitated-looking, which does not bode well for sleep. I snap off the light and climb into bed, my brain still racing.

Maybe I'm the one who screwed it up, by being naïve and dumb all those years ago. Everything was fine between us until that stupid alternate-universe episode late in Season Three. It was pure fan service, an effort to raise dramatically slouching ratings. In this version of the *Starlight* world, Skye had never been adopted, so she and Byron were not raised as siblings. And thus Skyron was born.

Actually, that's not true. Skyron existed from pretty much the beginning—people seeing what wasn't supposed to be there between Skye and her brother and writing fan fiction, *so much* fan fiction, about it—but this was the first time the 'ship was openly acknowledged by the show itself. So more like Skyron taking its first steps instead, I guess.

In this universe, the world was already ending. Brody was the enemy instead of Skye's guardian angel, and Byron was the love of her life, whom she was trying to protect.

And there was one scene. Just one, but it was more than enough.

Skye and Byron were taking a risk, having a picnic outside their underground shelter to celebrate a victory against Brody and the other angels who were trying to punish the surviving humans. But this Skye and Byron weren't awkward with each other; they'd been in a relationship for months, according to this timeline. This wasn't new to them, so it didn't have to be for us either.

It was just a grotty patch of fake grass on set beneath an apocalypse-dimmed sky (thank you, green screen), a small tattered blanket, and stale bread. But it changed everything. I'd had a crush on Eric for years before that, been half in love with him since our audition together and throughout our ensuing friendship, but this . . . when I'm ninety, I'll still remember this moment.

"Okay, let's try it again from Calista's first line," the director shouted, sounding weary. "And Jesus, can you two pretend like you like each other this time? Every other episode, you guys are practically eye-fucking, and the one time we need that . . ." He shook his head in disgust.

My face burned. And beneath my ragged and unraveling sweater—post-apocalypse chic—my heart was thumping so hard, I was pretty sure the boom was picking it up.

"Okay," I said. "Not a problem."

Eric, right next to me, said nothing, and I wanted to curl up and die. He'd been avoiding me all week, ever since we got the script for this episode. At first, I thought maybe it was because of his dad. Whenever Rawley Stone came by the set—which happened relatively frequently because he had an office at the same studio—Eric got super moody and crabby.

But then, at the table read, I'd finally figured it out. Eric had brusquely moved past this scene, refusing to run through even the few lines in it.

So it was the script that was bugging him—more specifically this scene. And me.

What, like I asked the writers to make up this scene? Okay, I might have *wished* for it—pretty much every day since the day Eric and I auditioned together—but I never said anything.

But now, it didn't even matter. His obvious irritation was draining away any anticipation I might have felt. And amping up my nerves a thousandfold.

For a moment, I longed for Chase. He wasn't even on set today, but at least he didn't make me feel stupid, childish and homely, like it was such a burden when we had to do stuff like this. He made me laugh by joking about the ridiculous flesh-colored nylon pieces we had to wear to look naked or about the unlikely placement of sheets.

People fluttered around us, making adjustments to hair, makeup and lighting, but Eric, at my side, was pretending I didn't exist. Great.

"Is everything all right?" I whispered to Eric, which was ridiculous, as we were both miked. But it didn't feel like a conversation to have at full volume. "I know this is awkward and weird, but—"

"Callie, it's fine," Eric said tersely. "Just . . . leave it alone, okay?"

Stung, I took a step away from him. Only to realize that I had to move back to be on my mark.

How exactly was I supposed to leave this alone? Our first take had been so horrible we hadn't even made it all the way through. Eric was stiff and wooden, and I was overacting in response, trying to pull emotions from him.

And it wasn't like we could skip it. The scene had to be done, whether we liked it or not. At this point, I would have been willing to forget my earlier fantasies and go back to a moment when he would actually look me in the eye.

As soon as the director called for action, I tried to shut my feelings away, to become Skye, with the guy she loves and fears losing. Which was not as hard as it should have been.

We tromped toward the patch of fake grass. "What are we doing out here?" I-as-Skye asked warily, hoping my nerves would read as her fears of being attacked from above. Only the audience was supposed to be aware that Hell had belched up zombies in response to losses the angels had suffered and that threats were now on the ground—and beneath it as well.

There was no response.

Uh-oh. I looked to Eric, half-expecting him to be looking past me for a prompt on his line.

Instead, he was watching me, hesitation flickering across his face, before it vanished and he seemed to come to a decision.

He grinned at me, all dash and charm.

My responding smile was reflexive—it was impossible *not* to smile back at Eric—and confused. It wouldn't be a consistency issue, as this version of Byron wasn't supposed to be the same as the other, but still. What was he up to? Because this was definitely Eric as Eric, not Eric as Byron.

"Relax," Eric said. "All the angelic bastards are on the other side of town, investigating an explosion at the old power plant."

Okay, so we were going with this, apparently.

"An explosion you set off," I said, injecting my voice with suspicion.

"I wanted to celebrate," he said, arching an eyebrow in that cocky expression I was all-too-familiar with.

"By getting us killed?" I asked, but I helped him spread out the blanket on the fake grass.

"There are some things worth taking a chance on," he said, his gaze fixed on me. His tone was mild enough, but I *felt* it, like a tug on the inside, pulling me toward him.

Oh. My foot caught on the edge of the blanket, and I nearly fell instead of sitting down gracefully, like the warrior this Skye was supposed to be.

But Eric caught my arm, keeping me from face-planting, and no one shouted cut, so we kept going.

"Here," he said, handing me a white cloth-wrapped bundle. "Eat."

I opened it between us, spreading the cloth to reveal a couple of lumpy, misshapen loaves of bread.

"Where did you get these?" I asked, trying to sound awed and enthusiastic about the possibility of eating them. In truth, previous experience told me they tasted like moldy paste. Or what I imagine moldy paste tasted like. But they apparently looked like bread made from scavenged ingredients and baked over a fire made of tires and whatever other toxic but burnable things one used in the apocalypse to stay warm, and that was good enough for our props department.

"I don't have to tell you all of my secrets," Eric said with a playful wink that stole my breath. And that internal tug grew stronger.

I cracked open one of the loaves and handed him half, mentally preparing to make my "oh yum, this is delicious" face.

But then Eric chucked the bread at me, unscripted. It missed me, veering off to my side.

My mouth fell open in shock, and he laughed.

What are you doing? I barely kept the question in check. Again, no one had called cut, so we were still rolling.

I dove after the bread, reclaiming it from the "grass." Food was supposed to be a precious commodity in this world—Skye would never let that go.

And when I returned to my upright—and scripted—position, Eric was holding up a thin gold necklace with a four-leaf clover charm dangling at the center of it.

"I got this for you," he said, his voice gruff with emotion. "I wanted it to be a surprise."

It was Skye's mother's, abandoned in their home months ago when the angels attacked. In the regular universe, it was Skye's only reminder of a mother she never knew. In this alternate world, it was a reminder of the mother she'd lost.

It was in the script—a soft, sweet moment to establish their relationship and feelings for each other. And to make 'shippers' heads explode.

But until that moment, I'd never really felt the emotions that were supposed to accompany the exchange.

And when I did, as it turned out, my feelings were neither soft nor sweet. In the least.

"You went into the restricted zone for this?" I demanded, refusing to take the necklace as I was supposed to. "That's dangerous, Byron. They would have killed you if they'd seen you."

"But they didn't," he argued, his dark eyes flashing. "And it's not fair that you should lose everything just because they—"

"But I haven't lost everything. Not unless you make me lose you, too!" My voice cracked, and to my surprise, my eyes were welling.

In theory, we were supposed to be saying these same words to each other but without this anger and heat. I was supposed to accept the necklace, and my sweet kiss of gratitude and love was to evolve into a lovely and gentle make-out scene, carefully choreographed to be swoonworthy. But the emotions were all off-kilter now, and there was this delicious tension in the air that wrapped around us. That certainly hadn't existed in the previous take.

Eric stared at me for a long moment, and I swiped the back of my hand across my cheeks to eliminate tears I wasn't supposed to be crying. Not yet.

You won't. That was Eric's next line, an idea proved false by the end of the episode when Brody kills Byron in an effort to make Skye surrender herself.

Remembering that, though, only made me cry harder.

Instead, Eric said nothing. Just reached over, the necklace still wound around his fingers, and pulled me toward him by the ragged collar of my sweater, until I was half in his lap.

His warm mouth covered mine, but this was no stage kiss. When his tongue brushed over my lower lip, I completely forgot about his coverage, my coverage, the fact that dozens of people were watching.

I chased that kiss and his tongue with my own, until his breath caught audibly in his throat. I'd had a little more practice with kissing since our audition, and the pleasure of hearing that noise from him was heady confirmation.

I wiggled around until I was fully in his lap, my knees on either side of him, and his hands gripped my hips tightly.

Above him like that, it was easy to sink my fingers into his dark curls, my thumbs lightly resting against his cheekbones, and change the angle of our kiss. Deepen it until we were both panting.

And he let me take control. For a minute.

Then his arm slid up my back, holding me close and safe, and I felt gravity shift. He was moving us to lie on the blanket. That wasn't a surprise, but the swiftness and the ease with which he accomplished it caught me off guard. And eagerness sent tremors through my arms and legs.

Breaking the kiss, he rocked back on his knees, pausing only a moment to whip off his shirt and toss it away from us. I didn't bother tracking where it went, my attention fully caught by the view before me.

I'd seen Eric shirtless before. The writers' room seemed to have been tasked with squeezing plot in around scenes featuring Chase or Eric half-naked.

But seeing Chase never affected me that way, and seeing Eric on a screen or even standing next to me was totally different than witnessing him directly above me, than *feeling* him above me. The scars and tattoos weren't his, except for the infinity symbol on his shoulder. Just part of this version of Byron. But all that glorious warm skin, and the muscles flexing as he moved—that was all him. The sight set off a craving in me that had me clenching my hands into fists to keep from reaching out to touch him everywhere at once. I wanted to make it—him—mine.

He never took his eyes off me, settling his weight on me carefully, bracing most of it on his elbows. But the heat of his body, so close, made me want to curl into him and never leave.

It was instinct, then, that made me part my legs, giving him access to be ever closer.

He dropped his head against my collarbone with a defeated-sounding moan, but then his mouth was moving against the exposed skin at the unraveling neck of my sweater, just inches above my breasts.

Never in my life have I so fervently wished for one or two already-loose stitches to give way and give me what I wanted.

I slid my hands around his back. Urging in silent gesture for him to let go and press against me fully.

He lifted his head with a wicked smile. "Your hands are cold," he whispered to me.

That might have broken the moment, made me remember what we were doing . . . or what we were supposed to be doing.

But his words held an intimacy within them, like it was just the two of us, like it was only ever the two of us.

"So warm me up." The response came easily, automatically, even though it wasn't in the script and didn't feel like anything I would normally have been bold enough to say. But I could taste the truth of those syllables coming from a core desire that I couldn't ignore any longer.

Heat flashed in his expression. And before I could respond, he pressed his mouth against the side of my neck in a trail of kisses that had me gasping and arching toward him.

And I was melting. I was a pool of Calista. I didn't care where we were or what was happening, as long as he kept touching me. As long as I could keep the heat and weight of him pressed against me.

Please, I begged silently. I locked one leg around his, as if to ensure that he wasn't going anywhere. It felt right in a way that I'd never experienced.

But then—

Background noise from somewhere, loud and repetitive, began to break through the haze.

It took my heat-fogged brain a moment to identify the sound. Clapping. Someone—lots of someones, actually—were clapping. And whistling.

Awareness returned in a sudden and cold rush.

My sweater had ridden up, the prickly fake grass was scratching my skin. The cool breeze of the air-conditioning units overhead cut through the heat of the lights and made me shiver.

I went still, awkwardness flooding me like blood returning to previously numb limbs. I wanted to curl into myself. Even though I wasn't wearing any fewer clothes than I had been before, I felt more naked.

Eric lifted up, his lips, puffy and reddened from kissing me. *From kissing me.*

"Welcome back!" someone shouted with a laugh. I couldn't identify the voice, and no way was I looking over there. "They called cut, like, five minutes ago."

I focused instead on the catwalk far above us. If I could be up there right now, or just invisible, that would be so much better. How hard was it to spontaneously combust when you actually wanted to?

"I told you to turn up the heat, not burn down the kitchen." That voice I recognized. Our director this week. He was trying to sound grumpy, but glee was leaking through. He knew what he'd gotten was good.

Eric straightened up slightly, pulling his weight from me, and lifted one hand off the blanket by my head to toss a salute at the director. "I aim to please," he said with a grin.

Oh, God. He did it on purpose.

The realization struck me belatedly, like pain flooding in only after you see the long stripe of blood on your flesh.

It paralyzed me momentarily. I wanted to run, to hide, to do both at the same time, but I couldn't make my body move.

"Calista seemed to agree!" someone called, and the catcalls and whistling grew louder.

Damnit. My face was on fire, so much so that my eyes were watering from it. And when a single tear trickled down the side of my face and into my hair, it released something inside me, giving me my motion back.

I shoved at Eric and twisted onto my side, turning away from everyone else.

He backed off, moving to his knees.

"Callie . . ." he began softly, reaching a hand toward me.

I ignored him, pushing myself to my feet and fighting the urge to run back to my trailer.

Running away would be the worst. But breaking down in

front of everyone would be the next worst. I would not let them see me cry. I would not let *Eric* see me cry. How could he do that to me? Just . . . make me forget everything else? How could he use me like that?

In retrospect, it's now perfectly clear that he knew how I felt about him, how I'd felt about him for years. And he hadn't hesitated to take advantage of it. Maybe that's why he'd blown the first take—maybe he was trying to get me to work that much harder, to care more when it counted. It was clever, manipulative. Exactly like Eric.

I took a deep breath, opening my eyes as wide as possible to keep the tears in, and stared off at the point on the green screen that would be our fake horizon once the visual effects guys were done.

"Why . . ." I swallowed hard, trying to push the words out. "Why would you do that?" It was like having a superpower and not using it responsibly. So, yeah, I was the dumb one, the young one who'd gotten lost in the moment, who'd taken playacting for reality. But he was the cruel one, the world-wise one who'd known exactly what he was doing.

"Calista, it's not . . ." Out of the corner of my eye, I could see him running his hands through his hair. "I didn't mean to . . ." He made a frustrated noise. "I told them this scene was a bad idea."

If I'd thought I'd been frozen in place before, now it was worse, like my lungs had locked up, refusing to move in or out.

"What?" I managed after a second. He'd talked to the writers about this? About me? He thought I couldn't handle it?

"Not like that," he said quickly.

"Then what was it like?" I asked through gritted teeth, but that didn't stop the hitch in my voice.

"I just thought . . ." He shook his head. "I thought it would be too much is all," he said. "And I was right."

I laughed, but it came out bitter and throaty from the tears I was working very hard not to cry. "I appreciate the concern, Eric. But you don't have to worry about me. Not ever again."

I started to stomp off, but Eric, still on his knees in front of me, caught at the side of my frayed cargo pants. (Apparently the apocalypse not only unravels sweaters, but it also throws fashion back a decade.)

"Wait. Please." His grip was tight enough to pull the fabric against my skin. I could have jerked away, but it was clear this wasn't a half-assed attempt to get my attention.

"Why?" I couldn't even look directly at him.

He gave a weary-sounding laugh. "Can you just stand there for a second, okay? Cal, please?" He flashed me a pleading smile.

Exasperated and humiliated and with my protective skin worn too thin already, I couldn't stop my temper from sparking to life. I glared down at him. "If you think I'm just going to stand here so you can keep the laughs going . . ." I began. But then I looked at him, really looked.

Like me, he was dressed in the latest post-apocalyptic wear. His worn black T-shirt with the artful tears and rips was still on the floor somewhere, so he was wearing just a pair of ragged cargo pants.

And the zipper at the front of those cargo pants was straining forward at the moment.

He was . . . oh.

Eric met my gaze defiantly for a moment, color staining his cheekbones. "Like I said, bad idea."

So, it wasn't just me. I'd lost myself a little—okay, a lot—but he had, too.

Relief and—weirdly enough, a shadow of the lust from a few moments ago—battled within me.

No one else seemed to have noticed. They were all going about their business to set up for close-ups. But at the moment, I was hiding him mostly from view. If I moved away, it would look weird if he didn't stand, and then it would be very obvious.

One might even say "hugely obvious."

Curiosity kept my attention focused on Eric and his . . . problem. It looked uncomfortable—for him—but positively intriguing to me. My experience with, well, anything was pretty limited. There were high school freshmen who'd rounded more bases than I had. I had more freedom now without my mom watching over my every move, but it wasn't like I'd thrown all caution to the wind and started riding around topless in limos and searching out guys in clubs to bring home.

Not unless it was the right guy.

"Not helping, Calista," Eric said under his breath, raising his eyebrows at me.

With a blush heating my face, I tore my gaze away, focusing once more on the metal latticework above.

Another few moments passed, and he finally got to his feet. "Thanks," he said gruffly, bumping my elbow with his as he passed.

When the episode aired—with our version of that scene instead of the scripted one—the internet exploded with joy . . . for about a day and a half before getting obsessed with something else, a kitten in a bowl or a doppelgänger for a young Leonardo DiCaprio in Canada or something.

The effects on us were more far-reaching. On a day-to-day basis, everything went back to a slightly strained version of normal between Eric and me. We never talked about what had happened that day, but it hung in the air between us for weeks afterward, especially when we were alone together. Which didn't seem to happen much after that. It wasn't like he was avoiding me exactly. But he stopped visiting my trailer to hang out, and whenever I went by his, he always had other people in there.

But that scene, it gave me ideas. It gave me hope that I shouldn't have had.

If that scene had never happened, I would never have asked him to . . .

I roll over in bed, pulling the cool side of the pillow over my heated face.

Well, I never would have gone to the party, either, and that's where things really went to shit.

In the end, though, it doesn't matter. The scene did happen. So did everything that followed. And Eric is not the person I thought he was. He doesn't care about anyone else besides himself and what he wants. I understand it; he didn't exactly have the best examples in his life. His mom dumped him off with his father when he was practically still a baby. And his father's version of caring is alternately ignoring Eric or condemning him for not living up to expectations. So, why should Eric take the risk? He'd learned early on that looking out for number one was his best—and only—option.

It just kills me because I see flashes of who he could be.

And that's the hardest thing to accept. I want Eric to be the better version of himself, the one I fell in love with when I was sixteen. Even the one who lost control that day on the set and was kissing me for real, for those few minutes. But I'm not sure that guy exists outside of my head. And I'm tired of looking for him.

So maybe I just won't anymore. Sometimes you have to let people—and old ideas—go. I can be done with Eric. It can be my choice.

The idea sends relief cascading through me like a series of small boulders finally rolling off my back.

I was young and foolish and in love once, and that left me open for hurt and spiraling disaster. But I don't have to do that again. I may have to work with him—or for him, in this case—but I don't have to love it.

Or him.

6

ERIC

Calista is waiting, right on time, at the glass doors of her dorm when my driver, Jimmy, pulls the car to the edge of the curb. Her backpack is slung over her good shoulder—I hate that there's a distinction now—and my coat is folded neatly over her arm.

As soon as she sees us, she waves to a sleepy-looking Beth and, pulling a roller bag behind her, pushes open the door in the predawn gloom. Without bothering to put on the coat.

Damnit, Callie, just wear the stupid thing. I drop my fist onto my leg in annoyance.

She's always cold. But not when she wants to make a point, apparently.

Her chin is set and her gaze fixed, like she's marching into war, as she steps down the stairs briskly. Jimmy puts her suitcase in the trunk. She smiles at him when he opens the door for her, but the smile vanishes completely by the time she settles in the seat next to me.

"Here." She gives me my coat, and I want to shove it back at her and tell her to stop being ridiculous.

But that's part of the whole "feeling too much" thing. Why should I care whether she wears a coat? Or if she's cold? It's not my business. And she's made that more than clear.

So I take it and fold it in a square to put behind my head as a pillow.

She smells of vanilla and mint, and now my coat does, too. Which is fine because it's not like I'll need it after today, anyway.

Jimmy shuts the door behind her, and she puts her backpack on the floor and then reaches for her seatbelt.

"It'll be at least an hour and a half to O'Hare," I tell her. "Maybe more."

"Okay." Her gaze flicks to mine and away as she nods. She looks bright-eyed and well-rested, if still slightly pissed. Clearly nothing was keeping *her* up until the early hours of, well, now. "It's fine. I have homework to do, anyway. My forensic accounting assignment is due the Monday I get back." The words come out as a challenge, as if she's daring me to deny her return.

But I keep my mouth shut as she pulls her laptop out of her backpack.

I stretch out my legs, careful not to veer into her space, and close my eyes. I'm never my best at this time in the morning, and after a sleepless night in a cheap-ass motel, I'm desperate to zone out.

But my eyelids keep flipping open. It's not that she's being loud or anything. She has her laptop out now, the keys clicking quietly, her forehead furrowed in concentration. It's more that there's this steady drumbeat of awareness in me that she's here.

Fuck.

I resettle myself in the seat, sinking lower, and shutting my eyes with determination.

That lasts for about five seconds. "We won't have time to stop for breakfast," I warn her, expecting a protest.

"That's fine," she says, without looking over at me. She pauses only to blow on her hands to warm up her fingers. Her feet are bouncing against the floor in a way that tells me she's trying to keep her feet from freezing.

It would help, at least a little, if she would just wear my coat. But I manage to keep from saying that.

"Jimmy," I call. "Can you turn up the heat?"

"I'm fine," Calista says.

"You got it," Jimmy responds, and a blast of hot air roars in from the vents.

"Maybe I'm the one who's cold," I point out, just because I can. In reality, my shirt is already sticking to my back.

Calista rolls her eyes. "Right. You're always, like, ten degrees warmer than . . ." She clamps her mouth shut, her cheeks turning pink. And her fingers go still on the keyboard.

I know exactly what she's thinking for the first time since I arrived. They always kept stage seven, where the main *Starlight* sets were, so cold. She was forever huddling in a coat or scarf or both. In scene, between takes, Chase used to scrub his hands over hers to warm her up. Or she would tuck her toes—which were, by the way, like blocks of ice—under my leg.

But not after that one episode, that one scene.

So warm me up.

After that, I stayed the hell away. Or at least, I tried. I really did. She deserved better than me.

"Maybe it's my thin California blood," I say, daring her to call me on it, to tease me for not being able to handle it when she's been freaking living with it for months.

But all she says is, "Maybe," in a completely noncommittal tone.

Is this the way it's going to be? Probably. I got what I needed. She's doing the show. That's all that matters.

But it doesn't *feel* like that.

Whatever. It doesn't matter. Giving up on sleep, I pull out my phone. There are always emails waiting now. Like I'm a responsible business person or some shit, with actual answers.

There's a text at the top of my screen.

Dr. Katie: How did it go? I'm here if you want to talk about it. Let me know if your flight changes.

I grit my teeth against the guilt. Even though I have nothing to feel guilty about. I did exactly what I said I would do: nothing more, nothing less. Her concern that Callie might remind me too much of my past mistakes and that I "might be tempted to spiral" amounted to nothing.

I'm here, I'm fine. Mission accomplished, just as planned.

Except, possibly, for caring too much about the girl sitting next to me. That I wasn't counting on.

It shouldn't surprise me. It's probably just leftover . . . *whatever* from all those years of looking out for her. But someone had to. Her mother was doing her best to drive her into the ground.

A mother I had just reintroduced into her life. Shit.

But it's what had to be done. Calista is an adult now. She can handle herself. And if she can't, that's her problem, not mine.

I unlock my phone, grit my teeth, and dive into the waiting emails.

For a long while, it's quiet in the limo except for the low murmur of the radio in the front with Jimmy, Calista's laptop keys clicking, and the buzzing hum of the road beneath the tires.

"Who's writing?"

Calista's question startles me from scowling at a location-scouting report. "What?"

"Who did you get to write the episodes?" she asks, her attention still seemingly focused on the screen in front of her.

"Oh." I smile. "Jude Graves."

Callie's head snaps up, and she stares at me. "Are you serious?"

Trying not to grin at her reaction, I lift my shoulder in a shrug. "She wanted to. It was part of the deal I agreed to for the option." I had to do something, offer her something she wanted to keep the project from going elsewhere. "She used to write for TV before she wrote *Fly Girl*."

"Have you met her?" she asks, shifting slightly in her seat to face me.

"Yeah. We've been working together for a few months. It's been kind of tricky breaking it down into ten-minute episodes without losing the heart of the story." I hear the words coming out of my mouth, and for a second, I'm surprised. I actually sound like I know what I'm talking about. But I've been working hard to try to figure this all out. No way am I going to let someone say I didn't earn this, that I'm only coasting on my dad's name and reputation. "Each one has to have an arc, but they have to build to—"

"What's she like?" Callie demands, closing her laptop with a definitive click.

I raise my eyebrows.

Calista, in general, is more reserved. She can turn it on and off as needed when the cameras are rolling. But in person, she's more reflective—not shy exactly, just more prone to listening than speaking. You can practically see the thoughts churning inside her head, though; she's just learned the hard way not to voice them. Especially back when I first met her, when Lori was prone to flying off the handle at any given moment, at anything she deemed a provocation—like the temperature in Callie's dressing room or the lack of gluten-free, dairy-free, sugar-free options at lunch.

Seeing Callie come to life, for lack of a better phrase, that third season without her mom dogging her had been amazing.

But I've never seen Callie as excited as she was about that book. I'd only asked about it, really, to kill time during a set up. But Callie had launched into a full description of the story and the characters. Which was interesting, yeah.

But I was more intrigued to see her face flushed with enthusiasm, and her hands flashing and darting as she explained. The book *meant* something to her. At that point, I'd never seen her so happy.

After reading it, I understood. Callie saw herself in Evie, a girl only valued for what she could do. It must have been a relief to feel less alone, though Calista had never talked about it that way.

When Callie was talking about *Fly Girl*, it was like someone had added color to a black-and-white picture of her. That moment left me with the unreasonable and impossible desire to be able to make her that happy.

"Jude is not what you'd expect," I say, shifting away from those dangerous—and ultimately pointless—memories. "I thought she'd be kind of a snob. You know, like one of those people who claims not to watch TV?"

And to be fair, the picture on the back of the book did lead one in that direction: Jude staring back at you with her glasses perched on the edge of her nose and her arms folded across her chest, looking like every pissed-off set tutor I ever had.

Callie nods.

"But she's not. She's little," I say. "Short and tough. She's from Jersey, and she says 'fuck' a lot."

Calista laughs. "I'm sure that endeared her to you."

"Hell yeah." I shift forward in the seat, trying to get a bit of cooler air. It is so hot in here, but Calista has her foot tucked under her leg. Another sure sign that she's still cold.

She fidgets with the edge of the laptop, where the outer shell has cracked. She needs a new one. It only takes a couple clicks on my phone to order the newest model of what she's using. My funds aren't what they were when I was playing by my dad's rules, but I have enough to get her a laptop if she's going to insist on doing homework the next couple of weeks. Since she probably won't buy one for herself. And her mother certainly won't do it for her. Fucking Lori.

"Will she, uh . . ." Callie begins, and then shakes her head. "I mean, I know that writers aren't usually there, but—"

"Jude is coming for a set visit. One day next week. She wants to make sure I'm not fucking it up," I say. "Her words, not mine, by the way."

"Are you serious?" she asks, her cheeks flushing with color.

"And she wants to meet you," I add.

She swallows hard. "I don't know. I mean, I'm not . . . Evie is such a great character, she has all this depth. I don't know if I—"

"So what you're saying is, you're not feeling your craft at the moment?" I ask with a feigned frown.

It takes her a second, then she snorts with laughter, clamping a hand over her mouth. "I forgot Chase used to say that," she says, her voice muffled through her fingers.

Whenever he was screwing up take after take, which happened to all of us at various points, he would say, with this deep and troubled expression, "I'm just not feeling my craft right now."

Completely understandable, but kind of hilarious to people like Callie and me who'd been working since we were little kids and—the only craft we were worried about was the kind spelled with a "K" that came with an orange cheese packet. (My dad's chef hated it, but Miss Claud, the nanny who took care of me until I was nine, wanted me to have some semblance of a normal childhood.)

"Callie, it's fine," I say. "She's seen the show. She knows you can do it." What Jude had said was something to the effect of, "She's a spitfire, huh?" Which, hey, close enough.

Callie nods, and I expect her to return her attention to her laptop. But she doesn't. She just keeps playing with that edge of loose plastic. "Have you heard from him?"

It takes me a second to put it together. "Chase?"

She nods.

We're walking a fine line here, right at the edge of territory that we, by unspoken agreement, don't discuss. Or, at least we haven't. And I really don't want to. Reliving one of my most shameful moments—and there's plenty of competition—is something I prefer to reserve for nights when I can't sleep and I'm left staring up at the stained ceiling of a terrible motel room.

In other words, nights like last night.

"No," I say. And I don't expect to hear from him. He made it pretty clear that he was done with me when he went into rehab for what turned out to be the last time. That's probably for the best. I screwed up his life almost as much as Calista's that night. My dad cleaned things up—before cutting me off—so Chase wasn't in trouble for the accident. But Chase is as much of a cowboy as exists in this version of the world—honorable to a fault—and his conscience ate at him until he couldn't stand it. So he had to cut me loose, along with everyone else who reminded him of who he used to be.

I understand that. That night changed everything for all of us. Even my sense of right and wrong, which was usually flexible enough to allow for almost anything, wouldn't stop bugging me about it—even now, years later.

It's why I'm here, why I'm trying to fix things for Calista, even if she doesn't want me to. Okay, it's *one* of the reasons why. She really is the best person for this role.

Hey, I'm trying to be a better person, not a saint.

"I wrote him a letter when I was . . . away," Callie says. "He never responded. I don't know if it even reached him."

I wonder what she wrote him. If she told him everything. I wince inside. Not that it really matters anymore. Chase wouldn't be around to give me that grave, disappointed-in-you look.

Or punch me in my apparently oh-so-punchable face.

"And since I didn't have access to the internet while I was at Safe Haven—"

"I'm not sure where he's living right now," I say. As selfish as it is, I can't stand to hear reminders of exactly how badly I messed up her life. "But he's back in the city, I know. And I think he's dating that girl, Amanda Grace." I hear the incredulity in my voice. "The one who got kidnapped and—"

"Yeah, the thing with his poster reminding her of home." Calista nods. "I saw some of the coverage."

"You think it's real?" I ask, shaking my head. Sometimes Chase could be a little too much of a good guy; it made it easy for people to take advantage of him. Nothing about this Amanda Grace girl seems like she's in it for the fame, but sometimes people can surprise you.

Calista lifts her shoulder. "He seemed happy from what I saw. And he deserves that."

"But talk about baggage, Jesus." Just the idea of that much commitment and risk, where one mistake would bottom out everything, makes me feel like I can't breathe. Or maybe that's still the superheated dry air in here. I tug at the collar of my button-down. "It has to be complicated as fuck, and—"

"Not everyone wants the easy, attachment-free option, Eric," she says sharply.

Ouch. That would be Calista dragging her foot across the line of which we do not speak.

I clear my throat, shifting uncomfortably. "Yeah, I guess." And I have to clamp down on the urge to say something asshole-ish, something that would divert the conversation elsewhere by making her seriously pissed. You know, something like, "Better him than me." Or, "Hey, damaged girls are always the most grateful."

But that will only further the endless cycle between us.

So I let the silence hang, even though it makes my skin itch.

"Who did you get to direct?" she asks after a long moment.

Safer ground, but still likely to cause trouble. But this kind of trouble I can handle. I think.

"Vincent Meyers," I say, bracing myself.

She groans, twisting to face me. "Oh, come on, Eric, seriously?" She slaps her hand against the seat. "You hired The Terrorist? He hates us. Hates *you,*" she adds, shoving the shoulder part of her seatbelt behind her and out of the way.

She's not wrong.

"Actually, I'm pretty sure he hates everyone," I say.

"Oh, that makes it better." Calista drops her head in her hands. "Do you remember that time he screamed at me because my phone went off during a take?"

I laugh. "Oh my God, he was so pissed."

"It wasn't even a call. Just a stupid alarm my mom put in there to remind me to drink more water. I didn't even know about it. I thought that vein in his neck was going to pop." She gestures at the side of her neck, moving her hand back and forth to indicate a pulsing mass.

"And then you kept missing your mark," I remind her.

She gives me a sour look. "Because you missed yours."

"The first time." Vincent is exacting as a director, but not always the best at communicating. "But after that?"

Calista avoids my gaze. "He was being a dick to you." She shrugs. "And he really wasn't clear."

Callie always had my back, fighting more fiercely for me than I would for myself. And I did the same for her. Until I ruined that, too. I feel that loss all over again suddenly, like it's fresh. A hollowed-out place beneath my ribs that just won't heal.

I clear my throat. "Vincent's good, though." One of his episodes of *Starlight*, the one with the bus crash where Brody has to choose between saving Calista and saving other innocent lives, made critics' year-end lists of best episodes and was our one and only Emmy nod. "He was willing to take the job at scale because he wants to expand his portfolio. Plus, I heard my dad wanted him for an episode of *Triple Threat* so . . ." I shrugged. That knife was particularly fun to twist.

Calista raises her eyebrows. "Really? Is *that* what this is about?"

"No!" I shift in my seat, kicking my legs out further. "It just doesn't hurt." I grin, but it feels more like a baring of teeth.

"Wouldn't be so sure about that," she mutters.

"What's that supposed to mean?"

"Just that . . ." She shakes her head. "Never mind."

"No, say it," I demand.

She huffs out an exasperated breath. "It's just, if you're expecting this to force him to admit that he's wrong about you, you'll be disappointed and—"

"I'm not. Expecting that, I mean."

She regards me steadily. "Just because it's the opposite tactic of pretending not to give a shit doesn't mean it's any better if he's still the reason."

"I told you," I snap. "It has nothing to do with him." A drop of sweat trickles down my temple, and I wipe it away as quickly as possible. "Besides, I don't think you're really the one to give me advice on dealing with pain-in-the-ass parents."

She stiffens, and I brace myself. But she just turns her head toward the front. "Jimmy, you can turn down the heat now. I think Eric is melting." Her voice is flat.

I hate this. We never used to snipe at each other like this. Argue, yes, debate even, but this is new and ugly.

"Calista," I begin.

"No," she says. "You're right. It's none of my business how you handle Rawley." She adjusts her position on the seat, angling herself away from me with her hand on her crappy laptop to keep it from falling.

"I didn't mean—"

"I don't care, Eric," she says. "I really don't." And with that, she opens her laptop again.

I close my mouth, clenching my teeth until it hurts.

The rest of the trip passes, slowly, painfully.

When Jimmy pulls up to the curb, it takes effort to wait until he stops the car.

At the trunk, Jimmy hands out our bags. I take Callie's before she can wrestle with it.

"I can do it," she says with a dark look. "I'm not broken."

Not anymore, and I'm not so sure about that. "Just leave it." I turn my attention to Jimmy and the clipboard he's holding out with the credit card slip. "Thank you for everything, sir," I say, scrawling a generous tip and my name across the bottom.

"Not a problem." He grins at us both. "Good luck, you two."

"Oh, no," Calista says immediately. "We're not . . . There is no . . . we're not a . . . two." She finishes awkwardly and long after he's already stepped away.

"Nice," I say as we start toward the sliding doors into the airport.

"I didn't want him to get the wrong idea," she says, hoisting her backpack higher on her shoulders. I catch the wince and the way her hand flies toward her arm. Her bad one.

"Give me the bag, Calista," I say.

"What are you, my personal bellboy? I didn't think you even carried your own bags."

I open my mouth to protest.

"Forget it, I'm fine," she says.

"Callie."

"Eric," she says back, just as sharply. Then after a moment, she shakes her head. "It's part of my life now. It hurts sometimes. That's just the way it is. Trying to avoid pain is how I got into trouble."

"I'm sorry." And for the first time, the words emerge easily. Because I am. So desperately and horribly sorry about the accident. I could, perhaps, justify the other events of the evening, chalk them up to overindulging and the multiple levels of shitty decision-making that came with that. But the crash? That was on me. If I hadn't chased after her. If I hadn't gotten in the car to argue with her. If I'd noticed exactly how drunk Chase was.

"It's not all your fault. You're . . . you. I should have known better," she says, her shoulders squared with grim determination.

I wince. "Calista—"

She pulls ahead of me, effectively ending the conversation.

She's quiet after that as we wind our way through the airport, retrieving our tickets from the kiosk and getting in line at security.

But she lets me help her load her backpack onto the security conveyor belt. And then she has to explain to the TSA guy that she has surgical pins in her arm, and she has a card in her wallet from her doctor. They take her away to be searched.

Jesus. I'm such an asshole.

When they finally clear her, I'm waiting on the other side with her backpack on my shoulders and both of our bags.

It's only been a few minutes, maybe ten, but she looks tired and withdrawn. "Thanks," she says, nodding at her backpack before holding her hand out for it.

"I've got it." When her mouth tightens, I add, "Please?"

She hesitates and then gives me a curt nod.

Before we start walking, I reach out with my free arm and pull her close, my cheek against her temple. The familiar smell of her, something soft and flowery in her hair mixed with vanilla, fills my head. It makes my throat tight with emotion.

"I am sorry, Calista." I struggle to find the words. "I didn't know how . . ."

She backs up to look at me, her expression softening slightly. "I know."

"Ready?" she asks a moment later.

I make myself nod. But that small portion of forgiveness actually feels worse than her continuing to hold tight to every ounce of hatred because the hate I understand. I've *earned* that.

7 CALISTA

Eric is conspicuously quiet as we make our way to our gate. He's shouldering all the bags, but he hasn't made a single complaint or even a sarcastic comment.

It's a little unnerving, actually. He's always looked out for me. But there was a line he wouldn't cross. Too personal, and he would back off, or push away with a joke.

The low-level yearning that had sprung to life the second I saw him yesterday, outside on the steps of Ryland, holding that dumb cigarette, is growing in intensity.

I've *missed* him.

Dumb, Calista. Don't do this. He blackmailed you into coming along, remember?

Definite asshole move. There is no excusing that.

And yet, he wouldn't have been able to do that if my mom and I weren't as complicated and twisted as we are. He was simply taking advantage of an existing conflict to get what he wanted.

That's manipulative and smart—exactly what I know him to be. Exactly what I have admired in him in the past, when it wasn't directed at me. Plus, the fact that his efforts are in the name of making *Fly Girl* the best it can be . . .

STOP.

I'm not going to go through this again. Eric is not the person I want him to be. He can't be, and that's not his fault. So it's on me, me seeing what I want to see and ignoring the rest.

Taking a deep breath, I turn to confirm with him that we're close—O'Hare is much larger than I remembered. "I think that's our gate up ahead. K12 . . ."

Only, as I turn, a woman rushes past me, almost knocking into me. "Eric!" She throws herself into his arms, and he stumbles back a step. But that does not stop her from attaching her mouth to his.

Oh, shit.

It's been a long time since we've had to deal with people who put the fan back in fanatic, but the pulse of panic electrifying my veins is all-too-familiar. That night at the MTV movie awards when Chase and I were swarmed by the crowd remains a frequent player in my nightmares.

I spin around, looking for someone, anyone, in a uniform. "Help! Security . . ." The words die in my throat as my gaze lands on Eric and the woman again. The kiss has ended, and he's smiling. He's dropped his bag off his shoulder and let go of my roller bag, and his hands are tight on the woman's hips, pulling her close.

Her fingers are in his hair with easy familiarity, and the sight makes my gut clench tight. *What? Just . . . what is happening?*

"What happened to your cheek?" She runs her fingers lightly beneath the bruise, frowning up at him.

He shrugs and gives her that devilish grin that I'm far too familiar with. "You know me, always charming. Until I'm not."

Suddenly it feels like I'm falling even though I'm standing still. The realization drops into place with the sensation of rushing air, like the ground is fast approaching in my eternal plummet.

This is not a playful encounter with someone he once hooked up with at a party. I saw that plenty of times with the gorgeous and scary-thin models he seemed to gather like lint on sticky tape.

Same thing with the bubble-breasted actresses who came around to his trailer. Once there was an issue with a girl who'd auditioned (and been hired) for daywork. She'd accepted the job for the express purpose of confronting him about his unfulfilled promise to text her.

Those girls were greeted with a peck on the cheek or mouth and that irresistible "don't hate me for not calling since the last time I saw you and we were both naked" smile.

This is not that.

This woman, whoever she is, is important to him. And judging by the amount of tongue on her end in that brief kiss, we're talking important in the sharing-my-bed sort of way, not like she-saved-me-thousands-in-taxes.

I can't breathe. My lungs are locked as tight as the Tupperware my mom uses as a secondary barrier to protect her expensive jars of moisturizer.

Eric is in love. With someone else.

I am such an idiot.

I don't think I made any noise—it would be difficult considering it still felt like I couldn't breathe—but something makes Eric look past her, meeting my gaze.

I should look away, but I can't. And my breathing resumes with a gasp.

Whatever he sees in my expression makes him lean forward to whisper a quick word to the woman. Then he grabs up our luggage and takes her hand, and with an uncertain smile, he closes the small gap between us, bringing her with him.

Oh, God. He's really going to do this. Please don't do this.

But Eric ignores my silent plea.

"Calista, this is Dr. Katie Wahlburg," Eric says. "Katie, this is Calista."

My empty stomach roils, sending a plume of acid up the back of my throat.

"Hi, Calista! It's nice to meet you," she says, pumping my hand with a firm effective grip. "I've heard so much about you." She's very pretty, but in a practical, non-Hollywood way. Her long chestnut hair is shiny and gathered up in an unartful pony tail that still manages to look elegant and pulled together with her long black coat, gorgeous knitted cowl, and battered leather bag. She's maybe even a few years older than Eric, putting her close to thirty.

With my jeans and Blake College hoody, I feel like a little girl in comparison, one with scraped knees and tears overflowing because my ice cream hit the sidewalk unexpectedly.

"I . . ." *Didn't know you existed.*

I want to say it, I really do, but that's a slash at Eric that will only hurt this seemingly nice woman. "Same . . . Doctor." I can't even look at him right now.

"Please call me Katie or Dr. Katie, if you have to." She gives a playful eyeroll. "Eric just likes being able to brag on the doctor part. No one calls me that except for the owners."

"The . . . owners?" I am not following this conversation particularly well, mainly because the blood rushing past my ears has reached a deafening level.

"Katie's a veterinarian at Sunrise Veterinary," Eric explains, squeezing her hand in his.

"For right now, but I'm hoping to start my own practice soon," she says, with the air of a topic long-discussed. So she's older, beautiful, has her shit together, *and* runs her own life.

If it were possible to create someone by simply checking opposites on a list, Katie would be that person for me.

"Oh." That is truly all I can manage.

Katie smiles at me, but her brows are furrowed with confusion. "Didn't he tell you? We met when he brought in Bitsy. He thought he broke her leg when he stepped on her accidentally, and you know how delicate those teacup breeds are."

She's gesturing while telling the story, and my brain can only comprehend a few pieces of information at a time. It's like she's speaking a foreign language—a few words sound familiar, but most of it is just gibberish.

Mainly because I have no idea what she's talking about—Eric, with an animal dependent on him?—but also because there's an enormous diamond ring on her left ring finger that is taking up all available computing space in my brain.

"Eric has a dog?" The syllables trickle out, sounding stilted.

Katie looks uncertain, as if I've just asked her what my own name is. "Well, yeah. His teacup Yorkie. Bitsy."

I don't even have words for this. Eric *proposed*? The rock on her left hand can mean only that.

My mind immediately produces an image of him on his knees in front of me, his dark head bent down until he looks up with that ring box balanced on his fingertips.

"You have a dog named Bitsy," I say through numb lips. Engaged. They are fucking engaged.

Eric sighs. "Not by choice. She was my mom's. She stayed with me the last time she visited."

So Eric has his own place now? Or does he live with her, with Katie? The sheer amount of new information in this conversation is making me dizzy. The Eric she's describing is not the one I know. Or knew.

"Mom got Bitsy to keep her company, then didn't bother to bring her home with her," Eric says, his mouth tightening. "Now I'm stuck with her."

The dog, at least, I understand now. He's not going to abandon a small helpless creature left behind by his mother. He was once in that exact same situation.

But none of the rest of it even remotely makes sense.

"Oh, stop, you love Bitsy and you know it." Katie shoves at his shoulder with her free hand, that diamond sparkling like it's doing so just to taunt me.

"He brought her in during my shift at the emergency clinic a couple of years ago. She's whimpering, he's dripping blood everywhere . . ."

"Lime-slicer accident. I was . . . being a dumbass," Eric adds.

Translation: He was drunk or high.

"Jumped back when it slipped and caught my hand. Bitsy was, as always, underfoot," Eric says. "I called for an Uber to the closest vet . . ."

". . . and I patched him up long enough to get X-rays for Bitsy, then I drove him to the ER," Katie says, beaming up at him.

They've obviously told this story before. It's like a two-person play. And I'm the audience.

"And now you're here," I say, my voice gravelly.

Her smile falters momentarily. "I was in Michigan for the week, and they were going to make me transfer in Denver, but I was like, 'duh, if I can get the change in Chicago instead, why not?'" She looks back and forth between Eric and me, as if expecting us to celebrate this development.

"Why not?" I agree weakly.

An awkward silence falls.

"I should go get . . ." But my head is spinning, and the rest of me just wants to find a quiet corner where I can have a minute to myself, to curl up and die. "Food," I blurt finally. "I should go get food."

Eric frowns at me, dark brows drawing together.

"And the bathroom," I add. He can't argue that.

"Oh," Katie says softly. "I'm interfering. I'm sorry. I know you two have lots to talk—"

"No, it's fine," Eric says. "We're boarding in ten minutes, Callie."

"You guys will still have plenty of time to catch up on the flight," Katie says with an earnestness that only makes me feel worse. I hate that she's so nice. "Last minute, I couldn't get anything but coach." She wrinkles her nose up adorably, holding up her boarding pass. "And I know how Eric feels about traveling with the common folk," she teases.

Nope, no, I cannot do this. I cannot stand here and have this conversation. And I sure as hell cannot get on a plane and sit next to Eric for the next four hours, pretending that everything is fine and I'm not bleeding out internally. True, he doesn't owe me anything. We were never . . . anything. Not really. He had every right to fall in love and get engaged to someone else. And I have no right to feel shredded over it.

But that doesn't change the fact that I do.

"Oh, well, that's just stupid," I say too quickly. "Here." Before Katie can protest, I've tugged her boarding pass free of her fingers, handing her mine.

She takes it with a startled expression. "Um, okay, but—"

"Now the two of you are together in first class. Perfect. Problem solved." Despite my best efforts, my voice cracks on the last word. *Shit.* "I'll just be . . . back."

"Calista." Eric's voice is dark with warning.

And I do not care.

I ignore him and keep moving. There's a bathroom directly across from our gate, but that doesn't feel far enough away. Then it occurs to me that possibly anywhere in the state is not far enough away. Any port in a storm.

I make a beeline for the doorway.

Eric is on my heels. He grabs my arm, careful to avoid my shoulder, and pulls me to a halt. "What are you doing? What is wrong with you?"

"The bathroom, Eric," I snap. "It happens."

"Bullshit," he says, releasing me. "I know you're pissed at me for everything, but you don't have to take it out on her. Katie's being nice—she *is* nice, a good person—and you're acting like a Grade A spoiled bitch."

I flinch, the insult biting deeper than I expected.

"That's not you," he says.

I know what to do. Tilt my chin up, summon my best imitation of my mother, and tell him that maybe he just doesn't know me well enough. Wouldn't that be a precious bit of irony?

But that's not what happens. "You're getting married?" The question slips out before I can stop it, and my eyes well with tears. Damnit.

His expression shifts from anger to surprise, his mouth falling open.

I want to bite my tongue off. "Never mind. Just forget it," I say in a choked voice.

"Callie," he says softly, and reaches out like he would touch me. But his hand falls short. "I didn't think . . ." Eric scrubs his hand over his face, his jaw tightening. "I wasn't . . ." He shakes his head, seeming more stunned than anything.

"I'll see you on the plane." I turn away from him before he can recover and beat a hasty retreat to the bathroom.

All the stalls are full, so I'm forced to wait in line. But thankfully no one seems to be interested or brazen enough to comment on the tears streaming down my face. I'm no longer famous enough for random strangers to recognize me.

An older woman passes me a tissue with a sympathetic smile. "Whoever he is, he's not worth it, honey."

But that only makes me cry harder.

Because once I might have agreed with her. He was too selfish, too shallow, too irresponsible. An arrogant player jerk. The flashes of more that I'd seen in him were obviously wrong.

Except they weren't.

That version of him that I fell in love with—affectionate, caring, driven, protective—that Eric did exist. Just not for me.

And somehow, knowing that I was right, but just not the *right one,* makes it hurt that much more.

8 ERIC

I wait at the gate, watching the bathroom door. They're calling for first class to board, and Calista hasn't reemerged. Any second now, they're going to start boarding groups in coach.

". . . and then my eighty-six-year-old grandmother says, 'That's what the shotgun is for!'" Katie laughs. "Can you believe that?"

I smile automatically, my attention fixed across the corridor.

"Hey." Katie nudges me. "You okay?"

"Yeah, I'm just . . ." I jerk my head toward the bathroom.

She follows the gesture with a frown. "Do you think she's in there getting high?" she asks in loud whisper.

"What? No." I shake my head. "It's just been a crazy couple of days is all. She just needed a minute, I think."

Is Calista going to miss the flight? Refuse to get on? It seems entirely possible after what just happened. Though I'm still not quite sure *what* happened.

Just Callie looking up at me, hurt, with her eyes shiny with tears, asking me about getting married.

Fuck. Fuck!

This should not be possible. She had . . . feelings once, I knew that. But that was years ago. Before.

"Please tell me you didn't go through with calling her mother, at least," Katie says, drawing my attention back to her. She's now watching the bathroom door with me.

I shift uncomfortably. "I didn't have a choice."

"Really?"

"It's the only way Callie would agree to it." I jam my hands into my pockets. "She's so damned determined to hide."

But now I'm wondering why, exactly. Her mother sent her away to try to clear the slate, taking advantage of the notoriously short half-life of most scandals. But Calista wanted a new life, something far away from Hollywood and her mistakes.

And me?

I don't know anymore.

"Maybe that says something, then," Katie says. "If you have to bully people into this project, maybe you'd be better off—"

I look at her sharply. "It's important to me." I don't want to have this argument again. Not here, not now. Katie and I rarely fight about anything, but the Michigan Plan, as she calls it, is responsible for a lot of escalating tension lately.

"And it's not bullying," I add, shifting my attention back to the bathroom door. I've seen several cycles of women come and go. It's not the line that's holding her in there. "I'm trying to fix things."

Katie raises her eyebrows. "By twisting her arm into doing a show she doesn't want to do?"

It's hard to explain. I know Callie. She does want to do the show. Or she would, if everything hadn't gotten all messed up. Except now, I'm not sure about that. About any of it.

I hurt her so badly. How can she possibly still care what I do or who I do it with? And yet she seems to. Everything is suddenly very confusing. And absurdly, I feel a spark of anger at Calista for making it all muddled.

"Come on," Katie says, looping her arm through mine and tugging gently. "Let's get our seats. Overhead bins are going to fill up fast, and you have Calista's bags, too."

I resist.

"Eric, if she's not coming, you can't exactly drag her onto the plane," Katie points out, amused. She nuzzles in next to my chin. "I know you don't want to hear this, but there *are* other actors who can play that role," she reminds me. "Lots of them."

"Maybe," I say, even as a voice screams inside me that no one is as right for Evie as Calista. Plus, we would miss out on the *Starlight* effect.

But Katie's right—I've used the one card I had to play, and that's it. If Callie decides to stay, then she does. The money I've already given to Lori will majorly screw with my budget if I have to hire another actor. But maybe that outcome would be for the best. I don't know.

"Or," she added hesitantly, "you could always just . . ."

Cancel. Close up shop. Quit before you even start.

Katie is convinced that I'll never be whole, that I'll never truly be better, until I'm away from everything that made me the dysfunctional wonder I am—Hollywood, fame, show business, and even California in general.

Katie's dream is to move back to Michigan where she can be near her family and start her own veterinary practice. And I'll do . . . something. What exactly, she's never been particularly clear about, though she's mentioned more times than coincidence allows that her dad is looking for a good right-hand-man at his real estate firm.

No. This industry may be desperately beyond-measure fucked up, but it's all I know, all I've ever wanted.

Katie must see it in my expression. "Okay, I'll stop," she says, pressing a kiss against my bruised cheek.

For now. She's supportive . . . to an extent. Pleased that I have direction, though less pleased with the direction I've chosen and hopeful it will change. Soon.

I let Katie pull me away and onto the plane.

Katie, always self-sufficient, stows her bag and then helps with Callie's. Maybe I should have left the bags with the gate agent if

Calista's not coming. But the thought of handing it over to the flight attendant makes me tighten my grip on her backpack and the battered laptop within, like having it here will summon her to follow.

Once we're settled in our seats—Katie on the aisle and me next to the window—Katie pulls a magazine out of her bag and starts flipping pages. "Calista didn't seem to know anything about your life now," Katie ventures. "Not about Bitsy or how we met."

Or that we're engaged.

I tense, warning bells going off in my head. Katie is not crazy dramatic, emphasis on *crazy*—she's not an actress, after all—and that's one of my favorite things about her. But I can feel the subtext here bubbling under the surface. "We haven't talked since the accident," I remind her.

"Until yesterday."

"Yeah."

She looks at me expectantly.

"It just . . . didn't come up." That sounds like an evasion, I can hear it, like the words are sliding sideways off my tongue, but it's the truth. "Honestly, I was so focused on getting her to sign on that we never really talked about what was going on with me."

She frowns. "Really?"

At the time, it hadn't really occurred to me how strange that was. Calista hadn't asked a single question about my life now, except as it related to the work. Okay, and my dad. And Chase. That made sense if she hated me, was only tolerating my presence because I forced her to via Lori.

But then she has the nerve to give me the big wounded eyes like I was hiding Katie? Like I somehow hurt her by having a life? And why the hell do I feel *guilty*?

That spark of anger returns. Why does she have to make this so confusing?

"Yeah, I don't know," I say curtly to Katie.

"Ladies and gentlemen, just a few more minutes and then we'll close the door and be on our way," the flight attendant says over the intercom.

No sign of Calista. *Shit.*

"Breathe," Katie says, without looking up from her magazine. She reaches over to squeeze my knee.

I grit my teeth to keep from snapping at her. She's just trying to help.

Because this isn't a big deal. I can totally hire someone else in the next twenty-four hours without hosing my entire production schedule.

Right.

A few seconds later, I catch a glimpse of Calista's bright blond hair as she rounds the corner onto the plane and steps into the aisle.

My shoulders slump with relief.

Callie moves with her head up, gaze firmly fixed on some point in the distance, and for a moment, I think she's going to breeze past us without a word. But then she waves at Katie.

Katie waves back. "Hey. Are you sure you don't want to switch—"

"Oh, no, this is fine," she says, already stepping past us, without as much as a word or a glance in my direction.

But even with as quickly as she's moving, I can see the faint signs of puffiness around her eyes. She's been crying. It's not as noticeable as it might have been, but Callie knows all the tricks around that. I don't know how many times I walked into her trailer to find her with her head tipped back and her mother applying cold cloths or those eye-pad things.

Sharp-toothed guilt returns to gnaw on me. And irrationally, that makes me even angrier. I reach for my seatbelt.

"What are you doing?" Katie asks, putting her hand over mine to stop me.

That is an excellent question. What am I doing? Preparing to have an argument on an airplane with my former . . . friend? Co-star? It feels like there should be a stronger word for whatever Calista is to me, but there isn't.

"She might want her laptop," I say. "She has homework that's due." Which is true, and sends another wave of that guilt through me. She was trying to make a life for herself, and I showed up and messed that up for her. I knew those facts before, but now, knowing what she might still feel . . .

During our *Starlight* days, I hadn't been aware of how deep those feelings went, not until she showed up at my trailer one night, about a month after we filmed that damned AU episode.

A knock sounded at my door as I was scrubbing the makeup off my face.

"Yeah. Come in," I shouted, without bothering to check. Or think.

"Hello?" a voice called uncertainly.

Calista. My heart sped up in spite of myself. I'd been trying to keep my distance, avoiding situations that left the two of us alone. Because every time she walked by, she left a wake that smelled of vanilla, even underneath the various scents of hair products and makeup, and it instantly transported me to that shitty blanket and fake grass and the feel of her warm and moving beneath me.

But she was barely eighteen, almost five years younger than me, and beyond that, so sheltered that she actually believed I was a good guy.

I wiped my face off on a towel and stepped out of the bathroom. "Yeah, hey. What's up, kid?"

She winced.

I frowned. "What's wrong?"

"Nothing. I just . . . I need to ask you something." Her gaze flicked down, her cheeks flushing as she realized I wasn't wearing a shirt.

I felt the heat rise in my skin, as if she were touching me instead of just looking.

Shit. Nope.

I backed up a step, grabbing a shirt from the floor. One of Byron's that was due back at wardrobe, as it happened, but it didn't matter. "Come in, sit down." I yanked the shirt on as she settled on the couch. "I've got a few minutes. Did your mom say something?" Chase and I helped her move out after she fired Lori, but Lori still found ways to interfere, like bringing her housewarming gifts—rugs and shit—along with healthy portions of guilt. *Zinnia needs braces. Poppy needs a specialist for her asthma. And you can't expect Dahlia's earnings to cover all of that—she's just a baby! I'm not asking for handouts, Calista. Just let me do my job. You need me.*

That kind of crap.

"No, no, it's not anything like that." Callie hesitated, pulling her knees up to her chest. She had already changed to her own clothes: yoga pants with a long loose shirt over them and white Converse. She twisted a loose thread from her shoe around her finger until the tip turned purple.

"Callie . . ." My phone buzzed on the coffee table impatiently, flashing a photo.

"Angelica?" Calista asked, her face carefully blank.

"Yeah, she's on her way." Angelica and I had been friends (who occasionally fuck each other) for years. Her father was a big-time agent, and we ran in the same circles. "There's a party tonight that's supposed to be—"

"I thought you had that thing with your dad tomorrow," Calista says.

"Another awkward lunch so he can tell me how disappointed he is in me one more time, while introducing me to assistant number four who is probably going to end up being wife number three? Yeah, I think I can skip that." More likely, I wouldn't even wake up until it was already over, which, as far as I was concerned, was the ideal scenario.

She shakes her head at me. "It's only going to piss him off."

"What, like you and Lori are super tight?" I snort.

"At least he's trying," she says.

"It's better when he doesn't. You and I both know that."

After a moment, she nods.

It was the one thing we had in common that others didn't understand—Calista and I were orphans. We just happened to be orphans who had parents somewhere in the world. Callie's mother was more manager than mom, too busy treating her daughter as an investment to ever stop and think of her as a kid. And these days, my dad preferred to pretend I didn't exist unless I forced the issue.

Sometimes I did, just to prove that I could.

Callie didn't say anything, just kept twisting that thread around her finger. "Do you ever think about what's next?" she asked.

"What, like, after death?" I grin at her.

"No, I mean, after this." She gestured around my trailer. "No one is saying, but they haven't picked us up for next season and the ratings are—"

"—in the toilet and buried under four feet of shit," I finished. "Yep." I dropped into the armchair across from her, trying to figure out where she was going with this. "Are you worried about getting another job without your mom? Because no matter what happens, you're going to be better off without her." If I'd been the worrying type, I might have been a little concerned for myself, given that most people still seemed to think that all I had to do was ask my dad for work. Which might have been true if we could stand to be in the same wing of the house long enough to have a civil conversation.

Not since I was about fourteen.

And because I had that reputation among others, getting callbacks wasn't always easily accomplished. Casting directors rarely took me seriously.

Fortunately, I was not the worrying type.

"No, it's not that," Calista said so softly I could barely hear her. "I just . . . this is the longest I've ever worked anywhere."

"I know," I said, trying to school myself into patience as my phone continued to buzz. This had to be important or Calista wouldn't have sought me out at the end of a very long day.

"And my family is . . . my family," she said, her mouth tightening.

Yeah, if I thought mine was bad, at least we had the good sense to avoid each other most of the time. Easy to do when Dad was always working and Mom now lived on another continent most of the time. Callie was not so lucky.

"I didn't go to high school," Calista continued. "I don't really have friends, not outside of work."

Ah, now I was getting it. When work was your entire existence, your family and your social circle, what happened when work went away? It wasn't just the paycheck, it was her actual life she was worried about.

I reached over and wrestled her hand away from the loose thread before she cut off her circulation for good. "You'll get another job. You'll find other friends. You're going to be fine, Callie." I squeezed her cool fingers and then let go before I was tempted to linger.

She nodded but seemed unconvinced.

"And if you don't?" I shrugged. "Who needs more friends?" I asked. "You've got me and Chase."

"Do I?" she asked.

"What do you mean?" If I were a smarter person, warning bells should have gone off then.

"I'm just afraid everything's going to change. And maybe I'm not going to find people that I feel the same way about." She lifted her shoulders in a shrug, then slowly raised her gaze to meet mine. "Or people who feel the same way about me." Her chin tipped up defiantly, as if she was daring me to deny something. Bright patches of color stained her cheeks.

Uh-oh. I suddenly had the sensation of falling, like gravity wasn't working as it should have been. It made me a little panicky. Surely she wasn't talking about what I thought she was talking about.

But if she was . . .

I stood in a burst of nervous energy mixed with frustration. "Cal, I think you're worrying too much about something that's not going to be a problem, and I have to go—".

"I'm not, though," she said. "Worrying."

I just looked at her.

She blushed. "I mean, yeah, I am. But not like that." She takes a deep breath. "I want . . . I need a favor."

Fuck. "Calista . . ."

Before I could say more, she unfolded herself from the couch and moved to stand in front of me.

Too close. I could feel her, like I was standing at the edge of an energy field. Her energy field. Like one of those auras Stepmother Two had always gone on about. I was caught between wanting to step back and push forward. To touch her, to bury my face in the softness of the skin where her neck met her shoulder and bite gently. To see if she'd react like she had that day on set, pushing her hips against me with a moan.

"There are things that I haven't . . ." Her face turned a deeper shade of scarlet. "Next year at this time, we don't know where any of us will be, if we'll still be as close. And I don't want to lose . . . this. My chance."

This is a bad idea. I should back away. I should just leave . . .

"What are you saying?" I asked instead, my voice gone to gravel, daring her to specify.

But her chin went up, responding to the implicit challenge. "I've never slept with anyone. I want you to . . ." She hesitated, and then rallied. "I want *us* to." She folded her arms.

Jesus.

"It doesn't have to be anything serious," she says quickly, her hands twisting together. "I just want it to be with someone I trust. Someone I care about." She met my gaze, unflinching. "Please."

"Callie, you shouldn't . . . that should be with someone you're sure of. Someone you love. A boyfriend or, fuck, I don't know." I stuttered out ideas that I wasn't even sure I agreed with, except in the sense that she deserved the best, whatever that was. Better than me.

"Do you not . . . is it . . . are you not attracted to me?" she asked, her chin wobbling.

I glared at her, irrationally angry at her for pushing the issue. "It's not that. You *know* it's not that."

"Then what is it?" she asked.

I rake my hand through my hair, trying to find the words to explain that it wasn't her, but me, even as a primal drumbeat throbbed in me. *Yes, yes, yes.*

But it was like she could read my mind, the doubt in myself. "I'm sure of you," she said, rising on her tiptoes, her hands balancing lightly on my chest.

Her breath fluttered against my cheek, and then she brushed her mouth over mine, so light it was barely there, but the touch of her lips sent electricity through me.

I closed my eyes. All the better to *feel.* And my hands moved automatically to her hips, keeping her steady. Pulling her closer.

She made a soft noise in her throat and curled her arms around my neck, pressing us together. And I couldn't stop myself; I slid a hand up and into her hair, tilting her head and taking control. Tasting her mouth until she gasped, her fingers wrapped tight in my shirt.

Opening my eyes, I pulled away from her, my gaze riveted by her kiss-reddened mouth.

For a moment, the thought of it filled my head. Her head thrown back against my pillow, her legs wrapped tight around my waist, her eyes fierce on mine.

But not just Callie in my bed. Breakfast the next morning, where she would insist on us trying to muddle through making pancakes for ourselves. Or a popcorn fight on my couch on our regular movie night (minus Chase, for once) that would result in me licking every place on her body where the salt may have stuck. Or just places that I wanted to lick. I wanted to see her moaning and shaking above me. To know that I was the one who made her feel that way, the *only* one. She deserved to have someone who would take the time to make her feel good instead of just focusing on getting off, and I wanted to be that guy.

It was so tempting, so much so that I caught myself taking a step back toward the bedroom, pulling her with me.

A pulse of fear stopped me.

It'll end badly. It always does. In tears or shitty texts and retribution. It never lasted longer than a few months. The thought of anything more permanent made me itchy. Because when you let someone in, you're giving them the chance to hurt you. To one day walk away.

Casual friendly sex between two consenting adults was one thing. No harm, no foul. But it wouldn't be just sex with Calista. I knew that already. It was too dangerous for both of us.

"Callie," I said softly. "I can't. Not with you."

Her face colored, and she pulled away from me. "Because I've never—"

"No!" I hesitated, feeling a level of discomfort I never knew existed. "Not exactly. It's just not a good idea."

She folded her arms across her chest. "Why not?"

"Because meaningless hookups are not who you are," I said, feeling dull satisfaction when just the words made her blush harder.

But she wasn't ready to give up. "That's up to me," she pointed out.

"I know you, kid," I began.

“Don’t call me that,” she said sharply.

I held my hands up in surrender. “Sorry. Calista.” I shook my head. “I just meant, it’s complicated. We’re friends, good friends, and I don’t want to ruin that with regrets.” Like I ruined everything—sometimes deliberately, sometimes not. I couldn’t take that chance with her, not and live with myself. Couldn’t stand to see her looking at me with so much hurt when it blew up in our faces.

“How do you know it would ruin things? It wouldn’t have to. It doesn’t have to be a big deal.” She edged closer to me again, and I felt my resolve weakening, like the ground was opening up beneath my feet. She knew the worst of me, had seen it for herself. And yet she was still standing here. And she smelled so good. It was too easy to imagine her hands on my skin, on my cock. Learning exactly what I liked. Learning what *she* liked.

“Except it is,” I snapped.

She raised her eyebrows. “*You* think it’s a big deal? Didn’t you lose your virginity to some makeup artist when you were, like, fourteen and—”

“Because I know it would mean something to you,” I said, frustrated beyond the point of being careful.

It took her a second, and when it clicked, she rocked back a step, like she was absorbing a blow. “And it wouldn’t to you,” she said in a slight, almost breathless voice. “That’s what you’re saying.”

No. If that were true, I’d already have us in the bedroom and missing most of our clothes.

“I need to go.” I stepped around her to scoop my phone off the table.

“Don’t bother. I’ll leave.” She mustered a tight smile. “You wouldn’t want to keep Angelica waiting.” Then she pushed past me, shoving open the outer door until it banged against the trailer.

“Callie . . .” But she was gone. That was what I got for trying to do the right thing.

Except that noble intention wasn't really the truth of it, not entirely.

Looking back on it, I vividly remember how hard my heart was pounding during that conversation, equally from fear and desire.

Not that it matters now, but I'd been right: It *was* a bad idea. Which I'd later prove to both of us.

I'd tried to protect her, protect us both, knowing I would hate myself if I hurt her. It was the one honorable thing I'd really tried to stick to. I'd messed that up, of course, and then taken it a step further to make sure she hated me. It worked. She said so herself yesterday, and I don't blame her.

Except now it doesn't seem like that's true. I don't understand this at all.

"At least wait until we take off and they turn off the seatbelt sign," Katie says, frowning at me like I've lost my mind. "She can't use her laptop until then anyway."

"Right." I tap my hands against my knees, my foot jiggling with excess energy. "You're right."

"Here. Something to read." Grinning, she hands me a magazine that's already open to a page.

Dos and Don'ts for the Groom-to-Be

"See, and it comes with a handy tear-out card in case you need a portable reminder that you're supposed to wear a tux and not get drunk before the ceremony." She rolls her eyes.

She's expecting this to make me laugh. And a week ago, it would have—the entire bridal industry appears to be centered on the idea that men are idiots and that the future bride best lock him down and keep him in line before his confusion wears off. Something Katie and I have joked about repeatedly. *Your shock collar came in. It matches my dress!*

Right now, though, the reminder of my planned future just makes my skin feel too tight. And it shouldn't. I have everything I want, finally. Katie doesn't take any crap from me, and she expects me to keep up. In work, in life, in taking my turn to walk Bitsy. If I don't, she'll cut me loose. Without hesitation.

She doesn't need me at all. And I love that. It takes the pressure off. I don't have to worry about hurting her, about screwing up and taking her down with me.

So I need to stay right here in my seat and pretend like everything is normal until it is again. If Calista wants her laptop, she can come and get it.

I force a smile at Katie. "You know me, always looking for more helpful tips. Does it say anything about walking and breathing at the same time?"

She laughs.

I'm not going to mess this up. I'm *not.*

9 CALISTA

My temples and face are throbbing from my crying jag in the airport bathroom and the pressure change in the cabin now that we're thirty minutes under way. But I did it. I made it onto the plane and past Eric and *his fiancée* without a single additional tear. Or vomiting.

Honestly, I think that should go up on my demo reel because that was some of my finest acting to date.

Right now, though, I just want this plane ride to be over and to be home. Not at my mom and stepdad's house, though, where my younger sister, Zinn, has taken over my former room. Or even back in my tiny dingy single at Blake.

I don't know where home is anymore. The thought sends a spiraling sense of panic through me.

The apartment I was renting the year and a half or so before my stint in rehab is long gone. It was bright and sunny, and I liked it. But I didn't live there long enough for it to ever feel like mine. And many of the days I was there are a bit hazy thanks to my pain management techniques at the time.

When is the last time I felt that safe-at-home feeling? I don't even remember.

I lean my head back against the headrest and close my eyes, trying to slow my breathing.

"Are you okay?" my seatmate asks.

I open my eyes to see her leaning over the empty seat between us with an annoyed frown. She's an older woman with tabloids sticking out of her shoulder bag and more spread out on the tray in front of her.

"The airsick bag is in the pocket in front of you," she says.

"Thanks, I'm fine," I say.

She returns to her reading, mumbling about sympathetic vomiting and the whole plane being a germ factory.

I shut my eyes again, willing myself to sleep and the oblivion that would accompany it.

I can't, though.

Instead, I stare at the darkness of my closed eyelids, pulling through threads of memory, searching for that lost sensation of home.

After a few seconds, it pops into focus. The interior of my trailer on *Starlight*. Except that's not quite right because for most of my tenure there, my mother would have been flitting around me, straightening my wardrobe, fussing over my hair, and scolding about carbs.

But in the vision in my head, it's my trailer, with Eric stretched out on the couch, waiting, semi-impatiently, for me to hurry up and finish removing my makeup so we could leave for movie night at his house. So the third season.

Or Chase, Eric and I stuck in some anonymously bland hotel, during a fan convention or a press junket, and playing Uno to kill time because those were the only cards available in the gift shop. Eric and I secretly colluded, using hand signals, to keep Chase from winning, something Chase protested vehemently once he figured it out. Which only made it all the more fun. "Y'all are a bunch of reprobates," he said in disgust, chucking his cards on the table.

Eric blowing powdered sugar at me across the craft services table, all over the dried kale my mother was pushing into my hand. My mother yanking me away in response.

Or when Eric and I sneaked into that hotel swimming pool in Germany and . . .

I stop, a belated realization forcing me upright, my eyes open. There's a theme here that's impossible to miss.

But how big of an idiot does that make me? Not just after everything that's happened between us but when he's obviously chosen someone else to be his home.

This is so messed up.

I make myself take another deep breath. *Do not panic. It's just two weeks. I can handle that.*

Two weeks of Eric every day and probably Katie, too. Bringing him, I don't know, homemade cookies and his bound-to-be adorable dog. Maybe homemade cookies *for* his adorable dog.

I groan, rubbing my forehead.

My seatmate lurches forward. "Do you need me to call the stewardess? I can't handle you throwing up on me."

I stare at her and open my mouth to respond, but then I see Eric charging down the aisle toward me. His mouth is a tight unhappy line, and his cheeks are streaky with color.

He shoves my backpack at me. "Your laptop. For homework," he says, biting off the words.

"Okay." I take the backpack, expecting him to turn and stomp off.

Instead, he stands there, far too close and looming over me, his hands on his hips. "I'm getting married," he says, the words tight, as though they're grating on the way out.

"I'm aware. I believe I'm the one who brought it up," I say, fighting the rising tide of anger.

He flinches, ever so slightly, at my words. And for a second, I feel gritty satisfaction at having scored a point.

Eric shakes his head. "You can't . . . you shouldn't feel anything about that."

I gape at him. "Are you serious right now?" I'm stunned. Not just that we're having this discussion but that we're having it *here*.

I can practically feel my seatmate pressing against my side to listen in.

"I was an asshole to you," he points out, like that makes any kind of sense.

"Yes. Thank you for the reminder," I say tightly. My jaw is aching with everything I want to say, all the words backed up down my throat and clamoring to be released. And I'm just weak enough to let some of them go, unfair though they may be. "It's not like I don't have enough of those." I lift my injured arm in example.

He reels back, his face blanching, and guilt tugs at me.

But then he nods and points at me. "Yes, exactly. That's what I'm talking about."

"I have no idea what you're talking about," I say, my voice rising in spite of myself.

My seatmate clears her throat in disapproval, and Eric's gaze shoots from me to her. "I'm sorry," he says in a deceptively pleasant voice. "Are we interrupting your study of botched plastic surgeries? Or celebrities with cellulite?"

An offended gasp is her only answer. I'm betting we have under a minute before she punches the flight attendant call button.

Eric's attention returns to me. "You need to learn to protect yourself better than that."

I can't figure out if I'm more confused or angry at this point. "Are you saying you want me to hate you?"

"Yes, because I deserve it," he says before clamping his mouth shut so tight that I can see a jaw muscle twitching.

In spite of everything, or maybe because I am a hopeless case when it comes to him, my battered heart gives a pathetic thump for him at those words. Because lots of people hate him—for various reasons, mostly for what he appears to be—and I know he believes he deserves that too.

But then he keeps going. "And because that means you've learned not to let people walk all over you anymore."

Fury returns in a sudden whoosh, blood pounding past my ears and into my already-throbbing head. "You are the one who came after me," I grit out. "You're the one who pulled me out of my life, a life that I chose, and forced me to be here."

He looks tired suddenly. "And you're the one who let me. You're the one who allows your mother to own you. It's your weakness."

I squeeze my hands into tight fists until pain shoots up into my damaged arm.

E-fucking-nough.

My hand flies up, and I slap at the call button myself, before my neighbor can do it. "I might still have things to learn, Eric, but it is *not* up to you to teach me," I say.

Emotion flickers across his face, gone before I can identify it. "Calista—"

"Sir, I'm sorry, but you need to return to your seat," the flight attendant says as she approaches. "We have to keep the aisle clear." It's a gentle scolding, with a smile on the edge of flirtation because it's Eric.

But she's not messing around, and neither am I.

I bare my teeth at him in the semblance of a grin, and he raises his hands in a sarcastic gesture of surrendering before backing away.

That's right. I win, asshole. The girl who would have "let" you do anything is gone.

The rest of the flight passes relatively peacefully. I try very hard not to listen for anything that sounds like Eric's laugh or Katie's voice from first class—it's none of my business what they talk about, even if it is pathetic little me.

Instead, I put my earbuds in and attempt to focus on my accounting project until my curiosity gets the better of me and I open the file my mom sent last night.

I don't even bother to read the accompanying email, paragraph upon paragraph, with some directed toward my agent, Mike.

Experience tells me that some of it will make me cringe, and she'll just say it all over again the next time I pick up the phone when she calls.

The PDF contains the scripts for ten webisodes of *Fly Girl*. Seeing Jude's name on the cover page sends an awed chill through me, raising goosebumps on my skin. The only thing missing from this moment is that I'd always imagined my name on there with hers instead of Eric's.

And as tempting as it is to blame him for taking this from me along with everything else, the truth is I walked away from this particular dream a long time ago.

I read through the pages, losing myself in Evie's world. It's good, really good, and my hand twitches at intervals, automatically reaching for a pen to scrawl notes for my performance.

Some of the writing and scene choices are not what I would have made, but that's because some of them are better, smarter. I see Jude's hand in the dialogue, definitely, but I can also see the work Eric had put into the form and function of each piece. Growing up on the sets of his father's shows—like *SpyWear*, the one about the supermodels-slash-international spies—had made an impact. Even in these short ten minute sections there are cliffhangers and emotionally cathartic moments, and they're doled out carefully and placed judiciously to keep viewers coming back for more.

By the time I'm done reading, even *I* want more. Damn him. My heart is aching for Evie and Cory. She's not sure of who she is without her abilities, and he's not sure what kind of life they might have together if she's not who she once was. They were balanced before, opposite sides of the same coin, and now he feels that they're too different. That she can't be a match for him anymore and that it's wrong (and dangerous) to try to hold on to her and their relationship if she has the chance to be a regular person again instead of a freak.

Wiping my stinging eyes—I might be relating to the situation a little more than I'm supposed to—I open a separate document on my laptop and jot down my initial thoughts on Evie before I forget them.

Then I pull up my copy of the novel on my phone, as if I don't already have parts of it memorized, and search for details, pieces of Evie that I can use to bring her to life.

The announcement to put away all electronic devices catches me off guard, so I have to hurry to get everything back in my backpack. And then to steel myself against another face-off with Eric or more awkward pauses with Eric *and* Katie.

My seatmate is standing up the second the seatbelt sign is off, of course, so dragging my heels isn't really an option. She'll trample me in her efforts to push into the aisle if I don't move fast enough.

First class is empty by the time we pass through, and for a second, I'm hoping that maybe Katie and Eric have just gone on entirely, leaving me to navigate the airport on my own.

But nope, they're waiting just outside the gate entrance, Eric scowling at his phone.

Katie nods hello. "You survive back there?" she asks with a smile.

"Sure, it's not a problem for *me*." Okay, maybe that's petty, lashing out at Eric's snobbish tendencies, but he doesn't even seem to notice.

He barely glances up, his frown growing deeper as he leads the way toward baggage claim.

"Is everything okay?" Katie asks, taking a couple of extra steps to pull even with him.

I'm walking behind them, behind the solid wall of their coupledom, feeling more and more like a third wheel. And a little kid. I'm a tricycle.

"It's fine. Just an accounting thing. Sam is freaking out," Eric says with annoyance.

I feel a flicker of interest. Part of what no one on the outside understands is how much Hollywood, whether it's television shows or movies, is all about the money. Who has it? Where is going? How can we get more of it? And on the forensic side, it's more like, where did it all go? And who might have been laundering or stealing it?

It's one of the reasons I chose my accounting major. That, plus, accounting is something that is either right or wrong. It offers concrete answers. And if you have those answers about the money, you have control. Or more control than the people without the answers, anyway.

Eric doesn't so much as glance back at me, even though he's pulling my bag for me.

"I can manage my own bag," I say, a little louder than is necessary.

Eric, in true asshole fashion, gives no acknowledgment of hearing me, just simply lets go of my roller bag without warning.

I'm forced to step to one side quickly to avoid stumbling over it, as Eric keeps walking.

"Eric!" Katie protests, stopping immediately. "What is wrong with you?"

"It's fine," I say, wrangling the bag into place behind me where I can pull it.

With a frown at his back, she pauses to wait for me. "I'm sorry. I think he's a little cranky today," she says with a conspiratorial wink as we start walking again.

I manage a sickly smile. "Yeah." Dr. Katie seems to be a genuinely lovely person, but that does not mean we are in this together. We are not going to have an "oh, that rascal Eric" moment, while she beams at him in fond exasperation. We are not friends or colleagues or . . . oh, God, roommates?

It dawns on me—far too late to do anything about it—that Eric never mentioned where I'm staying during filming. Unless he means for me to stay with my mom and stepdad, but I'm betting that, in spite of his recent scheming with Lori, he would do just about anything to prevent that.

"I didn't think to ask before. Do you know where I'm staying?" I ask Katie.

Please don't say, "With us!" Please, please, please . . .

Katie frowns thoughtfully. "Actually, I'm not sure, but I don't see any reason why you couldn't bunk with—"

"The production company is paying for you to stay at The Beverly Hilton," Eric says tersely over his shoulder as we enter the baggage claim area.

I'm surprised he could hear the question and that he's paying attention.

"A hotel?" Katie asks, taking steps to split the difference between us. "But Eric, it's so hard to be cooped up in one room for that long. Couldn't she just stay at your place since—"

"No, really, I'll be fine," I try. *Please stop trying to help me!*

"—you're staying with me anyway." She catches up to him and loops her arm through his.

"The hotel is close to all the locations where we'll be filming, and she won't be in the room that much," he says, scooping Katie's bag off the carousel. "I'll pick her up and drop her off."

Katie frowns. "But—"

"The hotel is fine," I say quickly.

"A hotel? You're putting the star of your show in a hotel?" A very familiar voice calls out behind me loudly. Too loudly. Heads are turning.

I cringe.

Eric's head whips around toward me, and his gaze focuses on something—someone—behind me for a second before ricocheting back to me.

His jaw tightens. "You've got to be kidding me."

"She asked me what time I was coming in," I say wearily. "She never said anything about showing up here."

It's Katie's turn to be confused, looking back and forth between us. "I don't understand what's—"

But that's all she has time for, or all I hear, as my mother grasps my shoulders and spins me to face her. She's a full four inches taller than I am. Some people have described her as a backwoods version of Daryl Hannah, circa 1991, and that is, sadly, fairly accurate. She's tall, thin, groomed to the hilt, and dressed like she's in front of an audience at all times.

"You're here!" she squeals, enfolding me in her embrace. Now, everyone in the vicinity is staring, but my mother doesn't care. She is in the "any attention is good attention" club.

Suddenly, I'm flashing back to every moment of cringing I've ever experienced, which is . . . a lot. And most of them feature my mother in a prominent role.

When I was younger, it wasn't like this. Lori used to be more like an older sister than a mom. She was only twenty when I was born. When I was five or six, she would take me out after auditions for those cheap McDonald's chocolate-dipped ice cream cones, the only treat we could afford. Half the time, the ice cream melted all over us and the interior of our crappy used Dodge before we could finish. And she didn't care. *Oh, well, we have to do laundry anyway,* she'd say with a laugh. *Better get our quarters' worth.*

But by the time I booked *Starlight,* everything had changed. *She* had changed. Suddenly this career—mine, ostensibly—meant everything, and I needed to "take it more seriously, Calista." There was no more laughing but a lot more shouting, at directors and casting agents. And sure as hell no ice cream. It was like the moment I hit fourteen, she didn't care about anything other than the work. Success only made it worse; the closer we got to achieving those Hollywood Hills dreams, the harder she pushed.

Behind my mom, Zinnia, my oldest half sister, gives an embarrassed wave. She's fourteen, and I could write off her embarrassment to just being a teenager and existence in general, but these days, our mother is capable of generating that reaction in the most stoic person of any age. Poppy, who's twelve, is next to her, with her nose practically buried in the crease of a book—Lori refuses to let her wear glasses in public, and as Poppy gets faint at the thought of touching her eye, contacts are out of the question. Dahlia Elizabeth, who is just six, is examining her distorted reflection in the dim metal of the carousel and holding her ruffled dress out as she executes a perfect mock-curtsy. She's been in the child talent circuit already for years, just as I was at her age. But she actually seems to thrive on it.

Yes, they're all named after flowers—in case, as my mother once said, they wanted to form a band. Never mind that none of us can carry a tune. And yes, Lori actually named her youngest daughter—deliberately—after the most famous murder victim/aspiring actress in Hollywood. Like I said, any attention.

This is my family. Minus my silent and always-fading-into-the-background stepdad, Wade. Lori probably made him wait in the car.

"Let me look at you," my mother commands, capturing my chin between her thumb and forefinger, pulling my face toward hers, and examining me as if I've been gone for years instead of months. "Calista Rae, did you not use the moisturizer I sent you?" she asks, scowling at me. Or she would be scowling, if her forehead was capable of moving.

She releases my chin and backs up a step, viewing me from head to toe.

"I'm glad I scheduled an appointment with Tim for you," she says after a moment. "What did I tell you about carbs?"

My face goes hot; I'm all too aware of Eric and Katie nearby.

The thunk of a suitcase hitting the floor sounds behind me, and Eric steps up next to me. "What are you doing here, Lori?" Eric demands.

She arches an eyebrow at him. "Nice to see you, too, Eric. Am

I not allowed to see my daughter? I don't believe that was in our agreement."

"I didn't think asking you not to stalk her was necessary, but clearly I was wrong about that," he says, just as evenly.

Inside I'm squirming, caught between being thankful for Eric's stepping in to defend me and being furious at both of them. He is every bit as controlling as she is, just for different reasons.

"I'm sorry," Katie says into the awkward silence. "I don't think we've met." She moves into the space between Eric and me, holding out her hand to my mom. "I'm Katie."

Mom takes her hand and shakes it, looking past her to Eric with an expectant expression.

"Lori Beckett, this is Dr. Katie Wahlburg, my fiancée," Eric says curtly. "Katie, this is Lori, Calista's pain-in-the-ass mother who isn't supposed to be here."

Katie gasps, but my mom just gives a tight little smile. "Mother/manager," she corrects. "And because she's so much better left to your influences, Eric? I think we both know better than that."

Oh,. God.

His mouth thins to a line, but he says nothing.

"These are my younger daughters, Zinnia, Poppy," Lori pauses long enough to wrestle the book from my middle sister's hand, "and Dahlia Elizabeth."

Dahlia, without prompting, drops into a curtsy, while Poppy waves blindly and Zinnia makes herself step forward to shake Katie's hand.

"Zinnia, keep your head up," Lori scolds. "It shows confidence. And it hides your double chin, darling."

Zinnia's face turns an unattractive shade of reddish purple as she moves behind Lori. She is, as I was at that age, nothing but coltish limbs, all knees and elbows. But Lori's imagination is especially honed to detect where potential fat cells might be thinking of gathering. Someday.

"Mom," I say sharply.

"What?" she asks. "You, of all people, know how easy it is to go from baby fat to fat fat."

"Jesus Christ," Eric mutters, rubbing his forehead. Then he glares at Lori. "Do you ever stop? Callie is not—"

"I'm right here. I'm fine," I say to him through clenched teeth.

He turns the force of that glare on me. "Really? Are you sure about that?"

I stiffen.

"Come on, let's get going, Calista. Wade is in the limo lane, waiting for us. Is this all you brought?" Lori locks her hand around the handle of my roller bag before I can process what's happening.

"What are you—" I begin.

"Stop." This time, Eric interjects himself between us. "What do you think you're doing?"

"I'm taking my daughter home, so she can visit with her family and relax in a comfortable environment," Lori says.

Oh, no. A sinking feeling, like my guts are slowly being emptied through a drain in my middle, takes over. But Zinnia and Poppy both perk up, looking hopeful. Dahlia appears to be in the middle of a tap-dancing routine with her blurry reflection and oblivious.

"No. We've made other accommodations for Calista," Eric says, grabbing the handle back from Lori. "It'll be over an hour each way to where we're shooting if she's coming from your house, not to mention the traffic—"

"I'll make sure she's there on time," Lori says.

"You're not allowed on set," he shoots back.

"Unless my daughter invites me."

Which I will pretty much have to if she's driving me back and forth every day. My mother excels at putting people in a tight corner and forcing impossible choices.

Because how am I supposed to tell her no when she's given up everything for me, for years? When my sisters are looking at me with such hope? When Lori used the last of her dwindling funds to put me in rehab? I'm not part of the family business; I *am* the family business.

She's beaten us. Even Eric realizes it, based on his thunderous expression, though far too late.

Damnit, Eric. You should have just left me alone.

He turns to me. "Calista, you don't have to do this. You know you'll be more comfortable at the hotel." His furious gaze demands that I speak up, stand up for myself.

But he doesn't understand. It's not just that I owe my mother, a concept Eric refuses to recognize in his own life.

It's more than that. I did this once before. I fired my mom, went out on my own. And in less than two years, I'd demolished my whole life. I had to be bailed out of jail. How am I supposed to trust my own choices when that's where they landed me last time?

My mother is infuriating and controlling and sometimes a bitch, but I did not end up an addict on her watch. That was all me. And it could be me again if I'm not careful. That's why staying away—going back to Blake—is so important. I can't be here anymore.

I open my mouth to respond, but Lori beats me to it.

"Eric's fiancée, you said?" my mother asks Katie abruptly, though I know she heard her perfectly well the first time. Her arch tone tells me she is in prime shit-stirring mode, and that is not going to end well for any of us. "How interesting. Eric certainly is capable of surprises, isn't he?"

I shut my eyes and waste a second wishing I was anywhere but here.

Because even Katie, completely new to my mother and her ways, cannot possibly miss what my mother is implying. Even though it's not true.

"When is the big day?" Lori continues. "Soon, I hope."

"Lori," Eric says in a warning tone.

But Katie, after a beat, seems to rally. I open my eyes in time to see her square her shoulders. "In January. We're starting the New Year off right."

That soon? I try hard to squelch the wail of dismay building inside me. It doesn't matter. It's old data. A complicated childhood crush that should have died years ago—that's all we are.

"Oh, how wonderful for you both. Sounds like you'll be too busy for much of anything else, then," she says ostensibly to Katie, but it's Eric who jerks as though she's struck him because there's no doubt those words are meant for him.

Too busy for a fiancée and my daughter, is what she means. And she doesn't care if Katie knows it, too, because any trouble that keeps Eric occupied keeps him away from me.

"We should go," I say quickly, making the only decision that's left to me.

Eric's head whips around. "Calista . . ."

"It'll be fine," I say, grabbing the handle of my suitcase from him. "I'll see you tomorrow morning."

"Call time is . . ." my mom prompts.

"Seven," Eric grits out.

"We'll be there," she sings out. "Come along, girls." She waves them ahead of her, and they walk toward the exit.

"Callie," he says.

I ignore him. "Katie, I'm sorry. She's just . . ." I shake my head.

She gives me a tentative smile. "That's okay."

"Calista!"

I follow my mom and my sisters, feeling Eric's gaze boring into my back the whole way.

10

ERIC

"Well, that was awkward," Katie says with a short laugh once we're settled in the back of the limo.

"That's Lori," I say, twisting around to look out the back window in spite of myself. It's not like I actually expect Calista to change her mind and look for us. But still.

"She is, as my grandma would say, a piece of work," Katie says.

Nothing out the window but other cars, jostling for position at the curbside pickup area. No sign of Calista, hair streaming behind her as she runs toward us. Toward me.

I shake my head and face front. "You have no idea."

"But you do." She sounds oddly curious.

"After you've seen that woman in action, you can't forget it," I say. "She used to have these caliper things, and she would make Calista lift her shirt, right there in front of everyone, so she could pinch her waist and take measurements."

"That's awful!" She frowns. "It sounds like abuse. How old was she?"

"Sixteen when I met her," I say flatly. Just thinking about it makes me curl my hands into fists. At the time, there wasn't much I could do about it. Just try to distract Calista and make her laugh when I could. "But Calista won't do anything to stop her."

I wish I knew how Lori held such power over Callie. Why the

hell didn't Callie just cut Lori off completely? She fired her once; surely it couldn't be that hard to do it again.

Of course, Calista wouldn't have to fire her again—at least not yet—if I hadn't forced her back under Lori's thumb.

Katie is silent for a long moment. "Is there something else I should know?" she asks finally.

"What?" I ask, startled.

"I mean, with you and Calista," she says, studying a button on her coat with more care than it deserves. "Her mother is terrible, no question." She hesitates. "But I've never seen you so aggressive before." She shudders.

Mainly because I've stayed away from asshole mode around Katie. It hasn't been necessary, and I don't want her to think of me like that. I'm trying to be the better person she sees when she looks at me.

"You care about her," she adds, a hint of vulnerability in her voice.

Careful. "It's not . . . it's more complicated than what you're thinking," I say, shifting my legs to stretch out. "The three of us were close."

Most people don't get it; it's not just work when you're together for sixteen hours a day, six days a week. The set becomes your home, and everyone there your family. Some of them even closer than your actual family. In my case, virtually anyone associated with *Starlight* would be closer to me than my own blood-relatives. But Callie and Chase in particular—though in very different ways.

I've missed *my* family, though I hadn't realized how much until now.

"You, Chase, and Calista," Katie says with doubt. "Two people you haven't spoken to in years."

"That's because I messed up that night with the accident."

"You said something you regret," Katie recites. "Then Callie got into the car with Chase . . ."

I nod. *Mostly.* Technically, it wasn't something I said so much as something I did. It makes me cringe thinking about it, and the fact that I'm hiding it from Katie only makes me feel worse. But I'm enough of a selfish jerk not to reveal the absolute depths of my fucked-up-ness to the girl I'm going to marry. I'm not sure she would understand. Cowardice is not something that fits into her worldview.

Besides, it's not like it matters now. I wouldn't make the same mistake again. Because I would never be in that same situation again.

"But before that happened," I say, "we were solid, the three of us. And you can see why we might have needed something like that." I jerk my thumb in the direction of where we left Lori behind. "You think Lori's bad, you should meet my dad."

"I'd like to," she says softly.

"No, you wouldn't. Trust me. My parents aren't like yours." Katie doesn't get it. She speaks to both of her parents on a regular basis. And her brothers and sister. They call just to talk to each other. Like, for fun.

My dad may or may not show up to the wedding and that would be bad enough. Even then, he might only come if he's concerned the media will make a big deal out of him not being there.

"Well, my family is yours now, too, right?" She wraps her arm around mine and snuggles close.

I try to relax into the seat and Katie, but all I can think about is Calista and what she's going through, trapped in that car with Lori, in that house for the next two weeks.

Frustration makes me grit my teeth. *If she would just stand up for herself . . .*

But you knew she wouldn't when you made that call to Lori.

So I'm as much to blame as Callie is. More so, maybe. Because I didn't let it stop me.

"So, I, uh, have a little confession to make," Katie says, distracting me from my thoughts. She's not quite meeting my gaze. "Speaking of family."

My heart lurches as my brain spins a thousand scenarios involving the words "family" and "confession."

I sit upright. "Wait, are you telling me . . . are you . . ." My gaze drops to her waist, where the belt of her coat is knotted, and I feel vaguely ill, my skin instantly clammy and the air too hot.

We can't even agree on where to live or what the next year is going to look like . . .

"What?" She looks up at me, follows my gaze. Her eyes go big. "No! No." She sputters out a laugh.

I slump back in my seat, my eyes shut, trying to get my breathing back in line.

"You don't have to look quite so relieved," she says dryly, but her smile wobbles around the edges. "It wouldn't be the worst thing in the world, would it?"

"No," I say quickly because I know that's the correct answer.

"When the time is right."

"Right," I agree. And I do. I mean, I think I want that. To be a father. To be a better father than my own, and to be fair, a rotting tree stump could probably pull that off.

But something about the idea still makes me feel unsteady and closed in. We've talked about it before, Katie and I, in a vague, someday sense. And I know to her, at thirty-one, her someday is probably a lot closer than my more distant vision.

It never bothered me before, but today, it makes me feel itchy and trapped.

Probably just because I wasn't expecting it, and tomorrow I'm starting the biggest undertaking of my professional life. Pressure on top of pressure. My stress has stress.

"So what is it, then?" I ask, taking her hand in mine, trying to make up for it.

"Okay, so you know we sent out the 'save the date' cards a couple of weeks ago," she says, and I get the distinct feeling she's hedging.

"Yeah."

"And you gave me the list of people you wanted them to go to . . ." She bites her lip.

I fight the urge to tell her that I don't care if the cards were late or if somebody was somehow missed. None of that crap has really registered with me. As long as it makes her happy. "It's okay, they'll get invitations and if they can't make it, no big deal."

"Okay, except the thing is I added someone, and I know you're going to be angry, but he's your dad and—"

I go still. "You invited my father."

"I sent a save the date card, and he called me." She furrows her brow. "I'm not even sure how he got my number. But he wants us to meet for dinner."

"No."

"He really wants to talk to you. To catch up, he said, and to get to know me. You know, your wife-to-be?" She tilts her head up to smile at me.

"That's what he said." It's not a question because I know he would say just about anything to get what he wanted.

"Yes, that's what he said."

"He's lying."

She pulls away to face me. "Eric, I know you guys have issues, not that you'll talk about—"

"He wants something else. He does not give a shit about you or me."

"You don't know that. You can't."

"I've known the man my whole life," I say through clenched teeth.

She shakes her head. "But how much of that had to do with work?"

All of it. Because that's all he cares about. But that's not the point.

"Besides, that was a long time ago," she points out. "And you've done so much, come so far since—"

"In spite of him, not because," I say. "'The best revenge is a life well-lived,' remember?"

That's what she said to me that night in the ER, a year and a half ago, when I was having my hand stitched. I was more fucked up than I'd like to admit, so everything came pouring out to the cute and sympathetic veterinarian who had come with me to make sure I was okay. It was a low point. I finally figured it out when I was in the back of an Uber, messed up out of my mind, with a softly whimpering teacup Yorkie in my lap: I had no one else to call. No one to come help me. All of my "friends" were too wasted or just didn't give a shit about anything but the next score, the next party.

Things weren't getting better—continuing to be the dumbass, spoiled brat my father thought I was didn't feel like a win anymore. It had cost me too much.

Plus, I was tired of being lost. All the reckless shit that had once made my heart pound—*how far can I go?*—now seemed old and worn out. I'd been living at the bottom of a bottle, or in the dust at the bottom of a baggie, just because I could. At first it was because it felt good—and because it irritated my father to no end to hear tales of his wastrel son and to be forced to clean up my messes to preserve his own reputation. Now, it was more out of habit and a lack of knowing what else to do. I wasn't even living at home anymore.

But that night, I could see all of that behavior for what it was—a tantrum. Me, proving to my dad that he was right, and there was nothing he could do to make me fall in line. If I couldn't meet his approval, I sure as hell would have no problem earning his continuous disapproval.

The issue with that approach, as Katie pointed out once I'd overshared all of this under the harsh florescent lights of the ER cubicle, was that ruining my life to spite him was still ruining my life.

The kindness of a pretty stranger in the middle of the night sometimes works miracles. Well, not immediately, but the next morning when I woke up with a throbbing hand and head and

Bitsy curled up on my pillows, I couldn't stop that conversation from circling in my brain.

Katie called me that day, and the next. Checking on Bitsy. And me. She came to my condo, brought me cookies, and examined the stitches on my hand. Taught me a few obedience tricks to keep Bitsy out from underfoot and away from danger, which Bitsy mostly ignored.

Katie was nice . . . and normal. Like, scarily normal. Her parents weren't even divorced. We kept talking, texting. She, it seemed, was someone who wanted to save me, make me better. And I, for the first time, wanted to be saved.

But now, sometimes I wonder if it's less about saving me and more about changing me into a version she likes better. To her, I'm not sure there's a difference. Her ideal Eric is someone she thinks I can be, whether or not it's who I want to be. At what point does it stop being saving and start being unrealistic expectations?

"I thought you wanted me to put all of this behind me. Move to Michigan, forget all this shit." I gesture toward the windows, the motion encompassing all of L.A., including my father.

She's quiet. "I do think a fresh start would help, more than you realize," she says eventually. "But that doesn't mean you should completely cut off your family, whether you're here or there. You've changed. Is it so impossible that he has too? Besides, I'm sure he's proud of what you're trying to do."

A few months after that night in the ER, I started trying to pull my life together. I auditioned for jobs that I would have turned my nose up at before. Making my own money, independent of my rapidly emptying trust fund, was the first step. It had to be.

It took me the better part of a year to get that work and income trickling in again and then to settle on what I wanted to do with it. Mostly because what I wanted was something I was afraid to want.

Calista was right. I always said I wouldn't ever be a producer like my dad. I never wanted anything in common with him. Now, though, I'm hoping it's not the occupation so much as the personality deficit that was the problem. But I still have my doubts.

"My father doesn't do paternal pride," I say. "Trust me." Maybe he did once. When I was little. I remember visiting him on set for *Spy Wear.* Everyone deferred to him, said hello to me. He was like a superhero, greeting the waiting crowds. And when I asked, he took me on a tour of the set, seemingly pleased by my interest.

Katie makes an exasperated noise. "My point, Eric, is that if you're so determined to stay and work in the same industry where your father is a leader, it's stupid to let those old wounds fester and—"

"So I either make up with my dad or move to Michigan, that's what you're saying?" I demand.

"No!" Spots of color appear high on her cheeks. She takes a deep breath and lets it out slowly. "I'm saying I want you to be happy. I want you to be whole. And when we get married, I want us to start our new life together on the right foot. And that means our families, too. Family is important."

Katie is a born fixer, whether it's people or animals. All she can see are ways to try to make things better. How can anyone resist that? She has been a force for good in my life, and she asks for so little in return. I should, at least, be grateful that it's not my mom she's trying to wrangle.

"Fine," I say with a sigh. "But please don't expect a tear-filled reunion with hugs and firm, manly claps on the back, okay?"

"I won't. Promise." She hesitates for a second. "But here's the thing . . ."

I raise my eyebrows. "There's another thing?"

"I know you're going to be busy with filming the next couple of weeks, but I figured the sooner, the better . . ."

I fill in the blanks. "Tonight?" I demand, sitting up straight, ignoring the protest of the muscles in my back. "You told him we'd have dinner tonight?"

"I thought it was worth a shot," she says.

"Oh come on, Katie." I slump, resting my head on the back of the seat. "I just got home, and I slept in a shitty motel last night. Seriously, the mattress was more metal than material, probably obtained from the nearest prison dumpster, and I think the mold in the shower was sentient."

"You are such a delicate flower," she teases. She is, after all, the girl who enjoys camping. Like, outside. Intentionally. Her whole family does it. So far I've managed to be busy every time it's been suggested.

"Damn right. But you wouldn't say that if you saw the roaches I slept with last night. I think one of them asked for my number." I lean in and kiss Katie because I can. This is nice. No angst, no drama. Other than my dad, but there's no getting around that.

Still, the dull throb of guilt is present, thinking of Calista. I wonder if she's doing okay, or if she's already regretting her choice.

But it was, in fact, her choice to go with Lori. I didn't engineer that.

"A good meal and deep emotional catharsis will go a long way to making you feel better, don't you think?" Katie grins at me.

I groan in surrender, rubbing my eyes. "Fine."

"It won't be that bad," she says.

"I'll hold you to that," I say, leaning back and closing my eyes.

"Don't worry, I have the rest of our lives to make it up to you," she says, curling into my side.

"Yeah." But for some reason, those words aren't as comforting as they usually are.

I haven't been to The Palm since I was a little kid. And that was the downtown location, rather than the newer one in Beverly Hills. But as soon as we walk in, I remember why it was one of my favorite places to eat. It smells amazing, and the cartoons and caricatures on the wall draw my eye. I always wanted to be up there. I even asked to go here for my tenth birthday, thinking that might have some sway with the whole getting my likeness on the wall. Look, I was ten, my dad was a famous producer, and his caricature was up there. Plus, I was technically a working actor at that point and had a vague idea of the celebrity that job entailed. So it kind of made sense at the time.

I'm guessing all of that is probably why my dad chose this restaurant for tonight.

Sorry, Dad, nostalgia isn't going to cut it. Though I am surprised he remembered.

The host greets us by name, ignoring my bruised cheek like a true professional, and leads us to a booth.

I probably should have spent the afternoon catching up on sleep; my temper is always on a hair trigger when I'm tired, and my dad only tests my limits further.

Instead, I got caught up reviewing everything for this week, going over emails, answering questions, responding to Vincent's increasingly caustic comments and notes. He's a great director and he'll do a good job, but holy shit, the man is a pain in the ass. I'm beginning to wonder if I didn't steal him from my dad so much as my dad willingly surrendered him.

"This place is great," Katie whispers to me as we walk to the back of the restaurant. "But did you see the prices? I looked them up online." Her eyes wide, she mouths, *Oh my God.*

You can take the Katie out of the Midwest, but . . .

I smirk. "Don't worry about it," I say. "Dad's picking up the tab, I'm sure." Mainly because that is in keeping with his magnanimous and generous persona, and regardless of what he thinks of Katie—he damn well better not upset her—he will want her to like him. If possible, even, to like him enough to side against me. It's messed up, but I've seen it happen.

And speaking of . . .

My father is already at the table and seated. It takes me aback slightly, to see him here, in my reality, with Katie next to me, my hand on her lower back. It's like two worlds colliding. Dad and I haven't been in the same room for almost three years.

He's wearing one of his dark, custom-tailored suits, the neck of his dress shirt open, no tie. California casual. I can almost guarantee he's not wearing socks with his shoes.

He stands as we approach—I'm right about the sock thing, pale, hairy ankles sticking out—but as he steps forward to greet us, he passes under one of the spotlight-type fixtures, and his hair seems whiter and thinner. In fact, overall, he just seems . . . smaller. It takes me a second to do the math: he'll be seventy this year. And for the first time in my recollection, he looks his age.

"Eric," he says in that familiar clipped tone. His gaze skates over my battered face, and I brace myself, waiting. "It's good to see you."

It's very hard not to raise my eyebrows at that, but conscious of Katie at my side and the high hopes she has for this meeting, I manage to maintain, I hope, a neutral expression. "Dad."

He shakes my hand and squeezes my elbow with his free hand. Ah, the Stone version of a warm embrace.

"And this must be Dr. Katie," he says, turning his attention to her. "I've done some checking on you, and you have a lot of very happy clientele, some of whom are very dear friends."

"Oh," she says, flustered but clearly pleased. "Thank you." Before I can warn her, she leans in to hug him, just as he goes for another handshake.

"Sorry! I'm sorry," she says as she tries to back-step. Her family members hug, for no reason sometimes, like when they pass each other in the kitchen.

"Forgot to warn you," I say. "Dad hasn't quite mastered the warm-and-fuzzy end of the emotional spectrum."

"Eric," he warns, but it's in this fake, jovial, *we're-all-family-here* voice, and I roll my eyes.

"It's lovely to meet you, my dear," he says, kissing her cheek and capturing her hand to lead her to the table.

I sit next to her before he tries it. I wouldn't put it past him. The man is shameless when it comes to women younger than he is. My mother is just turning fifty this year, and each of his wives has been progressively younger. Hayley, the most recent one—and the current one, I think—is only twenty-six or twenty-seven. The path from second assistant to first assistant to wife is a well-worn one in the Rawley Stone Production offices.

The fact that Katie is engaged to me wouldn't stop him either. My father has no compunction about being the living embodiment of a Hollywood cliché.

"I see you're up to your old tricks again, Eric," he says, jerking his chin at my face as he settles across the table from us. "To whom do I need to write a check this time?"

Next to me, Katie shifts uncomfortably, giving a polite laugh.

"I'm fine, thanks for asking," I say.

"Oh, calm down. I'm teasing." He inclines his head toward Katie. "Eric never did have much of a sense of humor," he says to her in a mock-whisper. "Always so sensitive."

Yeah, because it's funny to joke about paying to get me out of trouble when that's actually happened and I'm working hard to make sure it never happens again. It is simultaneously insulting and revisionist history—he cut me off after the accident, anyway.

"I think Eric is very funny," Katie says.

Oh, God. Don't, Katie. I try to send the thought to her, but she is far too used to functional families; the silent message passes right over her head as she beams at me with a bright smile.

"You do, do you?" he asks Katie, full of amused condescension. He points his finger at me. "Better not let her get away. She might truly be one in a million. A billion." He chortles at his own joke.

"Dad."

"All right, all right." He waves his hand at me. "I'll stop. I've ordered a bottle of—"

"Water is fine," I say.

He arches his eyebrows. "I knew you'd cleaned up your act. Hadn't realized you decided to give up good taste as well."

With effort, I keep my mouth shut. Because this is the game. Criticize me for being too excessive, and then critique my efforts to curb my habits. There is no way to win.

Beneath the table, Katie finds my hand and squeezes. "Well, it sounds lovely to me," she chirps. I understand what she's doing and why, but it still bugs me because even in this, he's winning. He's pulling her into this mess, forcing her to smooth edges that I don't want smoothed.

"So, tell me about the wedding plans," he says to Katie.

The two of them chat throughout the appetizer and salad courses about the location (Dad offers up the mansion for the ceremony even though we've already reserved a church), photographers (Dad knows just the guy), and reception food choice (you always need a good vegetarian option, according to my father).

"You are the wedding expert," I mutter, as our main course is delivered.

"Eric!" Katie stares at me, aghast.

"It's fine," my dad says. "He's quite right. I do have a lot of experience with weddings. Still working on getting the marriage part right." He gives her a charming smile, one that I recognize as similar to those in my arsenal.

I can't help studying him, wondering what he's up to. I would like to believe what Katie said, that enough time has passed and we've both changed to the point where a friendly—or at least, neutral—meal is possible. But . . .

He clears his throat as soon as the server takes our dessert order. "It sounds like everything is well in-hand, Katherine."

I wait for her to correct him—her name is not actually Katherine, but Katie.

She just smiles at him. "Thank you!"

"And Eric, I wanted to congratulate you on your new endeavors," he says.

I stiffen, waiting for the hidden sting, the slap that follows the caress.

"Your little project is generating a lot of interest."

Little project. I grit my teeth. Technically, yes, it is little, I remind myself. Small budget, web only. He's not wrong. It's just that he's so condescendingly right. "Thank you," I manage. I will not let him say I'm not at least *trying* to get along.

"I was teasing you about your taste before, but obviously, you haven't lost it when it comes to work. Or women," he adds with a wink, tipping his glass, salute-like, toward Katie.

I roll my eyes.

But Katie laughs.

"I knew my DNA would show through eventually," he says.

Of course it's all due to him. In truth, as much as I hate to admit it, some of it probably is. Not thanks to DNA, but the years he let me tag along to work and learn just by being there.

More like training by osmosis, rather than anything deliberate, but he won't miss the opportunity to try to take credit.

I don't have a response to that that isn't shouting or walking out—neither of which would go over well with the woman sitting next to me—so I clamp my mouth shut.

"And speaking of DNA, I wanted to make you an offer."

"Two tests for the price of one? Oh, come on, Dad, wasn't this issue resolved a long time ago? You just said so yourself." It feels good to let loose, just a little, to demonstrate the sharp edges of my tongue. Now that talent, I definitely inherited.

Next to me, Katie gives a strangled gasp.

My father barks out a forced laugh. "Always a wit, aren't you, Eric?"

"Always," I say with a tight smile.

"Fine, smartass," he says, putting down his wineglass. "Here it is: I want you to come work for me."

My mouth falls open. "I . . . you what?"

He smirks, another expression familiar from the mirror. "I want you to come work at RSP." He holds his hand up as if staving off my protests. "You'll have your own division. You can work on all this digital, web-only stuff. That is obviously the direction the world is heading." A faint hint of distaste colors his tone. My dad is old school. Always television. Always network television. He started as a writer and worked his way up, the "traditional way, the right way." It's a speech I've heard countless times growing up, usually followed by the refrain, "You have no idea what hard work is, what it means to actually commit."

"Think of the additional resources available to you," my dad adds. "We have much deeper pockets. You'll be able to explore a variety of projects and much faster. You can even keep the name, if you want." He waves his hand dismissively. "It'll just have a tag naming it as a division of RSP."

Eric Stone Productions is not a fancy name for a company and not particularly original—though I loved the logo, a rabbit's ears just poking out of a flipped-up top hat—but it is *mine.* I didn't want to go that route at first, but the truth is, if I'm going to try to capitalize on the whole *Starlight* connection at first, it only makes sense for people to know that it's me behind the curtain. Success or failure.

Katie makes an interested noise and loops her arm through mine, pulling me toward her slightly. "If you really want to do this, Eric, that could help," she says to me quietly, but not quietly enough. She's saying "if" like we're not a day away from filming. Like this business and my attempt to participate in it in a new way is a quirk I need to work through, and the sooner, the better.

"Why?" I ask my dad. I feel as if I'm being sold a pitch, and not just an innocent "if you're interested" kind of deal.

"Why would I want to work with my son?" My dad asks this like it's the most ludicrous question anyone could possibly conceive of.

"No," I say, trying for patience. "Why would you want to work with the son you obviously disapprove of and went to great lengths to remove from your life—"

"I wasn't trying to remove you from my life, I was trying to give you incentive to straighten up and fly right," he says, his voice rising. "And may I point out that it worked?"

I stare at him. "I don't believe you."

"It's a generous offer, but I think maybe it's something that he needs time to consider, Mr. Stone," Katie interjects, squeezing my hand.

I shake loose, irritated. *Katie, stop trying to fix things. This can't be fixed.*

"Please, Katherine, call me Rawley," he says, but his tone is flat now.

Because I've caught him. I'm onto something.

It only takes me a few more seconds to latch onto what it is. I should have seen it immediately.

"What about *Fly Girl*?" I ask.

"What about it?" he responds.

Not good.

"What would happen to it? Production starts tomorrow," I say.

"RSP will comp you for costs. Reimburse your investors." He waves a hand dismissively.

"You want me to just cancel it?" I ask. "No way. Forget it. It's taken way too much to get here." And now that I've stepped out on this particular limb, I find myself reluctant to retreat to the safety of the trunk, particularly if the trunk is my dad in this metaphor.

It feels like failure, but even worse, failure without really trying.

But deep inside, there is a tiny part of me that wants to consider the possibility. I wouldn't have to take the risk of falling flat on my face, of being that pathetic rich kid who thinks he's actually talented when it's just the power of his father behind any success he might have.

My dad makes an impatient noise. "Of course not. It would just be delayed."

I wait because I can sense the shadow of the other shoe hanging above me, about to drop.

He sighs. "Eric, you know it's a project far more suited to television. If RSP takes it on instead, imagine the scope. Think about what could be done with it."

Not "what you could do with it" but "what could be done." As in, absent me.

"And there it is," I mutter. The tread of that hypothetical shoe is now pressing hard into my neck.

I lean against the padded booth back. Because if he rolls my company into his, my projects would go with it. It's not about working for him or even his belief about the future of storytelling. *Fly Girl* would become his.

He ignores me. "You've done great work with the scripts, but think what it would be like with forty-two minutes of space instead of six?"

"Ten," I say.

"You'd still get credit for development. We'll list you as an EP. But the show will be glossier, more high-end."

Translation: the exact opposite of the spirit of the book and the scripts as they are now. He means exposed flesh, spandex outfits, and fight scenes where people are thrown through walls. Because that's the Rawley Stone trademark—hot, sexy action.

Fly Girl is a small production because it's meant to be small. It's a story about identity and love. Not tights and revenge sex. But Rawley's version would probably sell and sell well. The dichotomy sits uneasily with me. And I hate myself for even considering the possibility. But the truth is, it *would* be helpful to have a success in the bag early on. If only it didn't feel like I was selling my soul in this life and the next to get it.

"Of course we'd have to recast the leads with—"

"No." The word is out of my mouth before I've even had time to realize I'm considering speaking. It feels almost like someone else said it.

"Oh, I know you're attached to that troubled girl and her ridiculous mother, but do you honestly think anyone can see her as—"

I don't bother to repeat myself; I put my napkin on the table and stand up. There are certain lines I won't, can't, cross. And okay, yeah, sometimes those lines aren't quite as set in stone as I'd like them to be—no pun intended. But after everything I've done to Calista, dragging her here, only to have my father recast her role? That's not going to happen. "We're leaving now."

Katie looks up at me, wide-eyed. Then she scoots out after me. "It was nice to meet you," she murmurs to my father.

"Eric, damnit, don't be stubborn," he snaps. "You're too personally involved, that's never smart. You can't see what you're doing."

"Uh-huh." I step back to wait for Katie to stand and walk out in front of me. Miss Claud raised me right. "You know me, Dad, stubborn and stupid. Oh, and let's not forget reckless. I'm not sure why you're surprised." I bare my teeth in a grin. Fury pumps through my veins. I can't believe I let myself think for even a fraction of a second that this dinner was legit. I was right all along.

"You're going to embarrass yourself," my father says, tossing his napkin on the table and standing just as the server approaches with our desserts.

The server reads the tension and backs off.

"I'm trying to save you from that, Son, just like always," Rawley says, sounding weary and put upon, just like an exasperated, caring father. Perhaps it's not his writing and producing skills that should have won him such acclaim but his acting instead. This isn't about me, this is about him. He thinks I'm going to swing and miss, and the humiliation will be visited on him.

Fuck him.

"I'm not sure why I bother anymore," he says, shaking his head, more for Katie's benefit than mine.

I shrug as I turn away. "Honestly? Me neither."

11

CALISTA

It is shockingly easy to become an addict. Probably because no one, including me, ever sets out to end up that way. The addicts are always someone else. That stranger curled up and shaking on the street, the uncle with the bottle stashed in his favorite chair, the former celebrity who stumbles into the wrong house, thinking it's his. It's never you.

Everyone always thinks they're in control . . . until they're not. When I was in rehab, that was the common theme, especially among the first-timers.

With me, I never even considered the possibility that I was heading down a dangerous road. I wasn't drinking to excess like Chase, or like my uncle Chris, my mother's brother, who ended up drowning in his backyard pool. And it wasn't like I was seeking out dealers on the street. At least not at first.

I didn't have a problem. I was taking a doctor-assigned prescription. Yeah, maybe I was taking an extra pill or three to keep the pain at bay, but no big deal. They always write the instructions conservatively, so you don't accidentally overdose. At least, that's what I told myself when I was digging through my bag, frantic to find an Oxy that might have spilled out and caught in the folds of the lining.

It spirals so damn quickly.

One minute you're trying to figure out how to talk the doctor into giving you *another* refill or buying pills online, and the next some shady guy at a party tells you he knows someone who can get you what you need. And you find yourself in a dim corner somewhere buying freaking heroin, because this shady guy and his friend promise that it's better than Oxy, takes away the pain for longer. And it's certainly cheaper.

I was lucky. Relatively. I was busted early by an undercover officer, only the third or fourth time I bought heroin on my own and before I emptied out my *entire* bank account in pursuit of getting high.

But it took me some time to see getting caught then as good fortune instead of bad. In the moment, it felt like I was still in control, still with plenty of room between me and the bottom. I wasn't even shooting up yet.

And the moment I heard myself say those words aloud in rehab, in defense of my habit, it felt like I was falling down an endless tunnel, like Alice in Wonderland, my head where my feet should be, the world unrecognizable. I certainly didn't recognize myself in that moment. Like it would have been okay, more acceptable, if I'd been caught with a needle in hand? Then I would have known I was in trouble? Because snorting it, yeah, that was so much more acceptable.

The truth was I'd been in trouble long before that moment, and if I hadn't figured that out by then, odds were that I wouldn't have seen it later, either.

"Arms out," my mother instructs, body-fat calipers in hand.

In my former bedroom, now Zinnia's, I stand in the center of the room, wearing only a bra and boy shorts. The routine is as familiar to me as standing against the doorframe to have your height penciled in probably is to other kids.

Though, generally, I bet those other parents stopped measuring their children before the age of twenty-three.

We have to have a fresh baseline, Calista.

That's what Mom had said at dinner, during which the five of us—Lori, my sisters and I—ate meager salads: one cup of greens, a sliver of chicken breast smaller than my thumb, and no dressing. I'm pretty sure if she even knew I was thinking about croutons—like the crispy garlic-flavored ones I used to have from the Blake campus salad bar—her head would have exploded. There is no bread in this house. Except for the warmed dinner roll on Wade's plate. He got a petite filet, baked potato *and* a roll. The salad was just his appetizer.

My stomach growls at the thought of real food, and my mother glares at me, waggling the calipers in my direction. "That's the sugar! Your body is craving it."

But for the moment, the calipers are secondary. As is my apparent need for a sugar fix.

She examines my arms. And then my legs, between my toes, checking for track marks. She is more concerned about my other addiction. And that's something else you learn in rehab: You will always be an addict, no matter how long it's been since you've felt that warm rush of not caring, courtesy of whatever opioid you can get your hands on, flowing through your veins.

"I told you I'm sober. Clean. And you know I never used needles," I say, trying to bite back the frustration. Of all the things to be grateful for, my pathological fear of shots, leftover from childhood, had saved me from myself. For now, at least.

Lori shakes her head. "They said if you relapsed, you'd probably fall farther, faster." She pauses at the sight of the surgical scars on my right arm. She makes a small dismayed sound. "You've been using the scar cream, haven't you?"

"Yes." The scars have faded, but they, like that craving for chemical relief, will always be a part of me. "Good thing Evie doesn't have a swimsuit scene."

She stiffens. "It's not funny, Calista. Do you have any idea of the number of jobs you're going to miss out on because of those?"

I want to tell her, right then and there, that the jobs I want won't involve me removing my top for a love scene or bouncing along a beach in a swimsuit. That would cause quite a stir in the accounting department.

But I keep my mouth shut for now. There will be a time and place for that conversation, and while I'm mostly naked and vulnerable-feeling is not it.

"What's going on with the house?" I ask instead, trying to ignore the cold pinch of the calipers against my skin.

"What do you mean?" she asks, frowning, taking measurements and entering them into an app on her phone.

I raise my eyebrows. "The FOR SALE sign in the front yard?"

"This neighborhood." She waves dismissively.

"Mom, it's Valencia," I say. People give side eye to less-than-perfect lawns and compete to have the best stroller in neighborhoods like this. It's not exactly gangland territory.

"I just think it's time that we looked into moving into something that fits our needs better. We're jammed in here like sardines." She frowns at me. "Don't suck in. This is important. I need to know what we're working with here."

I swallow the urge to sigh. This house was purchased during the height of my—and therefore my mother's—earnings; I'm not sure they could even afford it today. But that's my mom: so focused on future golden days that she's willing to bet what she has now against something better rolling in at the last minute. Her philosophy has always been: *Act like you already have the success you're after.* Which is great, unless you're *spending* like you already have that success. "Mom, I don't think that's a—"

"Besides," she points out. "It's not like we can get by with only four bedrooms now that you're back. Zinnia deserves to have her own space, too, you know."

Living here again? For the foreseeable future? When I was fresh out of rehab and finding my balance again, it made sense. But as a permanent solution? No way.

"No, Mom. We talked about this. I'm taking a couple years to focus on my education. That was the plan, that's what we told everyone, and this one-time job doesn't change anything. Besides, I think it'll really help if I have the degree. Then I could even bring in income as an—"

"Oh, Calista, you have no idea." She shakes her head. "It's changed so much. People's memories are even shorter than what we thought. You'll be completely forgotten by the time you come back."

Exactly.

Then the implication of her words sinks in. "Wait, were you trying to get me work? I thought we agreed—"

"Exploratory conversations only," she says, tsking at me. "I just wanted to see what might be available to you if you were interested, and trust me, my darling girl, it's not good. Nothing like what you had in the past. Nothing like what you deserve."

The next thing you know, she'll be signing you up to audition for a local car dealership commercial or one of those TV movies where you get eaten by an ant-octopus-shark creature in the second act. All for her percentage.

That's what Eric said. I thought he was just speculating. But maybe it was more than that. Maybe he knows more than I do. A cold stab of fear pierces my stomach. If he hadn't offered me this job—okay, blackmailed me into it—what would I be doing instead? It sounds like I wouldn't have been at Blake much longer.

Lori frowns at the app on her phone and whatever calculations it's spitting back at her. "Though it looks like we have our work cut out for us."

I drop my arms to my sides, the right shaking and aching. *Boundaries,* my rehab counselor's voice sounds in my head. *You need to set them and keep them, even if it makes other people unhappy.*

According to Bonnie, my addiction came not just from the pain from my injury but also from my inability to deal with discomfort of any kind. Especially when it came to standing up for myself. I'd spent too many years trying desperately to keep my mom, agents, producers and directors happy. Add to that my inability to ask for help, even when I needed it, and I was a disaster waiting for a time and place to happen.

I take a deep breath. "Mom, this isn't what I want."

"Well, of course not. Getting back in shape is never easy. Fortunately, the advance from Mr. Fancy Pants will help with that." She rolls her eyes.

"Mom—"

"We'll start training twice a day, and by the time this little project is over, you'll be back to your—"

"Lori!"

She looks up at me, startled. "What?"

"I don't want this! I don't want to act again." The words echo in the sudden stillness between us, like a vast canyon has sprung up from between the floorboards. And the worst part is I can taste the hint of lie. It's not the acting that's the problem. Eric is right about that.

She takes a step back, her hands falling to her sides. "Well," she says, in a voice breathy with hurt and offense.

It's difficult, but I manage to resist the urge—and long-engrained habit—to apologize. "It's just that I don't think it's good for me to be here, doing this again. I mean, we saw what happened the last time—"

"Calista, I recognize that you're an adult and that, as such, you can make your own decisions," Lori says, setting down the calipers carefully on the nightstand. "But I want you to remember what happened the last time you went off on your own."

I flinch.

She steps closer to me, touches my cheek, though the cynical part of me registers it more as an evaluation of my cheekbones than a loving caress. "You just don't have the world experience to make good decisions for yourself, love. You need me."

I clench my teeth, even as tears sting my eyes. "But how am I supposed to get that experience unless you let me—"

"Let you make mistakes that break your heart? Destroy your future? End with you dead in a gutter?" She shakes her head. "I should have known. Every time Eric Stone is involved, you get all turned around and—"

"Eric has nothing to do with it," I snap. Actually, if anything, he and my mother were, for the first time, on the same page about my career and its need for continued existence, even if they disagreed about why and how.

"Oh, no?" Lori gives a bitter laugh. "Calista, darling, from the moment you *fired* me to stay for that third season, when everyone could see that the show was going downhill, it's always been about him."

My face feels like it's on fire. "I wasn't ready to leave," I mumble. "And it wasn't just because of Eric." True. I needed my version of family, and Eric was part of that, along with Chase. But if Eric happened to fall in love with me during that season somehow, too, well then all the better.

"Everything that followed that decision has been nothing but disaster for you. For us." She tucks my hair gently behind my ear. "The accident, surgeries, the pills. Getting arrested. You can see that, can't you?"

"Yes," I say. "But—"

"Just please, trust me this time." Lori took my hands in hers. "I only want what's best for you. Eric Stone is a necessary evil right now, but after this project is done, you never have to see him again."

The thought of the rest of my life passing without Eric in it sends a flurry of confusing and conflicting emotions through me: relief, despair and gut-deep longing. Like the desire for him is imprinted on my every chromosome.

I focus on my breathing, working to keep calm and ignore the thrumming desire to escape this conversation by any means necessary. I catch myself longing for the dry bitterness of a pill on my tongue. "You're right. I made some mistakes. Big ones. And that's what I'm trying to say. I think my path is somewhere else now. Not as an actress." Before she can protest, I hurry to continue. "I've been doing really well in my classes, and I think I could—"

"What? Become an accountant?" she asks. At least she's been somewhat listening. "Get a job in an office? Calista, please. You have a gift. It would be selfish to waste that, to hide behind an ordinary life." She turns away and heads for the door.

"Mom."

"Do you have any idea how many girls struggle to get where you are?" she asks quietly, her hand on the doorknob. "How many girls would kill to have the connections and opportunities that you have?"

Shame creeps up in me. "I know, but—"

She faces me, her eyes bright with tears. "I was one of those girls, a long time ago. Knocking on doors, auditioning for everything, trying to make my way to the top. But I gave up everything. For you. I was nineteen and pregnant and completely alone. My life was over."

I wince, even though I've heard this story before.

"Even your father wanted no part of you, and no part of me after I told him I wouldn't get an abortion." She dabs at the corner of her eye carefully with the tip of her finger. According to my mother, my father, whose name she refused to give me even now, took off immediately for New York and whatever acting opportunities he could find there, promising to send money that never arrived. "So there I was, a teenager in Los Angeles, single and with a baby on the way. My parents wouldn't even speak to me. I couldn't go to them for help. I had no one."

"Mom—"

"I could have been someone. I could have been a star. You've seen my reel."

I nod, my jaw clenched. She was good in the few parts she'd landed back in the late 90s before I was born. With a little more time, she might well have been able to accomplish everything she wanted.

"But instead, I worked three jobs, gave up on my acting dreams and did everything I could to provide you with the best life," she says in a trembling voice. "To give you the chance to make the most of the opportunities you were given."

Guilt settles on me like one of those lead vests at the dentist's office. "I know," I say in a small voice. "But those opportunities aren't . . ."

What *I* want anymore? Maybe, but how selfish does that sound under the circumstances?

She waits with her eyebrows raised.

I shut my mouth.

"You owe me. You owe us," she says simply. "I'll be blunt: Your sisters haven't been as fortunate as you in either looks or talent."

I wince, hoping none of them are listening.

"But they deserve to have whatever benefits can be afforded them. That is your responsibility as a member of a family that has done nothing but love and support and *pay* for you during your worst times." Her voice breaks. "Do you know how much that Safe Harbor cost? Do you realize what we could have done for Dahlia or Zinnia with that kind of—"

"I told you to use my money!" I protest.

Lori clucks at me. "Oh, sweetheart. Did you honestly think you had enough left for that? It's sixty thousand dollars a month. You stayed for three months. Both times. And that, combined with your—"

"Wait." I straighten, ignoring, for the moment, her jab at my relapse. "Are you saying there's *nothing* left?" Panic throbs in me. Lori has been in control of my finances since before rehab, as ordered by the judge. Once I finished rehab, the accounts were supposed to be mine again, but it had just been easier to leave them with her. She said she didn't trust me with them, and honestly, at the time, I wasn't sure I did either.

"Enough to pay your tuition this semester, that's about it," she says, sounding mournful.

I feel vaguely dizzy. "How is that even possible?" I thought I had a least a couple hundred thousand left, even after Safe Harbor. But it's been years, literally, since I've seen a bank statement. And as Eric pointed out yesterday, I haven't worked except for a few small jobs here and there since the end of *Starlight*.

"It doesn't matter." Lori smooths my hair, and I'm too stunned to jerk away. "The past is the past. But there's still time to fix it, for all of us. Starting now."

My throat aches with the desire to scream. How am I supposed to fight back against this? What boundaries am I supposed to set here? I don't have any money. I don't have a degree. I don't have any skills or experience in anything other than acting. It's not like I have anywhere else to go, someone else who will put me up.

"Be ready tomorrow morning for Tim at four-thirty," she says, turning and walking out, shutting the door on the conversation.

I drop onto the nearest bed, the one closest to the wall. I'm not sure which one's supposed to be mine, but the other bed has more of a stuffed animal collection, including Mr. Bug, a stuffed ladybug missing an antenna that used to be mine. Zinn appropriated it when she was four.

I'm trapped. After this project, it'll be another one, each slightly declining in quality or value until it's local only, the cheesy car dealership commercials Eric mentioned, if that. Whatever brings in the money.

And then what?

Whatever my mother tells me.

Suddenly I can't breathe. I can't do this. I have to find another way.

The money I'll earn from *Fly Girl* will be something. A start, maybe. Assuming I can get control of it. That has to be step one. But I've never opened a bank account in my life, never even thought about it. How pathetic is that? My mom has always taken care of that kind of stuff, including for the portion of money that was legally mine, that she couldn't officially touch. Money was an electronic umbilical cord between us, even after I fired her. The judge's ruling after my arrest just made it official.

Eric. I sit up straighter. He said my money would be mine. If he hasn't already set up an account in my name—*Is that even possible? I have no idea*—I bet he knows how to.

Of course, that's going to mean asking him for help, listening to his "I told you so"s.

The doorknob rattles suddenly, and the door starts to open. I brace myself, expecting round two with my mom. But instead, Zinnia slips in, dressed for her bed in a faded pink nightshirt, her damp hair hanging down her back. "Hey."

I clear my throat. "Hey." I frown at her. "Were you in the bathroom this whole time?"

"Better than in here with Mom," Zinn says, flopping on the other bed, her head disappearing in the menagerie of stuffed animals.

True enough. "Sorry for taking over," I say. "I really didn't think this would happen."

She shrugs. "It's okay. I'd rather share with you than Poppy. She snores."

I sigh. Poor Poppy. "It's her asthma, I think." Something else my mother refused to acknowledge except when absolutely necessary. A wheezy and nearsighted book nerd did not fit with her glamorous Beckett family image. Beckett wasn't even Wade's last name. It was my mom's stage name, passed down to us.

Zinn rolls onto her side to face me, propping her head on her elbow. "Are you going to stay?"

She seems so much older now, since I've been gone, not a little girl anymore but a teenager: all long legs, skinny elbows and a far-too-serious expression. I never saw her much when I was working. And she was ten when I moved out for the first time. After I finished rehab, we didn't cross paths much. She went to school, followed by some combination of dancing, singing and acting lessons. I was busy trying to keep my head on straight with NA meetings. But now that I think about it, I'm not sure if that's it or if there's just always been this distance.

"I don't know," I admit. "Mom wants me to."

"Did you like college?" Zinn asks.

I'm not sure how to answer that. "Some parts of it," I say cautiously. "I think it would have been different if I . . . hadn't been me." I make a face, but Zinn nods, seeming to understand.

"Did Mom tell you we're moving?" she asks.

"She said the house was for sale," I say. "It doesn't mean we . . . you're going to have to move."

"No, I'm pretty sure we are," she says. "I heard them fighting about it."

Fighting? Wade and my mom? I couldn't picture that. Wade would pretty much have to be on fire before he would even speak voluntarily.

"Dad lost his disability check, and now they can't afford it."

Disability? Wade owned some kind of shipping company, and he retired, as far as I knew, after selling the company years ago—not long after my mom married him and pressed him into chauffeur service, driving us into the city two or three times a week for auditions or work. I didn't know anything about a disability check.

I shake my head. "The house should be paid for, or mostly, by now."

"The bank is going to foreclose," Zinn says quietly.

Hearing those words, in that order, from Zinn sends a chill

across my skin. She's obviously overheard something. "I'm sure that's not true."

Really, Calista? It's Lori. The voice in my head sounds a lot like Eric.

And it would explain the urgency behind my return and why she'd jumped all over this offer, even though it was from Eric.

A heavy feeling settles in my stomach.

"I'll talk to Mom," I say.

After a moment, Zinn says, "I'm glad you're back."

The guilt and shame from earlier returns, making me wish I could sink through the mattress to the floor. Has it been that bad here that she actually thinks I can make a difference? We're both in trouble, then.

She rolls onto her back, staring up at the ceiling, and her stomach gives a loud rumble.

"Zinn, you need to eat more." At least I was grown, relatively. Who knew what that kind of deprivation did to someone her age? For the first eight, maybe ten years of my life, Lori was more focused on making sure we had enough to eat. But once she married Wade, and I started getting bigger parts, she developed this bizarre obsession with what we were eating. "Just keep it healthy" morphed into "document every calorie you consume," then got worse. There had been arguments about measuring intake versus output. No. Just . . . no.

"Can't," Zinn says matter-of-factly. "I'll get fat, and no one will want to hire me."

I flinch, hearing my mother's words out of her mouth. "Zinn, that's not true. And even if it was, you need to take care of yourself first." She's a freaking freshman in high school. She should be worried about making the show choir or getting good grades. Not getting work to bring in money.

Though that's exactly what I was doing at her age. She's a *kid. I* was a kid. I can see it so clearly now, in a way I couldn't when I was her age. No wonder Eric was always pushing food in my direction the first couple of years on *Starlight.*

If I stay and keep working, then Zinn wouldn't have to worry about anything other than being a teenager. At least for a couple years. Maybe that's the way it should be.

Zinn shakes her head. "It's all right." She reaches over the edge of the bed to pull a bottle of water from what looks to be a stash hiding behind the dust ruffle. "If I drink enough water, it makes it stop enough so I can sleep."

Oh, God. The worst part is I recognize that trick as one I've used. But it seems so much worse to hear about it from Zinn, in that simple, experienced tone. I used to spoon baby food—all organic and homemade, of course—into her mouth. She loved squash, hated carrots. Always ended up with those in her hair.

I don't know how to fix this, how to fix any of this. I'm not sure if I can.

12

ERIC

The alarm on my phone beeps in the pre-dawn hours, startling me, and I fumble across the kitchen table, past the various piles of paper and my tablet, to shut it off before it wakes Katie. I left the alarm set even though I've been awake for hours—just in case. I can't afford to be late, not today.

Removing my glasses, I drop them on the pages in front of me and scrub my hands over my face.

I've gone over everything. The budget, schedules, location reports, emails, contracts, invoices, permits. It's all as ready as I can make it. But I'm sure I'm missing something; I just don't know what. And my dad's words won't stop playing in my head: *You're going to embarrass yourself. I'm just trying to save you from that.*

"Shit," I mutter.

Katie appears in the doorway to the kitchen, Bitsy cradled against her. "Hey."

"Morning." I straighten up, the too-tight muscles between my shoulder blades protesting.

"You look like you need an assistant," she says, edging closer. Bitsy scrambles against Katie, her nails scraping against the silk of Katie's robe as she tries to get to me. For whatever reason, this crazy dog prefers me, the guy who is always almost stepping on her and who feeds her leftover potato chips and the dregs of my ice cream, instead of the person who can actually keep her whole and alive and healthy.

"I need about three of them," I admit. Then I frown at the piles of crumpled paper. "And possibly a filing cabinet. Why the hell isn't everything digital by now?"

Katie hands a squirming Bitsy to me, and Bitsy promptly wiggles free to plop herself in my lap, turning in circles until she's curled up in the space between my stomach and my hip.

"You slept on the couch last night," Katie says, taking down a coffee mug from the cabinet. Her back is to me, so I can't see her expression, but I can feel the tension in her, in the room.

"I fell asleep on the couch," I say. "There's a difference."

"Is there?" She holds up a second coffee mug in question.

I pick up my mug from last night, the cold greasy remains sloshing within, and make a face. "Yeah, thanks," I say. "It wasn't intentional," I continue, picking up the thread of the conversation. "That's the difference. I couldn't sleep, so I didn't want to keep you awake."

"I wouldn't have minded," she says quietly, pouring coffee into the mugs.

"I would," I point out. "You have lives to save today. Surgeries to perform. Anal glands to express, whatever that means. You need to be well rested."

She snorts with laughter. "Thank you."

"I mean, I don't know exactly what those are, but if I had them, I would not want my doctor to be sleep-deprived."

Turning, Katie shakes her head at me in amused exasperation and hands me a mug before sitting across from me with her own.

"I wanted to say I'm sorry about last night," she begins.

"You don't have anything to be sorry for." Except possibly not believing me when I tried to tell her about my dad.

"I shouldn't have pushed you into having dinner with him," she says.

"It's okay," I say. And I'm trying for it to be. There are bumps in the road with every relationship, right? Not that I would know from experience. This is my longest monogamous . . . anything.

Besides, Katie was genuinely trying to do what she thought was best for our future, and that's what matters. "You didn't know," I add. Now she does, though, and that's actually what's probably for the best.

She's quiet for a long moment, studying the rim of her coffee mug. Then she says, "Have you . . ." She hesitates. "Are you considering his offer?"

I freeze, coffee mug halfway to my mouth. "What?" In my lap, Bitsy makes a quiet grumbling noise, likely in response to the sudden rigidity in my posture.

Katie lifts her hand in surrender. "Just hang on," she says. "Before you lose your mind, I have a point."

I raise my eyebrows.

"Look, you've always said this is just a place to start. You want to build, you want to grow. You may not like your dad, but working with the resources he has might be a smart move," she says. "If you're sure you want to go through with this . . ."

"Instead of leaving everything behind and becoming a real estate broker?" I ask, more sharply than I meant to.

Her cheeks flush. "All I'm saying is, why start from scratch when you don't have to? You can get to where you want to be that much faster. Use him, use what he's offering."

And never make anything that's actually mine, always knowing that my dad can claim a hand in its success or ride my ass that much harder if it fails? No, thanks.

"Are you worried about money?" I ask. "Because everything is going to be fine, and I can always—"

"No! Of course not," she says, reaching out for my hand, and I let her take it, reluctantly. I'm too tired for this conversation. I can feel irrational irritation rising up, eroding my patience, and I work to stuff it back down. I'm only here because of Katie, because she believed in me enough to push me.

"I just want you to consider whether or not you're making this decision for the right reason. Forget your dad, forget his agenda. What about what you want? What about *your* agenda?" She squeezes my fingers, her gaze anxious but warm with affection. "Does this get you closer to your goals?"

I get what she's saying, but that just makes it clearer that she doesn't understand. It kind of feels more like she wants me to do whatever I need to get this out of my system, to succeed or fail on a faster timeframe so we can get on with our real life, whatever that looks like.

But to be fair to her, I'm not sure I entirely understood what I wanted until last night. Because it's not just about creating a great show, it's about doing it my way and *without* my dad's interference. Success or failure, it will be mine to bear alone. And yeah, maybe it makes me petty or stupidly stubborn to turn down what he's offering, to take the bigger risk, but that's the only way any of this *means* anything.

"Listen, I understand what you're saying, but it's not that simple. I need to do this without him. That part is important to me."

Her smile dims slightly. "Are you sure? I just feel like maybe there are . . . other factors affecting your decision."

I frown, gathering up my papers and stuffing them back into folders. I really need a better system. "Like what?" A more-than-twenty-year history of my dad acting like a douche seems like more than enough.

"Like Calista?"

I stop and stare at her. "Are you serious? She has nothing to do with this."

"You weren't telling your dad no last night until he brought up recasting," Katie points out.

"That doesn't mean I said no because of Calista!" Frustrated, I start to stand and pause long enough to pick Bitsy up off my lap before she falls. This dog. "That just happened to be the last thing he said before it finally dawned on me that I didn't have to listen to his particular brand of bullshit anymore."

"Okay, okay, I'm sorry," she says, holding up her hands. "I didn't mean to upset you. I just had to ask." She smiles, but the edges of her mouth are trembling. "I don't think you realize how different you are with her. How you guys look at each other."

I sigh. "I told you—"

"Family, I know. But sometimes it's easier for other people to see what you can't, and—"

"People always see what's not there with us. They have from the beginning." I clench my jaw and then force myself to let go when I hear my teeth squeaking from the pressure. "We're not like that."

"Not anymore?" Katie presses.

I relent. "There might have been a moment for it, once a long time ago. But no, we're past that." The memory of Callie's expression yesterday nags at me, her eyes wide with surprise and hurt. Not so far in the past for her, then, maybe. But that means nothing. It doesn't change anything. It can't.

Katie nods, but she seems unconvinced. "You know I couldn't do this without you," I say, leaning over her chair to nuzzle against her neck. She smells like sleep and that lavender soap bar in the bathroom, the one I got in trouble for moving in the shower because it dissolved. "Seriously. You saved me. I need you."

She pulls back, an unidentified emotion flickering across her face before it vanishes.

"What's wrong?"

"Nothing." She shakes her head, and then smiles at me. "You need me, huh? How much?" she asks, wrapping her hand around the back of my neck, pulling me closer.

"That sounds like a challenge," I murmur.

But then my backup alarm sounds, an old-fashioned telephone ring, loud and shrill, startling both of us and making Bitsy bark.

Katie pats the side of my face and then pushes me away. "Time to go to work."

"I can't work like this!" Vincent shouts in my general direction, when the power flickers for the third time in the last fifteen minutes.

It is the latest meltdown/screw up in a day that's been full of them. Starting with the warehouse co-owner, a dude I didn't even know existed, storming out and demanding our paperwork as soon as we rolled onto location this morning. I had it, fortunately, though it took me a few minutes to find it.

Now I push to my feet, my knees protesting—God, maybe I am getting old—and leave my mark in search of the power problem, and hopefully, a solution.

But before I get more than a step or two, the lights stabilize, and someone shouts, "We got it. Cheap-ass generator."

"Thank you," Vincent shouts back, sarcasm dripping.

With a sigh, I return to my mark and kneel on the concrete floor next to Calista.

She's lying on the ground, her eyes closed and her arm thrown over her head in a protective gesture that will do no good. Near her temple, her hair is matted with a mixture of corn syrup and food coloring, darkening the blond to a bloody red. It makes me feel a little queasy to see her like this. It's all fake, obviously, but I have real memories of pulling Calista, bloody and broken, from a very real car accident.

Chase hit a guard rail. We were lucky we didn't go tumbling off the edge of the hill. That shock of the crash still reverberates through me when I let myself think about it. After I freed myself from my seatbelt with shaking hands, I climbed out the shattered back window and immediately went to the bashed-in passenger-side door. Calista, unconscious, was half-in and half-out of the window, and bleeding. So much. I have a permanent—and horrible—sense memory of the weight of her head lolling against my arm, and her blood trickling, warm and wet, down my elbow. I was afraid she was dying. Amped too much on adrenaline and panic, I wouldn't let the EMTs take her at first once they finally arrived. In my head, it felt like letting her go, even to them, was giving up, that somehow my will was the thing keeping her alive.

This injury, though, is part of Evie's story. A knock to the side of Evie's head incurred while she is attempting to stop a warehouse robbery ends up stealing her abilities. Head trauma, traumatic brain injury—it's never made clear exactly what happened. And Jude's interpretation of it is that it might well be Evie's own subconscious choice to block out her superpowers, given that her family and friends only seem to value her for what she can do instead of who she is.

"You okay?" Callie asks me quietly, opening her blue eyes to blink up at me. It startles me and sends a reflexive wave of relief through me that is part due to the reminder that she's okay—no longer broken and unconscious—and part due just to her being here. It's a comfort to have at least one friendly face here.

Despite how we left things yesterday, she wasn't angry when she arrived this morning. Alone, without Lori. I'm not sure how she pulled that off. Callie just nodded hello and went straight to work. God love her. I couldn't take any more drama today, the first day.

Behind me, Vincent is muttering while we reset for another take, and I brace myself for another explosion.

"Being in charge is not like what I expected," I say to Callie. When I used to visit sets with my dad, he would stride through, surveying everything like a king with his kingdom stretched out before him. Sometimes people would approach to say hello or to ask a question, but it was all quick, superficial stuff, more to show deference than to get a needed answer. Whoever said it's nice to be needed must have had a severe inferiority complex. Because no one wants to be needed this much.

"There are always hang ups, you know that," she says reasonably. "You're just hearing about more of them this way."

"And in charge of fixing them," I say.

"The price of power?" she asks, arching her eyebrows.

"Yeah. I guess." I hesitate, but then continue. Calista will, of all people, understand. "My dad made me an offer last night. He wants me to come work for him."

Calista pushes herself up to her elbows, the neck of Evie's sweater falling off her shoulder, revealing pale, smooth skin and the start of several pinkish scars, and I have to look away. "Are you serious?" she asks.

I nod.

She narrows her eyes. "What's the catch?"

I point at her, triumphant. "Yes, see? Exactly." Calista gets it. Probably because her own parental situation is just as fucked up, only in a different way. "He wants me to turn over rights to *Fly Girl.* He'll rework it, recast, make it for television. He has the resources—"

She makes a disgusted noise. "So he can turn Evie into a stripper by day and superhero by night?"

I laugh because that's not far from the truth. I knew she would be as protective of Evie as I am.

"I hope you told him to fuck off," Callie says, lying back down in position. "And if you didn't, I'm sure Jude would."

I glance over my shoulder to where Jude is sitting, back behind the monitors.

From her chair, she's watching Vincent pace back and forth like a caged lion, and when she catches my eye, she gestures to him, not all that subtly, mouthing to me, "This fucking guy." Then she rolls her eyes.

Calista snorts.

As expected, Jude and Calista bonded immediately when they met this morning during the first shooting break, though there'd been a moment right at the start that made me wonder if I would be wrong.

Jude squinted up at Callie. "You're taller than I thought," she says. "Not tall, mind you. Just different than what I thought."

Her cheeks turning red, Callie went still, obviously expecting the critique to begin. *Too tall, too fat, too old, too inexperienced.* She'd heard it all before, mostly from her mother on various days with the rest of the *Starlight* cast and crew to witness it.

I made a move to intervene, but Jude continued.

"But then again, I'm just probably shrinking. Again." And with that, Jude let loose with a wheezy cackle that spoke to years of smoking.

Then she took Callie's hand in hers. "You are the perfect Evie," she said softly, her eyes bright with emotion. "Exactly what I pictured in my head all those years ago. I never thought that could happen. It's like seeing her come to life right in front of me."

Seeing Callie's face light up in that moment made me feel like I'd done something heroic—in optioning *Fly Girl*, in casting her as Evie, in introducing her to the author who meant so much to her—when really all I'd done is what I always do: what's best for me. It just happened to be good for her, too.

And speaking of which, I turn my attention back to Callie. "Listen, I didn't have time this morning, but I wanted to apologize for everything yesterday. I could have . . . I should have handled that better." Maybe by not springing a fiancée on her without any notice, given our rather tumultuous, though unofficial, history.

She stiffens before shrugging. "It's fine. I was just . . . surprised."

"Are you sure?"

"I think old feelings sometimes just hang on out of habit," she says. "That's all."

Her words leave an uncomfortable feeling in my gut.

"It was the first time I'd seen you in years. Of course things are going to be different. I just hadn't . . . processed that yet. That's all it was." Her gaze flicks past me to fix on a point on the warehouse ceiling above.

"Right," I say. "Good." Though it doesn't feel good or right. "And I'm sorry for all that stuff I said about you and your mom. I shouldn't have—"

Calista focuses on me again. "Actually, I wanted to talk to you about something," she says, sitting up. Her voice is hushed, and she's picking at the edge of her thumbnail with her index finger—the portrait of a nervous Callie. Her tension feels contagious.

"What's wrong?" I ask.

"My mom told me . . . she mentioned that she was having 'exploratory conversations' on my behalf while I was gone."

Damnit, Lori. I'd heard as much, but I was hoping that was just rumor.

"So, I just want you to know . . . I realize that it could have been a lot worse. She would have pulled me out of school and back here to do anything she managed to land. And I mean, I'm here playing Evie instead of being eaten by an ant-shark-octopus mutation, or whatever it was you said the other day. And that's because of you. So thank you."

I clear my throat. "You don't need to thank me," I say, my voice gruff. "You're here because you're good. You're the Evie I wanted, the Evie we needed."

She takes a deep breath. "I also wanted to ask a favor." Despite the makeup and the sticky, corn syrup blood, her cheeks are pale.

"Are we ready, people?" Vincent shouts. I don't think the man speaks at anything below a hostile screech.

I draw a breath to tell him we need a minute, but Calista shakes her head.

"No, it's fine. It can wait," she says hastily.

"Calista," I begin.

"Let's start at the top," Vincent calls out. It takes him only a second to zero in on me. "Anytime now, Mr. Producer," he says with a sneer.

I grimace. The guy was always a dick. Even more so now that he works for me, though it should be the opposite.

"We'll talk later," I say to Calista.

"Sure." She nods quickly before resuming her prone position on the floor, eyes shut. But I can't help but feel like I've missed a moment, something important.

13

CALISTA

I listen, keeping my body as relaxed and limp as possible on the cold concrete floor as everyone moves into position. Sometimes, the hardest thing is not to do anything. To be caught in a perpetual state of limbo, present but trapped, without the ability of action. Plus, keeping your eyes still so your eyelids don't move. That's tricky.

It's true for acting in scenes like this, where I'm here only for reaction—Cory discovering that Evie's been hurt.

But it's also true, I think, in life. Like this morning. After spending most of the night thinking about what I would say to my mom, how I would ask about the house and what's really going on, preparing to counter her every slippery side step to try and get the truth, it turned out not to matter. My mom woke with one of her migraines, and Wade drove me by himself, talk radio filling the silence. Normally, this would have been a cause for celebration. But not today. After all that buildup . . . nothing. It's a mixture of relief from avoiding the inevitable conflict and frustration at being thwarted. Plus, I doubt the migraine was anything more than her attempt to punish me for questioning her yesterday.

See, do you see how stressed-out and sick you make me? She may not have said it out loud this time, but I've heard it often enough in the past, every time sending a lurch of panic through me. For so many years, Lori was all I had. The threat of her leaving—or giving up on me—was more than enough to pull me back in line with whatever she wanted.

But I'm not a little kid anymore.

This morning, I tried to talk to Wade to get something, anything, about the house/financial situation. But he was his usual laconic self.

"Your mother handles that, not me. You know that, hon," he said.

I resisted the urge to groan. How could he not be worried about it? Then again, this is the man who happily turned over control to Lori in the first place. Maybe he didn't know enough to be worried. That was one way to live.

"Okay, but what about these disability checks? Zinn mentioned something to me about that," I asked, hoping I wasn't going to get my sister in trouble. Not with Wade, but with our mom when Wade inevitably reported this conversation to her. "I don't understand. I thought you were, like, a shipping company CEO or whatever."

He snorted. "Oh, Callie-girl, that was your mother. I think that is what she told people a long time ago, probably you, too. Truth is, old Wade was nothing but a long-haul trucker, working for one of those big outfits, 'til I hurt my back about fifteen years ago."

"What?" I asked, struggling to process this new information against what I'd always believed to be true. *She lied.* Not just to status-conscious moms and managers in the audition waiting rooms, but to me, too.

"Now, don't go blaming her. Your mother just likes to put things in the best light, that's all," he said with an easy shrug.

"Even if that light has nothing to do with reality?" I demanded.

He just laughed. "Oh, it always works out for Lori." He shook his head. "That woman, I swear, she just has to put her mind to it, and everything seems to fall into place. Don't you worry."

Yeah, it always worked out because she pushed me—and now Zinnia, Poppy and Dahlia—to be more and do more, pursuing her dream of being a star with us as proxies. But where had all that money gone? Where was the money she'd earned as my manager? Where was *my* money that the court had given her control over? No matter how little of it was left, it was—or is—still mine.

And here's the part I can't stop thinking about: If she lied about Wade, what else has she been lying to me about?

I try not to shift against the cold, concrete floor, even though it feels like it's beginning to burn where it touches my exposed skin.

"So you've got me running to Evie or not?" Eric asks someone. His voice echoes in the warehouse, making him sound very far away, when I know that's not true. His first mark is only about fifteen feet from me. The answer comes as a murmur, so it's not Vincent he's talking to.

Eric. I should have just blurted it out to him: *Hey, I need your help. If I can figure out how to start a new bank account, can you make sure my pay is deposited there, out of my mother's reach? Just in case. Because I have some concerns.*

Simple. Direct. Clear.

The trouble is, it feels like pushing a boulder off the top of a very steep hill and racing it to the bottom, while not being entirely certain I'll be able to stay ahead of it. It's making a choice that I won't be able to take back.

Eric will help me—yeah, I'm pretty sure about that—but he won't leave it alone, either. He won't let me handle it. He'll insist on getting involved, if nothing else just to yell at Lori, which is not to say she doesn't deserve it. But I need to find out what's actually happening first, before I can commit to doing anything. This is my responsibility, not his.

Except what, exactly, am I going to do? If my mom and Wade are losing the house, how am I supposed to stop that? Other than by giving them everything I earn and hoping they manage to figure it out? But I've already done that, and this is still where we ended up. I can't do that again.

"All right, people. Action!" Vincent yells.

I shove all the anxieties about my mom and money to the back of my brain and focus on being Evie, on being here.

Silence for a moment, then shouting from the other side of the warehouse. The rest of Cory's team are trying to get out before Evie's friends catch up with them.

No one actually sees Evie being injured; Cory, who, incidentally, is part of the team attempting to rob the warehouse, just finds her unconscious. The two of them have been sparring/flirting for years, on opposite sides of this world where special abilities have been gifted only to the few and the young. Evie is trying to help keep the world the same, but Cory and his fellow revolutionaries want to tip the structure of society to put the more powerful on top. *Take what you want, do whatever you want.*

Footsteps pound in my direction, then stop. "Evie?" Eric-as-Cory asks, his voice hoarse with surprise.

It takes effort not to tense up, to keep my breathing slow and even.

"Evie," he says again, the edges of my name—her name—rough with raw panic. Tears sting beneath my closed lids. Eric is acting, it's all pretend, and yet in spite of everything, it *feels* real. Or maybe I just want it to. Maybe some dumb part of me still wants to matter that much to him.

He runs the last few feet toward me, landing hard on his knees, half-sliding into me.

"Evie, Evie, come on, you gotta wake up. Evie!" He shakes me gently and then a little harder, before bending over me to check to see if Evie is still breathing, her heart beating.

The weight of his head rests lightly on my chest for just a moment, long enough that I feel the heat of his skin through my shirt, the tickle of his curls brushing my chin.

Then it's gone, and his hands are moving under me, grabbing me up roughly into his lap. My forehead rests against the warmth of his throat, which works convulsively, like he's trying not to cry.

"Help! Somebody help me!" he shouts. "Please! Call an ambulance."

Of course, the irony is supposed to be that Cory is now seeking help from the very system he was trying to disrupt/overthrow. But in the moment, it feels more like just a guy trying to save the girl he loves.

"Cut!" Vincent shouts.

I open my eyes and blink a few times quickly so the tears will retreat before falling or before Eric looks down and sees them. I'm still bundled against him. We're not moving because if we've nailed the take then we're moving to close-ups.

Eric swipes at his eyes and then runs his hand up and down my arm, like he's trying to bring the warmth back into my skin. "You okay, Callie?" he asks. "Didn't grab you too hard?"

Grab me harder. Don't let go. "No, you're fine."

"Did we get it?" he shouts over to Vincent, and his voice vibrates through his chest against my cheek.

"Son of a bitch! What do you mean there was a glitch?" Vincent's screaming reverberates through the cavernous space, and then something crashes to the floor.

"Shit," Eric mutters. He stands and puts me to my feet, making sure I have my balance before darting off toward the cameras and playback monitors.

I stretch, trying to warm up.

"Forget it, Stone! It's not worth my time or my effort. I thought you were serious about this, but this is a complete shitshow," Vincent says loud enough that everyone can hear. "I'm out of here."

"Vincent, wait, if you just . . ." I can barely see Eric through the tangle of equipment, starting after Vincent.

Uh-oh. I hurry toward Eric, catching up with him near the side door as it slams behind Vincent. "Is everything okay?"

Eric's gaze flicks from the door to me.

"He quit," Eric says in disbelief.

My mouth falls open. "He . . . what?"

"Everybody, just . . . let's take a break, okay?" Eric says, raising his voice so everyone can hear. The sound of whispering and talking increases, and a few people, members of Cory's team of thieves, drift toward the craft services table.

"Doesn't he have a contract with—" I ask.

"We don't want to force him to be here," Eric says grimly. "Trust me. If it comes to that, it's going to kill our production schedule, and then the delays will destroy what's left of our budget." He takes a hand through his hair. "Fuck!"

On a larger production, someone else would just step up. Actually, in a larger production, Vincent probably wouldn't have dared to quit in the first place. It's nothing I've ever seen happen before. So now what?

I've sunk everything I have into this. That's what Eric told me. His name is on it.

In spite of everything, my heart aches for him. He's really trying to change his life, to be the person I always knew he could be, but this situation is not going to help.

"I guess we need to stop for the day, and I need to find a new director," he says, rubbing a hand over his face. He looks exhausted already, and we've just started. "By tomorrow."

Except how is anyone new going to get up to speed in time to keep to the production schedule? That doesn't make sense. We'd have to shut down for at least a couple of days to let any new director catch up, and if the budget is that tight, that may not be possible.

Unless he gives up and hands it over to his father.

I can read the thoughts running through Eric's head right now as clearly as if they were posted on a monitor above his head, and frustration zooms to life in me. I should have known. The second there's trouble or complication, Eric will run. He always has, always will. "Don't," I say.

He gives me a strained smile. "Don't what?"

"I know what you're thinking. And you're not calling Rawley," I say fiercely.

"Calista," he begins with that world-weary smirk. "Kid, I know you think you understand—"

"Don't call me that," I say automatically. "You can't just give up and hand over control to him. Did you seriously think everything was going to go smoothly?" Forty-eight hours ago, I might have been relieved at the idea of the production shutting down. But now? Now I know better. I *need* this job.

"The director quitting was not something I had a contingency plan for, Calista," he says, raising his voice slightly.

"Boo hoo, we all have problems we weren't expecting," I snap, and behind me, I hear a muffled snort of laughter. A glance over my shoulder reveals Jude a few feet behind us. She waves her hand in an "ignore me" gesture.

I turn my attention back to Eric. "Get over it. This is one bump in the road. If this means something to you to keep going, figure it out."

"Callie, it's not that simple," he says, shaking his head.

"Because you don't want it to be."

"Yeah, I'm the one who wanted the director to quit!" he shouts.

"You are the one who hired The Terrorist!" I can't resist pointing out.

He rolls his eyes and leans against the wall, one leg crossed in front of the other. "I don't know," he says in an affected bored tone. "Maybe that was because he has the name and reputation—"

"For being a dick, but that doesn't matter now," I say. The solution is obvious to me, now that I've had a few seconds to think about it. "You should just do it."

"What?" Eric blinks at me, then his eyes go wide. "Direct?" He forces a laugh. "Are you kidding me?"

"Why not?" I fold my arms across my chest, ignoring the twinge in my damaged shoulder. "You know the material. On the really small web shows, sometimes it's all one person, writing, acting, directing, whatever. This isn't that different."

He glares at me. "You know it is."

"Why? Because you need other names to give yours legitimacy?" I ask, and he winces. Because yeah, I know.

"What kind of crap is that?" I continue.

"The kind of crap other people listen to," he hisses at me, straightening up. "I don't want to be that Stone kid just playing around with shit. I wanted to be taken seriously this time."

"So make them. You have the experience. That episode when we had Michael What's-his-face directing and his experimental style." I wave my hands around in an imitation of the director's woo-woo attitude. "You basically did it then. And you spent more time on *Starlight* behind the cameras than in front of them. You know what you're doing. Just . . . do it."

He leans closer to me, his jaw tight. "Calista, I'm trying not to fuck this up, remember?"

I pause. "You're good enough. You know that."

He jerks back, his gaze jumping to mine in surprise, and in that second, I know he remembers the last time I said those words. It's probably not fair to bring it up, but playing fair has never been one of Eric's priorities. Maybe it shouldn't be one of mine, either, when dealing with him.

Plus, I'm right. I was then, too.

"So," I say, "you can fuck it up by giving up and deliberately sabotaging yourself, which is guaranteed failure." His normal preference, at least in years past. "Or you can fuck it up by trying your best, which is only possible failure. Which one can you live with?"

"Neither," he snaps at me. But when he pushes past me and storms off, it's in the direction of the cameras.

My shoulders sag in relief.

"Wow," Jude says quietly.

Startled, I spin around to face her. I'd completely forgotten she was behind me. "Sorry," I say quickly. I stop, not sure how to explain what just happened. Eric and I have always helped each other, sometimes by pushing, just usually not quite that hard.

"That's okay. I guess I didn't realize you two knew each other *that* well." She eyes me speculatively, her green eyes glinting behind her glasses. "Just like my Evie and Cory."

"Lots of history is all," I mumble. "Working together for years, and then all the travel, fan cons and awards programs and—"

"And the accident," she says evenly. "The one that shattered your arm."

"How did you—"

"Oh, honey, writers are a terribly nosey bunch, and I wasn't going into this without doing my due diligence."

"But Eric's dad—"

She waves her hand. "—covered it up with all the right people, yes. But the truth is still available if you dig hard enough, and I like digging." She grins at me, and it doesn't *seem* threatening, but . . .

"It was an accident," I say firmly. If Chase is sober and getting his life back together, the last thing he needs is trouble from a mistake that wasn't even really his, four years ago. I'm the one who pushed him to drive me, to get me out of there that night.

"What happened?" she asks, leaning forward conspiratorially.

I just look at her.

"Oh, I'm not going to say anything to anyone." She holds her hands, palms up. "I'm on a flight back to Jersey in a few hours anyway. I'm just curious."

And if she knows the already damaging part, that Chase was drunk and driving, then it might be better to fill in some of the blanks. Enough to assuage her curiosity and keep her from asking other people about it, opening old wounds. "We were at a party. Eric and I got into an argument about . . . something that should have never happened. I asked our friend Chase to take me home, and we crashed. No big mystery or conspiracy. Just a dumb accident."

"Uh-huh," she says, sounding unconvinced.

And she's right to be skeptical. Everything I said was the truth. It's just only a fraction of the emotional devastation from that night.

I should have known from the second I walked out of my condo that night, dressed to kill, that it was all going to go wrong.

Chase, who'd come to pick me up, got out of the car, his mouth hanging open for a second in shock, before he managed to whistle. "Whose mind are you trying to blow tonight?"

I grinned at him. "All of them?" The gold mini-dress was slinky and smooth, making *me* feel slinky and smooth. The hem ended a good seven inches above my knee and my heels made my legs look even longer.

When I climbed into Chase's car, oh-so-carefully because in that short of a dress, flashing happens as easily as breathing, he just shook his head at me.

"Poor Eric," he muttered.

"This is not about him," I said quickly, face heating. And it wasn't. This was about me feeling good about myself. That being said, if he decided to weep with envy for his poor choices upon seeing me, I was fine with that.

The party was already well under way by the time we arrived, the valets scrambling to keep up with the arriving cars. Despite having attended plenty of parties in the last year, this one triggered a wave of nerves. Because it was Eric. Because he was here. Because I wanted, at the very least, for him to see me and recognize that I wasn't a kid anymore.

And I got what I wanted; it just didn't work out quite like I planned. But that's the past—ancient history, in fact—and it's not worth dwelling on. Not anymore.

"All right, let's pick up at the top of the scene," Eric calls out, his voice echoing. I can hear the uncertainty beneath the hardened edge of determination, but I'm hoping no one else can. "We'll finish this out and wrap for the day."

Next to me, Jude smiles in approval. I knew I liked her.

For a second, everyone goes still. "Where's Vincent?" someone asks.

I dart forward, leaving Jude behind. "Back to my first mark?" I ask, which is dumb. Because I only have *one*, given that I'm on the freaking floor the whole time. But it's the only question that springs to mind, and it, at least, does the job of deferring to him as the person in charge.

Eric gives me a curt nod. "Vincent quit," he says, raising his voice so everyone can hear him. "I'm taking over for now."

As I settle into place on the floor—the makeup person, Josie, rushing forward to dab me with powder—everyone else slowly returns to their marks. Sure, they're whispering and sending sidelong glances toward Eric, who is behind the monitors, but they're doing what they're supposed to do.

Eric takes his place at his first mark and nods at the cameraman. "Everybody ready?" Eric shouts.

He gets a variety of positive responses, including a couple of whoops and a few thumbs up.

"All right." Eric takes a deep breath. "Action!"

"Long day, sweet pea?" Wade asks when I collapse into the front seat of his old Lincoln hours later, after we've finally wrapped.

"Yeah." It took a little longer with Eric finding his way—and with taking a longer lunch break, thanks to Jude regaling everyone with tales about her early days in television—but once we got a rhythm going, it was a lot easier without Vincent screaming at us.

Wade makes a noncommittal sound of agreement or sympathy as he pulls onto the road. "Well, your mom has something special planned in celebration."

Suddenly my exhaustion fades, replaced by a spike of fear. "Special how? What does that mean? Celebrating what?"

He just smiles at me. "I don't know all the details. Guess we'll have to wait and see."

Normally, I would have spent the hour-long commute home reviewing my lines for tomorrow—we're shooting in an empty condo in Eric's building, apparently, one that will serve as Evie's home—or even dozing because long shooting days are exhausting, which I'd kind of forgotten, but now, all I can do is spin through various scenarios that would qualify as good news in my mother's mind. About half of them flat out suck by my standards.

Trying to push Wade for more information is pointless, so I check my phone again. No panicked messages from Zinn, who would likely be the first one to throw a red flag.

I text her. `What's going on?`

But there's no response.

When we pull into the driveway a very long eighty-three minutes later—thank you effing traffic—I'm a bundle of nerves.

The house looks the same from the outside. The Realtor's sign is still there, and no "SOLD" banner has been added, thank God. I don't see any strange cars parked nearby, and only the normal number of lights are on. So it's not like that time when I was ten and she tried to host a party for casting agents and "Hollywood insiders," whatever that means, and only the really sleazy types showed up.

Taking a deep breath to calm my nerves, I follow Wade into the house through the side door.

The scent of garlic is heavy in the air, and it makes my mouth water instantly.

That is the unmistakable smell of her famous lasagna, which means either someone landed a job or someone died. But since I'm already working, and my grandparents are both gone, I'm not sure how to interpret this gesture.

"You're home! Welcome back!" my mom says as soon as we

enter the kitchen. She rushes over to me and squeezes me tight, and it's as if the argument in my room yesterday never happened.

"We have the best news," she says, and it's only then that I see Zinnia standing in the back of the room toward the pantry, her arms folded over her middle. Bruises stand out in violent greens and yellows on her elbows; she has no padding to protect herself when she knocks into things.

"Tell them, Zinnia!" Lori commands.

"I got a callback on the daughter role for the show about the woman who is the head of the Secret Service," she says quietly, tucking her hair behind her ear.

"I'm telling you the audition was a total cattle call. Thousands of girls," Mom says in disgust, waving her hand dismissively. "But they knew quality when they saw it and chose our Zinn!"

"Congratulations, Zinnia," I make myself say.

She nods, and I've never seen anyone look more miserable at the prospect of possible success.

Wade squeezes her shoulders as he passes in her direction. "So happy for you, baby." Then he wanders out into the hall, and a few seconds later, I hear the TV in the great room click on to ESPN.

"Now, Zinnia, I'll have your smoothie ready in a minute. Dahlia, Poppy, let's go! Salads are on the table." Along with the smallest micro-slivers of lasagna. For them, not Zinnia.

Ah, yes, I remember this part of the celebration particularly well. Wade would eat what he could, but most of it would go to waste because the food prepared in honor of your accomplishment is not something you're actually allowed to eat.

When I was kid, I never thought to question it. But now?

"Mom, Zinn can have some lasagna. She needs the calories," I say, as Poppy and Dahlia take their seats at the table. "She looks like she's about to dry up and blow away."

Poppy glances up from her book, watching warily, and Zinn shoots me an alarmed look, shaking her head at me. "It's fine, I'm fine," Zinn says quickly, and it breaks my heart. How did I miss this happening under my nose?

Well, maybe because I wasn't living here, and then when I was, I was more concerned with my own problems.

Lori tsks at me as she pulls the tray of garlic knots from the oven and puts it on the stovetop, next to the glass pan of lasagna. "Bite your tongue, Calista Rae. Zinnia has just the physique they're looking for, obviously. We're not taking any chances between now and next week."

"If I'm working, why does she need to?" I ask, fearing I already know the answer.

"I want to work, Mommy," Dahlia chirps, tilting her head to the side and batting her eyelashes.

"You are, baby," Lori says, turning away from the oven to run her fingers over Dahlia's curls. "And you're doing such a good job!" Dahlia preens under the attention. It seems possible that she is one-hundred percent Lori's creation. An immaculate conception.

Mom turns away from Dahlia to give me a disapproving glance. "See, Dahlia understands."

"She's six, Lori."

"You're not having any lasagna either. I'll make a smoothie for you, too. We can't risk undoing any of the hard work Tim's managed to accomplish."

Seriously?

I step around Lori, grabbing a plate from the stack next to the stove and then a spatula from the drawer. With less care than necessary, I carve out a sloppy hunk of steaming lasagna.

"Calista!" My mom sounds horrified. "Stop!"

"Did I tell you I got an A on my Biology test this week, Mom?" Poppy asks loudly, trying desperately to either break the tension or shift the attention to herself. Poor Poppy. If anyone has to be wondering if they're adopted, it's her. But I appreciate the attempt to help, if that's what it is.

"That's great, Pops," I say. I slap the lasagna onto the plate. It's too hot and all the layers slide apart, but I don't care. As I grab a fork from the drawer, I catch a glimpse of movement from the corner of my eye and look up in time to see Zinnia vanishing from the kitchen.

Lori grabs my arm. "What are you doing?"

"I'm eating," I say, pulling away and plopping down at my seat across from Poppy. And Zinnia would eat, too. I'd make sure of it.

"I thought we were past this, Calista," Lori says, her voice frosty. "This is selfish and thoughtless behavior. Your career is not just yours. You know that."

But that's not going to work on me tonight. To make that point, I cut a bite away from the enormous piece of lasagna. A puff of steam rises up from the slice; I can't afford to be mumbling my lines tomorrow with a burned tongue, even to prove my point to Lori, so I put my fork down. For the moment. "Are you sure you want to do that?" I ask. "Lecture me about selfish behavior? Why didn't you tell the truth about what's happening with Wade?"

I sense more than see her sudden stillness behind me. "I don't know what you're talking about," she says primly.

But then she addresses my sisters. "Poppy and Dahlia, take your plates out to the living room with Daddy. Tell him I said you could watch the Disney channel for research."

That's all it takes for Dahlia to scramble down from her chair, but Poppy is slower to follow.

Behind those thick lenses, her gaze darts to me, and I nod. She's a good kid.

"Make sure you study their delivery," Lori calls after them.

"He wasn't ever a CEO, the money wasn't from his company," I say as soon as we're alone. "Not unless you count some kind of disability claim." Even saying the words out loud now feels surreal, like the familiar world is tilting to a new angle beneath my feet.

Our financial position is not what I thought it was, hasn't been, for literally years.

But that money had to come from somewhere, and I'm afraid I know exactly where.

"Oh, Calista, you always were such a stickler for details," Lori says with exasperation. "You of all people know that sometimes rough edges need to be . . . smoothed over."

"By lying? To me?" I demand. She doesn't respond. "What's happening with the house, Mom?"

"I told you, it's time for us to—"

I twist around in my chair to face her. "How long until the bank kicks us out?" I ask, surprised at how calmly the words emerge when my insides are hot and roiling with barely contained fury.

She spins away from the stove, grabbing my shoulders hard and shaking me. "Stop," she spits at me. "You're not going to ruin your sister's celebration dinner with all this negativity."

I jerk away from her, wincing at the dull ache in my right arm. "How is this negativity when it's just the truth?"

"I have a plan, Calista. This is none of your business," she says, with a haughty tilt to her head. "I'm handling it." She picks up the tray of garlic knots and begins transferring them to a basket.

"None of my business?" I stare at her in disbelief. "If it's my money and my career that are funding this desperate hope for financial redemption, then it is definitely my business."

"The judge gave me control over your money—"

"That's over," I point out.

"And besides, you're not the only earner now," she says. "Zinn—"

"Is a kid and has no desire to do this, except that she feels like she has to," I say. "Because of you."

She holds her hands up. "I'm not discussing this with you, Calista. Not until you can show me the respect I deserve." She storms out of the kitchen, and a few seconds later, I hear her bedroom door slam. Tomorrow would probably be another migraine day.

I slump in my chair, mind spinning to catch up.

My whole life, Lori's made me feel guilty for my existence, for trying to have any control over my life. When I messed up—and granted, I messed up big—she ranted for weeks in martyred tones about my selfishness in firing her, how I should have known better, how I couldn't be trusted to make good decisions and here was more proof . . . drugs, addiction, arrested! And I believed her, that I couldn't and shouldn't be in charge of myself.

But now it seems like maybe she hasn't done much better, despite her supposed expertise. All of their money—and I suspect some of mine—went to maintaining this house, this lifestyle, thanks to Lori's philosophy of living the life you believe you should have instead of the one you can afford. What kind of planning is that?

I'm not denying that I made mistakes. Clearly. But maybe Eric is right, and some of those mistakes were because I was on my own for the first time, with little to no experience in that arena. Mistakes happen the first time you do anything, particularly if you're a sheltered eighteen-year-old without any real idea of consequences. Because up until that point, my mom was always there to guide, steer, control. But surrendering that control to her again isn't going to fix anything.

We're past that point. *I* am past that point.

Lack of experience doesn't have to equal perpetual failure, no matter how much my mother would prefer that to be the case. It's just a learning curve to be conquered.

The only question is where to start. How do you take back something you never really had in the first place? It feels overwhelming. I can't just storm out. I can't leave my sisters like that. Banks don't foreclose for the fun of it. My family will be out of a place to live, likely soon. Maybe that's not my responsibility, but I'm not sure I can stand by and watch that happen to Zinnia, Poppy and Dahlia.

I remember what it was like to be poor and scared. To worry about making enough for Lori to pay the rent and keep the lights on. She used to try to make it fun: eating by candlelight and playing Hide and Seek—but mostly Hide—when the landlord came knocking. And when I was young, it *was* fun because I didn't get what was really happening. But I don't want that for my sisters, who are old enough to figure it out—especially Zinnia and Poppy.

I don't understand what happened to the Lori who used to buy me a Coke—not even diet—with the change from the cup holder and drive me through the expensive houses in the Hollywood Hills to pick "ours." She would talk about all the wonderful things we were going to see and do and buy as soon as the next check came in. I miss that version of my mom, even for as difficult as our lives were back then. We were in it together.

The woman who comes after me with calipers, harps about my weight and my choices, and reminds me of my worst mistakes to keep me in line—I don't know who she is.

Maybe it's time I stop looking for the old Lori, the one I haven't seen since before *Starlight*, and start looking at the one who's here now.

I pick up my fork with the bite of lasagna on the end of it. The pasta and cheese have cooled enough, it seems, not to burn my mouth. So I eat it, even though Lori isn't here to see my defiance. Because my defiance isn't about her, or it shouldn't be. It's about me—that's maybe the first thing, recognizing that.

So, baby steps, then. One thing at a time. That, I'm pretty sure, I can do.

14 ERIC

You're good enough.

I'm in my "home office" at my condo—basically an empty bedroom—with script pages for tomorrow spread out all over the desk's otherwise-pristine glass surface. I haven't used it for much until this last year. I'm not using it for much now, either. Calista's words from earlier today are playing over and over in my head, destroying my concentration. It's only the second time someone has ever said that to me—and both times it was Calista. Today, under slightly better circumstances than the previous.

I've wondered how much of that night Calista actually remembers. Plenty, apparently. It was probably wishful thinking on my part that she would somehow forget that moment. I'm not sure why that particular portion of the evening is more excruciating than the rest—in terms of low points, there are much lower, even that same night—but that is the one that sticks with me.

I knew I was in trouble the second I saw her in that gold dress.

I didn't clock her identity at first. I was riding a pleasantly warm chemical high, and my dad's house was full of people. Her hair was mostly up, trailing just a few blond curls over one shoulder. Plus that dress . . . it barely reached the top of her thighs, bent over as she was at the pool table, lining up her shot. A few inches shorter and the dress would have been a shirt.

Not that I was complaining. A hot girl with legs for miles at my party, leaning over my pool table and handling her stick like a pro? Fine by me.

The soft curve of her inner thigh was easily visible, and I was already imagining my hand gliding along that smooth skin to the warmth between her legs, stroking, coercing that heat to grow hotter, wetter. Just for me.

But then Chase's familiar and slightly too-loud guffaw of laughter snaps the spell.

From the other side of the pool table, he nods at me, lifting his overly full tumbler in a sloppy salute. "Told you," he says, seemingly to the hot girl in the gold dress.

Then the girl turns to face me with a knowing smile that, under any other circumstance, would have had me hard in an instant.

"Eric," Calista says, with that pleased-with-herself smirk, before reaching for the martini glass balanced next to her on the edge of the table.

Holy shit. The shock must be written all over my face because she laughs, all throaty and warm. It's like a siren song, with notes of soft sheets and warm skin pressed against skin. Calista, her head thrown back and throat exposed as she moans . . .

My dick is not getting the message that this is *Calista*. Fuck.

"Can I talk to you for a second?" I ask, through gritted teeth.

"Sure," she says, handing over her pool cue and her drink to Chase, who gives me a muzzy grin. He is well on his way to being wasted.

"How are you?" she asks, as she approaches.

"Oh, I'm great," I say grimly, taking her firmly by the elbow and leading her out of the game room. Guys are watching her like it's feeding time at the zoo and she's the last pallet of zebra meat for the entire enclosure. Sick assholes. They don't even know her.

Marcus, who played Skye's boyfriend for the first season, stops as we near him in the hallway and gapes. "Calista? Holy shit, you look—"

I shove into him with my shoulder, hard, as we pass.

"Damn, Eric," he protests. "What's your problem?"

I've always hated that guy. There was a good reason we left him behind in Mexico on that trip. "Keep walking, Marcus."

Calista twists around to wave at him and then eyes me. "You don't seem great," she says, suppressed laughter in her voice.

"How much have you had to drink?" I demand.

"Are you serious right now? It's a party. One of *your* parties."

That does nothing to make me feel better.

I pull her into the nearest unoccupied room, which, when I turn on the light, turns out to be a small closet full of shelved cleaning supplies. There are doors here at the mansion—my dad's ego trip made into brick, mortar and white stucco—that I've never bothered to open, especially here in the central part of the house.

"What's wrong?" Calista asks, rubbing her arm as I let go of her and lean around to grab for the door handle.

She doesn't move out of the way—to be fair, there's very little room to maneuver—and my chest brushes against hers as I fumble to shut the door. The light contact of her breasts against me sends heat through me, along with the urge to prolong the contact. To grab her and pull her against me.

But I make myself step back once the door is shut. It only kind of helps. I can still smell her, the vanilla of her perfume or lotion or whatever it is, even above the stronger scent of bleach and laundry detergent and whatever else is in here on the narrow shelves on either side of us.

"Did I hurt you?" I ask gruffly, nodding toward her arm.

"Of course not," she scoffs, but then she belatedly looks down to where her fingers are running over her skin, like she's surprised to see the gesture. She lowers her hand. "It just . . . no," she says a little more softly. "You didn't hurt me."

Her gaze meets mine and holds, for several seconds too long. It sends an electric charge through me. She liked my hands on her. That's what she means.

"What are you doing here?" I demand.

"In the closet? You brought me." She gives me a self-satisfied smile.

Definitely slightly drunk, and I'm not entirely sober myself. And we're trapped in close quarters now. This is a bad idea. The hem of her "dress" is brushing against my thighs and my hands at my sides.

It wouldn't take much effort to reach out and raise it. Touch her. Get her wet. Make her moan for me. Is she even wearing panties under there? I'm maybe two inches from being able to find out.

At the thought, my cock stirs painfully to life again, hard and throbbing against my fly.

Damnit. No, I'm not doing this.

"It's a party," she continues, folding her arms across her chest, which only raises that damned dress even higher.

I try not to look down. *God help me.*

"One that, I thought, I was invited to as a former cast member of *Starlight,* but now it seems like you've invited everyone in the greater Hollywood area," she says pointedly.

That, unfortunately, tends to happen with my parties.

Which is not my point. "No, I mean, what are you doing here dressed like that?" The Callie I'd known for years was more comfortable in yoga pants or those ratty, flannel PJ bottoms she used to wear to my house for movie nights. Or to play pool.

Now, I'll never be able to shake that image of her in that dress, and what I was thinking about, *about her,* out of my head, even if her outfit magically transforms into those awful flannel pants right now. It's not like I'd never thought about her in that way before, but I'd tried really hard to avoid it, and never in that kind of graphic detail. Flirty, touchy, yeah, but not heart-pounding, cock wet—*stop!*

"I can't dress up for a party?" she asks, raising her eyebrows, looking the slightest bit pissed for the first time.

"No! I mean, yes, you can." How did this conversation spin out of control so quickly? I am too wasted for this conversation. Or not wasted enough. "Is this about . . . what you talked to me about last year?" I'd tried very hard not to think about that conversation in the intervening months. "Are you here looking for someone to fuck you?"

Her sharp inhale tells me that I've crossed a line.

She moves closer, chin raised in challenge. "If I am?"

Jealousy beats powerfully against the inside of my chest, like one of those silverback apes trying to claim territory. "Jesus, Callie." I shake my head.

"What? Why is it any of your business?" She pokes me in the shoulder.

"These assholes aren't going to care about you. They aren't going to . . ." Make sure she feels good. Take care of her so she isn't more nervous than she needs to be. Make her come.

"You deserve better than that," I say, frustrated. "Some stranger pawing at you, trying to get off." I know these guys, I've *been* these guys.

"Why do *you* care?" she asks, her expression intent.

I open my mouth. *Because I want it to be me.* "Because I thought we were friends," I mutter. *Lame. Chicken-shit. Pussy.* I can't do it. She'll want more than I can give. Or I'll mess it up or both.

Her face falls. "Well, thanks, *friend*," she says. "But I've got it covered."

"Do you have someone already in mind?" I shouldn't ask, but the question is out before I can stop it. Marcus, maybe? God, Chase? My mind is creating all sorts of lurid images, and I hate them all. The images of Callie and Marcus and Chase and every guy at this party who isn't me.

"Maybe," she says after a moment.

Fuck.

"It's none of your business," she adds.

She turns away from me, but I reach past her to block her access to the door. She could duck under my arm if she wanted to, but she doesn't move.

"You're going to have guys crawling all over you," I say through clenched teeth. We are way too close now, with her ass pressed against me, and any attempts I've made at talking my cock down are over.

"Good," she snaps. "Glad *someone* will be." She glances over her shoulder at me, and despite the bite in her words, hurt and vulnerability play across her face. Then, to my shock, tears well in her eyes. "I've been in love with you since I was sixteen," she says with such weary sadness that it causes a physical ache in my chest.

"Calista," I begin, my voice rough.

She shakes her head. "And I get it, you don't feel the same way. But then just stop, okay? Let me go," she pleads, her words breaking into a choked sob.

It's that plea that breaks me, pushes me past all my well-reasoned objections. I'm causing her pain, and I never wanted that.

"It has nothing to do with what I feel," I say, my jaw tight. "I'm not a nice guy, Calista. I'm not good for you. Not good enough." I can feel the edge of fear pressing tight against my throat.

She turns to face me, her eyes red and watering but her gaze determined. "That's up to me, though, not you. And I'm telling you, you are good enough."

I don't believe her, but the force behind her words tells me that *she* believes it. And that's almost enough.

"You are the only one I want. You have always looked out for me, protected me, made me laugh, made me feel like I'm worth something. More than just a paycheck or a pretty face."

"You *are* worth more than those things," I say, unable to stop myself from touching her cheek with my finger, tracing the lines of the famous cheekbones her mother was always going on about.

She smiles, but it's filled with sadness and in direct contrast to the tears that are now cascading down her face and dripping off her chin. "You believe that about me, but not about yourself?"

Oh, God. "Don't cry, please. It kills me when you do. I just want you to be happy." Before I can talk myself out of it, and with my heartbeat thudding in my ears, I lean down and press my open mouth against the side of her neck. Her skin is satiny smooth and warm under my tongue.

She sucks in a harsh breath, and I feel her tremble against me. "Eric, please," she says in a voice so shaky with desire and uncertainty that I know it'll haunt my every waking moment from now on. It goes straight to my head with a rush that's so powerful it scares me for a second. "Don't do this if you're just going to pull away again. I can't handle it. It'll break my heart."

My eyes sting. "I'm right here," I say, each word grating and gravelly. "I'm not going anywhere."

I thread my hands through her hair, cupping the sides of her face, and then I lean down and brush my mouth over hers. Her hands clutch hard at my arms, and I can taste the salt of her tears. It just spurs me to do more, to make her feel more, to take away the hurt that I caused.

When I ease my tongue between her lips, she moans, her mouth opening wider beneath mine. Her tongue tangles with mine, every bit an eager participant. She's not the shy, nervous girl back in the audition room or even that day in my trailer.

She presses against me, wrapping her arms around my neck, and God help me, raising one leg up by my hips.

Lowering my hand to her raised knee, I pull her against me even more tightly, and she makes a soft noise, pushing forward instinctively, rubbing against my hard on.

It feels so good. My dick is hard and throbbing, ready for more. It wouldn't be hard to reach down and pull up her dress and flip open my fly so we can rub against each other with fewer layers in the way. Then I could just tug her panties aside and push into that tight, wet heat.

Assuming she's even wearing panties.

The thought of her bare, with only the fabric of her dress between us, makes my cock twitch with eagerness.

Shit. I'm going to lose it if I don't slow this down a little.

With a groan, I lower her leg to the floor, and she breaks off our kiss with a gasp. "What's wrong?" she asks, frowning up at me, her mouth all puffy and pink.

I touch her lips lightly with my fingers, and she sucks in a breath.

"Absolutely nothing, sweetheart." I grin at her, and she has enough presence of mind to roll her eyes at me. Then I turn her to face away from me, giving me access to the zipper at the back of her very short dress.

"Was this dress for me?" I ask, moving her hair out of the way, to kiss the back of her neck all the way to the edge of the zipper.

"No," she says on a moan, as I inch down the zipper to expose more skin. She's not wearing a bra. "It's for me," she says breathlessly. "It makes me feel good."

"Yeah, it does," I say, stroking the silky fabric before sliding my hands inside her dress. "Bet I can make you feel better." I touch the smooth, bare skin of her ribs and stomach before gliding up to cup her breasts. They are warm and perfect in my palms. When I run my thumbs over her nipples, they bud to hardness immediately, and I want to taste her. Want her to beg me to suck her.

She arches her back, pushing her breasts into my hands.

Fast. This is going fast. And I don't know how much she's done or . . . I need to try to think.

"Okay?" I manage, my voice hoarse.

"Yes." She nods and twists to face me, fusing her mouth with mine over her shoulder. The familiarity, the rightness, is overwhelming. Her tongue dances over mine, teasing, and any attempts at thinking evaporate.

I pinch one of those tempting, taunting nipples between my forefinger and thumb, and she moans into my mouth. My hips jerk involuntarily against her, and she grinds back against me.

"More," she says, catching my lower lip lightly between her teeth before letting go. And that is so hot I want to press her against the door, pull her dress up and plunge inside her. Claim her, make her mine.

I yank my hands out of her dress, over her noises of protest, and slide my palms down her sides to the bottom edge of the fabric. Brushing my fingertips beneath the hem, I trace the smooth skin of her upper thigh, but no higher.

She whimpers, and the sound goes straight to my head.

"Are you wearing anything beneath this dress, Callie?" I whisper in her ear.

Her cheek turns a lovely shade of pink, but she rallies. "Why don't you find out?"

But I'm not playing that game. I'm interested in another. "Callie," I say, adding an edge of sternness to my voice.

"Yes," she breathes. "Thong. No panty lines."

The thought of her in that mere scrap of fabric, in this dress, is almost as exciting as the thought of her bare. Just like I know her preference for flannel PJs, I happen to know Callie is not a thong girl on most days. Maybe she did this for me as well, though it wouldn't have mattered. I found her hot in battered cargo pants and a mostly shredded sweater, to the point where I nearly came in my pants in front of dozens of crew members.

I inch a little higher on her thigh, almost to her hip, until I feel the brush of lace. Heat radiates from between her legs. Her hand clamps down on mine, trying to pull me closer, but I resist.

"If I touch you, are you wet?" I ask, my voice hoarse.

She bites down hard on her lip, and for a second, I think maybe I've pushed her too far, too fast by asking. But then she nods. "Yes," the word escaping her in a hiss.

"Do you want me to touch you?"

"Yes." That answer came much more quickly.

"Are you sure you're ready for that?" When I skate my fingers over the fabric of her thong, it's soaked, and she makes a tight sound in the back of her throat.

Guess so.

Finding her clit, I circle lightly until she's pushing her hips toward my hand.

"I used to imagine this," she says between gasps.

"Imagine what?"

"You, suddenly looking at me differently one day, and then dragging me off somewhere to a corner on set or in your trailer and . . ."

I pause. "And what?"

"Don't stop," she protests.

"Tell me what happened in that corner," I say, amused but also turned on as fuck.

"I don't . . . I don't know."

"Liar." I pull my hand away, and she whimpers.

"You . . . you would do this." She grabs for my hand, fumbling, moving it between her legs.

She's so wet, the fabric is clinging to her. I resume petting her, light, soft touches that torture me almost as much as her.

"And what else?" I persist.

"I don't know, I never let myself go that far," she breathes.

She leans back against me, clutching at the leg of my jeans as if she's clinging to the side of a cliff for dear life.

Her questing hand rises higher, brushing over and then centering on my rock-hard cock. "Maybe this," she says.

It steals my breath. She's not even stroking, just touching, but it's more than enough for me to lose control.

Shoving beneath her thong, I run my fingertips against her bare skin, through her drenched folds.

She gives a squeak of surprise, but it turns into a moan as I continue exploring her. "Please," she begs.

At her entrance, I pause, teasing her by sliding back and forth but not entering. "Do you want this?" Her head bobs frantically against my shoulder, and I slide a finger into her welcoming heat. She's tight, but I can feel her opening up for me, making room for my cock. "You are so hot and wet for me." I work a second finger inside of her, and she gasps, pushing back against me, driving me deeper. I can feel the ache in my cock taking over my whole body.

"More," she demands, breathless, urging me to move my hand faster, harder, and I have to grit my teeth to keep from opening my fly and sinking into her. She is getting close but not there yet.

But that's fine. I've got other ideas in mind.

"What are you doing?" she protests as I turn her around to face me, her cheeks flushed, beautiful.

When I sink to my knees in front of her, her eyes go wide. "I have fantasies, too." My voice is so guttural I barely recognize it. That is what she does to me.

She blinks down at me, color rising higher in her face. "You do?"

In answer, I slide my hands up her thighs, raise the front of her dress. The front panel of her thong—white cotton, help me—is twisted and practically translucent with dampness. I can feel the heat and smell the tang of her excitement, and my mouth waters in response.

"Spread your legs for me a little," I say hoarsely.

Calista hesitates. "I've never . . . I mean I don't know." Her hands slide up to the edge of her hem where I'm holding it, as if she might pull it down.

Rocking back on my heels, I grin up at her. "I have, and it's my favorite."

She blushes, which is adorable, though I would probably appreciate more if I couldn't see the pinkness of her tempting me through the gauziness of her panties.

"The only rule is that you let me know if you like something."

She frowns, but before she can say anything, I lean forward and press my tongue against her.

She jolts and then her hand sinks into my hair, pulling my face closer.

"Yeah, just like that," I murmur against her.

Pushing the material out of my way, I explore the soft folds of her with my thumbs and my tongue and lips. Setting a regular rhythm of my tongue against her clit makes her moan and squirm against me. She throws her leg over my shoulder and uses the leverage to pull me closer.

That's it, Callie. Come on, baby.

When I slide my fingers inside her at the same time, she quivers.

"Eric," she says in a faint voice. "I'm . . . I can feel . . ."

I pause. "I know, it's okay. You're okay." I brace my free hand on her knee, the one not over my shoulder, to help keep her upright and press my mouth to her again.

She's so damn close; I can feel the first clutches of . . .

The rattle of the doorknob behind me is the only warning we get. Somehow, in all of this, I managed to forget we are in a closet, in the middle of a crowded party, and there's no lock on the door. Fortunately, it's enough time for me to yank the front of Calista's dress down to cover her. She's breathing hard, a dazed look on her face. I'm not sure she even heard anything.

I'm still half-crouched and turning to stand when the door flies open.

"Shit," Calista says frantically, and I hear the sounds of fabric rustling.

"Oh, hey, sorry, bro." A guy with bleached, teen-idol hair that's trying just a little too hard stands in the doorway, a girl wrapped around him, and I raise myself to my full height to block his view of Calista.

He pauses, staring, and I take a threatening step toward him, thinking he's staring at Calista scrambling to put herself back together.

But instead, his gaze tracks me, and his forehead wrinkles in a momentary frown.

"Hey, I know you," he says, pointing at me, a clear liquor bottle in his hand.

"I don't think so," I grit. "Get out."

He ignores me. "No, no, I do." He nods at me. "You're Eric Stone, right? Your dad's some big-time producer or whatever." His mouth twists into a tight smile. "I'm Kyle. We used to go up against each other at auditions. But you know how that shit worked out," he says with a laugh that sounds forced and more than a little bitter.

All the warmth from the past twenty minutes with Calista drains away, leaving me feeling cold and empty. Brittle.

"Uh-huh." I could give him my standard answer, that I don't get jobs because of my dad. That if I do I never want it to be that way. But what's the point? No one ever believes me. Just one more talentless rich brat getting by on Daddy's connections. There are hundreds of us.

Behind me, Calista grabs for and squeezes my hand. I can feel the sympathy in the gesture, and it's hard not to pull away from her instinctively.

Kyle, whoever the hell he is, takes a long swallow out of the bottle in his hand. "What are you doing here, man?"

"This is my house," I say. What does this guy want?

"No shit?" he says, sounding surprised. "I didn't know that." He cocks his head contemplatively. "Then you should probably know that someone set the pool on fire."

"Fuck." I shove past him into the hallway, pulling Calista with me. Sure enough, out here, there's a distinct smell of something . . . singed, though the smoke detectors aren't going off yet. How the hell do you set a pool full of water on fire?

The closet door closes with a giggle from Kyle's companion.

Making a mess is one thing; I can hire a cleaning service like usual. But if something's burning, I'm screwed. "I need to go handle this," I say to Calista, but I can't quite meet her eyes. Out here, with the thump of the music unmuted, and party-goers pushing past us on either side, it just feels more . . . real. Like what happened in the closet took place in another universe or between two other people.

"I'm sorry." But I'm not sure what, exactly, I'm apologizing for.

"Eric." She turns toward me, leaning forward until I finally look at her. Warmth and affection radiates from her expression. "It's fine, really," she says softly. "It's not a big deal." She touches my cheek, running her thumb along my jaw. "You have host responsibilities. One of which is probably dealing with any and all fire issues."

I snort, but there's an uneasy pressure growing in my chest. *This is wrong. You are wrong.*

She presses her mouth against my cheek, and my hand involuntarily squeezes hers tighter. *I want to keep her. Keep her safe. Keep her happy.*

Keep her away from me.

"Meet you upstairs in fifteen?" she asks in a whisper.

Oh, God. My nod feels more like a convulsive jerk of my head than an actual response.

But she smiles at me and turns away, letting go of my hand to head toward the stairs and my bedroom.

"Wait," I say gruffly.

She pauses, and I zip up her dress, resisting the urge to kiss the top bump of her spine. Also resisting the urge to say, "Let it burn," and follow her to my bed.

Calista in my bed. I want that more than I've ever wanted anything in my life. But my mouth is dry with terror at the thought of it actually happening.

When I'm finished with the zipper, Callie turns to shake her head at me, amusement flickering in her expression. "Waste of effort," she says, shocking the hell out of me with a wink. Then she moves past me.

I watched her go until she was out of sight at the curve in the stairs, wasting precious pool-saving seconds, because I couldn't seem to make myself leave.

It was like I knew even then that I was going to destroy everything. Maybe I did.

Dropping my glasses on the pages in front of me, I rub my eyes with the back of my fists, pressing a little harder than is probably wise, as if the action will somehow obliterate the rest of that evening from my memories.

As it turned out, the pool wasn't on fire. Just a deck chair or two, which were already sinking to the bottom. And once I kicked out the firebug asshole (he wasn't hard to pick out—he was still flicking his lighter on and off while he watched it all burn; Jesus, these former Nickelodeon kids are messed up), I was free to go back upstairs.

Except it couldn't be that easy. Not with me.

Of course, it wasn't like I was all that clearheaded that night. Or that I, even on sober days, had a great grasp of why I wanted to push so hard against someone who genuinely cared about me.

I didn't *want* to think about it. I hated myself back then, and that made Callie's feelings for me all the more confusing. I didn't deserve her because she was clearly wrong about me. Wasn't she?

I just wanted to obliterate the situation so I wouldn't have to feel so unsure about who I was.

And I succeeded beyond all expectations.

You're good enough. The fact that Calista is still willing to say that to me now, after all of these years, after everything I've done, is unreal. She believed in me then and believes in me now. What have I done to deserve that? A fuck lot of nothing.

And yet . . . I want her to be right. I want to believe that her belief in me is justified.

My phone lights up, casting a harsh glow, and a text message arrives with a buzz.

```
Katie: Where are you????
```

She must have just gotten home from her shift at the emergency vet clinic.

With a sigh, I pick up my phone.

```
Sorry. Lots of work to do. We're shooting
over at my place tomorrow, so I'm here.
```

My phone rings a half second after the text goes through. Katie. Shit.

I answer it. "Hey."

"Is everything okay?" she asks, sounding worried.

"Yeah, just kind of a crazy day. Tons of prep work for tomorrow. Didn't want to take over your kitchen and then ignore you like an asshole." Why does all of this sound like a lie? It's true. Just not all the details. I don't want to tell her that Vincent quit.

"How was work?" I ask.

She's quiet for a long moment.

"Katie?"

"Why did you pick up Bitsy?" she asks.

"I thought she might drive you crazy, looking for me," I say. Right now, she's curled up in my lap, snoring.

"You're very considerate of my peace of mind," Katie says with ice in her tone. I've never heard this from her before, except that one time, early in our relationship, when she was angry with me for staying out all night at a Kurosawa retrospective and then missing our lunch date because I accidentally overslept. She didn't understand why I went. *You've seen all the movies before!*

It was easier then just to give in, but not this time.

I grit my teeth and then make myself take a deep breath. None of this is Katie's fault. "Look, it was a long day, and—"

"And you can't talk to me about it? I come home to an empty

house. You're not here, the dog is gone, and you've taken some of your stuff—"

"I just wanted to spend the night at my place, so I'd have more time to prepare."

"Why do you suddenly need more—"

I make a frustrated noise. "Because the director quit today, okay?"

"Oh," she says, and relief is clear in that single syllable. "Why didn't you just say that?"

I shake my head in disbelief. "What did you think was going on?" I ask, but I'm pretty sure I already know.

"Nothing," she says, but the real answer is loud and clear in the ensuing silence.

Calista.

"I just didn't understand," Katie says with a laugh that sounds a little forced. "So, did you find someone else to fill in?"

"No, I'm just going to do it." As soon as the words leave my mouth, I feel the thump of dread in my chest along with my heartbeat, and I realize that I was avoiding more than just telling her that Vincent had quit.

"You're what?" she asks.

"I'm filling in as director," I say slowly, as if I'm testing each word against my tongue. But instead of the expected panic, I feel only a calm certainty that it's right, tempered with a little nervousness.

"I don't understand," Katie says, and I can hear the frown in her voice. "I thought you were acting in this just to capitalize on the *Starlight* connection."

"I was. I am."

"Then why are you directing now, too? This was just supposed to be a starter project. A test."

"We can't find anyone to fill in who knows the material as well as I do, and we're on a tight schedule. You know, speaking as the executive producer," I add, trying to rein in my natural sarcasm and not quite succeeding.

"I'm sure that's not true," she says.

I roll my eyes. "Katie," I begin.

"I'm just worried about you," she says. "You're taking on so much."

"And you think I can't handle it," I say.

She sighs. "Eric, I don't ever want to keep you from trying something new. But I think we need to be reasonable about what one person can accomplish and where your strengths lie."

I grimace. "You're afraid I'm going to lose it. Head straight for rock-bottom again."

"Well," she hesitates. And she doesn't need to say any more.

She's right. I have a history of spiraling in response to bad shit happening. Bad shit that I usually had a hand in causing. But the idea of being judged against my past mistakes when I'm trying so hard to make different, better choices makes a hard edge of resentment rise up in me. Is it so wrong that I want to be seen as someone who can change? That I can maybe have a shot at not dragging that history of bad decisions around with me everywhere for the next sixty years or so, like a trunkful of concrete chained around my ankle?

"Well, fuck it, maybe you're right," I say. "We should just cancel the whole damn thing right now."

"That's not what I'm saying," she says with an exasperated noise.

"Then what are you saying?"

Katie's quiet for a long moment. "I'm sure your dad could—"

I go rigid. "No."

"Eric—"

"What is your fixation with my dad?" I ask. "He's not a good guy, and he sure as hell wasn't a great father. Why do you think he's going to be my savior?"

"I don't think that. But you're doing it again, making choices based on what you think he thinks of you or how he'll judge you. If it were anyone else in your situation, it would be insane to think about them ignoring the resources you have right at hand. You want to be successful, but only on your terms."

"Hell yes," I say.

She sighs. "Don't you think that's giving your dad too much power? Again?"

The faint condescending note in her voice—*poor, dumb Eric just doesn't get it*—pushes me over the edge. She's not my therapist. She's supposed to be my girlfriend, my fiancée. "So I should let you do it instead?"

She sucks in a sharp breath.

I rub my hand over my face. "I'm sorry, I didn't mean that. I'm just . . . tired." But it's more than that, too. It's finally clear to me that she really doesn't understand. And she's not going to. No matter how many times I've tried to explain my messed-up family, she doesn't get it. It's just an experience completely missing from her life; she doesn't know how to relate. Maybe there are just some things that you can't understand unless you've lived through them.

And maybe I don't want someone like that to have so much say in my choices. Shit, that's probably not good.

"I'm not going to let you use this as an excuse to push me away," she says, her voice cracking with tears or exhaustion or both, and guilt pulls hard at my gut.

Never let it be said that the woman doesn't know me. But I'm beginning to think she may not understand me, and that might be the bigger issue.

15

CALISTA

"Remember, you need to keep your chin tilted up. Otherwise, this angle is going to do nothing for your cheekbones *and* make your face look fat," Lori says, her fingers under my jaw. The empty condo in Eric's building where we're filming today is huge. But the condo's bedroom, which is crowded with people and equipment, is hot, and it's only getting hotter as the lighting changes are made. And my mother is right on top of me, making adjustments. I can feel stress-sweat trickling down my spine.

"Mom," I say through gritted teeth. After last night, I expected her to avoid me, claiming more stress or another migraine. But instead, she's doubled down on her suggestions, interference and general pushiness.

"It would help if they weren't using all white sheets," she says with a frown, fussing with the covers over me, straightening them. "It's only going to make you look larger."

You'd think a few hours of filming in a bed—not a love scene, but Evie slowly recovering and coming to the realization that her powers are gone—would be somewhat relaxing. But not with my mother here.

"Don't forget to cry," Lori says to me, fluffing out my hair around the bandage on my left temple, much to the exasperation of Josie, who just fixed it. "It shows your range."

I could argue with her, make the point that Evie's not sad, more relieved at this point, so crying would be an emotional miscue, but at this point, I just want her to back off.

"Are we ready?" Eric calls—rather pointedly, it seems, in the direction of my mother, who is the only person not where she's supposed to be.

"Yes," I say, maybe a little too loudly. "Why don't you go wait by the monitors, Mom?"

But Lori lingers for a moment, her gaze scanning my face.

I brace myself, waiting for the commentary about my chins or wrinkles or shininess.

"You're such a beautiful girl," she says softly, her eyes growing bright with tears. "You know that? I'm so proud of you. If I'd had your talent . . ." She shakes her head.

My mouth falls open.

Before I can respond, she steps away.

What was that? I sag back on the pillows as Eric approaches.

"I'm sorry," I say to Eric. "I don't know what she was—"

He shakes his head, dismissing my words with a quick wave of his hand as he gets into position on the windowsill. Cory is sneaking in to see Evie. "Forget about it. It's Lori." But for some reason, those words sting a little today, like a slap against sunburned skin.

Yes, she's terrible sometimes—maybe even most of the time. But she's my mother.

And yet I don't know if I can trust her.

"Eric," I say in a quiet voice, after checking to make sure the boom isn't directly overhead yet. "I need to talk to you." My stomach aches. My mother will never forgive me for this when she finds out. And Eric . . . I trust him with this, but he'll be frustrated. And angry. On my behalf, yes, but also with me for not doing something sooner. For hesitating even a split second to turn on Lori. He doesn't understand the pull of that family loyalty, misguided or not. Nor does he understand that it's my mistake to make.

He slides down off the window ledge and steps over toward "my" bed. "What's up?"

I open my mouth to spill just the necessary details—separate account, money to be deposited there, away from my mother—in what might be my only chance today.

But he looks so tired, dark circles under his eyes and his skin almost pale with weariness.

Maybe I shouldn't have pushed him so hard yesterday. "Are you okay?" I ask.

"Didn't sleep well," he says shortly, staring at a point over my head. "Personal stuff," he adds a moment later.

It shouldn't bother me. Once he might have told me all about it, usually with that sardonic smile as cover, his favorite method for trying to pretend that whatever it was wasn't really bothering him. But we haven't been in each other's lives like that in years.

Still, it feels like he just shut a door in my face.

"What did you need?" he asks.

"I . . . how is the footage from yesterday looking?" I ask. *You are such a chicken-shit, Calista.* But even the new me, firmly committed to baby steps of change, is not quite brave enough to press my nose against that barrier and risk it being slammed again. Eric is just as likely to help me right now and then not speak to me for years. He's done it before. If I break ties with Lori and then Eric decides our friendship is getting too complicated—say, after his upcoming marriage and impending happily-ever-after with Katie—then I'll have no one. Again. And maybe that's for the best, maybe that's what I need, but I'm not sure I'm ready for that yet.

Eric raises his eyebrows at me, and I brace myself for that knowing look, the one that pierces through my bullshit and forces the truth out of me.

But then he simply answers, "Fine." He pauses. "Good, actually. We should be able to edit together a trailer from everything this week."

"Oh. Good."

"Is that all?" he asks, a faint crinkle appearing between his eyebrows.

In the distance, I can see my mother hovering. "Yeah, sure. That's all." *Damnit.*

He opens his mouth as if he's going to say more, but then he shakes his head. "Okay, people, let's do this," he says, raising his voice. Then he's back to his mark.

This morning's scene is a simple one. Cory, worried about Evie, sneaks in to see her, only to learn what Evie herself has recently discovered: Her powers are gone.

My eyes are shut until Eric's warm hand closes over mine, startling me even though it's in the script.

"Evie."

I open my eyes.

He rubs his hand over mine. That's Eric, though, not Cory, warming my ice-cold fingers. "You okay?"

I nod against the pillows behind me, affecting a wince at the motion.

"Thought you had a harder head than that," he says with a gentle smile, tucking a piece of hair behind my ear and eyeing the bandage on my forehead.

"I guess not," I say. "Did anyone see you come in?"

"No. I was careful." He hesitates, then adds, "Stevens is out. Can't take that risk again." He sounds grim and a little pissed off. "I told him before we went into that warehouse that you were off limits. He never should have touched you."

I stare down at my toes, which are poking up beneath the blanket like distant snow-covered mountains. "You didn't have to do that."

"He's dangerous. We're not looking to hurt anyone, just taking what's ours." He sits on the edge of my bed, his body angled sideways so the camera will get his profile and mine. It's awkward in real life, but it will look good on screen. "And maybe convince a few of the good guys that we're not so bad while we're at it." He smiles at me, but I keep my attention focused on my toes.

"Because robbing warehouses full of paper goods will do that?" I ask.

"Never underestimate the recruiting power of a good origmaist."

That draws my gaze to him. "You made that word up."

He grins. "Maybe. I'll never tell. In truth, though, we were actually looking for the warehouse full of cookies."

I snort with laughter and then clap my free hand over my mouth.

"That's better," he says. "You'll be back out there driving me crazy in no time." He leans forward to kiss me.

It's supposed to be nothing more than a brush of his mouth over mine, after which I'm supposed to break the bad news to him in a "clear, matter-of-fact tone that might be shock or the early stages of acceptance."

But to my dismay, my eyes begin to sting and water. "I don't think so," I say in a choked voice before his lips even touch mine. Damnit. I had no intention of following my mom's advice, but in the moment, I can't seem to stop myself.

Eric pauses for a half second and then, professional that he is, backs off the kiss and rolls to his next line. "You're going to let one little bump on the head—"

"It's not that simple," I say, forcing the words past the lump in my throat.

"What, did they finally figure out that maybe deliberate gene mutation isn't all it's—"

"It's gone," I say.

"What's gone?"

"All of it. The strength, the speed. The faster healing. I'm not . . . the same." *I'm not like you anymore.* And the sensation of loss is almost crippling, like a hole tunneled through my midsection, taking out all my vital organs.

Eric/Cory stares at me, his hand tight and growing tighter on mine.

I suck in a pretend-pained breath, and he drops my fingers like they've burned him.

"Did that . . . did I hurt you?" he asks, his eyes wide with astonishment. And my contrary brain retrieves a memory of Eric saying that same thing to me. When he very much had not hurt me.

Stop. I force my head back to the moment in play and my job.

"Nothing broken," I say, but I flex my hand quickly with a grimace.

"But I could have." He sounds horrified at the idea.

"Yeah," I admit softly. "I guess."

"Evie?" Alexa, Evie's older sister—played by the adorable Leelee Shoop, who was a day player on *Starlight*—calls from the other room. "Are you awake?"

"Yeah, just give me a second," I say, turning my attention toward the door—or where the door will be when it's back on its hinges.

Eric-as-Cory is at the window almost instantly, one leg slung over the sill. "I'll . . . come by and see you later," he says hastily.

"But . . ." I keep my gaze focused on his position, ignoring the movement as Eric drops to the floor behind the bed before the camera pans to show the empty window.

After a second, his head pops up. "Okay, let's cut." He pushes himself up off the floor. "Did we get it?"

There's a rush of excited whispering as people shuffle around, and I sit up and raise my hand against the lights to see what's going on.

"Looks good, Son," shouts a very familiar voice from somewhere behind the camera. It takes me only a second to place it. It's much heartier today, with false enthusiasm rather than scalding disappointment.

Oh, shit. Rawley.

I look to Eric immediately. He appears to be frozen in place next to the bed, his face a careful mask of indifference.

"Eric?" I ask.

"Ten minutes. Let's take a break and get set up for close-ups," Eric says as he moves around the bed and charges out into the hallway.

"Wait," I call after him. "Eric, maybe you shouldn't—" Then, an all-too-familiar—and fake—tinkling laugh trickles in from the hall, sending a shiver down my spine.

My mom is out there.

Of course she is, if Rawley is nearby.

A booming—and equally artificial-sounding—laugh joins my mother's giggling.

Rawley Stone has always looked at my mother with the faintest hint of lip-curling distaste. If the two of them are talking and laughing together . . .

"That can't be good," I mutter.

Shoving the covers back, I scramble to follow Eric's path, threading through cameras and cords and crew, to the hallway and down to the empty living room. It's not dressed for filming because we're not using it.

I stop at the threshold. My mother and Eric's father are standing near the big picture window, standing too close together for this to be a small talk between awkward strangers. Instead my mother is beaming up at him, like he's the guy with the Miss Universe crown to hand out, and as I watch, she laughs again and taps his arm.

"What are you doing here, Dad?" Eric asks.

"Good to see you, too, son," Rawley says.

"No, it's not." Eric's hands are clenched into fists at his sides.

"Eric," my mom says in a scolding voice. Then she turns back to Rawley. "I, for one, am always happy to see *you*."

I wince.

Rawley steps away from my mom to face off with Eric. It's hard not to see the similarities between father and son, though it's reflected more in tense shoulders and arrogant expressions than in actual physical characteristics.

"Now don't get all tetchy," Rawley begins.

"Tetchy? Really?" Eric asks, his eyebrows raised. "That's old even for you."

Rawley gives him a sour look. "I simply called Katherine to confirm some details for the big day and she mentioned your director issues."

Eric rocks back slightly at the news. "Katie?"

Oh, no.

For *anyone* to bring Eric's father down on him for *any* reason is a level of betrayal that goes beyond a reasonable expectation of forgiveness. In Eric's world anyway. How could Katie not know that?

"Everything's fine," Eric says, raising his voice just enough that the pretending-not-to-be-eavesdropping crew will definitely hear it.

Rawley lets the ensuing silence hold for a beat too long, which somehow simultaneously conveys his doubt and makes Eric sound like he's overcompensating. "I'm sure," he says, eventually. "But just in case." He reaches into the inside pocket of his suit coat to produce a folded slip of paper.

"What's that?" Eric asks, making no move to take it.

"Names for possible directors," Rawley says, as if Eric's just asked him what shoes are for. "I know Vincent can be difficult. So I made a few calls on your behalf and these candidates are—"

"No," Eric says.

"Eric, don't be stubborn." Rawley shakes the paper at him. "If you're going to turn down my offer of employment and insist on doing this yourself—"

Something clatters to the floor loudly in the room behind us, reminding me and everyone else that this is not even close to a private conversation. And the people listening have jobs and money at stake.

Oh, crap. Now, suddenly, it's very clear why Rawley is here and didn't just send that list by email or text if he was so worried. He's trying to sow discontent and/or doubt in this project under Eric's leadership.

His own son. He wants to win that badly. Or wants Eric to lose. Either way.

Rage on Eric's behalf bubbles up under my rib cage, and I can't stuff it back down.

"We're all set here," I say, moving to stand next to Eric. "Thanks for stopping by."

Rawley barely glances in my direction, but my mother is glaring at me. "Calista," she says through a tight smile.

"Leave now," Eric says through his teeth to his father, and there's more than a vague threat implicit in his tone.

And for a second, I think it's actually going to happen. Eric's going to have to drag his father bodily out of here.

Which is not going to be good for any of us or morale.

I look to my mother, who just lifts her shoulder in a minute shrug.

In other words, no help coming from that direction. Fantastic. *Thanks, Lori. Way to thank the guy who gave you a loan so you could pay your bills this month.*

Eventually Rawley lifts his hands, the slip of paper between his fingers. "There's no need to overreact," he says mildly. "Just trying to help."

I want to shove him right out the window.

The depth of my fury surprises me. I've never liked Eric's father, but this is a whole new level of murderous intention.

Then again, it might have to do with the stiffness of Eric's posture and the battered weariness radiating off of him, like this is a battle he's fought before and he's just so tired of fighting.

I know that feeling.

Letting the paper flutter out of his hand to the floor, Rawley turns and walks away, shutting the door very precisely and carefully on his way out.

"You were incredibly rude, Calista," my mother says tersely as soon as the door is closed.

I ignore her, and she sweeps away, probably to drag Josie in for a touch-up. Again.

"Are you okay?" I ask Eric.

"She called him," he mutters. "I can't believe Katie called him." He scrubs his hand over his face.

I stay quiet. I want to reach out to him, curl my fingers around his arm in reassurance. But he's not mine to touch, not mine to reassure.

"Katie doesn't want me to direct," he says with that quick flash of a smile. "Actually, she doesn't want me to do any of this. If she had her preference, I'd quit everything and move to Michigan with her."

My face must show my shock.

He shrugs. "She thinks it's too much for me. Better that I get a fresh start somewhere else."

"Why?" I ask, unable to stop myself.

"She thinks it's not healthy to stay. That eventually, I'll fall back into bad habits, make the same stupid mistakes, and I don't know . . . wreck things, I guess."

It occurs to me that Eric and I have the same problem: Just because someone loves you—or claims to—doesn't always mean they understand you.

"Bullshit," I say.

"I don't know. I'm not exactly the responsible type. Look what I did to you." His gaze bounces toward my shoulder and then away.

It takes my breath away to hear him reference that night so directly. "You didn't do anything. I made all those choices myself."

"Yeah, but if I hadn't been an asshole—"

"How about if I had more guts to call you on it?" I ask. "Instead I ran off like a sulking baby." I pause. "Okay, not a baby as they don't usually run. A sulking toddler, maybe."

The corner of his mouth quirks up.

"But my point is the same. We can play this game all day. We've both made shitty decisions. No one made me get in that car with Chase, and no one forced me to buy heroin when the pills stopped working."

Eric flinches. "Calista, I—"

Then I speak before I lose my courage. "I think my mom's pushing so hard to sell me on jobs right now because she's burned through all of her money. And what was left of mine. They're going to lose the house."

"What?" He sounds shocked.

"I know. It's bad." I wince in expectation.

But when I dare to look up at him, Eric is regarding me steadily, without the judgment or the "I-told-you-so" frustration I expected.

"Are you all right?" he asks.

Relief rushes over me. "No. I'm pissed," I admit. "I need to set up a separate account. Something she doesn't have access to," I say, careful to keep my voice down. "But I don't have a car. I don't even have access to whatever you need to switch it from the other account." Shame rises high in me, flooding my face with color. I'm an adult—and an accounting major, for God's sake—and I have no idea what bank my mother is using to supposedly keep my money. I don't even have the freedom to move around without judgment or questions. This is not the life I want.

"I'll help you," Eric says immediately. "We can figure it out."

"Thank you," I say.

"Of course."

Silence falls between us, but he still looks troubled. The urge to hug him—something I once would not have thought twice about doing—is overwhelming.

And in a moment of weakness, I give in.

I close the distance between us, lifting my arms to wrap around his neck. Rising to my tiptoes, I feel the rasp of his stubble against my face and then the tickle of his curls. It's an instant link to the past.

His breath is warm against the space where my neck meets my shoulder, and my heart trips in an uneven rhythm.

And yet he's not hugging me back.

My face burns. I start to let go, but then his arms close around me, so tight that my ribs ache but in a good way. I missed this. Missed him.

I want to tell him that he's making the right choice. His father is a jerk, and Katie is, at best, misguided. (Or possibly a heartless, clueless bitch, but that might just be my opinion.) And I want to stay right here forever, the sounds of the crew fading into the distance, leaving nothing but the two of us in our own little world. The solid pressure of his chest against mine, the familiar scent of his skin against my nose. L'Occitane. His mother buys him the same gift basket of shower gel and shampoo every year for Christmas.

But I make myself let go and step away. "Back to work?" I ask.

Eric gives a barely noticeable jerk of his chin. "Yeah." But then he touches my hair, tucking it behind my ear. "Thanks, Callie."

As I leave, a quick glance over my shoulder shows me Eric standing where I left him, his hands shoved into his pockets, staring out the window at nothing. My heart breaks for him. Yes, he's messed up in the past. But if *I* can see that he's legitimately trying to do things differently, I don't know why others can't.

Or maybe that's the issue. When I was in rehab, one of the things they teach you is to expect that your relationships with everyone in your life will be altered because of your choice to get clean, your addiction, or both.

When you change, people are uncomfortable with it. It's not even just that they're worried you'll revert to who you were before. It's more that you no longer fit in the tidy mental box they've assigned to you.

In my case, when I became an addict, when I was arrested, when I was sent to rehab, all of that messed with my box assignment for other people. But when I got clean, it was the same thing.

We're always clawing our way out of someone else's definition of us.

It's no different for Eric than it is for me.

Damaged. Weak. Can't be trusted. Scared.

Spoiled. Impulsive. Reckless. Selfish.

Plenty of awful boxes to be in.

But I'm wondering now if the larger challenge is escaping the box we've given ourselves. Or believing that we deserve to.

16

ERIC

"You're quiet tonight," Katie says, expertly twirling noodles on her fork.

The kitchen in her apartment is dimmed. Candles flicker on the table and the counter behind us, providing romantic lighting. Theoretically.

At the moment it just feels dark. I can barely see the fork in my hand, and the chicken parm on my plate—Katie's specialty and an apology for our fight last night—is a dark, amorphous blob.

Weirdly, that's what I feel like at the moment, too. I'm just here, shapeless and dim. A faded shadow.

I should be angry. I *am* angry. Intentionally or not, Katie sicced my father on me. I spent the rest of the day feeling like I was playing a role when the cameras *weren't* rolling. "Director." Someone who knew what he was doing. Someone who was in control.

No one asked me anything directly about my dad and what he'd said, but I could feel it like a riptide pulling beneath the surface. Invisible from the outside but utterly deadly if it catches you.

But this is Katie. She believed in me when no one else—okay, almost no one else—did, and she pushed me to do something with myself. Granted, she doesn't like what I chose, but still. I don't know what would have happened if she hadn't. Being angry at her *feels* wrong. Jesus, she saved me from myself. I owe her. Don't I?

I don't know.

Shit. In the past, when things got this complicated, I didn't exactly stick around for the conversation. I just stopped texting.

"Maybe it's just because Bitsy's not here tonight. It's weird how dogs fill up the silence," she says, an odd catch in her voice. Clearly, she's picking up on the tension as well.

But then she clears her throat and takes a swallow of sparkling water. "How did everything go today?" she asks. "Day two of directing." She offers me a smile and a thumbs up around her fork.

It seems a little forced, but she doesn't sound like she's baiting me. Does she really not know?

I eye her carefully, though it's hard to pick out nuances of her expression in the dimness. "It was fine. We've got another day there tomorrow," I say. "Thursday we're off for Thanksgiving. And then we'll pick back up on Friday. Over the weekend, I'm going to cut together a trailer with our editor."

"Oh, that reminds me, I put a turkey on hold at the store," she says. "We just have to pick it up tomorrow."

"Okay." I hate turkey.

"And I know, I know you don't like sweet potatoes." She holds her hands up as if to stop my protest. "Or pretty much any traditional Thanksgiving food. But I have my grandma's recipes for everything. And I promise you, once you try these, you'll totally change your mind."

She seems absolutely certain of herself, and something about that just flips a switch in me. The anger that was lying dormant beneath my indecision flares to life.

I don't like Thanksgiving because my father used to insist on a huge formal meal, and I would have to sit there for hours with whatever executives or actors or agents he'd invited over. No spilling, no fidgeting. It was not about family or tradition. It was another opportunity for him to show off and for people to be grateful for it.

Katie knows that. I've told her that story every year at Thanksgiving, and she still doesn't believe me.

I put my fork down. "What if I don't?"

She laughs a little. "What?"

"What if I don't change my mind?"

"About Thanksgiving?" she asks, regarding me with a frown. "I don't understand what—"

"My dad showed up today."

She freezes, her fork in mid-air.

"Offered me a list of directors who could do the job. In front of my entire crew."

She meets my gaze defiantly. "He called me. I didn't call him, Eric."

"But you told him."

"I didn't know it was a secret!" She takes a breath. "He's your father, he's family—"

"No," I say. "We're related because we have to be, but we're not family."

"Eric."

"The man has taken every opportunity to make me feel small, unwanted and a total fuck up. Starting with when he told me I only existed because my mom wanted more money in the divorce settlement."

She sucks in a breath. "That's awful."

"I was fourteen," I say tightly. "And he was pissed because I said something dumb on the set of one of his shows and people started talking. It got back to him."

"I didn't know," she says.

She didn't *want* to know.

"And then how about the time a few years ago, when he started dating my friend Angelica even though he was old enough to be her father—her grandfather, even? That was not about her, it was about me and taking something away from me." I shake my head. "We have a messed up and twisted relationship, and I need you to stop trying to fix it. Stop trying to fix *me*."

Those last words surprise even me.

"I didn't think I was," she says, pulling her napkin from her lap and carefully folding the edges together. "I was just trying to help you."

"But it's my life," I say. "My career. My admittedly screwed-up relationship with my father. Mine."

"Ours," she says softly. "*Our* life. I thought we were in this together."

I make a frustrated noise. "Yeah, okay. But the thing is, I don't feel like you're trying to help me as much as change me into someone else." I should probably take her hand, but I don't. I'm struggling to find the right words. Finally I land on: "I'm never going to be a real estate agent, Katie."

She sniffles, tears running a glittering streak down to her chin.

"And I can't do this if you think I'm not good enough as the person I am, right now. I already have enough of that in my life."

"But if you could just let go of these ideas that are holding you back—that you have to be at war with your dad, that you have to follow in his footsteps to be a success—you have so much potential," she says wistfully. "For a good life, a happy life."

Like I'm one of the strays she treats that, with an intense flea bath and a lot of house-training lessons, will one day make a good pet.

I know that's not exactly what she means, but that's what it feels like.

I stand up and put my napkin on the table. "I can't do this right now."

"What?" Alarmed, Katie stands up with me.

I start toward the door and she follows me. "I don't understand," she says. "What are you saying?"

"I need some time to think."

"Think about what?"

"Us. Everything." I grab my jacket off the chair and shrug into it.

"You're kidding me, right?" she asks as I pull open the door. "It's like you're a different person this week. A couple of fights and suddenly you're . . ." She trails off.

Even though I know better, I have to ask. "I'm what?" My hand stills on the doorknob.

"You're different," she says, her voice going flat. "Ever since you went to go pick up Calista Beckett."

I turn to face her, a denial ready on my tongue. But then I realize she's right, just not in the way she means. Seeing Callie reminded me of who I was, the good and the bad. Calista believes in me without reservation, even though she's the *last* person who should, and somehow that makes it easier to believe in myself. "Yeah, I guess I am."

"You didn't tell her we were engaged," Katie says.

I stare at her. "Are you serious? She knows. Of course she—"

"Because she asked," Katie points out. "You didn't say anything when you went to pick her up."

I grit my teeth. I cannot believe we're arguing about this, of all things. What difference does it make? "No, you're right. I didn't mention it within the first ten seconds of talking to her for the first time in three years. Sorry, I was a little busy with other things."

But a tiny voice in the back of my head whispers that if I really wanted Calista to know, if I was as sure about my choices as I was supposed to be, then I would have told her about Katie and I getting married *without* her asking. It would have just come up. It might have even helped convince her that I'd turned my life around and wasn't such a complete screw up anymore.

Except maybe, on some level, I didn't want Calista to know? Maybe I liked those twenty-four hours of just the two of us enough not to want to throw a wrench in the works?

I can't think about that right now.

"Are you sleeping with her?" Katie asks.

"What?" I ask, genuinely shocked.

"You heard me," she says, crossing her arms over her chest.

The question shouldn't slice at me, but it does. Because it contains her true opinion of me. I've done shitty stuff like that in the past, obviously, but not anymore. And she knows that. Or she should.

"I'm not," I say with a tight smile. "But I'm guessing you're not going to believe that." Her expectations are still set at the level of *Eric Stone, Complete Fuck Up.*

"I knew you were still in love with her," she says. "The second I saw you two together. And she is completely head over heels for you." A soft sniffle tells me she's crying again.

Shit.

"Katie, it's not like that. We just have history together. So she gets it. Gets me." I shift uncomfortably. "Everyone thinks that it's more than that, but it's not—"

Her laughter is choked by her tears. "Everyone thinks that because it's true, you just don't see it."

Frustration rises in me. "I think I would know, being one of the two people involved."

I would, wouldn't I? Suddenly, I'm not sure, and it feels like falling down a particularly long and dark tunnel. No sense of up or down, just the wind whooshing past.

My feelings for Calista have never exactly been easy or particularly clear: affection mixed with guilt, doubt and a healthy dose of self-loathing.

But real love, the healthy, non-self-destructive kind, is not supposed to be that. Right?

It makes me feel a little panicky inside to consider otherwise. With Katie, it's always been very clear and very straightforward—this is good for me, she is good for me. Being with her was the right choice.

Although that no longer seems to be the case. Katie has always been ready to help, to make me "better." But she doesn't know me, the real me. So I'm beginning to think that no amount of changing on my part or guiding on hers is going to get us to a point where we're both happy.

I rake my hand through my hair, making it stand up everywhere. "Katie, I don't know what else to say. I just need to—"

She holds up her hand, cutting me off. "No. You go ahead. You 'think' as much as you need to. You guys just 'think' your brains out." She shoves my shoulder, pushing me out the door.

"Katie, it's not—"

"Eric, it may surprise you to hear this, but as little as you seem to think I know you, I do actually know a couple things pretty clearly." And with that, she slams the door in my face.

Yeah. That was pretty clear.

17

CALISTA

My phone buzzes, rattling my pillow and waking me. It's dark, too dark, and my bones ache with lack of sleep. It feels like I just went to bed.

In my few months of college, I got in the habit of sleeping with my phone under my pillow so I'd hear the alarm. But this is just a single buzz and then silence. Who is texting me in the middle of the night?

I frown, glancing over at Zinn in the other bed to make sure it didn't wake her. But her breathing is steady and even.

I slide my phone out from under my pillow, turning toward the wall and sheltering the screen against the curve of my body to keep it from lighting up the room.

2:33 A.M.

Crap. Getting up in two hours to meet with Tim is going to hurt. I stifle a groan.

But the text below the time is startling enough that it sends a not-unwelcome rush of adrenaline through me.

Eric: You awake?

I swipe to respond and then hesitate, my thumbs hovering over the keyboard for a second.

Why is Eric texting me this late/early? More importantly, where is Katie while he's doing it? The quiver in my stomach isn't quite as close to indignant disgust as it should be, and I feel a little guilty about that.

Finally, I type: `Yeah, what's up? Is everything okay?`

> `Eric: Talked with accountant. Just need routing and account numbers of new account to make the change you asked about.`

I lay back, pressing the phone against my chest, gratitude rushing warm over me. He did it. He's helping me. It's not like I doubted it exactly, but after everything that happened today, I wasn't sure if he would remember.

> `Me: You talked to your accountant at 2 in the morning?`
> `Eric: Amazing what happens when you keep calling. Eventually they'll pick up.`

I grimace, imagining exactly what the accountant thinks about this method.

> `Eric: You have new account set up?`

Shame burns my face anew. After dinner last night, I'd attempted it. Found an online bank, one I'd heard of, and clicked on the link to start a new account. But there are issues when someone else has been in charge of you your whole life.

I tried but . . . I type and then delete. Sounds too much like an excuse. *It was harder than I thought* . . .

I delete that too.

Finally, I just tell the whole pathetic truth:

`Me: Started application. But I don't have a driver's license, and I'm not sure of my social. And if I ask, Lori will flip.`

That's me, so completely dependent on my mom that I'm trapped. I do know how to drive, Wade made sure of that. But when it came time for me to take the road test, I was always busy working. And Lori took me everywhere anyway . . .

God, how did I think of myself as any kind of adult human without any means of getting myself anywhere or having access to my own information?

The typing dots appear, moving for far too long. Then they stop and vanish.

I take a deep breath.

But then the dots return, quickly replaced by a message.

`Eric: I have your social. Lori put it in paperwork. Hang on.`

A second later, my phone buzzes with a string of numbers that looks vaguely familiar.

`Eric: Good to go? If not, I can set up for you tomorrow.`

A wave of affection for him makes my throat tight.

`No, I've got it with this. Thank you!!!` And without thinking, I tap the heart emoji.

Only after it whooshes away from me, too late to recall, do I realize that that symbol could be grossly misinterpreted, not just by Eric but by Katie, too, if she's watching over his shoulder.

Sorry, I add quickly and send.

Eric: For what?

I shake my head. If he's not going to comment on it, then I guess I won't either.

But I find myself reluctant to end the conversation. Why are you up?

Eric: Couldn't sleep.

I type, I hope it's not bc of your dad. I told you he's full of shit.

It takes him a few seconds to respond, just long enough for me to wonder if I've overstepped my bounds again. Really, it should be Katie who's reassuring him, not me. Though if she's the one who thought it was a good idea for Rawley to show up, maybe not.

Eric: Thank you.

Then a second later . . .

Eric: The Love Boat is on. MeTV.

Catching myself before I groan aloud, I roll my eyes instead. Eric's secret obsession with old television shows, particularly ones that have not aged well, has been going on for years. *The Love Boat* is, incredibly, a favorite, along with something called *Fantasy Island*.

Me: TLB again? Still?
Eric: What? It's soothing.

Me: It's repetitive. People get on the boat, drama ensues, people get off the boat.
Eric: Says the girl who saved the world how many times in a season?

Maybe it's the late night or the surge of giddiness I'm feeling at having taken those first steps to do what I need to do, but in this moment, it feels like all the years and the distance between us never happened. It reminds me so much of those early days on *Starlight*, the stupid conversations about nothing that we would have to pass the time between shots. Eric would lecture me about *The Brady Bunch* or *90210*, and when he bored of that, we'd argue over absolutely pointless categories of discussion. *Best road-trip food*—not that I'd ever taken a road trip or been allowed to eat any of the things I named. *Best thing you've ever stolen from a hotel*—my answer, the extra soap, was deemed pathetic by the judge, Eric, who had apparently actually unscrewed a painting from the wall, shipped it back to L.A., and then hung it in the pool house at his dad's place. Not because he liked it, but because it was horrifyingly bad. *Friendliest letter in the alphabet*—Q, obviously, but only the capital one. Because of the tail. When I confessed this to Eric, he just shook his head.

Me: No comment.
Me: And you just like TLB because it's Aaron Spelling's instead of your dad's.

Back in the day, Rawley was always chasing after the legendary Mr. Spelling, trying to one-up him, and when that failed, getting his revenge by rebooting thinly veiled versions of Spelling's classics.

Eric: Not my fault that Rawley's cheap knock-off never made it past the pilot

stage. How many people want to watch crew members hook up with new passengers every week?
Eric: Dirty Dancing on a boat. Fucker, please.

I snort, hearing his sarcastic voice in my head, and clap a hand over my mouth.

Me: Oh, come on. Of all people, you can't get behind the story of an older guy awakening a younger girl's sexuality week after week?

It slips away before I recognize exactly what I've said.

Nice, Calista. I wince. I didn't mean it that way; I wasn't specifically talking about us.

Though it's certainly not an inaccurate description of our time on *Starlight*. And that night at the party, in the closet, before it all went to hell.

If I touch you, are you wet? Oh, help me. The way he talked to me, put his mouth on me, like he knew exactly what I needed . . . I shake my head, pushing those thoughts away, just as I have every time since that night. But this time, they don't go so easily.

I know, it's okay. You're okay.

Sometimes at night, when I used to have the room to myself and when that need wouldn't go away by focusing on something else, I would let myself remember, let myself touch myself and pretend it was him, pretend that that night had turned out differently.

Sad *and* pathetic? Check.

The typing dots return, then: `Well, not every week.`

I smother my laugh against my covers.

The phone buzzes in my hand again.

Eric: I missed this.

Maybe I'm not the only one feeling closer and bolder in the dark. Me too.

His dots return and vanish. And then come back. Calista . . .

Suddenly, I'm panicking, afraid of what's coming next. *Calista, I have a fiancée. Calista, I'm getting married. Calista, I'm so glad we're friends.*

All of which would be completely justified. I just . . . can't handle the slap down right now, as deserving of it as I might be for feeling this way about someone else's significant other.

Particularly when that significant other hurt me in the past.

Except right now, all I seem to be able to remember is the good stuff. And the really, really good stuff.

No, just . . . no.

I type as fast as my thumbs will allow: Okay, good night! Hi to Katie. Talk to you in a few hours!

My heart is pounding as I lay there and wait for his response.

Eventually, it comes.

Eric: Good night. See you tomorrow.

The disappointment welling in me is only slightly abated by a grim sense of victory at having ended the conversation before it became necessary for him to remind me of these new boundaries between us. I know they're there, and I know better than anyone how much it hurts when someone violates the rules you thought were understood.

I click my phone to sleep and stuff it back under my pillow.

But my mind continues to replay the conversation, examining it from every angle and searching for nuance.

Damnit. I'm over this. Over him. I refuse to fall back into the sinkhole of misery that held me for months after the accident. Not just because of my arm, but because of that betrayal the night of the party.

I was so stupid that night.

With legs like jelly, my heart thundering like there was a finish line in my near future, and my panties damp and twisted, I walked upstairs and went straight for Eric's room. I'd been to his bedroom before, not for anything salacious, just waiting for him to get ready, which always took *forever*. This time, though, everything felt different.

It embarrasses me to think about it now, how easily I just went to his room and curled up on his bed—possibly smelling his pillows, pathetic is apparently a pattern for me—and *waited* for him.

Waited for him while he was . . .

I bury my head under my pillow, remembering, my face hot with shame.

Fifteen minutes passed after I left him, then twenty, then a half an hour. The party was still raging on, and I didn't hear any sirens or smell smoke. But I was starting to worry about Eric—how bad was the fire? Was he okay?—and maybe the first bit of doubt was beginning to set in.

I could hear people just outside Eric's room, and thinking, hoping, he was among them, having been caught in a conversation he couldn't escape, I got up and went out to check.

A cluster of three or four people hovered in the hall, looking at something in the guest room. Given the whispers and giggles from the watching crowd, I was guessing that someone had forgotten to close the door all the way.

I rolled my eyes. Great.

Not exactly an uncommon occurrence at parties like these, even in my limited experience.

To this day, I'm not sure what drove me to step forward and peer through. Maybe it was a familiar sigh, a whispered name, I don't know.

But I do know that it took me several seconds longer than it should have to piece together what I was seeing in that dim room, so many arms and legs tangled together, bodies thrusting and gyrating with all of the theatrics you'd expect from porn, I assumed.

And right as I was about to step back, vaguely embarrassed for them and myself, I recognized a profile in the shadowy and dim room. Eric. On that bed, with those girls. Angelica and her friend. The naked line of his body, muscles working as he pumped into the girl beneath him, the other writhing around both of them. His hair was rumpled and his face flushed while he bit his lip in concentration and effort.

Because yeah, as if he somehow had a magical sense making him aware of my presence, he looked straight toward the door. Right to where I was standing, mouth open in mute horror.

But he didn't stop. Didn't pull away or apologize. Didn't even have the decency to glance away.

Just stared right at me, as if he wanted this moment to be burned into my brain.

Mission accomplished.

I never expected that heartbreak would come with an actual, physical sensation of something rupturing, but that's exactly what it felt like. My heart breaking free from its position in my chest, leaving me to slowly bleed out on the floor.

In spite of the years that have passed since that night, my eyes well up with tears that spill over, dampening the sheets beneath me.

What I told Eric today is true: I should have marched in there, shouting and hauling him out by his . . . ear. Or at the very least stood, refusing to run away and daring him to continue. Not because he owed me anything as a girlfriend, but as his *friend*. That was a shit move to pull on anyone, let alone someone you supposedly care about.

But hurt like that, it crushes something inside you, kills it, making it impossible to breathe, to fight. You just want to get away and do everything you can to *never* feel that way again. I was used to my mother doing whatever she wanted, moving me around like a doll that didn't matter. I was not, however, expecting that from Eric.

I don't really remember running down the stairs or even how I found Chase, but I can vividly recall tugging on his arm, my face wet with tears, and leaving fingernail marks in his skin in my desperation to leave.

And then Eric chasing both of us down the driveway, barefoot, his shirt off, jeans barely buttoned. To stop me? To apologize? To keep me from getting in the car with Chase, who was more drunk than I realized?

I honestly have no idea, even now. I'm not sure why any of it happened. Eric could have simply let me go, just like I asked him to in that closet. It would have hurt, but less than what actually happened. Instead, he seemed driven to prove that he was exactly as awful as he claimed to be.

It remains a remarkably painful series of events, one that altered the whole course of my life—and Chase's—in under fifteen minutes.

My breath escapes in a shudder, muted by the pillow above me. The memory of that night is what I need to keep in mind.

That and Dr. Katie.

Though even that, the existence of Dr. Katie as Eric's fiancée, and everything I've seen from Eric since he showed up on campus, tells me that he's maybe not quite the same person he was before.

But that doesn't make him mine, either. And logically, I'm not sure I would want him to be, after all of that.

I just have to convince the rest of me.

"Let's try it again. Calista, are you ready?" Eric asks.

I need to date again. Maybe that's the issue. I've slept with two people in my whole life: Dylan Bradley, who is now happily married to his former co-star Scott, and Dean, a guy who was in rehab with me. (I'm honestly not sure of his last name. Yeah, it was not my best decision. But I was making lots of less-than-stellar choices in those days.)

I wasn't in love with either of them, which okay, fine. But that's where my sexual experiences stop. If you don't count the closet.

No wonder my feelings for Eric are lingering. I haven't put myself out there to meet someone new—I mean, who wouldn't love to be introduced into the whirling mass of chaos that is my life?—so my focus is too limited.

Right now, all I can see is Eric because that's all I've let myself see.

Though today, God help me, he is very worth seeing. He's in full-on director mode, seeming more comfortable and in control with every minute that passes. It's as if a switch has flipped in him and he's stopped waiting for someone to laugh and tell him he doesn't belong. He's committed, more than I've ever seen, and it is a *good* look on him.

Of course it doesn't hurt that he's somehow sexier with rumpled hair, a day of stubble, and wearing his glasses instead of his contacts. His dark green Henley fits him snugly, too snugly for my ability to concentrate today. I know the muscles beneath that fabric. They're the ones I used to feel when he pulled me close to ruffle my hair or to hug me. But I want—

"Calista?" Eric asks again, raising his eyebrows.

I jolt in my seat at the desk in "Evie's" condo and nod, pretending I don't feel the heat swooping in across my cheeks. Josie steps in with powder for a quick touch up and gives me a good-natured wink.

Great, so it's obvious to everyone, just like on *Starlight*.

Enough. I need to focus on work.

Wednesday's final scene is the last in a series showing Evie's new, superpower-free life. We've already shot short sequences showing confusion from friends and family who've relied on her to use her abilities to help them, whether it's stopping a crime or putting in a good word with the mayor about a traffic ticket or opening a stubborn jar of salsa. They don't know how to react to the new Evie, and it's clear Evie is feeling lost without the powers that defined her, no matter how much she hated that particular aspect of being what she was. Like never being able to take a night off from "hero-ing."

But now she's permanently "off," and in a way, that's just as frustrating.

Now it's Evie alone at home. She's trying to not look at crime reports for her city, which she can do nothing about anymore, and is instead searching for colleges, majors, a life. And yet none of it feels like the right fit because her previous life is all she's ever known.

I relate probably more than I should. Looking at it now, I can see why this book meant so much to me when I was sixteen.

Reflexively, I glance toward my mother, who is remarkably quiet today. She even thanked Eric this morning at the craft services table when he handed her a lid for her coffee.

It's giving me a deeply uneasy feeling. Or maybe that's just guilt. I haven't set up my account yet, but it's first on my to-do list tonight as soon as I can get a few minutes of privacy. Even if I have to lock myself in the bathroom.

With an effort, I drag my attention back to the scene.

"Action!" Eric calls.

We do the scene again, and this time, Eric is nodding at whatever he's seeing. "I think we're good."

This morning, he just jerked his chin in greeting, as if our text conversation had never happened. Which is for the best. And honestly, it felt like something out of dream anyway, a side step away from our current reality. Only my puffy eyes and stuffy nose indicated that it had definitely occurred in this version of the world.

After a short break to set up, we cruise through the close-ups, and we're done.

"Okay, that's a wrap for today," Eric says. "Thanks, everybody. Have a great Thanksgiving tomorrow!"

To his credit, he doesn't grimace at the "T" word. I know how much he hates all the major "family" holidays.

As people clap, sounding both excited and tired, it occurs to me then that we're almost halfway done. We're only shooting Monday through Friday next week. Then . . . I'm done.

And I have no idea what's going to happen next. Am I going back to Blake? Am I staying here?

The uncertainty makes my stomach pitch violently. Even worse, though, is the idea that I don't even know what I *want* to happen.

"Calista!" My mom sweeps in, wrapping her arm around me and giving a squeeze. "You did such a great job today, baby."

I blink at her.

She tips my chin toward her, squinting at my face, but then she lets go, apparently satisfied with whatever she sees.

For the first time in my life.

"Okay, let's go," she says. "You need to change. We're already running late."

"Late for what?" I ask with a frown. "You didn't say anything about going anywhere this morning."

She waves her hand impatiently, as if I've asked something irrelevant. "I'll explain on the way."

She starts walking away and then turns back to press a fruit-and-nut bar in my hand. "So you don't get crabby."

I gape at her. "This is . . . you want me to eat this?" Lori's stance on bars of any and all varieties is well-known. *You might as well just smash a king-sized Snickers in your face, Calista,* she once said to me.

"What?" She taps the wrapper with her fingernail. "It's gluten- and dairy-free." She reaches out and touches my face with a fond expression. "Come on, come on. Let's go!"

Who are you and what have you done with my mother?

But despite her persistence, I linger for a moment, watching Eric, his head bent in consultation with one of the lighting guys.

I want to say something to him. I just don't know what.

Eventually, I give in to my mom's prodding and leave, trailing behind her. Talking to him is a bad idea anyway.

Halfway down the hall, my phone buzzes.

My heart picking up a beat or two, I pull it from the pocket of Evie's robe.

`Eric: It's done. Check your email.`

I slow to a stop and click over to my email.

"Calista," my mom urges.

"Just a second," I say.

There's one new message from Eric, no subject line. But inside is a string of numbers, a user name and password, and a link to an online bank.

It takes a second for the meaning to soak in—he's taken things into his own hands and set up an account for me, likely linking it to my paycheck.

I turn abruptly and stalk back the way I came.

"Calista Rae—"

"In a minute!" I snap, and she gasps in response. "I forgot something," I add.

I push through the door, step around the equipment, and find Eric pretty much where I left him, only he's alone now. He looks up when I stomp closer, as much as one can stomp in slippers, eyeing me warily.

"I was going to do it," I say, waving my phone at him.

"I know that," he says.

"So why did you do it for me?" I demand.

He stares at me. "I was trying to help."

I step closer to him. "I don't need someone else making decisions for me, Eric," I say, my voice low and through my teeth. "I'm trying to get away from that."

He takes a deep breath through his nose, and exhales loudly in frustration. "Calista, there's a difference between controlling and helping. I know Lori doesn't act like it, but there is."

I open my mouth to protest.

"Everybody needs help sometimes," he says, sounding tired. "And as for that," he tips his head toward my phone and presumably the information in his email, "you can change anything you want. You have all the information you need. Close the account, move it, I don't care. I just wanted to help. Okay?" He grimaces. "I know it doesn't make up for everything, but it's . . ." He shakes his head. "Forget it."

He walks away, leaving me standing there.

I close my mouth, belatedly realizing it was still hanging open; now from shock, though, rather than anger.

"Thank you," I manage, though he's too far away to hear me.

My mind is caught up in replaying that interaction, so I'm not paying much attention as I exit the condo and my mom hustles me to the wardrobe area and shoves clothing at me. Different clothes than I wore this morning, as it turns out.

And it's only after we've been in the car for about thirty minutes, with Wade at the wheel, that I recognize this route.

"Where are we going?" I ask, sitting forward in the backseat.

"It's a surprise," my mom says with a tinkling laugh.

And it is and it isn't, when we pull up to the gates at Foxstar Studios, my home away from home—or really just my home—for the three years of filming *Starlight*.

A wave of homesickness washes over me, though none of what I loved or remember would be here or the same. Our trailers are gone, assigned to other actors. I won't find Chase and Marcus shooting hoops between takes, with Eric mocking them while simultaneously texting some girl.

Wade gives our names to the guard, and we're issued passes. So, clearly, someone's expecting us.

"Why are we here?" I ask. It's after nine at night, way too late for meetings or auditions—not that I've prepped for either one. I don't know if I even want a meeting or an audition.

"This is a special opportunity, Calista," my mom says, twisting around in her seat to face me. Her excitement is pure, missing the anxiousness that often threads through her these days. This is more like the old days, and seeing her like this sparks a reflexive excitement in me.

"What is it?" I ask. "Wait. Are we in talks for a *Starlight* reunion episode?" It's the only reason I can think of for us to be here, and just the idea sends a rapid cascade of emotions through me: uncertainty, anxiety, anticipation. But the primary one is joy. I would love to see everyone again, awkward as it might be for some of us.

"It's not something that comes along every day," Lori says, clapping her hands with glee. Then she stops and regards me. "This is important. You need to take it seriously." Her forehead pinches in her version of a frown, which is to say it's more of a faint line of dismay.

I stare at her. "Of course I would take that seriously. What are you . . ." My words dry up as soon as Wade pulls into a parking space in front of an office, one of the smaller buildings. The little sign in front, caught in the glow of Wade's headlights, is fairly discreet, considering.

But right now, the bright white reflective letters are screaming at me: RSP PRODUCTIONS.

18

ERIC

When I turn the key in my door, I can hear Bitsy scrambling across the floor and barking her little head off.

My head hurts and my back aches from carrying tension in my shoulders all day—the price of being in charge. I'm ready for tomorrow to be a day off, even if it is Thanksgiving. It seems every part of my life is in turmoil. Work. My dad. Katie. Calista.

I feel like I'm in one of those action-adventure movies from the eighties, where the floor is dropping out from under me in every direction.

And even *trying* to do the right thing—helping Calista—isn't enough to make it stop. If anything, it just made the pieces in that direction crumble that much faster.

"Just give me a second, brat," I tell Bitsy through the door, fumbling for the knob with all the folders, script pages and my tablet in hand. The last thing I need is for her to hurt herself trying to get to me.

When I get the door open, Bitsy immediately leaps at me, dancing on her hind legs. It's enough to make a smile pull at my reluctant mouth. At least someone's happy to see me.

After bending down to scoop her up with my free hand, I kick the door shut and stumble toward the living room, trying not to drop anything.

My general plan is to let everything fall on the couch, a soft landing for Bitsy and the tablet, head directly to the shower, then order take-out, possibly. If I don't fall asleep first.

And no thinking allowed. It will all be there tomorrow.

A few years ago, I would have headed to a club or thrown a party to drown out all the shit in my head. But now, a hot shower, some broccoli beef, and maybe an episode of *Fantasy Island* sounds better.

But that plan is swiftly derailed when I walk in to find the couch occupied. Katie is sitting on the far end, her overnight bag at her feet.

I stop, startled. Both by her presence and the flash of irritation it triggers. I work to squelch the irritation—it's not fair, and I know it.

Katie gives a small wave. "Hey."

"Hey," I say, struggling to keep my grip on a squirmy Bitsy. "Stop," I tell Bitsy in the low voice that usually snaps her to attention.

Katie smiles at me, but her eyes are red and watery. My heart sinks. This isn't going to be good.

"I hope you don't mind, I used my key," Katie says. "I didn't want to wait in the hall."

"Of course not, that's why I gave it to you." I shuffle toward the couch, the empty end, leaving a trail of papers behind me—damnit—and put Bitsy down.

She wags her tail at me and immediately whines to be put on the floor. Oh, no, I know this game. She wants down so she can jump at me and demand to be picked up again. Jesus, this dog.

I leave her where she is, though I have to keep an eye on her to make sure she doesn't take a header off the couch in a misguided attempt to get down on her own.

"What's up?" I ask Katie, trying not to sound too curt. But I meant what I said last night about needing time to think, and right now, I'm too tired for more drama.

"You'll need to remember to give Bitsy her heartworm pill every month. You can't forget," Katie says, her voice sounding choked.

"What are you talking about?" I drop everything else—papers, folders, tablet—on the coffee table. And only then do I see the small gray jewelry box on the corner of the table. Her engagement ring.

And sure enough, when I turn to look at her, her left hand is bare. "Katie," I begin.

Katie shakes her head. "Don't, okay?" She takes a breath, but it sounds clogged and rattle-y with tears. "I've been thinking about this a lot."

I push Bitsy over carefully and sit on the edge of the sofa. "It was one fight," I say, rotating my shoulder, trying to get the muscles to loosen up. I've been skipping the gym this week, and this is the punishment.

"It's not the fight. Well, it's not just the fight," Katie says. She folds her hands in her lap, her index finger tracing the blank space where her ring used to be.

"I'm not sleeping with Calista," I say tightly. Yes, my feelings toward Calista are confusing, and I've been thinking about her a lot more lately. And that might be a problem in and of itself, but I haven't *done* anything.

"I've had time to think about it, and I believe you," Katie says, after a pause.

"Thanks," I mutter.

"But why not?" she asks.

I stare at her. "What?"

"Why aren't you sleeping with her?" she asks very carefully, as if each word is an egg that needs to be cushioned.

I stand up and pace away from the couch. "Because . . . I'm not that guy anymore. Because we're together." Or we were.

I turn to face Katie.

"Not because you don't feel that way about her, though." Katie nods to herself, as if I've confirmed something she only suspected.

My temper flares. "Katie—"

"Eric, I don't want to be your prize for good behavior, a symbol that you've changed." Then she gives a bitter-sounding laugh. "And I really don't want to be your security blanket."

"What is that supposed to mean?" I demand.

She holds her hand up. "Hear me out." But she doesn't say anything for a long moment. "I always knew it was risky. We are really different. We don't have the same experience of the world."

I want to argue with that, but I can't.

"You're not supposed to expect to change someone, but you were already changing. And I thought if I could help you, maybe then we would grow together. And it seemed to be working. I mean, we had fun together, right?" She tries to smile through her tears.

I jerk my head in a nod.

"But when I saw you with her, I realized that it was different. This," she gestures to the space between us, "is safe for you. You don't feel that same kind of passion." She swallows audibly, as if forcing herself to choke down something.

I make a frustrated noise. "Passion doesn't *mean* anything. Calista and I have torn each other apart over the years, sometimes literally." Hurt and inappropriate lust, two predominant themes in the years we've know each other.

Katie looks toward the ceiling, and she's smiling, but tears are rolling down her cheeks. "I don't want to be your mature choice, Eric. I want you to want me the way you want her. As crazy and scary as those feelings might be." She takes a deep breath. "I *deserve* that."

"I do want you." But even to my ears, the sentiment rings hollow. The shape of the right words without the depth of feeling behind them. Shit.

"Because you see me as a sign that you're on the right track, that you're getting your life together, even as you fight with me about what that life should look like." Katie shakes her head. "We want different things. You have something to prove, and I get it. I do. But I don't want to be an *accomplishment* for you."

I open my mouth to protest, but I realize, too late, that she might be right. The growing-cold feeling in my gut—it's not sadness, or even hurt. It's fear. And not like I'm afraid of what it'll be like to wake up without her, more of what I might *do* without her.

Like she's the guardrail there to keep me safely on the road, and I'm the car that might careen out of control without her presence.

That sucks. For her. For me. For both of us, I guess. Because that's not a relationship, that's some messed up, codependent shit. At least on my part. Though it might not just be me because I still think Katie was probably happiest when I was at my most messed up and in need of fixing.

"So . . . what happens now?" I ask, my shoulders slumping.

She bites her lip. "I don't know exactly. I think I can still cancel the invitations. And we'll have to let everyone know."

I wince.

"I'm keeping my dress," she says with a small laugh. "I look good in that thing."

"I hope that you'll still . . . I would still like to see Bitsy," she continues, wiping her face with the side of her hand. "And you. Just maybe not for a while. I'll text you another veterinarian recommendation."

She stands and picks up her overnight bag. "My stuff," she says with a self-conscious shrug. "I'll leave your key on the table at my place. You can get it when you . . ."

When I box up the rest of my belongings. A process I'd already started a couple of days ago, even if I hadn't realized that's what I was doing. Pulling away.

"Katie . . . I'm sorry." I don't know what else to say.

"I know."

She passes me, going the long way around the coffee table to leave plenty of room between us. But then she pauses at the threshold of the living room. "You deserve to be happy, too." She sounds choked but utterly sincere. "To go after what you really want, what you're afraid to let yourself have."

I'm not sure it's that simple. But I don't say anything. Because what else is there to say?

With that final pronouncement, she leaves the room, and a few seconds later, the door to the hall clicks shut quietly.

No shouting, no accusations. Just over. The swiftness of it is stunning, the ultimate band-aid removal. And it hurts a little, but not . . . enough. I sag against the back of the couch.

It's not supposed to be that easy to end the relationship that was going to be the rest of your life. But everything with Katie was easy. And I used to think that easy meant right or better. Now, I'm not so sure. Now, I'm wondering if easy is a cop-out.

19

CALISTA

"Welcome!" Rawley greets Lori and I as soon as we walk in, gesturing for us to proceed through the reception area to his office. It's small in here, nothing like the sharp, glossy look of RSP's main location. I've been there a couple of times, once for an audition and once with Eric, after Rawley issued a command performance. I never made it past the waiting room either time.

I've always had the impression that Eric's dad doesn't like me very much, which works out well because the feeling is mutual.

Once Lori and I are settled in the black leather chairs in front of Rawley's desk, with him in the massive chair behind it, he smiles at me, all artificially white teeth and fake emotion. "I'm so happy you could meet on such short notice, Calista." He rocks back in the chair, crossing his leg over his knee. Like this is a casual, between-friends conversation.

"So short I didn't even know I was coming," I say, with an equally false smile. I do not trust this man. Whatever slight physical resemblance he and Eric may share is lost beneath Rawley's smooth, lacquered layers of polish, like varnish on a wooden mask.

My mom gives a nervous titter. "Calista."

Rawley's gaze skims toward her and then zeros in on me again. "I wanted to speak with you, Calista, specifically."

Because I'm special.

"I've watched your work over the years, and I think you've really got something special." He makes an emphatic gesture, his fist closed, his thumb pressed forward, like the presidential thumbs-up.

What do you want? The itch to shout at him grows beneath my skin. But he is a powerful man in the industry that keeps my family fed and housed.

I force the corners of my mouth up. "Thank you. I appreciate that."

Next to me, my mother makes a quiet noise in the back of her throat. To anyone else it might sound like she's clearing her throat, politely. But it's a sign, an audible elbow to my ribs, to be more effusive, more grateful.

I stay silent. I will not crawl to ingratiate myself with this man who treats his son like he's used gum that somehow got stuck to the bottom of his life and won't let go.

Rawley blinks, clearly taken aback momentarily. Then he clears his throat and puts his feet on the floor, pulling his desk chair forward. "Listen, I can see you're a straight shooter, and I admire that. I asked you and your mother here because I have a unique opportunity that I think would be perfect for you."

Dread pools in my stomach and then slowly begins stretching out tentacles. "Really?" I ask.

"You've heard of *Triple Threat*, obviously," he says.

I nod. It's his latest show, a trio of young, attractive, diverse women who solve crimes at the behest of a mysterious benefactor. The twist? The benefactor may or may not be evil, and they're trying to determine that along with the solution for the case of the week. In other words, a thinly veiled take-off of the old show *Charlie's Angels*. But it's already renewed for a second season.

"We have a recurring role that I think would be perfect for you. A troubled teen hacker who may have insight into Mr. X's true motivations." He picks up a heavy-looking silver pen from his desktop, as if he's ready to sign this deal into existence right now. "She also may or may not be Veda's daughter." He raises his eyebrows at me, indicating the significance of this, expecting me to be impressed.

Veda is the tall, blond, Nordic-looking one. I think.

"Wow," I manage. In truth, if it were any other producer, any other show, and if I had any indication that the offer was genuine, I might have been excited. Or at the very least tempted to consider it, given that I'm still not sure what I want for my life. Because if nothing else, *Fly Girl* has reminded me how much I miss having that on-set family. The shared experience of working on something together.

Not to mention, the money. More than enough to help my mom and Wade with whatever is going on with the house.

"It would be at least five episodes for this season," Lori says eagerly. "With the possibility of more." She looks to Rawley for confirmation.

He gives a magnanimous nod, clicking his pen lid on and off. "We are considering making the role a series regular."

So even more money, then. The faintest flicker of excitement moves within me. I could maybe save up enough to finish school. And if I've gotten my mom and Wade straightened out on the house by then, I could be free. Really free.

"Depending on how the rest of the season plays out," Rawley adds quickly.

Ah. So Veda's possible teenage hacker daughter will probably die in a mysterious accident as soon as Rawley can cut me loose. The season finale shocker. That feels more likely. But still. A recurring role on a network show is not a small thing. It would be a huge boost to my career (that I'm not sure I want) with a paycheck (that I desperately need).

But I still don't understand what's motivating this sudden generosity. Why me? Why now?

"That's incredible," I say, and I mean it—in the sense that it fails to meet any level of credibility. "I don't know what to say."

Rawley waves his hand in the manner of a generous king overturning a death sentence. "You don't have to say anything. We're just so pleased to be working with you," he says, and to his credit, the words flow smoothly.

But before I can respond—or even figure out how to respond—he continues, his brow furrowing. "There is just one small complication."

Here we go. I school my expression into pleasant blandness.

"You know how it is, always complicated with scheduling and casting." He rolls his eyes as if he has as much control over those things as the weather. "We would need you to start next week."

My mouth falls open. "*Fly Girl* is still filming next week."

But of course, Rawley already knows that. And he can't quite hide the smugness beneath his faux-troubled expression.

Suddenly, his long game is very clear.

"Don't worry," my mom steps in. "Mr. Stone has already said they'll arrange to buy you out of your existing contract. No harm, no foul." She beams at me, but it feels like her eyes are drilling desperate holes in my skin.

We need this. You need this. Do you know how rare chances like this are? A producer offering you a job that you didn't even have to audition for?

I can hear her in my head without her saying a word. Suddenly, I'm wondering if *this* is what was behind her sudden change in attitude toward me over the last day or so. The compliments, the kindness, the fruit-and-nut bar, even. Was she manipulating me?

That sets off a terrible ache in my chest that I can't examine closer. Not here, not now.

If I leave *Fly Girl* now, it'll shut Eric down for weeks until he can find someone else to play Evie—a prospect that sends a sharp arrow of loss through me. *Fly Girl* is my dream project, too, not just Eric's. Maybe my involvement isn't precisely what I thought it would be all those years ago, but the end result is the same—I'm helping to transform a book I love into a show I'm proud of. And recasting this late in the process may, quite possibly, kill the project entirely.

Rawley is sabotaging his own son. Even worse, he thinks I'll go along with it. That he can buy my loyalty because he's purchased my mother's. That I'm the kind of person who will turn away from Eric because his father offers more. How many people have already done that in Eric's life?

Anger on Eric's behalf roars through me, like a fire turned loose on a pile of dead leaves.

I stare at Eric's dad. "Why?" I ask.

My mother gasps.

"Why do you want to hurt him so badly?" I continue.

Rawley jerks back, his mouth falling open slightly. I've cracked his veneer.

But he recovers swiftly. "I assure you this has nothing to do with my son, no matter what you may think. My motivation for offering you this opportunity is based on nothing but your talent and a fit for our show."

"Calista," my mother hisses at me.

I ignore her, continuing to watch him.

He laughs abruptly, surprising me. Then he holds up his hands in surrender. "You want the truth? Fine. Here it is: Regardless of my reasons, you should take this opportunity and run with it. Who else is going to give you a chance? You had a modicum of talent and looks, but now you're damaged goods. Unreliable. A former junkie."

I flinch.

"Everyone knows it. And offers like this aren't going to come along very often in your future, if at all. You need to look out for yourself." He points his pen at me.

His words are too close to my mother's and to the secret, panicky fears I've tried hard to shove down. Hearing them aloud from such an authoritative source makes my stomach turn with nausea.

Without an education, I'm not trained for anything else, and if I can't work as an actress, how am I going to survive? How is my family going to survive?

Rawley leans forward. "What do you think your loyalty will

buy you other than a footnote on some digital embarrassment that will be forgotten before it's even released?"

I shake my head. "Eric's doing a good job. He's working really hard, and it's obvious to anyone that he knows what he's doing. You should be proud of him. He clearly learned a lot from you."

Distaste mixed with another not-quite-identifiable emotion flickers across his face and then vanishes.

It takes me a second to pin down what I saw.

Fear. Uneasiness.

"You don't want him to do a good job," I say slowly.

"That's ridiculous," he says with a false, hearty laugh. "I just don't want him to embarrass himself. And me." But he's glaring at me.

I ignore his response. "Why? Because you're afraid he'll eventually overshadow you?" Eric knows *everyone* in Hollywood; he's charming when he puts his mind to it. He's never chosen to use those connections for anything other than a good party, but if he did, he'd be a force to contend with. Rawley is still cranking out hit shows, but his audience is getting older, and he's tied to all the traditional means of storytelling while the industry changes around him toward more of what Eric is trying to do with *Fly Girl.*

It's just a guess, little more than a stab in the dark, based on what I know about the two of them.

But Rawley's face flushes a deep red beneath his tan.

Apparently my aim is true, even in the dark.

My mother makes a quiet, pained noise and stands abruptly, pulling me up by the wrist with her. My hip collides with the armrest, almost knocking the chair to the floor. "Thank you so much, Mr. Stone. We are so excited about your offer."

He nods grudgingly, his chin jutting forward, as if he's just barely holding back a retraction of his offer.

"Come on, Calista. We've taken up enough of Mr. Stone's

time." She tugs me toward the door, and the motion sends an ache through my damaged shoulder.

"Lori," I protest.

"Ms. Beckett," Rawley says, making both of us stop and turn to face him.

"Take the offer or don't," he says, each word an icy bullet. "But I guarantee you this will be the last offer of any substance you'll receive in this town."

"We look forward to working with you," my mom says with a smile, as if he's not overtly threatening me. *Us*.

She leads me out of the office, releasing me only after we're outside again.

Without another word, she climbs into the front seat of the car, Wade waiting patiently at the wheel.

Rubbing at my shoulder, I pull open the door to the backseat reluctantly. She's going to yell. Or worse, cry.

But to my surprise and unease, she remains silent as Wade pulls out of the parking space and off the studio lot.

"Rawley Stone doesn't want me for that role or any other," I say into the quiet over the soft murmur of Wade's talk radio. "He doesn't even *like* me." I exhale sharply. "He's just using us to ruin Eric. That's it. We're pawns to him. Something to use and get rid of when and how he sees fit. You get that, right?"

I'm not expecting a response, so it takes me aback when she says, "Well-paid pawns who can use the exposure."

I stare at her, at the back of her perfectly straightened and colored blond hair. "Maybe," I say after a moment.

"Do you know what a recurring role on a Rawley Stone show means? A comeback. It means you're stable and steady enough to be employed, and others will—"

"I'm not going to let him use me to hurt Eric—"

Lori gives a disbelieving laugh. "What has Eric Stone done to earn that loyalty, Calista? Use you when he needs you and then push you away? Call you when he needs to feel better about himself, and break your heart in the process?" Her gaze meets mine in the rearview mirror. "Oh, yes, I know all about it."

I shift in the seat uncomfortably. She's not wrong. "He's changed." And I believe that, but it sounds weak out loud.

Lori sighs. "I am trying to get us back on track, Calista. But I need you to work with me on this. Your choices don't affect just *you*," she says. But it's not in the high-pitched, panicky tone that she usually uses. She sounds tired and angry.

Frustration, built up over years, explodes in my chest, driving out words that I have never spoken before. "And why are you all *my* responsibility? Why is my life more yours than it is mine? I know rehab was expensive, I know that having me ruined your life, but how long am I going to pay for those things?" Tears sting my eyes. "How big does the check have to be? How many years of my life do you own for that?"

She stiffens. "Calista, we have all sacrificed for you to become—"

"I never asked you to!" I lean forward in my seat, against the shoulder belt digging into my neck. My heart pounds in a frantic rhythm. "I told you, I don't even know if I want this anymore. I'm not even sure I ever did."

Lori swivels in her seat, her mouth agape. "You used to beg me, *beg me*, to take you to auditions."

"When I was five and it was fun! I was playing dress-up, pretending. I never wanted to be your cash cow."

"I've given my whole life for you to achieve what I never could," she says, slipping down into her seat and facing forward. "And you're not even grateful."

I shake my head, my teeth clenched, until I can force my jaw open enough to speak. "Not when you do it because it's what *you* want. I want to make my own choices, try to find a life that makes me happy. Don't you understand that?" By the end, my tone almost sounds pleading, and I hate that.

She holds up her hands. "Fine, Calista, don't take the job. And we'll all suffer the consequences." My mother, the martyr.

The last of my patience evaporates, and I choke on a frustrated laugh.

"You want to talk about consequences? Where's my money, Mom? I know *I* didn't spend it, even with rehab. What do you think a lawyer would say about that?"

She sucks in a breath.

"You think I'm selfish, only making choices for myself? Fine. Now you can be free of me and my selfish whims. You can do what you want. Maybe even get a job where you earn the money instead of relying on me." The words land like a slap.

"Calista," Wade says sharply.

"I'm not doing it," I say, folding my shaking hands in my lap. "I'm not going to give Rawley Stone what he wants."

Neither of them respond to that, and the rest of the car ride home is in uncomfortable silence.

At home, my mom hurries into the house, leaving Wade and me to follow more slowly.

"She's embarrassed," he says quietly as I scoop up my backpack and we head toward the door. "She knows she screwed up, borrowing from you, not planning well enough."

Stealing. He means stealing, I remind myself.

"She doesn't know how to fix it. But she's trying, Calista. This Rawley guy's job, I guess, could really make a difference."

The frustration I felt in the car increases, making it harder to breathe. "I understand that," I say, trying to keep my tone level. "But her solution for fixing it is me. It's always me."

"She doesn't know how to do anything else," he points out. "Your career is yours, but her career is you."

I know what it's like to be faced with the idea of being out of the only job you know how to do, but it feels like I'm screaming for air here. Like I'm drowning, and my mother is standing on top of me so she can breathe. So Wade and my sisters can breathe. How can she not see that?

"I talked with her last night. The house is going to be foreclosed on in a few months if we can't sell it or come to an arrangement with the bank," he says in that slow drawl. "I'm sure we'll be fine, even if we're living in an apartment somewhere. But you know your mother."

Yes, I do. And my mother is all about appearances. It would kill her to be downgraded in life that far.

And so what? Maybe that would be good for her.

That's what I want to say. But what about my sisters? And then there's the issue of where I'm supposed to go. After my big speech about living for myself, it seems incredibly hypocritical to keep living with my mom and Wade, wherever they end up, relying on them to keep a roof over my head. But with little money and only one semester paid for at Blake College, I am at loose ends, with no plan.

Unless I follow the one my mother has in mind.

The slow-boiling panic in me picks up speed and force.

"Just think about it," Wade says, leaving me behind at the threshold into the house.

I stand there for a long moment, on the outside. The warm air ruffles my hair and tickles against my skin. I really have missed it here. Would it be so horrible to stay?

But the idea of working for Rawley makes my stomach churn. Especially when I imagine telling Eric.

But I can see his face the moment I tell him: the surprise followed by a flash of hurt and then that determined blankness. He won't be angry. He won't yell or accuse me. He'll just shut down and pull away. It'll be like seeing him at a distance, even when we're in the same room. And there will be no coming back from it because he'll see it as choosing his father over him, as so many people have done in so many ways. And he'll be right.

I will lose the only person who ever made me feel like I was good enough just being me. That I didn't need to be *more*, thinner or prettier or just better in some indefinable way. I will lose the last part of my *Starlight* family, a trio that on some days felt—and continues to feel—more real than the one I'm related to by blood.

I wrap my arms around my middle, holding myself tight, like I might break apart otherwise.

I can't do that.

When I finally cross into the kitchen, my mom is there fussing over Zinn, who has an ice pack pressed against her forehead.

"What happened?" I ask, my own problems forgotten as I rush in, shutting the door behind me.

My mother doesn't respond, ignoring me as if I'm not there. The sound of *SportsCenter* drifts in faintly from the living room.

"I fell at school today," Zinn says with a grimace, lowering the pack so I can see the purple bump rising above her eyebrow.

"Fell? How?" I ask. Zinn is not the clumsy type. "Did someone push you?"

She doesn't say anything at first, darting a glance at my mom. "The nurse says I fainted," she mutters.

Because she's not eating enough. Damnit.

"You'll be fine," my mom says to her. "Your dad said the doctors don't think you have a concussion. The goose egg should be mostly gone by the time you have callbacks next week, and whatever's left we can cover with makeup." She pats Zinn's shoulder reassuringly.

Realization washes over me in a cold rush. Zinn is determined to live up to my mom's expectations. Because she feels like she has to.

And my mom is going to let her. If I don't fall in line, Lori's going to use Zinn (and Poppy and Dahlia) to take my place. Or she's going to try, anyway.

"Come on, sweetie, let's get you upstairs. I think I've got

something that will help take that swelling down even faster," Lori says to Zinn.

"Mom," I say, my voice cracking and crumbling under the pressure. "You can't. Don't do this. She doesn't want it."

She ignores me and hustles Zinn out of the room. At the doorway, Zinn gives me a look over her shoulder, half-imploring, half-resigned.

Spots dance in my vision, and I can't breathe.

I cross the kitchen on shaky legs and yank open the back door, trying to suck in enough air to make this dizzy feeling go away.

But it remains, even with the breeze against my face and the open night sky above me.

What am I going to do? What am I going to do? The question is on a relentless loop in my brain, just repeating over and over again like one of those emergency flash flood warnings.

To save Zinn and my family, I have to say yes to Rawley's offer. To save myself—to have any part of *me* left—I need to say no.

My stomach churns up acid into the back of my throat, and I swallow hard.

I can't . . . I need to get out of here.

The drive to escape forces my feet forward, and I start walking, past the car, down toward the end of the driveway. Our house is all lit up, looking warm and homey from the outside. A home we will lose.

I blink back tears. I can't be here right now. But I don't have anywhere else to go.

Helping isn't the same thing as controlling. Eric's weary voice sounds in my head again, the words playing back from earlier today, and it sets off a deep and powerful ache in my chest.

I hope, I pray, he's right. And that I'm right about him. I need to be. I need *him*.

With fumbling fingers, I pull my phone from my pocket and press his number.

Eric answers on the second ring. "Calista?" he asks, sounding cautious and somewhat surprised.

"Hi." Just hearing his voice makes my eyes well up and spill over with tears. I take a deep breath. "I need help." Possibly the hardest words I've ever had to say.

"What's going on? Where are you?" His voice sharpens.

I turn to stare back at the house from the foot of the driveway. "I'm home, for now. Things have gotten . . . more complicated." A noise somewhere between a laugh and a sob escapes me.

"What happened?" he asks, and I can hear the dark anger in his voice. He suspects it's Lori. No, he *knows* it's Lori.

I take a deep breath and tell him. Everything, from Rawley's offer to Zinn's injury and my fears about what it means, both now and for her future.

He doesn't say anything, and the silence, but for faint rustling indicating movement on his end, unnerves me.

Wiping under my eyes, I try to control my breathing. "I need to get out of here. But I don't have anywhere to go." The admission costs me, a price that I cannot afford if he runs, if he can't be the person I believe he is. "I just . . . I'm afraid I'm going to give in, and I don't want to."

Hearing the words aloud makes the entire situation—my entire life—real. More real than I can handle at the moment. I crouch at the foot of the driveway, my backpack sliding down my bad arm, my knees against my chest, tilting the phone away from my mouth, away from the anguish and panic I'm trying to muffle but is somehow escaping in these loud, barking cries.

"Stay right where you are," Eric orders, his voice distant for a moment. Then he's back closer. "I'm sending a car. I'm having them bring you to my place."

It takes me a second to get enough of my breath back to speak. "Thank you. I'm sorry to interrupt you and Katie." Thinking of them, of her next to him in bed or on the couch, listening to this panicked and tear-filled conversation and shaking her head with pity, makes me flinch.

He sighs. "It's fine. She's not here. We ended things."

Shock makes me forget everything else momentarily. "What?"

"It's a long story," he says, each word threaded with an odd tension. It doesn't sound exactly like sadness or even disappointment. I'm not sure what it is. "I'll tell you more later."

It clicks, then. "So you're at your condo." I'd pictured letting myself into his empty home with a spare key from the doorman or a neighbor.

"Yeah." He's quiet for a moment. "Is that okay?"

Yes. I want to say it, but I'm afraid of how it will come out—desperate, hopeful, longing, too much of all of those things.

"Of course, it's okay," I say, striving for a normal tone. "It's your place." And he's being a good *friend*, taking me in.

Eric stays on the phone with me until the car arrives, which is quickly enough that he must be a good customer or he offered an enormous tip.

I climb into the car—a shiny black sedan—shut the door behind me, and sink into the leather backseat with relief. But as the sedan pulls away, leaving my house and my family behind, it feels like I'm making an irrevocable choice, forging a new path. And that sends a nervous or possibly excited shiver over my skin. Because I'm not sure what the destination is or what might happen along the way.

20

ERIC

I'm waiting in the open doorway to my apartment when Calista steps out of the elevator onto my floor.

She doesn't realize I'm there at first, so I have a few seconds to observe her. Her shoulders are hunched forward protectively, and her gaze is fixed on the carpet, as if its pattern holds whatever answers she's seeking.

It crushes something inside me to see her looking so sad.

I almost speak up right then—a joke, a sarcastic comment, anything to divert her, to make her laugh or roll her eyes—but as soon as I open my mouth, she takes a deep breath and straightens herself up, lifting her chin with a determined expression.

Her eyes widen when she sees me. "Hey," she says, slowing for a moment.

"Just wanted to make sure you got here okay," I say, which is a lame excuse for what amounts to eagerness. Eagerness to help, to make her feel better. To make her not regret trusting me.

I frown as she approaches. "That's all you brought?" I ask, nodding at the backpack over her shoulder.

"It's all I had with me. Clothes from earlier today, wallet, passport. I couldn't go back in there. Not tonight." She shakes her head.

When I step back to let her in, she smiles up at me. Her eyes, normally a very clear blue, are so red and watery they look painful.

"I don't know how things got so messed up," she says. "How we got so messed up."

"Callie." Her name escapes, fueled by the ache in my chest. It hurts me that she's hurting like this. I'm going to kill my dad.

I expected nothing less from her mother and my father, though the lengths they're both willing to go is definitely an unpleasant surprise. And something I'm going to have to deal with. I shove down the impulse for destruction temporarily—it's my natural state, to destroy things. Shouldn't be too hard to come back to it. But for the moment, I want to make sure Calista is okay.

The door closes behind her, sealing us off from the rest of the world, from the family members who doubt us, want to control us. Fuck them all.

"Maybe you were right. We're cursed." Her smile wobbles.

Nope, she's not okay. Instinctively, I open my arms to her.

She steps into me, so fast that the motion rocks me back, and buries her face against my chest with a muffled cry. It's enough to make my eyes sting.

I wrap my arms around her, pulling her tight, trying to give as much comfort as I'm receiving. We're in this together.

"It's okay, we're going to figure this out." I smooth my hand over her hair, the familiar vanilla scent of her shampoo or lotion or whatever drifting up to me. It brings me immediately back to those early days on *Starlight*.

Home. It smells like home. Only not the giant monument to ego that my dad had built. Or even the barely-lived-in-emptiness of my condo. It's something more than that.

"I don't know." Calista moves her head against the fabric of my shirt. "I think we're just screwed."

In spite of everything, that makes me laugh. "Hey, I'm supposed to be the cynic here, not you."

She gives a snort but makes no move to pull away. If anything, she presses closer, drawing in and exhaling a deep breath that I feel through my shirt.

"And if we're cursed, it's with a fuck-ton of talent, astonishing good looks, and shitty luck with the people who are supposed to love us," I add grimly, running my hands over her back, shoulder blades to ribs.

She gives a hiccuping laugh, then sighs. "I'm sorry about Katie," she says after a moment. "Are you okay?" She looks up at me, resting her chin against my chest.

And it's weird because in that moment, with her here next to me, almost like we're slow dancing in the entryway to my condo, I do feel okay. More than that, I feel a sense of rightness that's been missing. Which is a little scary—enough to make my heart beat too fast.

Is this what it's supposed to feel like? This strong, overwhelming feeling, as terrifying as it is irresistible? A few years ago, when I felt this, I bolted. Straight into the arms of someone else. Okay, two someone elses. Leave it to me to mess up beyond all recovery.

But this time, I don't want to go anywhere. Which is also scary.

"Yeah," I say. "It's all right." I should step back and let Calista go, especially if we're going to have this conversation right now. But I don't want to. I've made that mistake before. Actually, even worse than letting her go, I pushed her away.

"What happened?" she asks, shifting to rest her cheek right over my heart. I wonder if she can hear its new, faster rhythm.

"She asked if I was sleeping with you."

Calista looks up in outrage, pushing back from me.

"I told her I wasn't."

"I'm aware," she says dryly. "Did she believe you?"

"I think so."

Her forehead creases with a frown. "So what's the problem?"

"She wanted to know why I wasn't."

"What?" she asks, shaking her head in confusion.

I take a breath and try to find the words. "She doesn't think I feel the same thing for her that I feel for you."

She makes an exasperated noise. "Of course you don't. She's your fiancée, the woman you're going to marry. She has her life together. She's perfect." Her mouth twists in a wry expression.

"She's worried I feel more for you than for her," I clarify.

Surprise, then wariness, floods her face, and suddenly she's backing up a step, pulling free of me. "Oh. Well, I'm sure you set her straight," Calista says, folding her arms across her chest, her eyes anywhere but mine. The air between us pulses with unanswered tension.

So, this is it. My pulse picks up another beat or two, and my palms are sweaty. If nothing else, another sign that I care more than I'm comfortable with. I can give Calista some generic response, basically pinning the whole thing on Katie's suspicious nature. And then Calista and I would go back to something resembling normal, the new normal we've established in the last week.

"I could have," I say. "But I started thinking about it."

"That's never good," she says with a faltering smile, trying to tease, even as she takes another step back from me. She's retreating, seemingly without even realizing it.

"And I think she's right."

Calista freezes.

"Callie, the night of the accident," I begin.

"I don't want to talk about it," she says quickly, turning away from me. "It's over and it doesn't matter anymore." She starts toward the living room, leaving me in the entryway. "Where's Bitsy? I've heard so much about her. Will it bother her that I'm sleeping on the couch?"

In her voice, I hear her mother, desperately trying to make everything light and manageable.

She doesn't have to pretend with me. Or she shouldn't have to.

And that's what pushes me to keep going with the truth. "I was afraid."

She stops, a mere shadow at the end of the hall, on the edge of the living room. "What?"

"That night. I was . . ." I rub my hand over my face. "I told myself you cared too much and you were going to get hurt if things went further."

She makes a small sound of distress.

"But the truth is, you meant too much to me. I was scared shitless." A strangled laugh emerges from my throat. "I wanted more, I wanted everything, with you. But I also knew that I would probably screw it up somehow. I couldn't handle that. I was an idiot, a coward. It just took me until now to figure it out."

She faces me. "But you hurt me intentionally. You made sure I would see you."

I wince. "I know. It was stupid, and you have no idea how sorry I am. I just . . ." I take a breath. "It felt somehow like I would have more control if I destroyed it, destroyed us, before I really tried and then ended up messing it up anyway." I rake my hand through my hair. "I wanted you to find out I'm a worthless piece of shit on my terms, I guess."

She's quiet long enough that it unnerves me. "Calista?"

"Do you really think that?" she asks.

"What?" That's not the response I was expecting.

"That you're worthless?"

The temptation to pass it off as a joke, to make some smartass remark about my resale value being drastically lower than my sticker price, rises in me. It's what I would have done in the past, but now everything feels different. Or I'm trying to make it feel different.

I sigh. "No . . . yes. I don't know. Sometimes?"

She steps toward me. "You're not," she says fiercely, and her anger surprises me. "And if you don't care about it for yourself, then you should remember that you're insulting me and everyone else who cares about you when you say that or even think it."

"That list is fairly short," I say with a bark of laughter.

She starts to turn away.

"Okay, okay, I'm sorry." I hold my hands up in surrender, and she stops.

"Other people may see you that way," she says sharply, "valuable only in your connections or who your dad is, but I know you better than that."

"I know." I swallow hard. "And that means more to me than you can imagine. I guess that's why I freaked out that night." I shake my head. "I didn't realize it was supposed to feel like this. That caring about someone was supposed to be fucking terrifying." I give a shaky laugh.

She edges closer. "But you know that now? Because of Katie?"

"Not in the way you're thinking," I say. "She ended it because she didn't want to be the right choice on paper."

Calista stays quiet.

"She was. I mean, she was good for me, and I cared about her. But that wasn't enough for her. She wanted me to feel . . . more." I hesitate. "And for better or worse, I've only ever felt that way about one person." It feels like I'm standing on the edge of a cliff, naked, to say that out loud.

"You didn't look freaked out."

I blink. It takes me a second to trace back to what she's talking about. She'd seen me that night, I knew that, but I was never sure how much she'd seen. I was a little distracted.

"You looked like everything I wanted," she continues, the ache of longing and hurt evident in her voice. "Only with someone who wasn't me."

"Callie," I say. "I am so sorry. I was an asshole. A stupid asshole. I don't . . . I can't . . ." I trail off as she closes the distance between us slowly, like she's expecting me to bolt, or perhaps she's considering each step with the full intention of stopping or retreating.

But then she's in front of me, her fist curling in my shirt, and a blend of fear and arousal makes my heart throb even faster.

I couldn't turn away now if someone lit the house on fire. Again.

She licks her lips, not necessarily in a seductive manner, but more like an uncertain gesture.

But it sends a pulse through me, and I groan. "Callie." I want her mouth on mine, on me.

I bend my head toward hers, and she rises up on her tiptoes to meet me, her hand still clutching my shirt.

Her lips are warm and smooth, and when I touch my tongue against the upper one, she makes a soft noise, her mouth opening beneath mine. I lick inside, and she moans.

I'm lost then. Sliding my hands to her hips, I pull her tightly against me. It's less than what we've done in front of cameras, on demand and on cue, but this is just for us, and that makes all the difference in the world.

Her hands slip up over my chest, leaving a trail of heat in their wake, and to the back of my neck, where she sinks her fingers into my hair. Then she presses against me, arching into the hardened ridge of my cock, until a gasp escapes her mouth, the air brushing over my cheek.

"Callie," I murmur, turning us until her back is against the hallway wall. She wraps her leg around my waist, or tries to, and when I curve my hands under that very fine ass to help her keep her balance, she pulls herself up fully against me.

And I can't resist the urge to thrust against her, the memory of her, wet and tight around my fingers, coming through loud and clear. I want to be inside her. But more than that, there's a driving desire to have that moment of togetherness, not just me inside her because it'll feel good, but the two of us joined in a way that will change everything between us.

I want us to be one, Calista-and-Eric, cemented together in a way that we've never been before.

I bury my nose against the side of her neck, the warm scent of her flooding my senses. Trailing my mouth down her neck to her collarbone, I pause to nip at the soft skin, and she squirms against me. "Eric," she whispers.

"I know, baby, I've got you." The heat of her against me is making me kind of crazy, but I'm determined not to rush this.

Using the pressure of my body and the wall to keep her in place, I slide my hand up under her shirt to cup her breast, my thumb caressing her nipple, hard beneath the soft lace of her bra. When I tweak it gently, pinched between my thumb and forefinger, she jolts against me, and my mouth curves against hers in a smile. I cannot wait to explore every inch of her, finding all the places that make her cry out and tremble.

Then she stops, her whole body tensing up.

Concerned, I pull back. "Callie? Calista? Did I hurt you?"

Her eyes are shut, and she's breathing hard. She pushes her hands against my chest, and I let her down, gritting my teeth against the slide of her body against mine. "What's wrong?" I ask, the strain in my voice more evident than I'd like.

She shakes her head rapidly, her tongue darting out to her kiss-reddened lips. "This is a bad idea," she says breathlessly. "Every time we get tangled up, we end up hurting each other. Actually, I end up getting hurt. I'm . . . I can't do that right now. Not again."

I stare at her, the shock taking a second to sink in, like the pain of a slap. I might not be able to turn away, but she can, even though she can barely look at me when she says it. It's that scar tissue showing through, from the damage I did before. She doesn't trust me. And I probably—no, definitely—deserve that. "Calista, I'm here. I'm not going anywhere."

But she stares down at her hands, locking her fingers together. "If you need me to leave, I understand completely, and I'll—"

I exhale sharply, trying to get myself under control. "Christ, Callie, no. You don't need to go. Even if it's not like that. Even if *we're* not like that. I will always want you around."

She searches my face for a long second, and then nods, evidently assured by whatever she sees there. "Okay."

Which is good because it's the truth. I just have to talk my dick down long enough to believe it.

The silence is awkward with the lingering heat between us and our still-accelerated breathing.

I inhale through my nose, trying to slow it all down. "Okay, so, uh, let me just get sheets for the couch. I have some around here somewhere. You can take my room. I cleaned it up yesterday." Basically when I moved back in. "But let me get Bitsy out of there first. She kind of gets territorial over my pillows."

Calista shakes her head. "I'm not kicking you out of your bed. The couch is fine."

"Callie."

"Eric. It's fine."

And there's enough steel in her voice that I know better than to argue.

I give up with a shrug. "Whatever." It comes out sounding angrier than I mean it to. But I'm not angry with her, just myself. We can't seem to figure this out between us, and maybe we're not meant to. Maybe I blew the one chance we were ever going to have. If so, I have to live with it—another mistake. But this one hurts so much more than the others.

21 CALISTA

Eric's couch is uncomfortable. The cushions are too . . . soft. It's like sinking into marshmallows. Or maybe it's that the leather beneath the sheet is too slippery, or that the entire thing is tipped too much, so I keep rolling into the crevice between the cushions and the back.

Or maybe it's just me.

I let out a slow breath, staring up at the darkened ceiling. Eric left on the stove light in the kitchen—"In case you need to find the bathroom in the dark," he said gruffly—so I can just make out the decorative swirls in the ceiling above me. Some kind of imitation-Art Deco design that's probably expensive.

It's quiet in the condo. My phone is silent because I shut it off after the barrage of texts my mother sent in response to my message that I was fine, with a friend, and she should NOT call the police. With my issues, I'm sure she was already imagining me facedown in the gutter with a needle in my arm.

After Eric took Bitsy out for the last time, an hour or so ago, he went to bed with a barely audible, "Night" in my general direction.

There's no sound from his bedroom. I strain for the sound of him moving beneath his covers, the rustle of fabric or a soft inhale or exhale. But there's nothing beyond the occasional faint jingle of Bitsy's tags as she moves or adjusts. For all our closeness over the years, Eric and I have never slept together, literally slept. I used to fall asleep sometimes during movie nights—there's really only so many Michael Bay-orchestrated explosions one can endure before numbness sets in—but I'd wake up to Eric gently shaking my shoulder or tickling my feet until I screamed with laughter or begged for mercy.

Turning over, I stare at the coffee table, where my clothes are folded. With the sheets, Eric had handed me one of his old T-shirts. A *Starlight* shirt for a charity event we'd both supported back in the day. It's worn—probably one of his workout shirts—and far too big on me, enough so that I can pull my knees up beneath it, curling into myself. But it's little comfort.

I hurt him tonight. Eric. I saw it in his face. And maybe he deserves it for some of the crap he's pulled. How am I supposed to trust him with my heart—or anything else—after what we've been through? What he's put me through.

A tear slips down the side of my face, dampening the pillow case.

But I love him. I've loved him . . . it feels like forever. Corny as it sounds, it's like my life had one of those photo filters that dulls everything and makes it look bleached out until the day I walked into the *Starlight* auditions.

Until he stepped between my mother and me like she didn't exist. Treated me like a person instead of an object. I would love him forever for that alone.

But love doesn't fix anything or solve your problems. In my experience, it just makes things worse. Gives someone another way to hurt you. A better grip to cause you pain or bend you to their will.

And yet I'm lying here, trying to listen for the sound of him breathing. Wishing I was in there with him, curled up at his side. Wishing I'd had the courage to say yes instead of no.

Yes, odds are, we would mess each other up, break and bend each other. His relationship with Katie just ended, and there are bound to be repercussions from that. I couldn't figure out how to sever myself from my family, or if I even should. I hate his father and would have zero hope of disguising that, and yet, he probably should have a connection with the only parent who hasn't essentially abandoned him.

But worst of all, I'm realizing that I don't trust myself to make good decisions, and if Eric is one of those decisions, how is that supposed to work?

More tears trickle down to the pillow, and I draw in a quiet breath, trying not to sniffle.

The problem is, none of that changes the essential nature of what I feel. I am . . . empty out here without him. I miss him when he's only thirty feet away. And no, I don't know what's going to happen tomorrow, but that doesn't change tonight.

That doesn't change that we're here. Together.

My pulse skips rapidly when I sit up, as if I've surprised myself.

Wiping under my eyes, I push the sheet and blanket off myself, standing with a light-headed sensation that is not entirely unpleasant. It feels almost like an out-of-body experience, except somehow I'm hyperaware of my skin, the brush of his T-shirt against my thighs. The cool air against the bends of my elbows and knees.

My hands are shaky, trembling at my sides, as I start past the edge of the couch. I've never understood that phrase, your heart in your throat, until right now. My heartbeat now resides just below my tonsils, keeping me from fully swallowing.

An anticipatory shiver dances over me when I imagine his big, warm hands on me, and I slip down the hallway, the chilled air skating over the already heated and aching place between my legs, heightening the sensation.

The door is mostly closed, open only a few inches. I'm not sure if that gap is for Bitsy or if, as my heart tells me even now, he's keeping an eye—or an ear—out for me.

I don't knock, just widen the gap enough for me to step inside. In the very faint light from behind me and the moonlight through the uncovered windows, I can just make out the shape of Eric's bed in the center of the opposite wall. My eyes adjust quickly, and then

I can see him, shirtless and propped against the pillows on the right side, his dark hair tousled against the lighter pillowcase.

Bitsy, on the pillow next to him like a little queen, sits up, her tags jingling, and she barks once.

Eric shifts, and he sits up. "Calista? Is everything okay?" he asks, his voice raspy.

He reaches for the light on the bedside table. "No, don't," I say quickly.

"What's wrong?" he asks.

"Did I wake you?"

"No, I was just . . ." His words trail off as I approach the opposite side of the bed. "Calista."

I pick Bitsy up, pillow and all, and put her on the floor. She gives a woof of discontent but doesn't otherwise move.

Eric is watching me, and I can feel his dark-eyed gaze on me like heat on my skin.

Peeling back the covers, I slide between the sheets.

"Calista, you don't have to—"

"Shut up," I say softly and scoot toward him.

The warmth radiating off him reaches me first, but the initial skin contact—my leg against his—steals the breath from my lungs. He's so hot. Literally—and figuratively—in this case.

Ducking under his arm, I curl up against his bare chest, shivering at the contrast between his skin and the cooler air.

He automatically pulls his arm tighter around me, and my nipples tighten almost painfully in response to the press of his body against mine.

"What are you doing, Calista?" he asks with wariness.

"What does it look like?" I slide my hand across his chest, and he jumps.

"Damn, your hands never get any warmer, do they?" he murmurs, but he catches my fingers and presses them against his skin.

"All my blood is busy elsewhere," I say, leaning over to kiss just above his flat, brown nipple, which has perked to attention. He's warm, and he smells good, like Eric, whatever combination of deodorant, soap and skin that is. It's as familiar to me as the scent of my own shampoo, only more comforting and a lot more exciting.

I nuzzle down the center of his chest, tasting his skin, like I want to brand that flavor on my tongue forever.

He sucks in a harsh breath. "Are you sure? I don't want you to regret anything." His voice is rough with want, but pain and uncertainty are mixed in there as well.

I hesitate for a second—wrestling with my desire and my self-confidence to follow through, but it's Eric—before clasping my fingers around his and leading them between my legs.

"Warm enough for you here?" I ask.

"Jesus, Callie," he says with a sharp exhale. He rolls to his side, facing me, and strokes me between my fingers until I get out of the way.

His hand slips beneath my panties, and I gasp.

"Any more questions?" Though it comes out more like a breathless moan because his hand feels so much better than my own, his fingers bigger, warmer than mine. He's toying, tracing a path from my clit to my entrance, but without penetrating.

And it's killing me. I push my hips up, begging without words for him to push in, but his hand moves back, avoiding.

"How are you so wet already, Callie?" he murmurs, leaning over to kiss the side of my neck. I arch my head back to give him more access.

"I was thinking about it . . . about you . . . ," I say, closing my thighs around his hand. "For years."

He groans and pulls free to tug my panties down my hips and over my ankles.

With shaking hands, I grab the back of his neck, pulling him closer, and he settles his weight partially on me. His erection presses hard against my hip, which makes me squirm to try to twist into him, to center him over me. I ache with a throbbing emptiness that feels like it might never end. I need Eric.

But he resists. "We don't have to hurry, Callie." His hand cups me, his middle finger just barely penetrating. I am going to lose my mind.

I slide my hand from his neck, over his chest, and before he can stop me, down the front of his boxer-briefs.

His erection is even more impressive in my hand, hot and tight beneath the fabric. It makes my mouth water. I run my fingers over the length of him, squeezing just a little.

His eyes close and his breath escapes in a rush, his hips moving convulsively, pressing into my palm. I love the muscle that jumps at the back of his jaw.

In response, his finger pushes inside me, and I arch up into his hand with a cry. The relief, temporary as it is, is a rush.

My hips work up and down, seemingly without my conscious choice. "Please." It's not enough, not even close.

When his eyelids flutter open, his dark-eyed gaze is glassy, and that sends a thrill through me. I flatten my hand over him so that the top of his boxer-briefs slide down and I can briefly feel the press of his heated flesh. It sends a delighted shiver of anticipation through me; I want that heat and hardness in me.

He makes a low noise in the back of his throat. "Shirt off."

I struggle upright enough to free the fabric from beneath me. As I'm pulling it over my head, he shifts position. A second finger presses into me, tight, wonderful, still not enough, as his mouth closes hot over my breast.

I can't move for a second, sensations rioting over my whole body, my brain short-circuiting temporarily.

He pauses, releases my nipple with a soft pop, and the cool air where his mouth was makes me shiver. "Calista? Callie?"

"I'm okay," I manage, muffled by the fabric of my shirt still.

Eric's leg slides between mine, and he pulls his hand free,

replacing it with the heat and pressure of his thigh. I whimper and press against him. It would take a stronger person than I am not to wiggle for that small relief of friction.

Then he helps me finish pulling my shirt over my head, releasing it where it was caught behind me.

I blink up at him, the flushed spots of color high on his cheeks, his lips puffy from kissing me. The dark stubble across his jaw. The faint spray of freckles across his nose that I can't quite see but know are there just from studying him over the years.

I love him.

My heart swells, and my eyes grow damp in spite of the clamoring of my body. "Hi."

His smile flashes in the dim light. "Hi. You okay?" A flicker of something that looks like wonder crosses his expression, like he can't believe we're here, that this is happening.

I nod and push myself up on my elbows to brush my lips over his. It's not the deep intense kisses of a few minutes ago, but gentler, slower.

Touching the side of his face lightly, I run my thumb over the familiar shape of his cheek, trying to tell him without words how I feel. Love, not just lust. Our history compacted into a single gesture, every moment, every touch and hope in that movement.

He catches his breath and kisses me back, just as slowly, deliberately, his mouth and tongue soft over mine.

Somehow the slowness accelerates the need in me to a fever pitch even faster. Bracing myself on one elbow, I reach up and trace the lines of his chest and stomach over me, dipping beneath the waist of his boxer briefs to wrap my fingers around him.

I stroke my fingers up and down his length, and his mouth goes slack over mine for just a second. And when he resumes, there's nothing gentle or soft about it.

His mouth ravages mine as he thrusts into my hand, and I feel the dampness of his excitement at the tip of him. When I touch there, circling him with my thumb and forefinger, he tears his mouth from mine, and his arm, braced against the bed by my head, trembles. "Callie."

"Take these off."

The words are barely out of my mouth before he pulls away from me, and when he returns, we are skin to skin and the sensation makes me dizzy with desire.

He moves to kneel between my legs, and I widen my position to accommodate him, my thighs trembling a little with excitement and too many workouts this week. Eric braces himself, hands planted on either side of my head, and then presses against me.

He groans. "You are so wet," he says, rubbing against me, and I press back in counterpoint.

The tip of him pushes into me, and we both go still. Temptation flashes across his face, the same temptation I feel. I had every test known to mankind before, during, and after rehab, and I'm on birth control—have been since I was fifteen, my mother was taking no chances with contraception or my complexion—but in the moment, even the possibility of a baby with his black curls and dark eyes, a connection to him forever, doesn't utterly terrify me as much as it probably should.

But he shakes his head and reaches across me to the nightstand and fumbles in the drawer. "Condoms."

He straightens up with one caught between his fingers, and I reach down to touch his erection, caressing him until he shudders and pulls away to roll on the latex.

When he returns to me, he grabs my wrists and pins them gently over my head with one hand.

His one free hand does its best to drive me crazy, pinching one nipple and then the other while I gasp, following with his lips and tongue to soothe and suckle.

Until I'm straining against the grip of his hand, trying to reach his mouth with mine, trying to raise up to force him to take me deeper into his mouth.

He lifts his head at one point. "Am I hurting your arm?" he asks, his forehead creased with a worried frown.

I shake my head. "No, no. Keep going."

He returns his mouth to my breasts, but then I feel the sweet pressure of him at my entrance as he pushes that first inch inside. It's tight, slow going, and I feel the stretch, but it feels . . . God, it feels so good.

My head rocks back against the mattress, my chin tilting toward the ceiling. *Yes.* "Eric. Please."

He pulls back and presses forward again, that first inch moving smoothly this time and then deeper. In spite of myself, a moan escapes.

I buck against him, meeting his thrusts until he's all the way in. Filling me, making me feel tied to him in a way that my imagination failed to adequately convey.

Then I lock my legs around his hips, holding him in place.

He stares down at me, the heat in his expression making me wetter around him.

But I'm not giving in, not letting go.

He retreats as far as my locked legs will allow and slams forward into me in a short, digging thrust that sends a shockwave of sensation through me, stealing my breath and snapping my eyes shut. My fingernails curl into the side of the hand that holds me captive.

"Callie?" he asks, his voice low and rough.

"Don't stop!"

He resumes, our position making him work that much harder, and every grunt of effort from him makes something inside me curl tighter and tighter. It's a building feeling, one I recognize from nights alone in my bed, but my fingers are no match for Eric above me, the dampness of his sweaty skin, his bare chest rubbing mine, his cock buried deep inside me.

But the enormity of the impending tidal wave that just won't crash yet—why won't it crash?—is a little scary, even as much as I desperately want it.

I open my eyes. He seems focused inwardly, his own eyes heavy-lidded and his mouth a tight line of concentration. That muscle that I love at the back of his jaw is taut and standing up beneath his skin.

"Eric?" My voice cracks with the pleading question, and I don't even know exactly what I'm asking him to do. I just *need* more.

His gaze snaps to mine, reading something in my face.

"It's okay," he says, emotion softening the planes of his face. He releases my wrists. "I'll get you there."

He pauses for just a second, bracing himself on the mattress, and then his big hand slides between us, coasts over my abdomen and down to my clit, pressing it back against me gently.

Pleasure spirals through me, and I suck in a desperate breath. *I love you. I love you, I love you.* The words are bubbling up in me, and I can't stop them.

"Don't freak out," I manage, my hands on his sides, where I can feel his muscles working. "But I need to . . ."

He looks up at me, his gaze fierce. He's willing to give me anything. "What do you need?" And God, that makes me love him even more.

"I love you," I say. And a second later, everything goes tight and still in me, while ripples clutch all around him, sending that tidal wave rushing over me. I gasp.

He groans, dropping his head down to my collarbone. "Not freaking out," he says through clenched teeth.

Then when my legs go slack, he plunges inside me with renewed vigor, thrusting a few more times until I feel him pulsing inside me. "Definitely not freaking out," he says.

22

ERIC

When I slide beneath the sheets after disposing of the condom, Calista gives a throaty laugh that sounds utterly sated and seductive. It hits a pleasure center in my brain, and I want to do anything and everything to hear it again.

"What's so funny?" I ask, bending over to scoop Bitsy off the floor from where she's come around to beg to be picked up. She gives Calista a baleful look and then settles at our feet with a deep, disgruntled sigh.

"We are the worst role models," Callie says, sounding so relaxed, almost lazy with pleasure. I've never seen her like this before. And it sparks pride in me to have made her feel that good.

Propping myself on my side, I smirk at her. "Speak for yourself."

"Not that." She lightly taps my chest in remonstration. "I just mean, 'Demon Baby.'" Her expressive eyes go wide, and she watches me expectantly. "Don't you remember?"

It takes me a second. And then I groan.

During the second season, the network had some kind of weird initiative to show the consequences of drinking for teens. Every series with main characters under the age of 21 had to include a storyline illustrating the dangers.

Most shows went with dream sequences or found a way to tie it in to the current storyline that made a little bit of sense. But *Starlight*, under the guidance of our brand-new and overeager showrunner, the same dude who later brought in zombies, decided to go for broke.

Lilah, one of Skye's few female friends on the show, gets sloppy drunk and, as a result, has unprotected sex with one of the angels from the cadre sent to help Brody with his mission of protecting Skye. She ends up pregnant with a demon child. Talk about consequences.

Calista's eyes dance with mischief and laughter. "'But Skye!'"

"'It was only for a few minutes!'" we finish together, and Calista's shoulders tremble with laughter against me.

"Oh, my God, Harper hated that scene," I say, shaking my head against the pillow. The actress portraying Lilah was thirty at the time, playing seventeen. And apparently, as she put it, *a stupid seventeen.*

"Who could blame her? It was ridiculous. And insulting." Calista sniffs.

"Well, considering we were brother and sister, I'm pretty sure they would have dreamed up worse consequences for this." I gesture at our naked bodies. "Probably demon *twins*," I say solemnly.

That sets her off in another fit of giggles, including a fucking adorable snort, and she shifts to her side, curling up against me, her back pressing against my chest.

Neither of us mentions what she said. And other than that Harper reference, we don't discuss that we very nearly had unprotected sex, something I've never done in my whole life—not with Katie, not even during my drunkest, highest nights. Something that even now sets off a surge of desire, a longing to bury myself in Calista with nothing between us.

She holds nothing back from me. She never has. And I want that closeness, even if I can't make myself say it, can't make myself say the words that she so freely and generously gave me. I've never said those words to anyone.

Calista's breathing slows, her body softening into mine. I wrap my arm carefully around her waist, keeping her pressed against me. I want to keep *her.*

When I wake, the sun is shining, and cool fingers are questing below my waist, tracing lightly over my painfully hard cock.

"Callie . . ." I squeeze my eyes shut.

The sheet rustles away, letting the almost frigid air-conditioning access my skin, but before I can protest, her mouth brushes over the tip of me.

My hips arch helplessly, and she lets me push past her lips into her hot, wet mouth, working her tongue against the underside. Then her hand wraps around my base, squeezing and sliding.

I moan.

And she releases me with one last long lick. "Too soon?" she inquires, and my eyes snap open.

Forget what *Starlight* casting said—Calista is the angel, kneeling next to me, the early morning light spilling through my window, her hair golden and lit by the sun, her expression heated and filled with shining affection that I probably don't deserve.

"No, not too soon," I say gruffly, leaning up to guide her head back down.

With a smile, she complies.

Watching her take me in, my dick wet from her mouth, is almost as much of a turn-on as the sensation. But as good as it is, it's not as good as being inside of her. And after only a few minutes, I'm getting too close to the point of no return.

"Wait, Callie. Wait." I tangle my hands in her hair, carefully, to get her attention.

She raises her eyebrows and slows but doesn't stop. And I can see the glimmer of mischief and challenge in her expression. She wants me to lose control.

Goddamn, this girl. My eyes roll up toward the back of my head. She's comfortable enough with me to stand her ground, push back for what she wants, and I might be the *only* person in her life she feels safe enough to do that with.

But not now. Not this.

"Calista, I want to come inside you." Urgency makes me blunter than normal.

Eyes wide, she stops immediately and releases my cock, crawling over my body to position herself over me. "Why didn't you say that?"

But before she can say more, I roll her over onto her back, then pull away.

Her head pops up from the pillows. "What are you doing?

"Trust me?"

She nods.

I grab a couple of pillows and stack them, then I guide her onto her stomach, her elbows and knees supporting her. The pillows will provide that extra friction she needs.

"Eric?" She sounds uncertain, until I stroke the soft, wet folds between her legs and she moans.

I lean over to grab a condom from the nightstand drawer.

"Wait," she says, when I return.

I stop. "What's wrong?"

"I want to be able to see you."

Remembering how it felt to watch her suck me, I understand the desire. And fortunately, there's an easy fix.

It only takes a few seconds of rearranging so that we're facing the foot of the bed, and the mirror above my dresser. I grip her hips in my hands, lining us up. She catches her breath. "Oh."

"What?"

"We look good. Well, you do." Her gaze moves hungrily over my reflection, making me feel huge. "I like seeing your hands on me. I like watching the way your muscles work." Her cheeks flush with the admission.

I stroke my palm over the smoothness of her ass. "It's not me, it's you. You look so beautiful." And she does, spread before me on her elbows and knees, her hips angled up toward me. Her hair spills forward over her shoulders.

With a soft noise, she pushes against the mattress and into me.

I pull back long enough to roll the condom on.

"I'm on birth control."

She says it so quietly, I barely hear her, but my heart almost stops in response.

"If you want to . . . I mean, it's safe that way," she continues. "Next time."

We're . . . that would definitely be crossing a line. But just the thought of being bare inside of her makes me harder.

My eyes meet hers in the mirror, and I push into her. She's wet but tight, grasping around my cock, and I have to grit my teeth to go slow.

She gasps once I'm fully inside, her hands clutching tight at the sheets.

I pull tighter on her hips, my hands locking on, thrusting as she pushes back against me, and the sound of our bodies meeting with a slap only drives me to go faster.

She shudders, her expression one of fierce intensity and pleasure, and drops her head.

I love watching her, watching us move in the mirror, the furrow of concentration in her forehead, the way she dips her hips lower to catch the pillows against her clit.

It's not long before I can feel the first ripples clutching around me. "Eric," she whispers.

"Go, baby, just go." I manage to hold on while she comes, barely. But then that white-hot heat spreads through my lower back, and I press myself into her as deep as I can, pouring out in jerky spasms until there's nothing left.

"I love you," she says again, sounding dazed, her voice muffled by the pillows.

I love you, too. The words are there, but I can't seem to make them come out.

23

CALISTA

The warm glow of satiation fills me and surrounds me as I make my way from the bathroom to the kitchen, trailing a hand along the wall as much for the sensation as balance. My skin feels warm, tingly, even with the rapidly cooling water dripping from my still-wet hair.

After a shower together that resulted in a lot of water on the floor and a very thorough cleansing with hands and soap in inappropriate places, I'd toweled off and nabbed Eric's shirt from the floor—over his mock protests—and set off in search of food. I would have stayed, not really wanting to be out of touching-distance, but I'm *starving*. I don't ever remember being this hungry, even back in the days of kale-only lunches.

Behind me, still in the bathroom, Eric belts out the opening of an old theme song, *Gilligan's Island*, I think. Just to make me laugh. The man is gorgeous, but he can't sing. Never could. During those movie nights when he would tickle me to wake me up, he would also sing—for the express purpose of torturing me, I think.

I stop in the hall, my hand flying up to my mouth to block the giggles. "Eric, stop!"

I don't know if he hears me, but he sings louder.

Tears from laughter dampen my eyes. Is there such a thing as sex-drunk? Because if so, I am. Even the thought—sex-drunk!—makes me giggle again. Apparently, good sex leads to giddiness. Definitely a new experience for me.

I take a deep breath, steadying myself, and continue to the kitchen. I love him, I love being here. I love imagining that this could be our every Thursday. Or, at least, our every Saturday.

In the kitchen, I head immediately to the refrigerator, my stomach rumbling. It dawns on me when I touch the handle that I hadn't had dinner the night before. No wonder I'm hungry. Not that it had occurred to me until my other needs were well-addressed.

I feel a too-satisfied smile pulling at the edges of my mouth.

Yanking open the fridge, I brace myself for the blast of cooler air wrapping itself around me while I search the contents.

The cold is still a shock, as is the inside—in that *there's nothing here.* Condiments in the door. A few bottles of beer and a magnum of expensive champagne with the cork already popped. A single egg of indeterminate age or source rests directly on the glass rack, next to an open but mostly empty carton of Chinese food.

Whoa. How does he survive like this?

Then it clicks. He doesn't. He wasn't living here. He was staying at Katie's. He'd had a fiancée. Until, from the sounds of our conversation, last night. Maybe the day before. The champagne . . . is it from when he proposed? Surely not.

But the chill—from the refrigerator or that thought—makes me shiver.

I love you. I heard my own breathy voice echoing back at me, and I squirm in discomfort. It sounds so yearning and needy.

I was making declarations of love, offering sex without a condom, and he hadn't even had time to restock his fridge between ending his engagement with Katie and starting . . . something with me.

Cringing, I feel my face flush hot with embarrassment. It's not that he can't have two serious relationships in quick succession, but . . .

Has he even fully moved out of her place? I don't remember seeing boxes anywhere. I'd like to believe that it's because he packed light, somehow having a sense that the relationship wouldn't work out. But he had proposed to her.

Suddenly I'm feeling vulnerable, exposed in a way that has nothing to do with the shortness of this T-shirt and the fact that I'm not wearing anything under it. Yes, he said last night that I'm the only person he's ever felt this way about. But what does that mean in Eric-land? Are we going to reach a certain point where he panics and does whatever it takes to extract himself? God, am I that "whatever" for he and Katie? Am I his panic-reaction to cold feet?

I want to trust him. I want to trust the choice I'm making, the choice I made to be with him. But it feels like I'm out here all by myself, like I'm the one taking all the chances, giving up all my control. By my decision, of course, but that doesn't reassure me. My track record for personal decisions includes those that would have led to actual track marks. So.

"Hey." Eric steps into the kitchen, wrapping his arms around me, startling me. In spite of my worries, my body immediately responds to the warmth of him behind me. His bare chest against my back, the velvet of his worn jeans brushing against my legs.

"Hey," I manage.

"What's wrong?" He twists around to look at me.

"Yeah. Just . . . no food." I tip my head toward the empty refrigerator.

It takes him a second, but understanding registers in his expression, a faint tightening. "Yeah. I, uh, had a food service before." He runs his hand through his damp curls.

"When you lived here."

"Yeah."

We're silent for a moment, and everything we've been ignoring rushes in to fill the void. Like how this thing between us happened very quickly—or years too slowly, depending on your perspective—and it doesn't really change anything. My mother is going to push me to sign with his father, and his father is attempting, with this same move, to assassinate Eric's one and only project. His future.

He takes a deep breath. "Calista . . ." he begins, his hands falling away from me.

"If you had more eggs or ramen," I say quickly, closing the refrigerator door like it'll close the door on whatever he was going to say, "I can cook the shit out of ramen." I don't want to talk about it. Not right now. I just want this bubble of blissful ignorance to last a little longer.

His eyebrows shoot up. "Ramen," he repeats slowly.

"You know, the curly noodles in the styrofoam cup?" I prompt.

His lip curls up in disgust.

I laugh in spite of myself. He's such a snob. "Poor college student here," I remind him. Actually, poor person in general. The years before Lori married Wade and my career took off, we survived some pretty lean times. Vegetables came in the form of chicken pot pies we ate for dinner, sometimes for weeks in a row. I think that's partially why she's gone so crazy in the other direction . . . because she can.

But thinking about my mom makes uncertainty and guilt rise up in me, and that, in turn, makes me angry and frustrated.

"Let me take Bitsy out while you get dressed, and then we can go get something," Eric says, but it sounds more like a question. His gaze searches my face.

Bitsy, hearing her name, comes scurrying in from the bedroom, where we left her sleeping. Apparently, we'd kept her awake last night. She paws at him, and he bends down to scoop her up, which makes my heart ache and kicks off a yearning that has nothing (and everything) to do with wanting him. Handsome man being responsible and taking care of something little and helpless, it's a genetic predisposition. I can't help it.

I nod, and naked relief shows on his face.

"But it's Thanksgiving Day," I point out. "And not everyone has your antipathy toward holidays. A lot of places are closed."

He snorts. "Nice vocab word, college girl." Hesitation flickers, then he asks, "What do you normally do for Thanksgiving?"

The pulse of love I feel for him in that moment almost takes me to my knees. Because I can guarantee that if I told him we usually ate raw octopus while sitting on the roof of the Capitol Records building, he would try to find a way to make that happen for me. Even though he hates the holiday. All holidays. Except, as he's fond of saying, Arbor Day. Just to be a jackass.

I shrug. "Lori cooks. I'm allowed double calorie intake, usually, if I promise to double up on a workout the next day," I say mockingly. I try to smile, but it feels too tight on my face.

Eric shakes his head in disgust.

The worst part is, I'll miss it. I hate Lori controlling me, but living without it feels like walking on a tightrope. Blindfolded. Above a tank of starving sharks.

And I have to wonder if she's pulling the same crap on Zinn today. With that callback next week? Probably.

That thought makes the guilt in my chest throb that much harder. Damnit.

"If you want to go home, I can—"

"No," I say sharply. Then I shake my head. "No," I say in a softer voice. "I'm exactly where I want to be." I hope. I think.

Eric loops his arm around my neck, pulling me closer, and Bitsy pushes her cold nose to sniff my elbow, making me jump and him laugh. "We'll find something. Brunch. People eat brunch on Thanksgiving, right?" He kisses my forehead, sending pleasant shivers through me. "We'll figure it out."

After one Bitsy walk—she gets her revenge for her sleepless night and me in Eric's bed by taking forever to find the perfect place to pee—we're off to what is likely the only brunch place in Hollywood that's a) open and b) not serving some version of the traditional holiday meal. The promise of cream-cheese-filled waffles and bacon is more than enough to convince me.

The sun is shining, the palm trees are rustling in the breeze, and the haze hasn't kicked in yet. It's one of those perfect Southern California days. Made even better by the fact that it's Eric behind the wheel, day-old stubble on his jaw, his eyes hidden behind sunglasses but his mouth quick to smile. His hand rests on my knee as he drives, and he laughs when I point out the typo on the sign in front of a boutique store that changes it from advertising a sale to something vaguely pornographic and kind of confusing.

We have to park a few blocks away, and when we amble up the sidewalk, which is virtually deserted thanks to the holiday, Eric reaches out and takes my hand, lacing his fingers through mine. The simplicity of it, how natural it feels, steals my breath.

I'm still trying to recover when a photographer comes out of nowhere, stepping in front of us on the sidewalk to snap pictures as he walks backward.

Eric tenses, his whole body going rigid and his hand tightening on mine, which only makes me realize how relaxed he was a few seconds ago by contrast. "Leave. Now," Eric says, moving to block me from view as best as he can without letting go of my hand.

"Are you guys together now?" the paparazzo, in his forties and Australian by the sound of the accent, persists. "Eric, aren't you engaged to someone else? A doctor or something? How's rehab, Calista? Are you still clean? Want to roll up your sleeves and show me?" He's trying to get a reaction.

I clamp my jaw shut, my teeth squeaking in protest. I've been trained too well, at this point. This has been Eric's life as Rawley's kid, probably for as long as he can remember. But I was dropped in at the deep end with *Starlight*, and those were hard lessons I don't have any desire to repeat. I know how the game works now, and the media is always harder on girls. Especially girls like me, the ones who've made mistakes. They're always easier on the guys, even when they misbehave. That's macho. When a woman does it, she's a bitch. Or an attention whore.

Back in the day, Eric and I would have had to coordinate to keep Chase from punching guys like this. And then sometimes the two of them would ignore me and go after photographers on my behalf, which didn't help. That's where the second season rumors about the three of us sleeping together—all of us at once—came from, I'm fairly sure.

As if the pap can read my mind, he switches gears. "Have you seen Chase Henry? He's here in town with his new bird. Some kind of *Starlight* reunion in the works?"

Almost in unison, as if we'd planned it, Eric and I raise our free hands, middle fingers up, in front of our faces. Eric sticks his directly in front of the guy's camera, which is, admittedly, not quite as bad as hitting the photographer, but definitely more aggressive. It's not just a rude gesture; it'll make the pictures unsellable in the US. Decency laws, I think. I don't remember the exact terminology anymore.

What I do remember: To win against the paparazzi, it's always best to hit them where it hurts—right in the dollar signs.

The pap groans. "Oh, come on. Just a couple more."

But we keep walking toward our brunch destination, our fingers up until he finally gives up and drops back.

"Asshole," Eric mutters as he pulls open the door to Buttercup. "Are you okay?" he asks as the noise from the surprisingly large brunch crowd inside drifts over us.

"There's probably a high-value catch in here somewhere," I make myself say with a shrug. "He was just killing time." But the pain from his remarks still sizzles, like the aftereffects of a hand accidentally pressed to a stove. No matter how many years have passed, if I'm still at all in the public eye, I will be remembered for my mistakes rather than my (albeit limited) successes. Oh, and whatever plastic surgery I might or might not have had. And who I'm currently sleeping with, of course.

It's this kind of thing that makes me long for my imagined life as an accountant. To be fair, I don't know exactly what it's like, but I'm betting no one whispers about Botox or asks you to roll up your sleeves to look for track marks.

Eric pulls me closer, wrapping his arms around me, pressing his mouth against the top of my head, and I shut my eyes, letting the familiar comfort of him—this is something he would have done even before last night, though we would likely have been more careful about maintaining some distance—ease some of my tension. I bury my face against his T-shirt, wishing I could be even closer. I'm wearing one of his shirts with my yoga pants from yesterday, but it's not the same. More like I want to crawl inside with him. Crawl inside his skin and live there, perhaps.

"Two, please," he says over my head to the hostess.

I tilt my chin up against his chest, on the verge of suggesting that we order something to go and retreat to the safety, sanctity and solitude of his bedroom, when he stiffens, his arms going taut around me.

"What's wrong?" I ask.

But his attention is fixed on something—or someone—in the distance, deeper in the restaurant.

Uh-oh. My mom? His dad? Oh God . . . Katie?

My stomach roiling, now with dread on top of hunger, I twist around in his arms to follow his gaze. It takes me a second to figure it out, to realize that the paparazzo outside hadn't just randomly asked about Chase, as I'd thought.

No, Chase Henry, our former co-star, former friend, the one whose life we accidentally turned upside down in our night of selfish stupidity, is sitting at a table in the far corner.

His blond hair is shorter than I remember, and maybe a little lighter. And he's not alone. Directly across from him, a pale but familiar-looking redhead—Amanda Grace, I'm almost positive—speaks with animation, gesturing with her hands. He laughs at something she says.

"He seems okay," I venture, even as guilt scrapes away at my insides. How does that old song go? *We used to be friends.* Do you ever get over that weird dichotomy of staring at someone who is now a stranger whose face you used to know as well as your own? I literally spent years kissing Chase Henry. We weren't ever like that with each other off set; the chemistry we manufactured on screen didn't exist in the real world. At all. But we were family. It's Chase's voice I hear in the back of my head sometimes, that slow drawl in gentle warning when I was about to do something stupid, like skinny dipping in the hotel pool on a dare: *Callie.* Just as I hear Eric's urging me on, the devil in his laugh.

The two of them are older, so they spent more time together off at bars I couldn't get into or my mother wouldn't allow me into. But the three of us were friends.

At least until I messed it up.

"Do you think we should go over there?" I ask.

"Jesus, no. Why? He hates us." Eric's body is practically vibrating with tension behind me. "Well, he hates me at least," he adds with that cocky laugh that he uses to pretend he doesn't care.

"We owe him an apology. I do, anyway. He never would have driven that night if I hadn't pushed him to. You know how careful he was," I say.

"He was an alcoholic no matter what, Callie," Eric says a little too sharply.

"Yeah, but I'm the one who almost got us all killed," I point out, trying not to feel hurt at how quickly he dismissed Chase as an alcoholic. I'm an addict. I will be one forever, though I'm clean now and plan to stay that way. I know now, better than ever, what Chase was going through then, although he hid it well. Too well.

"It's over now. Let's just leave the past in the past, or whatever," Eric says. He slides his hand down my arm to lock his fingers with mine. "Come on, let's just go. We'll find somewhere else to eat."

I twist around to face him. "What happened?"

"Nothing." His gaze remains firmly fixed at a point over my head.

"Eric."

"Nothing. Literally," he says flatly. He tugs gently, trying to pull me toward the door.

But I stand my ground and refuse to move. Something is wrong here. I'm missing something.

Eric makes an impatient noise. "Look, he cut off contact with me back then, and he was right to do it. I was dragging him down, and I was an asshole, okay? Everybody knows this."

"Okay, but things are different now, and you said he was one of your only real friends—"

Eric gives a bitter laugh. "Calista, I doubt he feels that way now, and even if he did, I don't deserve it."

I wait.

He shifts uneasily, letting go of my hand to fidget with the sunglasses hanging from the collar of his T-shirt. "There had to be a story about that night, what happened. How we ended up in the car."

I nodded. "A story to give the police." I'm sure Rawley had to make up something—along with whatever "favors" he had to trade in to keep Chase and possibly Eric from going to jail.

But Eric shakes his head. "Not just for the police."

Regret and shame are etched in the lines of his face, and I can't figure out why.

And then it clicks. Chase used to black out, easily, when he was drinking. He'd be moving around, talking and laughing just like normal, and have no memory of it in the morning. We were always having to fill him in on what happened the night before.

Oh, Eric. "What did you say to him?"

24

ERIC

The problem with making shitty decisions is that even when you think they're well in the past, they somehow manage to come back and take a chunk out of you, destroying your future.

"Callie," I begin, though I don't know how I'm going to finish. She will hate me for this. I hate me for it; though at the time, it felt more like survival than anything else.

"Are you ready? Your table is right this way," the hostess chirps at us, gesturing us forward, leather-bound menus in hand.

Neither of us move.

"What did you tell him?" Calista asks evenly. She's not going to let me off the hook without answering.

"That he was driving us to another party." That is, in fact, partially true. While I was trying to talk Calista down and get Chase to pull over, Chase had been rambling about finding another place to go, that it would make Calista feel better, without even knowing exactly what was wrong with her. If he'd known that, he wouldn't have bothered going anywhere. He would have just punched me.

"I said that he insisted on it." In my head, I can see it all over again: visiting Chase in the hospital and trying desperately to find a way to make everything go back to normal. Pretending that what I'd done that night hadn't mattered. That we would go on like nothing had happened. It was an impulse in the moment; I had no way of knowing that he wouldn't eventually talk to Calista and find out the truth. Though, if I'm being honest, I was fairly confident she wouldn't give him the details. She was—and is—private that way.

Calista's eyes go wide. "That's . . . you didn't tell him about what happened? Why I was upset and why I asked him to drive me—"

"Yeah," I say through clenched teeth. "I know, okay?"

"You let him think it was his fault?" she asks softly, sounding wounded on his behalf. "No wonder he fell apart."

I can't even respond. I just shake my head.

"Um, are we ready?" The hostess tries again.

"In a minute," Calista says to her. "I'm sorry. Go ahead and take someone else."

Her voice is chilly with politeness, and I steel myself for Calista to walk away. I deserve it.

Instead, she steps to the side, allowing another couple to reach the hostess, and waits, her arms folded carefully over her chest, favoring the right one a little in the way it's angled.

I exhale loudly in frustration, not with her but with myself, and follow her over. "I was . . . not making good choices," I say in a low voice. "I knew I'd messed up and lost you, and I knew what he would say if I told him what happened."

"He would have hit you," she says without an ounce of sympathy.

"Which I could have handled, but you know Chase. He wouldn't have ever spoken to me again." Loyalty. It's the primary operating system for Chase—like I said, a cowboy.

After a moment, she nods.

"Of course, he stopped talking to me anyway because he, unlike me, figured out that when your life is continually going to crap, your actions might have something to do with it rather than just shitty luck. He cut me loose, and his life got better. End of story." I draw in a breath. "Better that he think I was an asshole than a coward, okay?" It strips something away from me to admit it, but it's true.

"You put yourself ahead of him," she says.

"Yep, just like always." Because how can I deny it? That is certainly who I was, who I'm trying not to be anymore. Then I force a smile. "Now, if you're going to leave me here in a fit of moral outrage, then you'd better do it before the chick with the menus comes back and starts asking questions." It hurts like a fresh scalding burn to imagine her walking away, but I'm not stupid enough to pretend otherwise. Why the hell would she stick around with even more proof—that she probably didn't need—that I'm not the person she wants me to be?

Calista rocks back, as if startled. Then her expression softens.

My heart sinks. "No," I say, shaking my head. "Don't. Don't do that."

"Do what?" she asks, her eyes shiny with tears.

"I can see your brain clicking away," I accuse. "You're tallying up the missing mom and the asshole, absentee dad and the poor-little-rich-boy lonely childhood. Don't you dare fucking feel sorry for me."

She laughs with a sniffle, raising her hand to her nose. "Oh, fuck you, Eric. I'm allowed to feel sorry for you. When you love someone, you feel what hurts them. Plus, it's not like you're having any trouble feeling sorry for yourself."

"What's that supposed to mean?" I demand.

"Come on," she says, taking my hand and leading me deeper into the restaurant. Straight for Chase's table.

Fuck. "What are you doing?"

"We're going to apologize. Like I told you before, we both messed up that night."

"Calista—"

"Your dad isn't worth your time, he's a lost cause," she says over her shoulder. "But Chase? You screwed up with him, and instead of even trying to fix it, you just wrote him off because you were scared he wouldn't forgive you."

Her truth-filled words are an arrow to the soft spot I try very hard to keep hidden.

I wince. "Calista, I'm pretty sure he's not going to—"

She stops, turning to look at me. "Would you have done the same thing to me? I mean, if you hadn't needed me for *Fly Girl*?"

I want to lie and say it's different. But if I hadn't been forced to take the chance, and if I hadn't had the ability to twist her arm (through her mother) to guarantee some measure of success . . .

"It doesn't change how I feel about you," I say gruffly, avoiding her gaze. "I just didn't know—"

"I know," she says. "That's what makes it worse."

But when I dare to look at her again, she's not pissed; she's wiping away tears. "You would have just let it go. Let me go, no matter how you felt. No matter how *I* felt."

"Callie." I try to pull her closer.

"You're an idiot." She shakes her head and pulls me toward the table in the corner that Chase is occupying.

"No argument there," I mutter.

But for all her brave words, her fingers tremble in mine, and she hesitates before making the final approach.

I lean forward, her scent filling my nose. "He's not angry with you. I guarantee that. I don't know why he didn't answer your letter, but he doesn't blame you."

She nods. Then she takes a deep breath, straightens her shoulders, and keeps walking.

The girl with Chase—Amanda, I guess—sees us first. She pauses, her fork midway to her mouth, her eyebrows going up. "Chase," she says, jerking her chin in our direction.

Guess she's a fan.

Or he's told her about us.

The latter idea makes the overwhelmingly sweet, syrupy smell in here turn my stomach. God, is this going to be a scene? That's the last thing I need, a flare up of *Eric Stone, Spoiled Brat Wreaking*

Havoc, when I'm trying to be *Eric Stone*, *Producer*, instead. But hell if I'm backing away now and leaving Calista here on her own.

Chase twists in his chair, his face paling as he stands. He takes in Calista first, and then me behind her.

"Hey," Calista says hesitantly, waving with her free hand. "We saw you and thought we should say—"

She doesn't even get the full sentence out before Chase encloses her in one of those giant bear-hug things he does, lifting her off her feet. Her hand lets go of mine so she can hug him back.

For a second, I'm transported back to set, watching the two of them together. Smoldering at each other as Brody and Skye, enough to make me act out and do or say something stupid—like chucking a pencil at them—to ruin the take, even if I didn't at that point understand the true motivation behind my actions.

He sets her down gently, but doesn't let go of her. "Are you okay? How are you?" His hand belatedly leaps away from her arm as if fearing that her injury is still too recent.

She laughs, and a tiny ugly part of me is jealous. "I'm fine. It's okay, really."

"Good, I'm so glad," he says, shaking his head. "I really thought that it might—" He cuts himself off abruptly, swinging around to face the girl at the table.

"I'm sorry," he says to her quickly, that drawl that used to drop panties left and right around us surfacing. Then he turns to us again. "Calista, this is Amanda. Amanda, this is Calista." He hesitates and then adds, "And Eric."

Ouch. Guess I know where I stand now.

"We used to work together," Chase finishes.

"I'm aware," Amanda says, amused. "It's nice to meet you both." She waves but doesn't get up to shake our hands.

And Chase, as much as he's standing to speak to Calista, also appears to be protecting Amanda from anyone getting any closer.

Yeah, like I thought. Baggage. But justifiably so, given what I remember of her story, and as much as the cowboy, moral-code-of-honor shit used to get under my skin sometimes, it's legit with Chase. He's a good guy.

"I'm so happy you're doing all right," Chase says to Calista. "When I didn't hear back from you, I thought maybe—"

Calista holds up her hand. "Wait, what?"

He frowns. "I wrote you when you were in . . . Safe Haven." He lowers his voice in deference.

She shakes her head. "I wrote to *you* when I was in Safe Haven. You didn't get my letter?" she asks. "They said they would mail it for me."

He looks confused. "I was moving around a lot then, but no."

Suddenly, a possible answer is quite clear to me.

"Cal, did anyone censor your mail while you were there?" I ask.

"No. I mean, I don't think—"

"Did someone have to give a list of approved contacts?" I press. "People you were allowed to have contact with?"

Over her head, Chase meets my eyes, his mouth tightening. He gives a short nod. He knows what I'm thinking.

It clicks for Calista just a second later. "My mom . . . I guess."

Her mom, who already thought we were bad influences, who wouldn't have hesitated to limit Callie's contact with the outside world if it would strengthen her control over her daughter. Control that was, at that point, court-ordered.

"Shit," Calista mutters, much to the disapproval of the elderly couple at the nearest table.

"It's fine. You're here, you're doing all right. That's all that matters," Chase says soothingly.

I give in to the petty impulse of marking my territory and reach out to take her hand.

Chase notices, as does Amanda. Her eyebrows go up.

"Would you like to join us?" Amanda asks, and Chase looks back at her in surprise.

"I'm sure they have other places to—" he begins, and she shakes her head at him, a tiny motion that seems to deflate his objection.

"Amanda is right. We should be going," I say. There is no possible way this can end well, and the sooner we get out of here the better.

Callie's hand tightens on mine. "Just for a minute," she says to them. "We don't want to interfere."

Shit. Even after that not-awesome revelation about Lori, Callie's still going to make me go through with this. Fine, but it's only going to be that much worse and last that much longer if we have to abandon our seats and possibly our meals as well.

It takes only a few seconds for Chase, wearing an expression of patient resignation, to signal to the very-eager-to-please server, who hustles over two additional chairs. Amanda scoots her chair to the far side of the table to make room, and Calista drops neatly into the seat next to Chase—putting herself between us, which is probably smart. Then she takes my hand again, linking it with hers and resting them both on the table top, which is probably not smart.

"Please tell me you're not serious with this," he says to Calista, nodding at our hands.

I tense. "None of your business, Henry."

He ignores me. "It's a bad idea, Callie," he says, like I'm not even there.

"Chase," Amanda says, tapping him on the shoulder in warning.

I take a more direct approach. "Shut the fuck up, Henry."

"Both of you, stop," Calista snaps. "I'm an adult now, remember? Capable of making my own decisions."

Making her own mistakes. I can read it in Chase's expression even if he doesn't say it aloud. And you know what, he's probably right. But screw him anyway for thinking it.

Amanda clears her throat loudly. "So are you here in town for the holidays?" she asks, directing the question toward Calista. "I read somewhere that you were in college now. In the Midwest, I think?"

Calista nods. "I am. Or . . . I was. Things are little complicated right now. But I'm working on a web series with Eric at the moment." She turns to Chase. "Remember that book that I used to read and reread? *Fly Girl*? Eric bought the rights. I'm playing Evie, and he's producing it." The pride in her voice makes me want to cry.

Chase sits up straighter. "I thought you weren't acting anymore." He sounds suspicious, shooting a glance at me.

Calista hesitates. "I wasn't. But this was a project I couldn't pass up." Her voice is too cheerful, too much like her mother's in that moment. It's as much of a tell as Calista has for when she's lying.

Shit. I shift uneasily in my seat.

Chase is quiet for a long moment, and Amanda, who seems cool, tries to fill in the awkward gap. "That's so exciting! So are you—"

"Jesus Christ, Eric, are you making her do this?" he demands.

His words sting, even though they're not far from the truth. Or perhaps because they're not far from the truth as it was in the beginning, anyway. But hell if I'm going to show it. I force a smile. "Yeah, that's me, the puppet master."

"Eric," Calista says sharply in reprimand. Then she turns to Chase. "Nobody's making me do anything." But she sounds tired.

"She'd do anything for you, and you know it," Chase says to me. "And her mother will do anything for cash and another credit for Callie's filmography." That, I assume, is directed to Amanda, since the rest of us know all too well what Lori is capable of.

Calista winces.

Amanda notices and frowns. "Chase, I think maybe you should just let them—"

But Chase, as predicted, is way too far into honorable-cowboy mode. He pushes his chair back, turning more fully toward Calisa. "Callie, you don't understand. After the accident . . ." He shakes his head. "I screwed up. I know that. And I will be sorry for the rest of my life for whatever impulse drove me to pick up the keys that night."

Calista stiffens. "Chase, it wasn't like that. You were—"

"And I know you and Eric have been friends for a long time, but he's not a good influence," he says, barely even glancing in my direction, and Amanda makes an exasperated noise.

I snort, unable to stop myself, even as fury swells to a swirling mass in my chest. "So you're the only one allowed to change? The only one allowed to make up for past mistakes? How convenient."

Chase's gaze snaps to me. "If I thought for a second that it was genuine, and you truly cared about what was best for someone else—"

"You know what? Fuck you, Henry. You don't know me." I shove my chair and stand up. "And I'm not perfect, but you sure as hell aren't either."

But next to me, Calista stays seated, and my heart falls. She's going to stay. It's Katie all over again.

I take a deep breath against the pain in my chest. Fine. Whatever. Guess that solves all of her problems. Chase can give her a ride back home, then, too. And she can start work on Monday with my fucking dad. I start to turn away.

But then she speaks. "Do you know why we came over here?" she asks Chase quietly. Beneath the softness of her words is a hot molten layer of anger, and I stop.

"Callie, I—" his words cut off in a grunt as Amanda's elbow reaches his ribs.

"To apologize to you."

He rocks back, startled. "What, why?"

"That night, in the car, you were talking about another party, but that's not why we were in the car."

His eyebrows shoot up.

"We were in the car because I begged you to drive me home. I was drunk, and I didn't know or care how drunk you were. All I cared about was getting out of there. We could have died because of my hurt feelings."

Chase's mouth tightens, and he looks over at me.

Calista exhales loudly. "Yeah, it was because Eric hurt my feelings, but so what? Running away, forcing my friend with a drinking problem to drive when he was always careful not to? That was my selfish choice, me putting myself above everyone else. Including you. Eric was trying to stop us. That's why he was in the car."

Amanda glances at me, and I give a short nod. I tried. I really did. Short of lunging into the front seat and yanking at the wheel, there was nothing more that I could have done that night. Other than not creating the situation in the first place, but that required a little more foresight—and a hell of a lot more maturity—than I had at the time.

"But he lied, then," Chase says, after a moment, still processing what Calista is saying. "When I saw him in the hospital, he said it was my idea, that I was driving because I wanted to go to another party."

Here we go.

"That is what you said that night. But the truth is you would never have been in the car that night if it weren't for me . . . for us," Calista says, folding her arms over her chest carefully, in deference to her damaged arm. I step closer, resting my hand lightly on the top of her good shoulder, letting her know I'm still here.

"He let me believe I was responsible," Chase says slowly.

"Which was a chicken-shit thing to do," Calista says without hesitation. "Because he knew you'd blame him—even though I'm as much at fault as he is. And he didn't want to lose you as a friend. It was dumb—criminally stupid—to lie, but that's why we are here. To apologize."

"Are we ready to order?" The server, a tiny blond girl, steps up next to me, either unaware of the tension or not caring.

"He wants to apologize?" Chase rears back in his chair. "I haven't heard so much as a fucking sorry from him."

"I'll come back," the server squeaks, practically running in the opposite direction.

Swallowing a sigh, I turn my attention to my former friend, his face flushed with anger. The ridiculous stuff we used to get up to, back in those days when we didn't worry about anything other than having fun. It all feels like a thousand years ago.

"I am sorry," I say, the words coming out stiff, my jaw tight. This is pointless. Chase has, as I tried to tell Calista earlier, already made up his mind about me. But I'll do it, lay the worst parts of myself bare, if that's what she needs. And as much as it grates on me, Chase does deserve the explanation. "It was a shitty thing to do to you, to make you blame yourself, especially when we were all struggling. I was desperate and feeling shitty about myself, and I knew you'd be pissed if I told you the truth. I didn't want to lose you and Calista both, so I tried to push it back on you. It was stupid. Cruel, even. And I am sorry." My voice cracks, and I clear my throat. "But I am trying to be different, to be better."

Chase shakes his head with a sound of disgust. "Forget it. I don't want to hear it."

"Chase," Amanda says in surprise. "If we're talking about second chances . . ."

Calista pushes up and out of her chair. "You're a hypocrite," she says to Chase.

"Calista," he begins, rubbing the back of his neck.

"You were okay with apologizing and us forgiving you when you thought you were responsible, but when it's us—"

"It's not you," he says. "It's him. You're not seeing this clearly."

She's silent for a long moment, during which I start to wonder if he's convinced her and panic takes hold in me. "It's not, though," she says finally. "It's both of us. He's the one who told me not to come over here, that you wouldn't understand or be able to forgive *us*. But I was sure—*sure*—that you would because we were family once."

Chase flinches.

"He was right, I guess," Calista says, but then her smile goes tight. "But then again, so was I. Because only family treats family this badly."

Calista pushes past me to march away, her head held high, and I follow, stunned.

She took my side. She did it.

"We've elected to eat elsewhere," she says as we pass the server, who is hovering, watching greedily. This is definitely going to make it onto the gossip sites somewhere. "The company sucks here."

Calista is shaking her head and muttering to herself as she stalks through the restaurant to the sidewalk outside. Then she pauses and turns to me. "I am so sorry, Eric," she says. "I should never have tried to—"

I catch her chin in my fingers and tilt her mouth up to meet mine, cutting off her words with a fervent kiss, using my mouth and tongue to convey what I can't seem to say.

Her hands slide up to catch at my waist, pulling me closer. I back us up until we are against the wall of the café and far too close for public decency. There's a driving ache in me to feel her skin against mine, to bury myself inside her and just *be*.

"What was that for?" she asks breathlessly, when I finally pull away, my heart full to overflowing. It's a warm feeling I'm not used to.

"Thank you," I say. "For trying. For believing. In me."

She touches my cheek, running her thumb lightly over my mouth. "Of course," she says, her eyes shining with unshed tears again. But it's not pity this time, it's love. I can see the difference now.

Smiling at me mischievously, she slides to the side, out from under me. "So how strongly do you feel about food right now?" she asks, tugging on my hand to get me to follow her. As if I wouldn't. "Because I could definitely be convinced to order in." She winks at me.

As she turns to lead the way back to my car, the words that have been churning beneath the surface inside me finally break through. "I love you."

Granted, I'm saying them to her back, but I'm saying them.

She stops dead, her hand clutching tight around mine, and then slowly turns to face me, her expression uncertain, as if she's misheard me.

"I love you," I repeat, nodding in confirmation. It's easier to say it the second time, even with her facing me.

Calista closes the distance between us and locks her arms around my neck. "Let's go home."

25

CALISTA

The short drive home takes forever, but I do my best to entertain myself, my hand on Eric's knee and then traveling higher, stroking him through his jeans until the muscle at the back of his jaw is jumping.

He grabs my hand and puts it back on his knee firmly, with his hand on top to keep it in place.

"I would prefer that we not die before I can get us home and fuck you senseless," he says, his voice rough with strain.

His words send a shiver of anticipation through me, so I'm mostly good the rest of the way. Though honestly, can you truly expect me to keep my hands to myself at a red light? Especially when the heat in his gaze is enough to set me aflame. And if I can't touch him, all I want is to feel his hand stroking between my legs.

But no.

Once we're at his building, he pulls me through the lobby without a word, past the doorman—who greets us—and into the elevator. In the elevator, he locks his arm at the elbow, forcing us to keep our distance for that fifteen-second interval.

When the door pulls back, he charges down the hall so quickly, I'm practically tripping to keep up with his long legs.

Once the door to his place is open, I'm expecting him to yank me inside, slam the door shut and start tearing off my clothes. Eagerness makes my heart beat faster. That would not be a bad ending to an unexpected morning.

But instead, he closes the door after me and leans closer, bracing his hands on the door on either side of me.

The brush of his mouth is sweet and soft over mine, and the touch of his lips, so light it's barely detectable, only heightens the sensation, sending electric shocks zipping through my veins.

I moan.

He dips his head to kiss along my jaw, more of those whisper-soft kisses that make me feel small and delicate and valued.

Which is nice, but . . .

I clutch at his T-shirt, trying to pull him closer, but he won't move.

His mouth moves, warm and open, down my neck to my collarbone, and I scoot closer to him, trying to wrap my leg around his waist, but it's impossible without the door behind me or his help.

I make a sound of frustration.

"Callie," he says against my skin. "Just let me, okay?"

With a shudder, I lower my leg and take a step back against the door.

I'm rewarded for my acquiescence a moment later. His big, warm hand skates beneath the hem of my shirt—his shirt—and rests lightly on my stomach before curving to my side and sliding up to cup my breast through my bra. His thumb skims over my nipple, and I buck against him—or I would if he weren't keeping that distance between us.

Shaking with need, I'm not above begging. "Please. I just . . . want." I don't know how else to describe this feeling. It's more than lust or desire, both of which I've felt before. This is more like needing air. Something I must have. Immediately.

Before he can stop me, I'm tugging my shirt over my head, and he groans, closing his eyes.

I take advantage of the moment, reaching beneath his shirt to slide my hands over the smooth plane of his abdomen and then moving them higher, peeling him out of his shirt—which he allows, temporarily removing his hands from the door behind me before returning them.

Leaning forward, I bury my nose against his skin, taking in the scent of him, the soap we used together in the shower, the smell that is just him. I use my lips and my tongue to make my way across his chest, then I start to slide down his body.

And his hands come off the door to clutch at me, pulling me up against him.

"Callie, damnit, I'm trying to . . . make love to you." His cheeks flush adorably as he says it. I'm not sure if it's embarrassment or frustration. Or both.

"So do that," I say, panting. "But it doesn't have to be ceremonial. You love me, and I love you, so . . . fuck me senseless?"

He exhales sharply, nostrils flaring. "Yeah."

Tugging at my hand, he leads me to the bedroom. On the way, we shed the rest of our clothing, wrestling ourselves out of it. In following him and not watching where I'm going, I trip over one of his discarded shoes, and he catches me, scooping me up in his arms, bride-style. He grins at me, but it's this fierce, possessive expression—like a declaration of "mine"—and I love it.

In the bedroom, he sets me on the edge of the bed. Bitsy, on her pillow, regards me with suspicion before Eric picks her up, pillow and all, and carries her out of the room. I watch him go, the view of the muscles working in his backside more than enough to keep my attention.

After shutting Bitsy in his office, he returns to the bedroom, closing that door as well.

"She is going to be pissed about that later," he warns as he crawls up the bed to lie next to me.

"Too bad. My turn to have you to myself," I say.

He strokes my hair away from my heated face. "Hey, Callie."

"Hey."

I turn my head toward him, kissing him, enjoying the feel of his tongue moving over mine with us lying skin to skin and the anticipation slowly building.

The stubble on his jaw is slightly rough against my face, but the sensation just ties me even more tightly to the moment. His hand skims over my body from my collarbone, down my injured arm, to my hip. It feels light and worshipful, like he wants me to know he's here and appreciative but not demanding.

It is the easiest and most natural thing in the world to tug at his shoulder and let my legs fall open. He moves on top of me in answer, supporting his weight on his elbows.

The warmth of his body against mine takes my breath away. It's like curling up under a sun-drenched towel after getting out of the ocean on a windy day. But his erection pressed against the center of me—not pushing inside, not yet—is even hotter. I rock my hips against him, and his eyes close for a second as we slide together.

"Calista," he says, his jaw tight.

Then he opens his eyes, and the heat in his expression makes my chest ache. No one has ever looked at me like that before.

He lowers his head to press open-mouthed kisses across my chest and down my breasts, suckling one nipple and then the other until I'm writhing under him, trying to press even closer.

As he slides down past my ribs to my stomach, I smooth my hands over his hair, his neck and shoulders, desperately touching wherever I can reach, enjoying the feeling of his muscles moving beneath his skin but always wanting more.

He continues to work his way down my body, and when his mouth closes over me, I gasp, my legs clutching together.

He looks up at me with a wicked grin and then scoots down farther to settle in, his shoulders nudging beneath my legs and his hands gripping the inside of my thighs to keep them apart, to make room for him.

His tongue flicks lightly against my clit in a series of teasing touches, and my fingers tangle in his curls. I'm trying hard not to tug at him or press him down, just to make him hold still where I need him to be, and . . . oh, God.

My hips lurch up toward him, and he gives a soft, distinctly smug-sounding laugh against me. But the vibrations from the noise spiral through me, and I'm lost for a second.

"Eric."

"Hmmm?" he asks, just before he delves down, his tongue just barely penetrating my entrance.

Swallowing a gasp, I squeeze my eyes shut to keep from losing focus, my grasp on the words I want to say. "Not like this. Please. I want you inside me."

"I am."

I can feel the first clutches of an orgasm looming. I'm close. And impatience for what I want makes me a little more grabby. This time, I do lock my fingers into his smooth curls and pull—probably not as gently as I should—until he looks up at me.

"I want you to come inside me," I say, paraphrasing the words he used yesterday, the ones that sent heat coursing through me.

That catches his attention, and then, suddenly, he's moving back up my body.

His hands brace on either side of my head, and he rubs against me, his cock hard and ready, and I lock my legs around his waist.

Groaning, he reaches between us to position himself, and the tip of him fits snugly against my opening. I arch my hips in welcome.

His gaze flicks to mine, in question, and I nod. I'm sure.

"So wet for me," he says with a groan as he pushes in. "And warm. I think . . . know why the rest of you is always so cold."

My laugh emerges rather strangled-sounding.

He bites his lower lip in concentration as he thrusts and withdraws, carefully working his way inside me, until I prop myself up to kiss him, taking his lower lip between my teeth gently instead.

Something about that action makes him lose a little control, and he's pushing in harder now, his gaze fierce on mine. He pauses once he's fully inside me, bare, with nothing between us, and lifts a hand to caress my cheek.

"I love you," he says, sounding a little amazed.

"I love you, too." The words are barely out of my mouth before he's thrusting into me, fast and hard.

Yes.

I push back against him in counterpoint, just as fast, trying to keep up with the escalation, but I'm tipping over the edge before I can stop myself. The spasms bubble up and around him, clutching at him.

I dig my fingers into his shoulders, grounding myself against that sensation of falling, and a moment later, his whole body shudders, and I can feel him pulsing inside me.

He collapses on top of me.

"Am I crushing you?" he asks, out of breath.

"Not yet."

He shifts upward as if to pull away.

"Not yet," I say, wrapping my arms around his neck.

I want this moment to last forever.

But it doesn't, of course. Eventually, once he's recovered enough, he pulls away, leaving me feeling empty and cold. He leaves the room, and the water runs in the bathroom a few seconds later. Then he returns with a wet washcloth in one hand and his cell phone in the other.

I raise my eyebrows.

He grins at me, waving his phone at me before approaching to put it on the nightstand. "I'm going to order pizza. Does that sound okay?"

In response, my stomach gives an embarrassingly loud gurgle, all the louder and more humiliating for being naked on his bed when it happens. I clap a hand over the offending region, my face going hot. "Um, yeah, it sounds great." I sit up and grab for the sheet at the bottom of the bed.

He laughs. "Wait," he says, settling next to me.

Before I realize what he's up to, he's already dabbing the warm washcloth between my thighs, cleaning up the dampness he left behind.

If my face was hot before, it's downright radioactive at the moment. I clear my throat and reach to take the washcloth from him. "I can do that." This feels more intimate, somehow, than what we just did.

He nudges my hand away. "I've got it."

It occurs to me that, although he would deny it until the sun collapsed in on itself, Eric might have a secret nurturing side. No one has ever looked out for me like he has, even before this change in our relationship. And for as much as he rolls his eyes about taking care of Bitsy, it's clearly a fond exasperation. He cares for her without complaint even though he could have easily given her up to a shelter when his mom flaked out on her. And Bitsy adores him.

My guess is he's putting forth the effort that he wishes someone would make or would have made for him, and it breaks my heart to think about that.

I blink my eyes quickly to keep tears from spilling over. Unfortunately, not quite fast enough.

When he looks up at me, he freezes. "What's wrong? Is it too hot?"

"Nothing. It's just nice." I touch his bristly jaw. "*You're* nice."

He mock-scowls. "Don't tell anyone," he says, pointing at me. "You'll ruin my reputation."

When he returns the washcloth to the bathroom, he comes back with my shirt, his boxer-briefs, and Bitsy at his heels. After a brief argument about green peppers—I am pro, as it's at least something vaguely healthy and green, and he is con, for the same reasons—our Thanksgiving meal is ordered and on its way. The start of a new tradition.

While we wait, we curl up beneath the sheets, talking about everything and nothing in particular, his arm tucked underneath my pillow and his body curved protectively behind mine. Bitsy is at the bottom of the bed with her back to us, like we don't exist—he was right, she is pissed.

"Listen, I want to talk to you about something," I say in a moment of comfortable quiet.

Eric tenses, and I turn over so I can see him. He's watching me warily.

"I'm going to talk to my mom tomorrow. I'm finishing what I started. What's important to me," I say.

"Okay," he says slowly.

"*Fly Girl* is important to me. I'm proud to be a part of that project," I say. I hesitate and take a deep breath, studying the stitching in the hem of the sheet covering us. "And I want to finish my semester at Blake. It's only another month or so, and I don't want to lose those credits. I can have them transferred to somewhere around here if I want." I'm offering this last part in the most casual tone possible. I don't want him to feel like I'm suddenly rearranging my life because of him. But I also would like to continue . . . whatever this is. I'm not ready to let it—or him—go.

"I'm sure my mom and Wade are going to need some kind of financial help, so I'll probably have to work and go to school. It isn't exactly what I wanted, but it'll be a lot easier to do that here rather than Indiana."

I'm not exactly expecting a shout of joy from him or a declaration of eternal love, but something indicating that he's amenable to the idea of my remaining in close proximity would be nice. But there's nothing but silence.

When I dare to glance up at him, his expression is troubled. My heart feels like a leaden weight in my chest. I've overstepped. Now he's going to freak out and back away as fast as possible.

"What's wrong?" I manage to ask.

He doesn't answer right away. "I hope you don't think . . ." He shakes his head, seemingly struggling with words. If so, it's for the first time since I've known him. Possibly for the first time in his entire existence. "I want you to stay . . ."

"But . . ." I prompt him, my voice dull, trying to ignore the rising feeling of nausea.

His eyes widen. "No, not 'but' like that. I want you to stay. Hiding away in Whereverthefuck, Indiana is a total waste," he says, a faint hint of his familiar sneer returning. "But I . . ." He swallows hard. "I hope you don't think I was manipulating you to make that happen. With this." He waves a hand in a vague gesture over the bed and our bodies beneath the covers.

He pulls his arm out from under me, and I immediately feel the loss of that closeness. "I wouldn't do that to you," he says, as though someone is accusing him of it.

I stare at him. And it takes me a second to understand that that's exactly what he's expecting, whether from me or someone else.

"Right," I say slowly. "Because, of course. You plotted for seven years in a carefully crafted scheme to make me fall in love with you at this exact moment, never mind that it isn't exactly the best moment for either of us, so you could manipulate me into keeping a job I want to keep."

He makes a face at me and yanks the pillow out from behind me, only to bop me on the head with it.

"Hey," I protest with a laugh, grabbing the pillow from him and tucking it under my head.

"You know what I mean," he says. "Someone will think that. *Lori* will think that," he adds darkly.

I sigh. There's not much I can say to that because he's right. "Yeah, well, Lori also thinks that gluten is evil. Not, like, just bad for you, but actually evil. Sent to test our will and make us fat."

He snorts.

"Besides, as long as we know the truth, nothing else matters, right?"

"Right." But he sounds less than sure.

However, before I can try to convince him further, the buzzer sounds, indicating that our pizza has arrived.

Grinning, Eric rolls over to his side, holding his fist toward me. "Rock Paper Scissors?"

"Um, I have no money, remember?" A fact that makes me squirm with discomfort. If Eric is worried that someone might think he manipulated me into staying, I'm worried that same anonymous someone might accuse me of staying for the wrong reasons.

He shakes his head. "Yeah, no. I mean, who has to put on pants to answer the door?"

I pretend to frown at him. "You put pants on to open the door?"

He reaches over to tickle me, and I shriek. "I guess that means it's me," he says.

With a faux-grumble, he shoves back the covers to stand and tug on a pair of jeans.

"Pants are overrated," I call after him as he steps out into the hall and heads toward the front door. Though he does look great in them, especially with the top button undone and no shirt. Hell, I'd take that as a tip, if I were the delivery person.

"Good to know. Maybe I'll let you talk me out of mine again later, sweetheart."

I sit up. "Please. You should be so lucky," I respond, raising my voice so he can hear me.

He doesn't answer right away, and I think he might not at all. Then he says, so quietly I'm not even sure I'm supposed to hear it: "Yeah, I think I am."

Squeezing my arms over my chest, as if that will somehow capture and contain his words inside me, I flop back onto the pillows, with a smile so wide it feels like it might crack my face. Or my heart.

26 ERIC

It is, without a doubt, the best Thanksgiving I've ever had. Actually, probably the best holiday in general. There was once a pretty good Arbor Day party that I threw myself—that used to be the high-water mark. But not anymore.

Calista and I spend most of the day moving between the bedroom and the couch, eating pizza and then Chinese, taking Bitsy out, watching old movies, and touching each other whenever possible.

I didn't know it could be like this. This much fun. Simple stuff makes her happy, like giving her the green peppers off my pieces or remembering to mute the kitchen scene in *Jurassic Park* because the raptors scare the shit out of her. (She watches with her hand half-covering her face and her cold toes curled up and tense under my leg, even though I know for a fact she's seen the movie at least twice before.)

Friday morning comes too early, but at least it's accompanied by Calista rolling over in my bed to bury her face against my shoulder when the alarm goes off.

I slap at my phone, fumbling for the snooze, while Calista manages to drag herself to the shower.

"Come back," I mumble, blinking at her blearily.

"Come join me," she says, her voice raspy with sleep.

I groan. "I can't. If I do, we'll never get out of here on time. I can't be late. I'm the director." I still kind of love hearing that out loud.

She grins at me. "Yeah, you are. And the producer," she adds. "So you really can't be late." But then she pulls her shirt over her head and tosses it at me, hitting me in the face, before strolling off toward the bathroom. Naked. I can just see the curve of her breast as she rounds the corner.

Okay, I'm up.

Maybe we can be a little late. I throw back the covers to follow her.

My phone buzzes on the nightstand. I barely glance at it as I reach for it, assuming it's the snooze going off. But when I look at the screen, it's a call coming in. And from a number I recognize.

Generally speaking, a call from your bank first thing in the morning isn't a good sign.

Dread curdles in my stomach.

The shower turns on in the bathroom, the spray sounding like rain or one of those relaxation apps, as I answer. "Hello?"

The woman on the other end introduces herself as my personal banker, something I didn't even know I had. And then she proceeds, in a very understanding but firm tone, to ruin my day, and quite possibly my life.

Ten minutes later, Calista emerges from the shower, towel wrapped around her body and her hair dripping down her shoulders. "Hey," she says. "I thought you were going to . . . what's wrong?" She stops at the foot of the bed.

Shaking my head, I stare down at the numbers I scrawled on the back of a receipt I found in my nightstand, trying to make them make sense, with my phone pressed to my ear, ringing endlessly on the other end.

"Eric?"

I scrub my hand over my face, my foot jittering against the floor. "Payroll didn't go through this morning. Insufficient funds."

Her mouth drops open. "What?"

"I don't know. There should have been more than enough. I covered it with my personal account for now, but that just about emptied out everything I have left. And now my fucking accountant isn't answering." I shout the last part into my phone, which stubbornly refuses to connect with a live person on the other end.

"It's the day after Thanksgiving," she points out. "He's probably on vacation with his family."

"I don't pay him to be on vacation," I snap.

I sense more than see Calista's recoil.

"Sorry," I mutter. A little too much of Rawley in me in that moment. "Actually, it sounds like I may not be paying him at all." I smile tightly.

"It's probably just a weird little glitch is all," Callie says, moving to my side. "Routing number got mixed up or an invoice hit twice or something."

An invoice would have to hit a lot more than twice, but I want to believe it's possible.

I look up at her for the first time. "Does that happen?"

Callie shrugs. "It can." She hesitates. "Do you want me to look at it? I might be able to see what's wrong, if it's something simple. Your accountant will have answers, I'm sure, but if you don't want to wait—"

"Yes. God, yes." I hand her the receipt and then lead the way to my desk, pulling out my file folders of invoices and statements and random sheets of paper that seemed important.

Calista looks at the pile of stuff and then me with a sigh.

I hold up my hands. "I know, I know. That's why I hired someone, okay?"

"I shouldn't judge. I didn't even have my own freaking account until this week." She shakes her head. "How about access to an online statement? Someplace I can see all the transactions."

Grabbing my iPad, I pull up the site, log in, and hand it over to her. Tucking her towel more securely around her—I love this girl, she's willing to help me before doing anything else—she settles in my desk chair. She clicks through the pages, looking, her forehead crinkling as she studies the screen.

"Anything?" I ask.

"Eric."

"What?"

"You're looming," she says, gently but pointedly, her nose almost brushing mine as she turns to face me.

She's right; I'm literally hanging over her shoulder even though I have no clue what I'm looking for.

I straighten up and step back, holding my hands up in surrender. "Sorry."

"Just give me a couple minutes. Go shower, get dressed. We still have to go to work," she reminds me.

Like I'm going to be able to concentrate on anything else. If we can't figure this out, then next week, I won't have anything to . . .

I shut that thought down swiftly. It'll get figured out. It has to.

I'm showered, dressed and back in the room in record time, so she's still frowning over the screen when I get back. But now she has a pen in her other hand, writing down numbers on a piece of paper as she scrolls through with her thumb.

"What is it?"

She hesitates, biting her lip before looking up at me.

"Calista."

She makes an exasperated noise. "Look, I don't know for sure," she says. "I'm just taking classes in this, and I'm not even close to an expert."

"But?"

She sighs. "But this seems . . . odd to me."

"What does?"

"It looks like you have a bunch of receivables being paid twice but to different companies. Actually, all of the doubles go to the same company, and I can't figure out why," she says with a frown.

I force myself to take a slow breath in and then out. This is why I hired an accountant. To have an expert keeping track of everything. But now I'm wondering if that was a mistake and I should have kept my hand in it more. "I don't understand. Can you show me?"

She points to the screen at one transaction and then another one that posted a day later. "See? The exact same amount, but two different companies?"

She shivers and it breaks into my concentration, making me aware that she's still sitting here, not dressed, in the air conditioning with her hair dripping wet.

I turn the chair away from the desk. "Callie, you're freezing. You should go get dressed."

She scowls at me and swivels back. "It's not just that one time either. But not every time either. It's . . . random. But about every third payment or charge for say, camera rental, or whatever, you have an identical one to this company." I lean over to see, and she slides her finger up the screen, showing me. "It's the exact same amount, to the penny. And that's weird. I think."

"What's D&G Inc.?" I ask.

"I have no idea. I Googled them. Nothing came up. Your accountant will probably know."

"My accountant who is either a criminal or criminally negligent," I say flatly. And I'm the idiot who hired him.

"Eric." She twists in the chair, putting her hand over mine on the back of the chair. "I don't know that I would go that far." She hesitates. "Not until you talk to him, at least. But I would definitely talk to him."

"And say what? Are you stealing from me?"

Her silence holds a beat too long.

"Are you serious?"

"The only reason I can think of for there to be charges of the exact same amount is so you might not notice, if you weren't paying close attention," she says reluctantly. "And it would have to be someone who knows what your receivables are supposed to be . . ."

I grit my teeth. Of course this is happening. Why did I think I could do this again?

"Was he recommended to you by someone?" she asks.

"No, not exactly," I say. "My dad used to use his firm . . ." And once again, ego might be sharpening its teeth to bite me in the ass. I was trying to prove that I was good enough, to be playing on the same level in all aspects, but instead I was following blindly, possibly to the point of using someone who had been fired for a reason.

I turn away from her, struggling with the urge to slam my fist into the door. "Goddamnit."

"You can't do anything about it right now," she says gently. "And it's still costing you to have all of us for today, even if we're not working."

All of us. Including Calista, who needs the paycheck. Unless she wants to take that job with my dad.

My anger cools immediately and hardens into resolve, and I turn to face her. "I promise you, I will get this sorted out. I'm not going to fucking flake out on you. Not on this. Not like this."

Calista smiles at me, and there's such faith in that expression that it makes me dizzy with my own unworthiness of it. "I know," she says. "It's okay." She stands and starts for the door. "But we should get going."

As she passes me, I wrap my arm around her shoulders, pulling her against me. I breathe in her scent, which is even stronger with her hair wet, and press my lips against her cool temple. Her feet slide between mine and her arms go around my waist, holding me tightly in return. I could stay like this forever.

"Thank you," I say against her skin.

"For what?" she murmurs.

I don't know how to respond because there are too many answers. For helping me. For not seeing me as a total fuck up. For believing in me even when I don't deserve it. For forgiving me when I've made unforgivable mistakes. "For being you."

She leans back to meet my gaze, and the smile breaking across her face is something to behold. All light and joy. "You're welcome," she says.

And I wonder if it's the first time anyone has expressed that to her, gratefulness for who she is. Not what she looks like or what she can do, but the complete package of her intelligence, her caring, her willingness to love the unlovable.

Judging by her reaction, I think it might be.

That makes me want to spend the rest of my life showing her that gratitude, for how much better my life is with her in it.

"I love you," I say gruffly, but the words are hopelessly inadequate for the moment, for the feelings surging inside me.

"I love you, too," she says, her eyes growing damp. She reaches up and skims my mouth and then the dimple in my chin with her fingertip. "But you have to stop looking at me that way," she says, her voice dropping into husky notes. "Or we're really going to be late."

"Fuck it," I say, sliding my hand inside her towel to touch the soft smooth skin of her waist. "The perks of being the boss. Besides, I can be quick." I duck my head to bite gently at the soft skin beneath her jaw.

She laughs shakily, sliding her hands into my hair. "Not sure that's something you want to brag about."

Pulling back, I grin at her and tug her towel free, letting it drop to the floor. "No worries, sweetheart. I can make you quick, too."

27

CALISTA

Never let it be said that Eric doesn't keep a promise.

"Okay over there?" he asks with a wink as we hurry out of the elevator and down the hall toward the condo where we're shooting. Rather, as we try to hurry. I'm floating in a languid fog that is, well, kind of awesome.

"I am great." I sound triumphant. Which, quite frankly, isn't far from the truth.

He snorts. "Keep saying it that way and everyone is going to know exactly why we're late."

I shove his arm. "Yeah. I don't care."

Reaching out, he wraps his arm around my shoulders and tucks me against his side.

I know he's still worried about the money, what his accountant has been up to. But we're together, and in this moment, I'm confident that we can figure out anything that comes at us.

I am the happiest I've ever been.

That sentiment lasts all the way until we round the corner and the condo is within sight. The door is open, and the crew is moving in and out with lights and equipment. And my mother is standing off to the side, waiting, with a tense, worried expression.

The warm glow of my mood snaps, shatters, like glass turned brittle with the cold.

Eric slows, his arm tightening around me.

"She's here. Maybe that means she's willing to let it go," he says to me.

Maybe. But as soon as she catches sight of us, the concern vanishes, replaced by a murderous glare that, if it had physical form, would skewer Eric, pinning him to the wall. "I don't think so."

She starts toward us.

"Do you want me to stay?" Eric asks quietly before she reaches us.

"No," I say, even though my stomach aches at the coming confrontation. "I need to talk to her."

"Okay," he says, rubbing his thumb lightly over my shoulder before releasing me.

"Eric," my mom says in greeting once she reaches us. But her frosty tone would ice over a heated swimming pool.

"Lori," he says in a bland neutral that still somehow manages to convey his complete and utter disdain.

I hold my breath for a second, afraid they're both going to just throw down.

But instead, Eric turns to me. "I'll see you in a few minutes," he says, and it's exactly the promise I need to hear to ease some of my tension.

He touches my cheek, and then, with a devil-may-care smile, he leans down to kiss me. Gentle, soft, and over quickly, but an act of rebellion all the same.

When he pulls away, he nods at my mom. "Lori." And then he strolls past, hands stuffed in the pockets of his jeans, behaving for all the world like the playboy asshole he is rumored to be.

I swallow a sigh. Of course he couldn't resist.

My mother watches him go, grimacing like she's trying to swallow back bile.

"Are you okay?" she asks as soon as he's out of earshot.

I have to resist the urge to roll my eyes. "Yes, I'm fine."

She's quiet for a moment, then says, "For now, I suppose."

And in spite of myself, in spite of the happy glow I just had, her dire tone sends a foreboding chill through me.

I shake my head, dismissing her words and the idea. Lori is just being Lori. Sulking because she's not getting her way.

"Come on, let's go," she says, linking an arm through my elbow and pulling me toward the condo.

"I tried to call yesterday," I say. "No one picked up." Eric wasn't thrilled, but I had to do it. I just kept picturing Zinn picking at her food and Poppy desperately trying to keep up a conversation at the table. (While Dahlia sang quietly to herself, of course.) The guilt was eating me alive and would have ruined the rest of our day together. But evidently my family didn't feel the same way as no one picked up the house phone and my mom's cell went straight to voicemail.

"Mmm-hmm," is all she says as we cross the threshold and head to the bedroom, where the dressing room is set up for today since we're shooting in the living room.

Josie is already waiting for me, her brush in hand and her makeup case open, in front of a mirror leaning against the wall. But it's Zinn who catches my attention.

My sister is folded up in the corner of the room on a metal stool, studying pages in her hand. Sides, if I had to guess, for her callback. The goose egg on the side of her head looks even larger today, but that might be just because of the shocking shades of purple and green all around it.

"Oh, my God, Zinn." I pull away from my mom to hurry over to her. "This looks way worse."

"It's fine." She squints up at me. "Just hurts when I touch it. And I have a headache."

I turn to my mother. "Did you take her back to the doctor?"

Lori waves my words away. "He just said to keep an eye on her and let her rest."

"So why is she here?" I demand.

"Calista," Lori says sharply. "She's here, I'm watching her. I'm her mother, not you."

Maybe if you acted like it . . .

But I swallow the words for the sake of keeping our tentative peace.

"Besides," Lori says. "It's not like I could leave her at home alone."

I want to suggest that Wade could have stayed home with her instead of chauffeuring my mom everywhere, but thinking through that scenario—Wade parked in front of ESPN downstairs—it's probably better that Zinnia is here.

"And this is a good learning opportunity for Zinnia," my mother says. "A chance to see what happens when you don't listen to your manager." She looks around the dressing room with a sniff of disdain. Mainly, I suspect, because it's not actually a full-on dressing room, just a corner of the room shielded with screens for privacy. At the moment, one of the screens is tilting at a drunken angle, possibly damaged in the move from one location to another.

"Mom," I say in warning. But at least it sounds like she's a step closer to accepting my rejection of Rawley's offer. I want to feel relieved, but I can't shake the sensation that I'm still tiptoeing across a minefield.

"Sorry, Josie. I'll be ready in a second." I touch Zinn's shoulder reassuringly, though she doesn't look up, and then I hurry behind the screens to change into Evie's wardrobe for the day. Just jeans and a scoop neck T-shirt, both hanging over the top of the drunken screen.

I pull them down, and the screen topples over, clattering as it hits the floor.

"Shit." I stick my head out. "Everyone okay?"

Josie, who has stepped back and pulled her makeup case out of the way, nods.

Lori shakes her head in disgust. "If you were a regular on *Triple Threat*, this wouldn't be an issue."

"I told you, I'm not agreeing to that," I say quietly, disappearing behind the remaining screens to get dressed. She's probably only here to try and talk me into changing my mind.

"And why not? You have something against steady work?" she asks, louder than she should, as if she's expecting anyone within hearing range to weigh in. But beneath her words, I sense the challenge. If I object, I look like the spoiled child she's making me out to be. If I mention Eric's name, I'm a pathetic, lovestruck teenager all over again. She wants me to cave.

I square my shoulders. *Boundaries. Gotta have them,* Bonnie's voice sounds in my head.

"First, it was a recurring role he offered, not a series regular, which you already know," I say calmly. Once again, my mother's vision of the future is outpacing reality. "And second, because I am not doing it." End of story.

My mom is quiet just long enough to give me the hope that maybe, just maybe, this conversation is over.

"Did I ever tell you that I auditioned for Rawley back in the day?" my mom asks, her voice taking on that wistful, dreamy tone that's threaded through every one of her early-nineties-Hollywood memories.

"Yes." It's one of her favorite stories. "During his teen-soap-opera phase." I step out from behind the screens, and Josie sets to work on my hair in front of the mirror. "You made it to the second-to-last round for Shannon, the new-girl-from-Iowa lead, but then you ended up as Skateboarder's Girlfriend #3."

"And Drunk Girl #1," Lori adds swiftly. "Later that same season without even having to audition. Then I was up for the part of Layla, the new girl in school. Right before I learned I was pregnant with you. I never got another role on one of his shows again."

The words hang in the air like an accusation, and I grit my teeth.

Josie makes an uncomfortable noise and fusses with her brushes.

Leave it to my mother to air our dirty laundry in public when it suits her. She would have been mortified if I did it. "Mom, can we talk about this later? Please?"

"All I'm saying, Calista," she says with exasperation, "is that you need to think about what you're doing. One wrong decision can ruin your life."

It's hard not to flinch at that.

She steps closer. "Don't let a man who pretends to care about you take everything from you," she says in a hard voice. "It happened to me, I don't want to see it happen to you. Eric Stone doesn't give a shit about you except what you can do for him. He'll use you, and then he'll throw you away, just like before."

I should never have told my mother what happened the night of the accident. Heat crawls in a slow burn up my neck and into my face. "Josie, I'm sorry, can you give us a second?"

Josie nods hastily, her ornate earrings jangling. In our shared reflection in the mirror, her cheeks are almost as pink as mine. "Sure. I'll be . . . out there." She gestures awkwardly toward the hall. "Just yell for me."

But before she vanishes from the mirror, she gives me a sympathetic look and squeezes my shoulder. My mother's abrasive moments on set are legend, but this one is a new low.

I take a deep breath and turn to face my mother, who simply raises her eyebrow, as if daring me to challenge what she's said. "I've made a decision. I'm not working for Rawley Stone."

She opens her mouth.

"I'm not," I say before she can interrupt. "And that's my choice, not Eric's. And not yours."

"Of course you say that now," she says gently. "He's muddled your thinking with sex."

"Mom," I say sharply, with a glance toward Zinn, my *fourteen-year-old* sister, who is listening avidly.

"My baby, listen to me." Lori steps in front of me, cupping my face in her cool hands. "I know you probably think you love him. You've thought that since you were sixteen. But he's trouble. Believe me. He wants you right now because you're new, you're different, and he needs you to capitalize on your reputation." She smooths my partially-styled hair away from my face, which will surely piss off Josie when she returns. "You were *Skye Danvers*," she says with awe in her voice that seems weirdly detached, like she's talking about someone else besides me.

"But in six months, once the novelty has worn off, once this project has bottomed out and he's bored, he'll be moving on to something else, to someone else. He had a fiancée just a few days ago, didn't he?"

Those words strike my lingering concerns with unerring accuracy, blowing them up and sending slivers of fear in every direction. "He loves me," I snap.

She cocks her head to one side with a pitying look. "I'm sure that's what he says now. But Eric Stone doesn't need the money or this crappy project." Her mouth purses in distaste. "He's playing. That's all."

Except he's not. I've heard the excitement and the passion in his voice when he talks about *Fly Girl*. It's the same way I feel about the project. Hell, he just emptied out his own personal bank account to make payroll. Which, okay, is maybe not a great sign in terms of money management, but it's not his fault his accountant is (possibly) cheating him.

"You don't know him," I say, pulling away from her.

"Oh, sweetie. I've known plenty like him," she says.

"Like my dad?" I demand. "Just because he took off doesn't mean that Eric will do the same thing. The situations aren't even remotely—"

"It doesn't mean that he won't, either," she points out. "What I'm saying is that work, taking care of yourself, that's what will keep you safe."

The irony of *her* saying this to *me* makes me want to scream. "Until I'm too old or too fat or 'not what they're looking for' too many times," I say, my ire rising. "I told you, I don't want to do this anymore, the relentless auditioning and dieting and rejection. Always feeling like I'm running on a wheel and I have to keep up or be thrown off. I have a plan." The time away with Eric allowed me to think, to come up with a solution that will work for all of us. Well, not Lori, not entirely. But she'll have to live with it. "I'm going to finish this project, and I'll share the money, whatever you need to keep the house, but I want to get my degree and—"

Her laugh has a desperate quality to it.

"What?" I ask.

"My darling girl," she says. "Do you think they foreclose on houses for missing a payment or two? The money from this," she waves her hand around to indicate *Fly Girl,* "*adventure* isn't going to save us. At best, it holds everyone off for another month or two. That's all. And if you want your degree, how exactly do you think you're going to pay for it?"

I lift my chin. "There are student loans, and I can take small acting jobs if I transfer back to California—"

"Um, Calista?" It's Josie at the door, fidgeting anxiously with a hairbrush in her hands.

"I'm so sorry, Josie, I just need one more minute with my mother."

"Okay, but it's just there's a delivery for you, and the guy needs you to sign . . ."

I watch, flummoxed, as she steps back and a flushed and sweaty guy in a delivery uniform rushes past her into the room and presents me with an enormous vase of pale pink roses mixed with baby's breath.

I have no idea what this is about. Eric is not exactly the send-roses type of guy. Which is a good thing because I hate roses as a romantic gesture. They're so easy, no forethought or knowledge required. If there's a woman involved, send roses. (The guy from rehab sent me roses once.)

The delivery guy holds out a clipboard and a pen for me. My mom steps up and takes the vase so I can sign.

I scrawl my signature across the bottom, but before I have a chance to look at the sender's information, assuming there is any on the form, he pulls the clipboard away and hustles out the door.

"Oh, look, a card," my mom crows, pulling it free from the pink buds without hesitation. "'Congratulations, Calista! Looking forward to a most-productive future together. Rawley.'"

She holds it up so I can see, and even from here, Rawley's name—in big, block letters—is plainly visible.

Sickness spirals through me until I feel like I might actually throw up. "What did you do?"

"Exactly what I'm supposed to do, as your mother and your manager," she says briskly. "I'm protecting you from yourself."

28

ERIC

The problem with working low budget is that you don't have money for the niceties that normally come along, unquestioned, with higher-end productions.

Like security. To keep random people from just walking in.

I'm talking with Dave, one of our lighting techs, when I see the delivery guy come in with flowers—a disgusting shade of pink—and assume at first that it's something our set decorator, Kelly, has approved for a scene. But when the guy disappears down the hall and reappears a few seconds later without them, it triggers an alarm in the back of my head.

The only thing down that hall is the dressing room, where Calista is.

"Can I help you?" I ask, stepping in front of him.

"Just dropping off some flowers, man," he says with a grin. "Are you the director?"

"Yeah."

"Then this is for you." He pulls a shoebox-sized package, wrapped in a bright silvery paper, from his messenger bag and holds it out to me.

"From who?" I ask, refusing to take it.

"Come on, man." He waves the package at me.

"Hell no," I snap. "And get off my set."

He makes an impatient noise and steps closer to me. "Chill, bro. It's from one of those production companies downtown."

Production companies . . . my father has an office downtown.

With a clenched feeling in my stomach, I snatch the package from his hands.

"Hey, can you sign for—"

"No, leave."

With a mournful sigh, he turns away, muttering about a lack of tip.

I tear off the silver wrapping, which is perfect, with razor-sharp edges. An assistant's work for sure. I recognize it from every birthday present I've ever received from my dad.

I inch the box lid off cautiously, as if there's a good possibility a rattlesnake is going to leap out and bite me.

In the end it is both more innocuous and more venomous than that.

Beneath several layers of tissue paper, I find a red baseball cap with the RSP logo embroidered on the front. A card lies on top, blank except for one word, "Welcome!" in my father's handwriting.

It takes me only a second to put the pieces together. My father. Callie. This is a declaration of victory, as clearly as if he'd just knocked over the queen on my side of the chessboard.

I charge down the hallway to the dressing room, where Callie is staring at her mother in abject horror, while Lori beams at the vase of pink roses.

"What the hell is this?" I rip the baseball cap out of the box and hold it up. "My father is congratulating me? What did you do, Lori?"

"Oh, my God," Calista whispers, her face paling. "Eric, I had no idea—"

"She didn't," Lori affirms smoothly. "I took care of it yesterday."

"Yesterday was Thanksgiving," Callie says, as if this is a misunderstanding that logic will clear up. "No one does business on Thanksgiving." She sounds panicked.

"Yesterday . . ." It clicks. Calista's attempt to call home yesterday. "You were at my father's house. His Thanksgiving Day schmoozefest."

"He invited us," Lori says defensively. "He called the other night to discuss some additional details—"

"I bet." More like dear old Dad figured out he wasn't going to win so easily and needed to add a little more fuel to the fire. "How much more did he offer you?"

Lori doesn't even have the shame to look guilty. She lifts her chin. "Recurring at twice her *Starlight* rate, with the possibility of series regular next season."

So while Calista and I were laughing, eating pizza, and feeling free for the first time in either of our lives, the walls were closing in on us the whole time. We just didn't know it.

"You have until Monday to finish up with Calista. You'll get more than enough to put together a few episodes, if you want, and then you can wait until hiatus to continue. Assuming you're still interested." Lori's tone indicates that she strongly doubts this.

Fury lights within me. "She's not a child anymore," I say, stepping closer to Lori, who cocks her head but takes a most gratifying step back. "You don't make decisions for her. Her contract with me stands, and legally, you can't force her to—"

"Who says I'm forcing her to do anything?" she asks, with the gall to sound offended.

"I don't know, maybe the precedent of Calista's entire life? You harping over her shoulder about what she eats, how much water she drinks, where she goes, when she sleeps." I shake my head in disgust. "Jesus, no wonder she went over the ledge when she fired you. She has no idea how to be a person without you micromanaging her every breath. Heroin has to be easier than you."

It's a quiet sound, a gasp barely audible over the noise around us, but I know exactly who it is, what I've done.

I turn. Callie is watching me, her blue eyes wide and filling with tears. "Calista, I—"

She pushes past me and flees the room.

Fuck.

Lori looks slightly shaken, but her smile curls with satisfaction. I can almost see the feathers sticking to her lips.

"You are pathetic, and you don't deserve her," I spit at Lori as I follow after Calista.

"And that, maybe, is the one thing we have in common," she calls after me, sounding tired but triumphant.

Her words hit the mark well enough that it causes a hitch in my step.

I catch up with Calista in the hall outside the condo, where she's stopped, seemingly at a loss of where to go next. "I'm sorry, I never should have said any of that." I reach out to touch her, and she twists away. "Lori just pissed me off. She has no right to do that to you. Or to me."

"Do you believe it?" she asks, studying the floor.

"I don't know what—"

"That I don't know how to be a person without her?" she asks, her chin jerking up in defiance. She's sad, yes, but there's anger burning deep in there, too. Not at Lori. At me.

"I think she makes it harder on you that she should, and you're nicer to her than you should be." *Softer.* That's what I want to say. Somewhere inside herself, Callie is still waiting for her mother to pat her on the head and say *Good job, you're good enough.* I gave up on that from my dad ages ago. I'm not saying that makes me better or smarter than her, but in this situation, it makes me stronger. "It's a verbal contract at best, Callie. Made without your consent. You don't have to do this."

"The money is gone," Calista says with a sigh.

"What?"

"All of my money. All of her money. Their house is next. I can't stop it."

Shit. "Callie, it's okay. This is not your fault." It's that of the judge who gave Lori access to all of Calista's funds when Calista was under her mother's "guardianship." But then, Calista never took that access back.

But she doesn't seem to hear me, folding her arms across her middle as if she's trying to be smaller. "She's just going to push Zinn down the same path. She's already doing it. That bruise on her head? That's because she fainted at school. She's not eating enough, afraid she's getting fat." She looks up at me then, sharply. "You remember what that was like? When I didn't know how to be a person and only ate what my mother told me to?"

I wince. "Calista . . ."

"She's going to do it to Zinn, if I'm not here. If she can't control me, she's going to use Zinn to get what she wants."

"But where does it stop? When are you done with her? When she can't land you regular work anymore, except for some soft-core porn bullshit?" I demand. "Or will you do that, too?"

"No!"

"Are you sure about that? Because I'm not. If she leans hard enough on you, I think you'll do whatever she tells you is necessary. And what kind of example does that set for your sisters?" I rub my forehead where pressure is beginning to build. "I don't have siblings, but I'm guessing they might look up to you. And do you honestly think she'll stop with you anyway? That she won't push the rest of them to follow you?"

"Where else am I going to go?" she asks. "What else am I going to do? I can't afford tuition. I need to work, and your dad has already said that he'll keep me from getting more jobs if I turn him down."

I jerk back. "You never told me that. He can't . . . Calista, he thinks he's all-powerful, but—"

"He's more powerful than a former addict who hasn't worked steadily in years," she hisses at me.

"I will help you," I say. "We will figure this out. Callie, please." It's as if I can feel her disappearing right in front of me.

She looks at me helplessly. "For how long?"

"What?"

"How long are you willing to help me?"

"As long as it takes."

"You're going to let me move in with you? What about my sisters?"

The thought is panic-inducing. My condo has two bedrooms, that's it. And I don't have the financial resources at the moment to pour into an insta-family. Not without tapping the last of my trust fund, and that would be taking money from my dad, which I've sworn never to do again. Rawley wins again.

Plus, I'm just figuring out how to be responsible for myself, let alone three kids.

My hesitation must show on my face because she smiles sadly. "That's what I thought."

I shake my head. "No, I'll do it. Whatever you need. We'll figure it out."

She just shakes her head with a tired-sounding laugh. "And how long until you resent me?" She swallows hard. "Until you're bored, frustrated, tired of being tied down and wanting to move on?"

I can't breathe for a moment. "That's what you think of me? Still?" That, more than anything, feels like the betrayal. She doesn't believe, not completely, that I've actually changed.

"I won't do it," she says. "I won't do that to you. I won't do that to *us*. I don't want to see us destroyed that way."

It's in that instant that I realize she's already made up her mind. She probably made up her mind the second she saw those flowers and figured out what they meant, what her mother had done on her behalf.

Something in me goes cold and hard. This is her version of goodbye. She's just taking a little longer to get around to it. "But this way you'll have, what? The memories?" I give a harsh laugh.

"What do you want from me?" she asks dully. This is not the girl who was in my bed just a few hours ago. It's a shadow of who the real Calista is, the version of her that exists when her mother is in charge. Small, scared, lesser, and it kills me to see her reduce herself that way. To fit into the tiny space her mother allows for her. But I don't know how to save someone who won't save herself. I don't know that I'm even going to be able to save myself.

But I can sure as hell answer her question. "I want you to grow a spine and do what *you* want."

She jerks her head up to meet my gaze. "Even if it's not what *you* want?" she asks, her words sliding in like a knife between my ribs.

"You think I'm like *her?*" I ask in disbelief.

"Aren't you?" She lifts her shoulder. "The two of you were just standing in there arguing over me like I wasn't even there. For different reasons, but it's control all the same." Her mouth turns up in a bleak smile. "Isn't that what someone means when they say they love you? They just want to control you."

I don't know how to respond to that. Yes, I want her to walk away from Lori, and yeah, that would benefit me, but I don't want her to do it for that reason. I want her to do it for herself.

But I have the feeling that explaining that would be like trying to explain color to someone who has never seen.

"You're right," I say finally. "There are limits. I'm not going to watch you destroy yourself for her. I won't help you with that."

She pales, and then she nods as if I've confirmed some horrible flaw in my character.

And that's it. With the clutch in my stomach, I can feel the finality of the moment. I've just signed away any chance of an "us" now or in the future.

"If this weren't about your father, you would understand. But all you see is him winning," she says, her voice shaking.

I roll my eyes. "Don't bring him into it. I hated what your mother does to you, what you *let* her do, long before—"

"Oh, but you didn't hate it enough not to use it against me," she points out.

I grit my teeth. "I told you, I'm sorry about that. It was just a means to an end. You were hiding, and I didn't want you to—"

"Make choices on my own?" she asks.

"That's not fair," I snap, though there is enough truth in her question to make me feel uneasy.

She laughs, wiping under her eyes. "What, exactly, about any of this is fair?" She pauses. "I love you. You are . . . home to me." She makes a choked noise, somewhere between a sob and a laugh. "I can't believe it took me this long to figure it out, and now . . ."

My eyes and nose are stinging now. "Please. Don't do this."

She shakes her head. "You have no idea what it's like. You aren't responsible for anyone. I'm responsible for everyone!"

I stiffen, her words slamming into me. "Because I'm a total fuck up, right? Just Rawley's spoiled-brat kid who's playing around with being an adult and—"

"That's not what I meant, and you know it," she says, glaring at me.

"I want to believe that," I say flatly. "But I don't."

She folds her arms across herself. "I don't know what else to say."

There isn't anything else *to* say. She's made her choice. And I have a crew waiting on me, equipment rentals that are costing me every minute, whether we're working or not. An accountant who is possibly stealing from me.

The memory of Calista frowning over my accounts this morning, trying to help me, tears at me, makes me feel as helpless as I ever have. Worse even than the time my father told me the truth about my existence. Worse than when my mother confirmed it.

Something in me pushes for a fight. But the wrong kind of fight, an old impulse that I thought I'd conquered: to break before I am broken.

I force a smile. "Well, then. Good luck with your life as Lori's slave," I say. "I hope she stops before she signs you up for *Saucy School Girls 3*, but I wouldn't count on it, sweetheart."

She gives a choked gasp. "Eric."

"But maybe you'll get lucky. Maybe she'll eventually switch her attention to the next generation. Because Calista, that's the only way you're getting free of her."

Spewing those words should make me feel better, like releasing the pressure behind all my hurt and frustration, but it doesn't.

So, of course, I keep pushing.

"You know I have to give my dad credit," I say, as I turn to head back into the condo. "He knew you better than I did, after all. Maybe I should send *him* a congratulations card."

She's crying then, and the soft sounds of her breath hitching in her throat slice at me. But I keep walking. Leaving her there alone.

29 CALISTA

Eric.

I want to call after him again, the urge so strong in me I can feel it pushing up against my lungs.

But I don't. Because what will change? We'll just keep tearing each other to shreds until there's nothing left.

I curl my arms tighter around myself and slide down against the wall until I'm sitting on the floor.

He's protecting himself, choosing to see it as me picking his father, my family, over him.

And . . . maybe he's right. But I don't know what else to do. How do I protect myself and my sisters and have him, too? I don't think I can.

I saw it, that flicker of uncertainty, when I talked about moving in together. When I talked about bringing my sisters. And why not? It's crazy. We're not even officially a couple. But that's the thing—it's never going to get any less complicated with me. Or, rather, I don't know how to make it less complicated without hurting people who don't deserve it.

But he has a point—one that's kept me awake at night at various points in my life—where does it end? How does it end? The path from former teen star to just-barely-not porn star is not an untraveled one. Desperation and lack of other marketable skills collide in an ugly way sometimes—that's why I wanted my degree, my nice, safe accounting office, a fallback plan.

Because as much as I would love to think that my mother would never, ever, sink to that level, I can almost hear her—"Calista, darling, don't overthink it! It's art, not some guy with a mattress and a camera. You'll transform the medium, and they'll all be knocking at your door, admiring your daring choices. And the money!" Yeah, that totally worked for LiLo.

"Calista?" Josie calls, then she peeks into the hall. Her eyes go wide as soon as she sees me on the floor. "Oh, Calista." She sounds sad for me.

"I'm fine," I say, but my voice cracks in the face of her kindness and then I'm crying again.

She doesn't say anything, just pulls me to my feet and ushers me back to the dressing room, her arm around my shoulders to block prying stares.

My mother is waiting, of course. "Oh, baby," she says, as Josie and I walk through the door. "I know it's hard, but you'll thank me later." She reaches out as if she's going to pull me to her.

"Don't touch me," I snap.

"Calista . . ." Lori sighs.

Josie seats me in the folding chair and immediately applies cucumber-patterned eye pads to take the swelling down. I may need a whole case of them before I can go back out there.

"You know we could just go home," Lori offers. "There's nothing that says—"

"No. I'm finishing what I started." As much as she'll allow anyway. I may not be able to give Eric next week, but at least this way, he should have enough to finish an arc. A much shorter story arc than he'd planned. Five episodes instead of ten, assuming he ends on the emotional low point that we're filming today—Evie and Cory realizing that they're now too different—but it would be something. Enough to prove that he's as good as I know he is.

But in the way of things, it's the worst possible section we could be filming today. Evie and Cory trying to have a normal date, kissing, holding hands, and watching a movie at her home instead of fighting on opposite sides of the superhero spectrum.

The problem is neither of them are normal, and without their antagonism between them, they have nothing in common. And then when Cory accidentally squeezes Evie's hand too hard, forgetting the strength difference between them now, he breaks a bone, and that devastates him. They are standing on opposite sides of an uncrossable divide, one that somehow didn't exist when he was a villain and she was one of the "good guys."

It is one of my favorite scenes in the book—mainly because of the absolutely crushing emotions. As an actor, the juicy, painful scenes are the ones you look for, the ones that give you something to work with.

But now, today, to go out and play that scene, one that feels entirely too close to home—I don't know if *I* have the strength.

Except I have to. I'm a professional. And beyond that, I refuse to leave Eric any further in the lurch than I already am.

I close my eyes tighter behind the eye pads, trying to focus on nothing more than the coolness of them against my skin. If I can't stop crying, they won't do much good.

"It's okay," Josie whispers. "Just take a couple of deep breaths."

I try, but it's hard to focus on anything right now but the clamoring in my head and heart.

The dull roar of noise, conversation and the moving of equipment coming from the living room grows louder for a moment and then drops down.

We must be close to ready. I take a deep breath and then another, trying to clear my mind. I can be Evie, I can do this. I'm certainly feeling some of the same emotions. But kissing Eric, even as Cory, I . . . he will taste like Eric to me, he will smell like Eric, and how will I stop myself from curling into him, from begging him to not give up on me, even when he has no reason to believe?

Home. He is home, and that means even more to someone like me—someone like him, too. Neither of us has ever known what it's like to have a person or a place that just accepts us for who we are. And now I'm destroying that for both of us.

Hot tears dampen the eye pads and then slip down my cheeks.

"Josie," someone hisses behind me. From the door, most likely.

I start to turn around, but Josie stays me with her hand on my shoulder. "Just a second. I'll be back."

The conversation is murmured at first, but the other person's excitement—I think it's Lydia, one of the PAs/interns—eventually comes through, raising her voice to the point where I can hear it.

"No, I'm telling you, that's what he said. We'll be paid anyway, but it's a wrap."

Yanking the eye pads off my face, I twist around in my seat. "What?" It comes out too harshly.

Lydia jolts, clearly caught off guard. "Oh. Um. We're wrapping today? I guess? Eric just said that we're done, and we'll be paid through next week?"

Rawley's contract buy-out.

"No." I stand up. "No."

My mother intervenes, stepping between the door and me. "Oh." She tuts over my swollen eyes, touching the sides gently. "It's for the best, Calista. Really. Now you'll have the weekend to prepare for Monday, and I think you'll see that more clearly when you're winning an Emmy for Best Guest—"

I jerk away from her, and suddenly any patience I had for my mother, any feeling of debt or obligation, is just gone, evaporated in the heat of my anger. "For the best. For the best. Are you fucking kidding me?"

"Calista," she says, shocked.

"What kind of delusion are you living in? This is not the

bathroom where we're practicing our acceptance speeches anymore, Mom. There's not going to be an Emmy. Rawley Stone is going to fire me the first second he can."

Her face flushes red. "He certainly will if you can't control your negativity like I've always—"

"Because that's worked out so well for you," I snap. "You want me to imitate you? Which part? Where you're dependent on your kids for a living? Where you're losing your house because you can't hold on to reality long enough to make sure the bills are actually paid instead of planning for a star-studded future that never shows up? Or how about the part where you wasted all of your money and then stole mine, too?"

Her breath catches sharply in her throat. "I didn't steal anything, I—"

"Thank you, Mom, for not aborting me. For not abandoning me like my anonymous father. Is that what you want to hear?"

The room around me goes deathly silent.

"Well, okay, thank you," I say. "Thank you for letting me live, for feeding me and keeping me alive. Oh, wait, except I was paying for all of that by the time I was, what, six? Seven? I think you've been well compensated to make up for those years now. And thank you for paying for my rehab when I screwed up, because, yeah, I did. My first time on my own, I blew it. Big time. Except, oh, wait, that wasn't my mother loving me, wanting the best for me, that was my manager looking out for her best interests."

Lori is pale now, but her chin is tipped up in a defiant way I recognize from the mirror. "Calista, I never—"

"So, if it's a job, you're fired. You're fired as my manager. You are fired as my mother. I cannot do this anymore. You have destroyed and taken from me until there is nothing left." The last words are wrenched out of me. "I am done. *We* are done."

I turn to Zinnia. Her mouth is partially open in shock, her eyes wide with tears, the pages in her hands crumpled. "I'm sorry. I'm so sorry, Zinn." The lump in my throat chokes me and it takes me a second to continue. "I can't anymore. And you shouldn't, either. We are not her toys, her playthings to live out the fantasy life she always wished she had. Stand up for yourself. Please. I should have done it sooner."

I start for the living room. I need to find Eric. I don't know if I can fix this, but I have to stop it from being ruined any more than it already is.

"I don't want you to be me," my mother says in a tight voice. "I never wanted that. I want you to be *better* than me."

"Good," I say, pushing past her with determination. "On that we agree."

She gasps, but makes no attempt to stop me.

Out in the living room, everyone is taking equipment down, packing it away. There's no sign of Eric.

I stop one of the sound guys. "Where is he? Where's Eric?"

He shakes his head. "Told us to shut everything down and then he took off."

I squeeze past a cart full of lighting equipment and bolt for the hall.

It's empty, and so is the elevator up to Eric's floor.

My heart hammering in my chest, I bang on the door to Eric's condo until my fist aches from it.

"Come on, come on," I murmur.

Bitsy is going crazy on the other side, throwing herself at the door, barking, scratching and panting. But he doesn't answer.

If he were in there, he would stop her. He wouldn't let Bitsy hurt herself. As much as she drives him crazy, he loves her. It's easy to see in how he takes care of her.

Takes care of her.

I sink to the floor in front of the door. He takes care of the people—and animals—he loves. That's what Eric does when he has the opportunity—which isn't often, given how infrequently he lets himself care. That's a defensive measure on his part. If he doesn't care, he can't be hurt or rejected. And those are feelings he's been dealing with pretty much since birth thanks to his messed-up family dynamics.

It's not about control for him. That is—was—my mother's way, not his.

Even his strong-arm method to get me on board with *Fly Girl* was more about trying to make up for what he saw as his past sins against me. Not the best approach, but he wasn't wrong. He recognized that I was hiding at Blake—from my mom, from taking risks—even before I did. And he felt responsible for putting me in that situation, for the accident that led to my addiction and retreat, for the end of my career.

He was trying to take care of me. Just as he always has, from the very first day we met.

I pull my knees to my chest and rest my forehead on them.

Parts of this mess could be undone. Eric has to come home eventually. I might, *might* be able to talk him into continuing *Fly Girl*. Maybe. But the rest of it? No. That's over.

Wrapping my arms around my knees, I squeeze them tighter against me as if that will help fill the hole in the middle of me, where my heart used to be.

Nothing has changed. I would still be dependent on him or my mom. I would have no plan, no . . . what did he say? *No idea how to be a person.*

He was right about that.

But I don't know how to change that. I don't even have a place to go for the night. I won't go home with Lori, and waiting here for Eric . . .

I shake my head. He'll never see me differently now. I've burned that bridge and salted the earth behind me.

My phone buzzes in my pocket, against my hip, and I throw myself sideways to get at it.

Please, please, please.

But it's just another text from Beth. A smiley-face emoji followed by a turkey and then the sick-looking emoji. `How's it going? So sick of leftovers and my family. Ready to be back "home" in Ryland.`

I start to type a banal response—`okay. Me, too.`—because how the hell am I supposed to explain everything that's happened? There aren't enough emojis in the world.

Inside the condo, Bitsy finally calms down enough to curl up, panting. I can see her little shadow in the crack under the door.

Right there, right on the other side of that door, I was home. That's what I want to type to Beth.

But it's too late.

And now I just want . . . I want oblivion. I want to just be gone. Like this place never existed, like this week never happened.

The good news is with the money in the account that Eric helped me set up, I know exactly how I can do that.

I say goodbye silently to Bitsy and the rooms beyond, to the future Eric and I might have had, and then I push myself to my feet.

30

ERIC

It is surprisingly hard to find an open bar in Hollywood at ten in the morning. Places that serve mimosas or Bloody Marys, yeah, but an anonymous, shitty bar where you can get wasted on cheap whiskey (because the cheapness is part of the punishment) without anyone looking twice at you? That's a real trick.

But I manage it because hey, I'm not a quitter.

I probably should be supervising the end of the shoot, making sure equipment gets returned, that nothing is lost or damaged. Hell, that someone remembers to shut the door of the condo that we were using behind them.

But I don't care. What's the point? I'll just send the bills to my dad. Again.

He won. He got what he wanted. And he can afford to take the hit. Plus, it'll make everything in his world right if I'm the screw up. Again.

As the bartender delivers my fourth shot, my phone, lying next to my keys on the sticky wooden bar in front of me, lights up.

Chase.

What the hell? Nope.

I send the call to voicemail, down my shot and signal for another.

Chase calls back almost instantly, and I send it to voicemail again. This is fun.

A moment later, a text flashes across my screen, also from Chase. `Pick up, asshole. I know you're there. I'm trying to apologize.`

So when he calls again, I answer. "Apology not accepted because you were right and have nothing to apologize for. Go away." I hang up.

He calls back, and I answer because at this point, it's clear he's just going to keep calling.

"What's wrong with you?" he asks.

"Everything or nothing," I say. "Depends on who you ask. I think most people are in the everything camp today." Chase probably is.

Calista definitely is.

She thinks I'm like Lori.

Maybe I am. I did manipulate her into coming here. But I wasn't trying to hurt her. I was trying to help her.

Of course, Lori probably thinks that, too. About herself, not me.

And some part of me worries that Calista is right, that maybe I just pushed her away—the only person who has ever cared about the real me, even the messed-up version—because of my dad. Because I was afraid of letting my dad win. And in pushing her away, didn't I let him win anyway? A different point, but the same game.

Game over now.

"Are you drunk?" Chase asks, his voice creased with worry, and I realize belatedly that I just said all of that out loud.

Chase doesn't wait for me to answer. "Where are you?" he asks impatiently. "What bar?"

"How did you know—"

"Alcoholic, remember? And we used to be friends. Plus, you're slurring worse than that night at our first Comic Con, and I can hear the pool game in the background."

I turn around. Sure enough, there's a pool table and a game in progress, with all the requisite clinks and cracks of the balls colliding. Huh.

"Good ears, man," I say to him in sincere admiration. "That's fucking impressive. How'd you . . . how did you even—"

"Where are you?" he repeats.

"I . . . don't know. Don't remember the name. Why? You want to join me? Hookers and cocaine again?" I snicker. This makes the man on the other end of the bar look up from his drink to glare at me. I might be being a little loud. It's hard to tell.

Chase sighs. "You know she wasn't a hooker and . . . never mind. I'm coming to get you." He doesn't sound happy about it.

"No! I don't want any of your . . . holier-than-thou lectures." I'm a little impressed with myself for remembering "holier than thou." "I know that you're better than me. I don't need to hear it all again. I messed up. I lost it all. Hurt Calista, just like you said. And Rawley wins again. But you know, I think . . . I think the lesson is . . . is not to make better decisions. But just that it's not worth trying at all. I think. Just easier to be Rawley's fuck-up kid with no responsibility. No caring, no—"

"Give your phone to the bartender," Chase says.

I'm already pulling the phone away from my ear before it occurs to me to ask. "Why?"

"I want to buy you a drink," Chase says. "You need something to drown yourself in besides self-pity."

"Fuck you," I say automatically.

"I'm serious. Give him or her the phone, and I'll buy you another of what you're having."

This sounds entirely logical. I give my phone to the bartender. His shirt says John. But it's a bowling shirt. And this is a bar. I think John may not even be his real name.

The bartender says something to Chase. Then he hands the phone back to me and pours another shot with a grimace.

"But I owe you a drink," I say to Chase. "I owe you many drinks for the shit that I said. For what I did. Except you don't drink anymore." I frown, trying to work through the logic of that.

"Uh-huh. We'll figure something out. Maybe you can give me back my car. The one you took from me in that card game." I hear the jingle of keys and the rustle of movement on Chase's end.

Not-John pushes the shot toward me. I take it and swallow the warmth in one go.

"But you wrecked mine in the wreck," I point out, and then immediately feel like shit for bringing up the accident. "I am sorry. I shouldn't have lied to you. That was stupid. But you, you and Calista . . ." Uh-oh, Calista comes out sounding like Calishta. That's not right. "You were my only friends. And I knew I'd already lost her because . . . because . . ."

"Because you were an idiot," Chase offers helpfully.

"Yes. That."

"And I didn't want you to leave, too. Fucking selfish, yeah? And pathetic."

Chase doesn't answer right away. "I'm on my way," he says after a moment.

Damnit, Not-John. "You gave him the address?" I demand. Not-John ignores me.

"Try not to run your mouth or look at anyone in that way you have," Chase says grimly. "I'm out of practice with bar fights, and Amanda will kill me."

"I doubt it," I say, spinning my empty shot glass on its side. "She seems to like you. It's that Texas accent."

He sighs. "Eric—"

"Do you love her?" It's painful suddenly to push those words past the lump in my throat. I love Calista. I do. But she didn't choose me. She can't. And I can't let go of that.

"I am not talking about Amanda with—"

"Do you?"

"Yes," he snaps. "Hell, she's the only reason I'm still here. She and I . . ." He makes a tired sound. "She reminded me that we know what it's like to need second chances, okay? So I'm giving you one. Don't make me regret it before I even get to you."

"I love her," I say. "Calista." I'm flooded with mental images of her, snapshots that I was apparently unconsciously preserving: Calista grinning at me over her shoulder on the way to the shower. Calista holding my hand in the car. Calista snuggled up next to me on the couch, her cold toes tucked beneath my leg.

Home. That's what she called me. And that's exactly how I feel about her. Like I have nowhere to go, nowhere worth going without her.

Oh, God, the ache in my chest feels fatal.

Chase is quiet. "Yeah, I know. Pretty sure I figured that out before you did. Like *years* before you did." He gives a tight laugh. "I mean, you started a company and picked the one project in the whole world guaranteed to mean something to her. Everybody on set knew how much she loved that book. Come on."

I sit up straighter on my stool, gripping the edge of the bar as the world swirls around me. "But yesterday, you said—"

"That doesn't mean I think it's a good idea," he argues. "I care about Calista. I want her to be happy. She deserves to be happy after everything she's been through. And you . . . you are not easy."

I want to be offended—and I am, maybe, a little—but this is coming from my best friend, whom I haven't spoken to in years, after lying to him about a car accident that he didn't really cause.

I swallow hard. "An excellent point."

He sighs. "Just stay there. Don't cause trouble, if you can manage it."

"Oh, I can manage *that*." I wave my hand dismissively, but when I see the angry guy at the end of the bar glaring at me again, I wink at him.

The gentleman in question slams his glass down and stands up—he's bigger than I thought.

Bring it on, motherfucker.

Maybe pain on the outside will make the pain on the inside go away.

"Were you drinking whiskey or swimming in it?" Chase asks with a frown, surveying me on the sidewalk outside the bar an hour later. I'm standing—okay, mostly leaning—against the bus stop out front. A big splotchy stain decorates the front of my shirt and down the side of my jeans. "And what happened to your face?"

I shake my head, which only makes my split lip and bruised cheek hurt more. And if they hurt now, sobriety is going to be even more painful. "Spilled my drink, and a couple of other people's, when that guy punched me."

"Which guy?"

"The one I winked at because he was being a judgy dick."

Chase sighs. "Do I need to go in and—"

"Nope, all handled. Gave them my credit card and my dad's name."

"That's going to end well," he says, grabbing my elbow and guiding me to his car at the curb.

"Bro. Is this a fucking Camry?" I ask with a disbelieving laugh as he pulls open the door.

"Shut up and get in," he says, his mouth twisting in a reluctant smile.

"Nice grocery-getter, Henry." I drop into the seat.

"Go fuck yourself, Stone."

"Not possible, even with my considerable talents."

Rolling his eyes, he slams the door shut, then walks around to the driver's side to get in.

I give him the address for my condo, and he puts the car in gear.

But he's edgy, uncomfortable, adjusting the a/c vents, looking at me and then away.

"What's the matter?" I ask, finally.

"It's just . . . I can smell it." His jaw tightens.

It takes me a second to realize what he means. The whiskey. We have shared more than our share of bottles. Years before. When he was still drinking.

"Sorry. Didn't think about that." I reach over, fumbling for the window controls. The glass retracts with a buzz, and air rushes in.

"Thanks."

"I am . . ." I try to find the words, which would likely be difficult under any circumstances but especially under the influence. "I don't know, is it weird to say this . . . I'm proud of you for doing what you did. For getting clean, for getting your life back together. I know how hard it is to do that." Or, at least, I know how hard it is to try. "And you were right to cut me off." I shake my head with a grim laugh. "I'm not even sure why you're here now."

He's quiet for a long moment. "When I moved out here, I didn't have anybody. Maybe some of our choices weren't great ones, but you looked out for me. Made me feel like I could belong out here. Kept me from running home to Texas, especially right in the beginning."

"Would have been a waste. You're talented." I rest my head against the back of the seat. "More than me. And that is not self-pity, that is just a fact." I could feel pain starting to move up from my jaw. Yep, alcohol is already wearing off. "I've been around long enough to tell, trust me."

"How did you like directing?" he asks.

"Loved it." If acting was focusing on one pixel of the giant picture, directing was taking a step back to be able to see all of it. Like conducting an orchestra instead of playing a single instrument. And right now that feels like another loss, another gaping hole in the tattered identity that I'd managed to string together. Because who the hell is going to hire me to direct when I can't even handle my own web series?

Chase nods, as if this was the answer he expected.

"I don't know if we can be friends anymore," he says after a long moment, where it's nothing but silence and the air rushing in my open window.

It's nothing less than I expected, but hearing it sends a cold stab through me.

"I'm not saying we can't," he continues. "I'm saying I don't know. So much of what we did back then was . . ."

"Based on being wasted? Or in pursuit of being wasted?"

"Yeah. And that's not me anymore. I can't go back in that direction. I won't." He shoots a wary look at me, as if expecting me to protest or try to talk him into it.

I hold my hands up. "I'm not going to tear you down. You're making something out of your life. What I was trying to do."

"You still can. Just because this one project—"

I shut my eyes, slumping in the seat. "What's the point? I'm always going to be Rawley's kid."

"Yep."

I open my eyes to stare at him.

"Did you expect that to change?" he asks, his eyebrows raised. "People are always going to judge us by our pasts, by our mistakes. By who our families are or aren't. But none of that matters unless you let it stop you."

I give him a sour look. "When did you get so fucking zen about everything?

"I took a yoga class once."

The mental image of tough-guy-cowboy Chase folding himself up into a ridiculous pose on a bright pink mat (like Stepmother Two) is enough to make me laugh.

"No, it's just . . . I've been figuring some stuff out for a while now," he says with a shrug.

"With Amanda."

"Yeah," he says, but in a voice that clearly indicates that line of conversation will go no further.

He's protecting her, I get it. I tried to do that for Calista. I wanted to protect her, but I managed to blow it. She couldn't trust me enough. Maybe that was smart of her, after all.

We're silent the rest of the way, but he insists on making sure I reach my condo. He parks in the turnaround and flips on the hazards.

"I can use an elevator," I argue as we walk—okay, I stumble—into the building.

"Good for you," Chase says evenly, nodding at the doorman/concierge at the desk.

In the elevator, I fumble for my keys, but once we're out on my floor, I don't want to go any further.

If I open the door to my condo, I'm going to see the blankets Calista piled on the couch yesterday when we were watching movies together. My shirt that she wore, still lying in a heap on the floor of my bedroom. The bathroom floor is probably still damp from our attempt to shower together.

I shake my head. "I can't. She . . ." I took a breath. "She believed in me, and I needed that, but I wasn't enough. And I said some shitty stuff." I scrub my hands over my face. "I should never have let you talk me out of that bar. I need another drink."

"You know you're an idiot, right?" Chase asks.

"Probably," I say bleakly. "But I'm not sure how to—"

"Come on." He takes my keys from my hand and drags me down the hall. "Which one?"

I tip my head toward the door, and Bitsy starts barking as soon as she hears the key in the lock.

"You have a dog?" Chase asks with a frown.

I sigh. "Sort of. It's a long story."

He gets the door open, and Bitsy races toward me. I bend down and pick her up.

"Dude. That is not a dog," Chase says. "That's an overgrown mouse. With a haircut."

"Don't listen to him," I tell Bitsy. "He's just jealous because you have better style."

"Go." He pushes me into the condo, and I make it to the sofa and collapse, with Bitsy in my lap. Calista's scent is all over the blankets, and I want to bury my face in them.

Chase reappears a moment later with a glass full of water and holds it out to me.

"Are you serious?" I ask.

"You can get drunk after I leave," he says. "But it's not going to fix anything, and you damn well know it. Putting off the pain until later doesn't make it go away."

I take the water and drink a token sip or two, expecting him to turn and leave now that he's done his duty, as my former friend.

"I have to get back to the theater for the show tonight," he says.

I nod.

But instead he stands there for a second before seeming to come to a decision. With a reluctant shake of his head, he sits in the chair opposite me. "Look, you can't make Calista believe that she's enough, that she's worth it as a person. Lori has done a number on her for years, and that's not going to just go away. You can't fix that for her."

"This pep talk is really helping," I say.

"Just shut up and listen. You can't fix that for her, any more than she can make you believe you are more than Rawley's son."

I snap my mouth shut.

"You both have to do that yourselves. But it would probably help if you hadn't given her an ultimatum. That was beyond stupid, and exactly what Lori does."

I straighten up. "I did not—"

"Yeah, you did," he says, exasperated. "Basically, you said that if she doesn't do what you want, then it's over, right?"

"But that's not how I—"

"Doesn't matter how you phrased it or even how you meant it. Matters how she sees it."

Isn't that what someone means when they say they love you? They just want to control you.

That's what Calista said.

"Shit," I mutter.

"Your dad is your weak spot. Her mother is hers. This?" He gestures in a way that encompasses the entire situation. "It's the perfect storm. Drought and high winds."

I roll my eyes at his colloquial Texas-ism, but that's just Chase.

"So?"

"So you expect her to get over her deal with her mom, but you can't do that with your dad?" He shrugs. "Why do you expect her to be better at this than you?"

"Because . . . because . . ." My rationale, which had seemed so clear a few hours ago, is shaky under the weight of his logic. "It's different. I've cut my dad off, but she's still letting her mother hurt her. I can't stand by and watch that."

He shakes his head. "I could argue that cutting your dad off has done jack shit in stopping him from controlling your choices except in the most obvious ways. But whatever, I'm not getting into that. My point is, don't watch. *Help* her."

"You just said I can't fix it for her," I point out, frustrated.

"You can't, but you can be there, showing her there's another way. That you're not going to freak out and leave every time she does something you don't agree with."

A slow sinking feeling settles over me. I think all of this is what Calista was struggling to tell me before. *Damnit.*

"But my dad—" I begin.

"—is probably going to gloat like a motherfucker," Chase confirms, his mouth tight. It seems he remembers Rawley's visits to set as well as Calista does. "But you have to decide what's more important." He shrugs. "Again, you expect her to ignore Lori . . ."

Even while I'm not capable of ignoring my dad.

Shit.

Chase must see the comprehension in my expression because he nods and stands.

"Why are you helping me with this?" I ask, trying to sit up straighter. "I thought you didn't want this for her. You said I wasn't easy."

Rubbing the back of his neck, he gives an exasperated laugh. "Who the hell is, Eric? I care about Calista. I don't want her to be hurt, but it's not up to me. And I'm pretty sure that Amanda's family would have much rather had someone easier for her than me."

I don't know what to say for a moment. And probably it's the alcohol, but I can feel a lump rising in my throat. "Thanks."

He nods and starts to walk away. Then he stops at the threshold to the hall. "You still surf?" he asks without looking at me.

"What?"

"Surfing. You used to go, didn't you, when we were working together?"

"I haven't gone in a while, but yeah." Used to go every weekend. Because I loved it. But it had the added bonus of pissing off my dad—slacker hobby, according to him.

"Good. I have Sunday morning off."

"*You* want to learn how to surf," I say in disbelief. This from the guy who'd never even seen the ocean until he moved out here, and even then, the expansiveness of it freaked him out a little.

He raises his eyebrows. "You want to go running instead?"

"Fuck no. Surfing is fine." I'll have to get my board out of storage.

"Amanda wants to learn," he says. "I want to go with her."

"She's coming wi—"

"No," he says sharply. "Not this time," he adds in a calmer voice.

I get it. I haven't earned that level of trust yet.

"Yeah, okay," I say. "I'll text you. It'll be early," I warn.

Chase snorts. "I am not the one with that issue. Not anymore." He gives me a skeptical look, with a raised eyebrow. "Maybe I better text you."

I give him the finger and he laughs.

But then he's gone, the door shutting quietly behind him. And I'm alone.

Well, not quite, with Bitsy in my lap and memories of Calista all around me.

Chase, much to my irritation, made several good points. Unfortunately, he didn't really offer much by way of execution.

How exactly am I supposed to help Calista? Especially now, when she probably won't let me, anyway?

I don't know. But I love her—so much so that it feels like I might not ever be able to breathe again without this hitch in my chest if I don't figure it out.

31

CALISTA

It's cold and gray in Indiana. And it's snowing again.

Somehow, in just a week, I've forgotten exactly how awful the Midwest is in November.

"Are you sure you don't want to stay at my house?" Beth asks, looking away from the road to me, her forehead creased with worry.

She cranks up the heat when she sees me shivering.

We're on our way back from the bus station in Merrillville, where she picked me up when I called her this morning. I spent most of yesterday at LAX, getting my original return flight changed to today instead of next Saturday. And then, with nowhere else to go, I tried to sleep in one of those awful plastic chairs.

Once I got to O'Hare, it was another trick figuring out the bus schedule to Merrillville, which is only about thirty minutes from campus. But I managed it.

And now I'm here, with nothing more than the sweatshirt I bought at the airport. I'm still wearing Evie's wardrobe. When I left the hallway outside Eric's condo, I just took the elevator down and walked out. No one even noticed.

I shake my head at Beth. "I just want to get to my room and sleep," I say, pulling my hands up into my sleeves for warmth.

Blake feels like an entirely different world from California: a gray one, a bleak one. Eric's not here—an absence that makes my chest feel caved in. But neither is my mother. And this, at least, is the one place where my name is on the paperwork because *I* wanted it there.

For the next month or so, anyway. After that, when next semester's tuition isn't paid, I'm sure I'll get to see my name on other paperwork, the kind that comes when they're gently—or not so gently—kicking you out. Even before I left, I'd gotten a couple carefully worded emails from the administration, as if they were smiling through clenched teeth, regarding my "plans" for tuition next semester.

"Do you . . . do you want to talk about what—" she begins.

"No," I say flatly. I can't cry anymore. I feel weirdly hollow inside.

"Oh. Okay." Beth doesn't say anything more on the way back to campus, but I can feel her concern in the glances she sends my way, the adjustments she makes to the heat and the vents.

When she pulls up in front of Ryland, she insists on coming in with me. "It's mostly empty, Calista." She pauses. "It's creepy." She shudders.

"I'll be fine," I say.

But Beth is right. As soon as we enter the lobby, it's clear from the dim lighting, the cooler-than-usual temperature, and the thick layer of stillness that this is not a typical day. It gives the building an abandoned feel that is definitely creepy.

But homeless former stars who've rebelled against their families and pushed away the one person who understands them cannot be choosers. Or something like that.

"I have some extra blankets in my room," Beth says. "And some ramen? The cafeteria here is closed. You'll have to walk all the way over to the union, and I think they're only serving lunch."

"Thanks, Beth. I mean it. Thank you for coming to get me, too."

She smiles shyly. "It was worth it to get out of the house and away from my brothers, trust me."

"That bad?" I ask, more to fill the eerie silence as we walk up the stairs. I hear music somewhere, or voices, in the distance. Or maybe it's the pipes humming?

"I'm the youngest," she says with a shrug. "They all love telling me what to do. And the noogies . . ." She grimaces.

"I'm the oldest," I offer. "I still have people telling me what to do."

"Sucks, doesn't it?" she asks.

"Yeah." Sometimes it does. Sometimes, though, it's hard to tell the difference between someone trying to help you and someone trying to keep you in line with what they want.

How messed up is that?

I open the door to my room—thank goodness my keys were with my wallet the night I took off from my mom's house—and the sight of the space exactly as I left it a week ago sends a pang through me. The chair where I hung Eric's coat still faces away from the desk, like he might have sat there himself.

I clear my throat. "You said you have ramen?" I ask Beth.

She nods and we hurry down the cool, dim hallway—only every other light is on overhead—to her room.

And I should have thought about it, I really should have, but I didn't, and as soon as Beth opens her door and I follow her in, I'm confronted by the enormous *Starlight* poster above her bed. Eric and Chase on either side of me.

Eric's too-familiar smirk steals the air from my lungs. I step toward the poster, unable to stop myself. I want to touch the paper, to trace his features in the photograph, since I might not ever see them again in real life.

But I keep myself from it, barely.

"Here, I found the—" Beth says, turning around from her closet with white Styrofoam cups of ramen in her hands. Her eyes go wide. "I'm sorry, I didn't think—"

"It's okay," I say, my voice low and guttural with repressed emotion.

"Oh, Calista," she says softly. "What happened?" She drops on the end of her bed, the ramen cups in her lap. "Why are you back *here*?"

She makes it sound like we're in the bottom of a collapsed mining shaft and running out of air.

The poster of the three of us keeps drawing my attention. "Have you ever . . . have you ever found the best thing—not perfect, nothing is perfect—but then it's gone and you don't know how to get back there?"

"No," Beth says softly.

"I feel like I had everything, but I couldn't fit it all together, and the worst part is, I still don't know what I should have done instead." My eyes well, and my vision goes blurry. "I just . . . I'm screwed." I force a laugh.

"Calista," Beth says. "What happened?"

So I tell her. Everything. From the time Eric and I left campus to when I boarded the plane yesterday.

Beth's mouth is hanging open slightly by the time I finish.

"Yeah," I say, wiping under my eyes. "A mess, right?"

"I didn't . . . I had no idea," she says.

"It's not all red carpets, stylists and award shows," I say. "We're as messed up as everyone else."

Her cheeks flush red, color rising all the way to her hairline. "I never meant that."

I sigh. "I know. I'm sorry."

"You know he loves you," she says, after a moment.

A sinking feeling begins in my stomach. "Beth . . ."

She stands up and starts pacing the length of the bed. "Look, I know you probably think I'm one of those pathetic Skyron-obsessed freaks—"

Yes. "I would never—"

"And I am," she says, meeting my gaze defiantly. "But I know the difference between fiction and reality, and Eric Stone loves you.

Not Skye. It has nothing to do with Skyron. I saw it when he was here."

"Look, Beth, I appreciate everything you're trying to do, but—"

"When we went to that party, Blackout, it was because he wanted to make sure you were okay," she insists.

"Because he didn't want me to go in the first place," I point out.

"No," Beth says sharply. "We were there, I don't know, for like fifteen or twenty minutes, and he wouldn't interfere because you were having fun, talking to those girls."

That party feels like a lifetime ago.

"He didn't even intervene when that first guy was bothering you because he saw you could handle it. He only went over there when Carter," she rolls her eyes, "started writing that . . . shit on your shirt." Her color deepens with the swear word. "You couldn't see it, so you didn't know. You couldn't protect yourself in that case, so he did it for you."

And took a punch to the face for it, as well.

The ache in my chest swells until it feels like it might break through my ribs. "Stop," I say raggedly. "It doesn't matter. I tried, I wanted to choose him, but he didn't understand why I couldn't just leave my sisters, my family—"

"Yeah," she says, sounding frustrated. "Because you can't save someone when you're still drowning."

I blink at her.

"It's like that thing they tell you on airplanes?" she continues. "When we went to Florida last summer to visit my grandma, it was the first time I'd ever flown."

Beth's only a few years younger than me. By the time I was her age, I'd traveled out of the country, flown on private jets. Of course, I'd also been audited by the IRS and never been to a dance. So maybe our experiences are just limited in different ways.

"But in the instructions, if you're paying attention, they tell you to put your oxygen mask on first before helping the person next to you." She nods to herself. "I think that's what he was trying to say to you. How are you supposed to save your sisters when you can't save yourself?"

I sink onto the edge of her roommate's bed. "It doesn't matter. It's too late. He won't forgive me for taking the job with his dad."

"But you didn't," she points out. "You're here."

"Yes," I say. "After I chose my family over him. And then bailed on everyone." I shake my head. "Maybe Eric is right. I don't know how to be a person without someone telling me what to do. Because this plan? Sucks. It's only good for about a month, until the semester ends, and I have no idea what I'm going to do after that." I've never felt so helpless and alone in my life.

Beth's forehead furrows with concern. "But Calista, that's what it's like for everyone," she argues. "No one knows for sure what they're supposed to do. And fighting back took guts. Guts that some of us don't even have," she adds, picking at the loose edge of plastic on a ramen container.

I wait, sensing she has more to say.

"I'm a business major," she says finally. "Do you know why?"

I shake my head.

"Because all my brothers were business majors. That's what my parents wanted, so that's what we are. They're paying for my tuition, so . . ." She shrugs.

"What do you want instead?"

She gives me a sad smile. "I don't know for sure. English, maybe?" She hesitates. "I do a lot of writing online."

"Writing like blogs or . . ."

"Mostly Skyron," she says. "But some Byrdy."

It takes me a second to decipher that sentence. I know Skyron is Skye/Byron so Byrdy is . . . "Byron/Brody. Really?" I grin for the first time in what feels like days. I'd love to read some of that. Bet Chase and Eric would both have something to say if they knew. Probably an argument over who would have made the first move—Byron or Brody.

She nods, pleased. "My dad says there are no jobs for English majors. But I'm one of the top fic writers in both categories in views and kudos."

"That's awesome," I say. I have no idea how it all works, but I vaguely remember hearing that someone got a book deal for a story they wrote based on an alternate version of Brody and Skye, with different names. So what she's talking about isn't impossible. Difficult, probably, but not impossible. Plus, there are all kinds of writing, not just fan fiction. Scripts, books, plays, advertisements.

"If writing is what you really want to do . . ." I begin and then stop.

"See, that's the thing, isn't it?" she asks softly. "First it's figuring out what you want, but then it's deciding what you want to do about it. What risk you're willing to take. Who you're willing to hurt."

She stands up then and hands me the cups of ramen. "Because the thing is, I'm pretty sure someone's always getting hurt when we make choices. It's just that sometimes it's easier to hurt ourselves than it is to believe we deserve what we really want and to take the chance of hurting someone else."

32 ERIC

It takes a minute for me to wake up enough to identify the noise penetrating my consciousness.

I spent most of the weekend in the editing room. And after surfing yesterday morning with Chase—he is both as terrible and determined as I expected—my whole body is achy and slow to rouse.

The phone. It's the phone.

But it's early. I squint at the windows in my bedroom to confirm, but yeah, that's definitely gray pre-dawn, not gray-from-rain.

Who the hell is calling before dawn on a Monday morning?

That thought alone is enough to catapult my heart into my throat. *Calista.*

I fumble for my cell underneath the pillow next to me. Bitsy grumbles and curls herself up tighter.

But the screen on my cell is dark.

Then I realize it's the wall phone. Which never ever gets used.

Except when unapproved visitors are downstairs.

I throw back the covers and hurl myself toward the kitchen, where the wall phone resides.

Well, that's what I try to do, but every muscle in my body is protesting.

Shit. I either need to quit surfing or do it more often.

I finally make it to the phone, breathless and sore, and grateful that Antonio hasn't simply decided I'm not home. "Hello?"

"Hey, Mr. Stone. I have a woman here. I've seen her here before but—"

"It's okay," I say quickly. "You can just—"

There's a clatter and the sound of fabric rustling. "Let me talk to him!" A shrill and familiar voice comes through the phone, loud and clear.

And my heart sinks. Not Calista.

"He *knows* me!" Lori shouts.

"Ma'am, I can't let you have the phone," Antonio protests.

"I'll be right there," I say to Antonio, and hang up.

I can't imagine what Lori wants at this point. But . . . however small the possibility that it's about Calista—a message from her—I have to at least see.

Plus, it's really not fair to subject Antonio to Lori, who sounds like she's in a mood. Why, when she's gotten everything she wants, I have no idea.

But she better not be here to complain about my dad screwing her over, because that I could have told her over the phone. Last week. Years ago.

I pull on clothes and head for the lobby, taking Bitsy with me. She'll need to go out anyway.

I'm barely out of the elevator before Lori is in my face.

She looks like shit, her hair plastered against her face and her makeup smeared from crying.

"Where is she? You send her down right now!"

I stare at her. "What are you talking about?"

"Mom," Zinn tries. She's over at the desk, watching her mother warily. Oddly enough, she's in her pajamas, flip-flops and a knitted beanie. What is going on here?

"I know she's up there." Lori tries to shove past me, and Bitsy starts barking.

"Ma'am, if you persist, I'll have to call the police," Antonio says, lifting the phone.

Lori stops, folding her arms across her chest. "Good! Call the police, they can arrest him for . . . for . . . kidnapping!" She sounds just short of hysterical.

"Kidnapping? Who the hell would I be—"

"My daughter!"

Jesus, Lori's really lost it this time.

"Lori, Zinnia is right—"

Zinnia's too-serious expression stops me, and she gives her head a tiny shake.

"Which daughter?" I ask, with a growing sense of dread.

"Which daughter? The only one whose life you're ruining!"

"You're looking for Calista?" I ask to confirm, mainly because I'm still confused. "But she's with you. I haven't seen her since Friday morning." When I said horrible, horrible things to her. Just remembering how we left it makes me feel ill.

"Oh, please, do you honestly expect me to believe that?" Lori scoffs at me. "She took off after you and we haven't seen her since. And she's due for her wardrobe fitting for *Triple Threat* this morning!"

It's clear which part of this Lori is most upset about.

Fear, deep and ugly, spreads through my gut. "When, exactly, was the last time you saw her?"

"Friday morning. After you shut down production," Zinnia offers quietly, edging closer, though she's still keeping a cautious eye on her mother, as if expecting a slap or a backhand.

Three days ago. The fear sharpens. A lot can happen in three days, particularly if you're feeling like your life has gone to hell. If people you trusted have stomped all over you. "We need to call the police." I shift Bitsy to my other arm so I can pull my phone out of my pocket.

Only then does it finally seem to dawn on Lori that I'm serious and I really don't know where Calista is.

"You don't have her upstairs?" Lori asks.

"First of all, she's twenty-three and a person, I wouldn't 'have' her anywhere. She's not a fucking doll, Lori. And second, no, she's not upstairs."

"Oh, my God. She's using again. She has to be. I should have known. When she yelled at me like that . . ." Lori shudders.

I pause in dialing. "Wait, what?"

Zinn speaks up then. "She fired Mom. Not just, like, as her manager, but as her mom." She sounds awed, and a tiny, gleeful smile plays around her mouth. The bruise on her temple looks better now. Or maybe it's just that the beanie is so brightly colored that it distracts from the injury.

"She screamed at me and then she left," Lori says. "God save me from my own children." She gives a dramatic half sob, like she's trying to hold back tears. But then she glares at Zinnia. "I've only ever wanted the best for them."

I'm not sure what's happening here.

Zinn pulls her beanie off with a grin then, revealing ragged and chopped sections of hair, some of them going all the way to her scalp.

Lori gasps, as if the sight is a shock all over again.

I raise my eyebrows in question.

"She wouldn't listen when I told her I didn't want be the Secret Service director's daughter. I want to play basketball." This last is directed at her mother.

"Secret Service . . . a role?" I ask, trying to piece this together.

Zinn nods. "But I don't want to do it, and Calista's not, so I shouldn't have to either."

Holy shit. She did it. Calista stood up to Lori. I try to keep my mouth from falling open.

Of course, she did that and then came to find me, only I wasn't here.

That thought immediately clips the wings of my exuberance. Hell, I'm surprised she even came looking for me after what I said.

Zinn jerks her chin at my phone. "Are you calling the police?"

I look down at the phone in my hand, another idea slowly bubbling to the surface of my mind. For Calista, there just aren't that many places for her to go, people that she trusts. And if she was willing to rebel that far against her mother . . .

"No," I say. "Not yet. I need to check something first."

It takes me a few seconds of scrolling to find the text conversation from last week, just a few messages back and forth with meet-up times and details.

```
I'm not going to ask if she's with you. But
have you heard from her? Is she okay?
```

The typing dots appear almost immediately.

Thank God.

```
Beth: She's here. She's fine. Sad, crying a
lot, but not hurt. Physically.
```

That last bit tears through me. Her pain, that's on me.

```
Beth: You should come.
```

I look up at Lori. "She's fine. Calista's safe."

Lori lurches toward me. But Bitsy barks at the sudden movement, and she backs off. "Where? Where is she?"

"If she wanted you to know, if she wanted either of us to know, she would have told us," I say, tucking my phone back in my pocket.

"You can't do this. She doesn't belong to you," Lori says, frustration pulling her mouth tight, forcing new lines into existence.

For a second, I feel a flash of genuine pity. It has really never occurred to Lori that it might end this way. "I think," I say, "the issue here is more that she doesn't belong to anyone. Not like that. And she's finally, thank God, figured that out."

"I'll just call the police myself," she says, as if that will solve everything. "I'll tell them she's using again. They'll find her."

Calista's an adult who left of her own volition, so I doubt it. But I'm not sure that point will register with Lori, so I go with the one that will. "And who will hire Calista then?"

Lori's face seems to collapse in on itself. Then she turns without another word and marches out the door, where Wade's Cadillac is waiting at the curb.

Taking a deep breath, Zinnia starts to follow her.

"Zinn?"

She pauses.

"You have a phone?"

She pulls it from the pocket of her pajama pants.

I take it and program my number in.

"If you need anything, I'm here, okay? If it gets to be too much at home, you call me. I will help you." Her sister is gone and unable to step in because I couldn't step up, but I won't make that mistake again in her absence.

Zinn takes her phone back when I hold it out. "Okay." She hesitates. "Are you going to bring Calista back home?"

"I . . . don't know. I don't think so."

"Good," she says with a decisive nod. "She deserves to be free."

"So do you," I say with a lump in my throat. Calista should have had someone looking out for her back then, when she was Zinn's age.

She grins at me, her shorn hair sticking up all over the place like feathers on a baby bird. "I'm working on it."

Then she turns and runs after her mother.

"Whew," Antonio says, slumping behind his desk. "I don't mean to criticize, but she's a friend of yours or—"

"No, Lori is awful. No question. Thank you for not letting her up." I watch Wade's Cadillac pull away, with Zinn waving in the window until Lori yanks her hand down. Definitely going to have to do something about that.

"Sure thing, man. Oh, hey, you have a package down here. Came in on Saturday, I think. You want it now?" He doesn't wait to hear my answer before unlocking the office door behind him and stepping inside. He reappears a few moments later with a slim, rectangular box. "Here." He holds it up.

I frown. My name is on the address label, but I don't remember ordering anything . . .

Then it clicks. The new laptop for Calista. To replace her old cracked one, one that she might not have if she left that quickly on Friday. I ordered it last Saturday, but it was out of stock at the time.

And it feels in that second like maybe this is a nudge, a push in the right direction. If nothing else, I can help her with this one small thing. And that's more than I've done before.

"One second," I say to Antonio. Then I pull my phone out and type another message.

Are you sure? I ask Beth.

Because I don't deserve Calista, is what I mean. Because I really messed up.

`Beth: No, not sure. But that's kind of the point, isn't it? There's a chance.`

A chance I have to take, but there's something I need to do first.

My father's current assistant—Madisyn, according to the nameplate on her desk—shows me into my dad's downtown office right away with a perfect, bleached smile. She's maybe twenty-two. Maybe.

"Eric." As soon as I walk in, Rawley closes the folder on his desk with a showy gesture. "I wasn't expecting you today, was I?" The smugness in his tone tells me he hasn't heard about Calista missing her wardrobe fitting yet.

I swallow the smartass reply that, thanks to years of practice, leaps to my tongue. *I'm pretty sure you haven't expected much of me, Dad, ever.* "No."

"I was sorry to hear about you and Katherine," he says, his gaze drawn momentarily to the square box under my arm.

Oh, I bet you were. I grit my teeth and nod in a manner that I hope passes as gratitude. I'm not here to start a fight. I'm here to end one.

"You should know better than to mess around with the talent you hired," he adds. "It's too public, too sloppy. Not to mention desperate." He laughs.

My hands tighten into fists. Calista is not just "the talent." And it wasn't like that. Isn't like that. But I know better than to argue those points with him.

"Have a seat." He gestures to the chairs in front of his massive desk.

"I'll stand."

He sighs as though I'm being overly dramatic. He and Lori really are a pair. "Suit yourself. What can I do for you?"

"D&G Incorporated," I say, enunciating each syllable carefully. I expect him to look shocked or bluster about not knowing what I'm talking about.

But he doesn't.

He rocks back in his chair, a smug smile playing on his mouth, and I feel sick. "Figured that out, did you?"

"It's yours?"

Rawley makes a dismissive noise. "You're smarter than that. I don't need to steal from my competitors to make them falter."

"But you knew. You knew what the accountant was doing," I say, trying to keep my temper under control.

"I knew what he was doing when I fired him from RSP," Rawley says, picking up a pen.

"But you didn't report him." Nor did he warn his only son.

"Sometimes it's useful to have someone who owes you a favor." He lifts a shoulder in a shrug.

"A favor," I repeat. I can feel my blood pressure rising, like the blood is boiling in my veins, giving off steam.

"Listen to me, Eric." He sits forward in his chair, the leather squeaking beneath his weight. "You were so bound and determined to shove what you were doing in my face, to spite me, I figured it might be useful for you to learn a tough lesson or two."

"So you told Sam to steal from me."

"Oh, no. I just . . . let nature take its course." He waves his hand, pen still grasped between his fingers, like he's casting a spell.

I want to say it doesn't surprise me, that I would have expected nothing less from Rawley, but I can't. This is a new low, even for him.

"Come on, son. You can't be angry. You should have checked his references." He points his pen at me.

"You're right," I say.

His eyebrows go up.

"But you're going to use that favor he owes you and get him to put all of that money back."

"Eric."

"Or I'm going to report you *both*. To the police, to the Producers Guild. To whoever will listen."

He scoffs. "They won't believe—"

"It doesn't matter. The scandal of the accusation, especially from your own son, will be enough." I smile tightly at him. "Think of all the time and money you wasted hiding my sins. Do you really want yours going public?"

My father is looking at me as if he's seeing me for the first time.

"What do you want?" he asks after a moment. The consummate businessman and negotiator. He's not going to whine about hurt feelings or injustice. He'd better not.

"The money back where it belongs," I say.

"Done."

"And if Calista comes back, you're going to keep the deal that you offered her, if she wants it."

His forehead furrows. "If Calista comes back . . . where—?"

I ignore him. "You know one of the reasons Katie and I didn't work out is because she wanted me to stop fighting with you. She was convinced that it didn't have to be a war between us. She wanted me to smooth things over."

Rawley smirks. "She is a smart girl. Better than you deserve. Better than that Beckett girl and—"

"Stop," I say, my voice quiet, deadly. "She was right, just not the way she thought. It's not a war, because it takes two sides to battle. And I'm done."

"We'll see how long that—"

"You don't talk to me, you don't come to my sets, you don't bother the people who are working for me. Understood?"

"Eric, I think you're—"

"Is that understood?"

He makes an exasperated noise. "Fine, fine."

"If I hear about you interfering in my business, or with the people I care about, ever again, I'm going live with every nasty detail I can think of and maybe even some made-up ones that would make Joan Crawford and her wire hangers look like Mary fucking Poppins. You get me?"

His face is flushed, ruddy with anger and surprise, but he gives a curt nod in acknowledgment.

I pull the RSP hat from the box and drop it on his desk. "You don't own my company, and you don't own me." I step back and turn for the door.

"I didn't think you had it in you to play dirty," he says as I reach the threshold, and I can't tell if it's admiration or censure in his tone. Either way, it doesn't matter.

"Like you're always saying, Dad, I am your son," I say. Then I walk out.

33 CALISTA

Beth was right. Walking all the way to the union cafeteria for food, through another foot and a half of new snow—thank you, lake effect—feels like more effort than a soggy grilled cheese and French fries are worth.

But it's Wednesday, and even with Beth's ramen supply and her checking on me once a day, I've run out of food.

So, Arctic adventure it is. At least my boots are still here, and Beth loaned me a coat.

I'm slogging my way back to Ryland with a grease-stained paper bag in one hand and an application for a food-services job in the other. I don't know what I'm going to do at the end of the semester, but it's ridiculous to pretend that it's going to sort itself out while I hide in my dorm room.

What I really want is to have the last week back, to reset and go into it knowing what I wanted and . . .

Within sight of the front door, I freeze. Someone is waiting outside, at the top of the steps. Dark curls tousled in the wind, shoulders hunched, in a familiar wool coat.

Eric.

I blink, trying to convince myself that this isn't me simply seeing what I want to see. A vision brought to life by desperation and exhaustion.

I approach cautiously, stopping at the bottom of the steps.

When he sees me, he gives an awkward laugh, his breath puffing out in clouds. "It's really fucking cold here. Worse than last time, even."

I don't move.

He pulls his hands from his pockets and holds them up halfway, a skinny box tucked under one arm. "I'm not here to try to control you, to make you come back."

I flinch.

"I just . . . I heard about what you said to Lori. I wanted to make sure you're okay." He looks nervous, uncertain.

"I . . ." I don't know what to say; there are too many words lodged in my throat.

"That was so brave," he says, swallowing hard. "Braver than I was, in just trying to piss off my dad. And I . . . I'm sorry for everything that I said. That I wasn't there to help you, to back you. I should have been. Not that you needed it."

"I saw Zinn," he adds. "She's okay." His mouth twitches with a smile. "Cut off all of her hair to keep your mother from sending her on auditions. I gave her my number and told her to call me if she needs anything."

"Thank you," I manage, forcing the words from a throat that feels painfully swollen with emotion.

"And I wanted to bring you this." He pulls the box out from under his arm. "It's a laptop . . . to replace your old one. I thought it would help for school."

I stay where I am. So he sets it carefully on the landing, in the barely shoveled pathway, and backs up a step, as if I'm a wild animal that will only approach cautiously, fearing capture. And maybe that's not far from the truth.

"I put the trailer for *Fly Girl* on there, too," he says quietly. "I've been working on what we shot. Not to talk you into coming back, but just so you can see how good you are. That you're going to be fine, no matter what you do." The depth of sincerity in his voice, backed with passion, makes tears spring to my eyes. No one has ever said that to me.

"You are enough," he says fiercely. "You need to know that, and I know I can't convince you of—"

"Why not?"

He closes his mouth. Then asks carefully, "Why not what?"

"Why aren't you here to convince me? Why aren't you here to talk me into coming home?" My voice breaks, and I wipe my face with the back of my hand. *With you. Why don't you want me with you?*

His expression softens then in understanding, and he shakes his head, his eyes visibly damp. "Because, fuck, Callie, I want you to be happy, wherever that is, whatever that looks like. With me or without—"

I fly up the stairs and throw my arms around him, colliding with him so hard it knocks him back a step.

But then his arms are tight around me, his cold nose pressed against my neck. I shiver both from the contact and from *him*, being here. With me. "Now who's cold?" I murmur against him.

"Still you," he says. "But I admit my blood may be taking on a slight chill."

I raise myself up on my toes to fit against him even tighter. I'm not letting go. "I don't know how this is going to work," I whisper, my tears dripping off my chin onto the collar of his coat. "I'm a disaster. I don't have any money. My mom is not going to give up easily." I pause. "I do have almost one-eighth of a college degree."

Eric laughs, and the motion brings his lips against the sensitive skin behind my ear. I squirm closer to him, sliding my hands into his coat. "It's okay," he says, his voice thick with emotion. "There are rumors that I'm kind of a disaster, too. In case you haven't heard."

"So, how—"

"I have absolutely no idea. But together, Callie. We'll figure it out together, yeah?"

"Yeah." I nod against his shoulder.

He leans back slightly to smile at me and tucks a strand of hair behind my ear. “Besides, two disasters are better than one.”

He kisses me then, his mouth warm on mine, his tongue light and teasing against my upper lip.

My hands curl tightly on his shirt. “I don’t think that’s how that saying goes,” I say breathlessly, when he pulls away. How quickly can I get us both inside and into my room? I need to feel his skin against mine, to *know* that we’re here and together.

Eric shrugs easily, with that casual confidence that made me fall in love with him all those years ago in that audition room. “Then we’ll make a new one.”

Sounds perfect to me.

EPILOGUE

CALISTA

TWO YEARS LATER

"I feel ridiculous," Eric mutters, tugging at the open collar of his shirt.

"Is it the formalwear that's not really formalwear or the not-formalwear on the beach?" I ask, trying not to laugh.

"Both?" he asks, making a face. "All of the above?" He rolls his shoulders in his tuxedo jacket, as if he's trying to get comfortable with little success.

"If it helps, you may feel ridiculous, but you look amazing," I say softly.

And he does. Beach wedding is a weird contradiction of terms and situation, but he's got it nailed.

His dark curls are loose, not slicked back, lifting and moving in the breeze off the ocean, and yeah, he's wearing a tux, but the shirt is open at the neck—no tie or vest—just the black jacket and pants, which are rolled up at the ankle. Because he's barefoot in the sand.

Like me.

His gaze darkens as he looks at me. "No, that's you. Amazing."

I grin at him. The pale pink floaty number is not my normal style, but it matches perfectly with the bride's bouquet. And, as it happens, the colors of the sunset streaking the Maui sky.

He steps closer, sliding his hand around my waist. "I mean, it's not that little gold shirt," he murmurs in my ear, sending a delicious wave of goosebumps over my skin.

It takes me a second to figure out what he's talking about.

I shove his shoulder lightly. "That was a dress," I say.

"If you say so." He smirks. "I liked it either way. I owe it a lot."

I roll my eyes, but he has a point. If I hadn't dressed to catch his attention at that party all those years ago, none of the events of that night would have happened. And to be fair, few of those things were good at the time, but the results now are hard to argue with. One of which we are here to witness today.

I twist around, and Eric pulls me closer, wrapping his arms around me from behind as we watch Amanda and Chase at the edge of the water with a local justice of the peace.

He, like Eric, is in a tux deformalized for the setting, and Amanda is wearing a simple white gown, her arms and shoulders bare, and her hair pulled up in dark-red ringlets. It's like she's declaring to the world that she has nothing to hide.

The look on Chase's face when she appeared at the edge of the beach made me cry.

We are serving dual purposes of witnesses and best man and maid of honor for this ceremony, which is technically an elopement, before the "official" family and publicity-heavy event next month. Her sisters will be her maid of honor and bridesmaid for the church deal.

But here, it's just the four of us. And that sense of family I used to feel about the three of us—Chase, Eric and me, during our *Starlight* years—hasn't changed, only expanded to include Amanda.

"So I guess you're going to need a new roommate, huh?" Eric asks, his mouth warm against my neck.

Amanda and I, both of us getting used to living on our own for different reasons, were a logical match when I moved back to California to work and take classes. She was quiet at first, and my poor friend-making skills, demonstrated in all their awkward glory, didn't help. But having Chase around a lot as a bridge helped. And watching her with Chase, God, the two of them light up the room and each other whenever they are together. She makes him so happy,

I was predisposed to like her. And both of us know what it's like to have a past that people are interested in when we are both more focused on the present.

So despite our differences, the roommate thing just worked. Or it did until my roommate went and got married.

I resist the urge to curl my arm up and around Eric's neck, to tangle my fingers in his hair. "Maybe," I say, doing my best to keep a straight face. "I mean, Zinn *is* dying to get out of the apartment with Mom and Wade." My mother still goes through phases where she doesn't speak to me, usually after she fails to sign someone else to the management agency she founded after I fired her for the last time. It's small and stays afloat mainly, I think, due to cash infusions from Wade—who's started, of all things, working as an Uber driver.

Eric doesn't react with a grumpy noise or a huff of mock exasperation at my having deliberately missed his point.

Instead, he finds my hand, linking his fingers through mine. "What if we found somewhere big enough for all of us? Zinn, if she needs a place to get away, and you and me." He sounds serious, with just the faintest hint of vulnerability in the question. Enough that I regret teasing him.

The decision for Eric and I not to live together was mostly mine. I didn't want the pressure of trying to figure out work, money and what exactly we were to each other to make our relationship collapse in on itself before we even got started. And I was scared.

"I think everything is calm enough now . . . if you want to," he adds.

He's right. Eric has six successful web series to his name now—including *Fly Girl*, which we finished after I formally turned down Rawley's offer and moved back at the end of the semester. *Fly Girl* won three Streamy awards, including Best Directing, and earned a Creative Arts Emmy nomination. Eric is in demand as a director and works regularly for a variety of television shows—except his father's, which pisses Rawley off to no end. And Stage Seven—Eric renamed his production company after where we started and *Starlight* was filmed, breaking that final connection with his father's name—is gearing up for its first feature film, another book I found and loved.

Eric and I have acted together a few times on the web shows—people will always, it seems, love seeing Skye and Byron Danvers in some way—and I help on the producer side sometimes, too, between acting jobs. I enjoy acting again now that I'm doing it because *I* want to. I probably will always take on passion projects, roles I can't pass up. But I'm just a few credits short of my accounting degree, and once I'm finished, I'll be able to do more as a producer at Stage Seven, which I'm looking forward to. I like being behind the cameras more than in front of them these days. Hollywood needs beautiful people, but it needs people who know how to read a balance sheet almost as much.

I still feel that pulse of fear at the idea of being dependent on someone I love, as I'm sure it probably still makes him nervous to commit to someone who could hurt him. With his abandonment issues and my fear of surrendering control again, we could circle each other endlessly.

We are, in fact, two disasters, but we're working on it. Taking it slow in the beginning only seemed smart, but that was then.

This is now.

"I think we're up," Eric says, stepping from behind me to start toward the water's edge where Amanda and Chase are waving us forward.

But I hear the stiffness in his tone, and I know what it took for him to make that offer and mean it. The accelerated thumping of my heart is still a little bit of fear—it probably always will be—but it's also love and a crazy level of excitement. To wake up with him every morning. To see his face as the last one before I fall asleep.

I tighten my grip on his hand and dig my feet in the sand to hold my place. "Yes," I say.

He pauses, glancing over his shoulder at me as if unsure he heard me correctly. "Yeah?"

"Yes, to everything. To all of it." The rush of giddiness triggers a grin wide enough to hurt my cheeks.

He steps back to me, framing my face with his hands. "I love you," he says, his voice rough with emotion.

I will never get tired of hearing him say that. "I love you, too."

He bends his head to kiss me, and I push up on my tiptoes to meet him, wrapping my arms around his neck.

"Did she say yes to the new place?" Chase calls, and Amanda grins. Of course they're both in on it.

"Aren't you kind of in the middle of something?" I ask, laughing.

"Well?" Amanda asks, her cheeks flushed with happiness.

I nod. With a smile, Eric presses a kiss to my forehead. His hand slides into mine, locking our fingers together in a firm grip. We're together now, finally, and that's not going to change. It took us the better part of a decade to work it out is all.

ACKNOWLEDGMENTS

This book almost didn't exist. Before we sold *738 Days*, I'd convinced myself that I had one good romance idea. And *738 Days* was it. (That sounds ridiculous now, given how many ideas are currently swirling around in my head, but that's what I thought at the time.) It was, quite simply, that lethal combination of self-doubt and the fear that comes with venturing into something new. And yet . . . I was intrigued with Eric and Calista the second they showed up on the page in Chase's story, and I couldn't stop myself from wondering about them.

All of this is to say, I'm so incredibly grateful to Suzie Townsend and Whitney Ross (my agent and editor, respectively), who saw things much more clearly. You guys, I *loved* writing this book. LOVED it. I'm here to tell you that that is not always the case, but it was this time. And I almost missed out on the experience because of . . . me. I'm sure there's a lesson in there somewhere about confidence and writing and sallying forth into unknown territory, but I'm still working that part out. In any case . . . THANK YOU so much to Suzie and Whitney!

Huge thanks as ever to Sara Stricker, Kathleen Ortiz, Mia Roman, and everyone at New Leaf Literary & Media. Thank you also to Amy Stapp, Ksenia Winnicki, Laura Etzkorn, and everyone at Forge Books who believed in *738 Days* and *Starlight Nights*. That means so much to me!

I cast all of my books in my head. It just makes it easier for me to picture what's happening in the story. And when I first started work on *Starlight Nights,* I was having a terrible time finding someone to "play" Eric. That combination of arrogance and vulnerability is not an easy thing to pull off without looking like a complete jerk. So I owe Melissa Landers big time. She pushed me into watching the exact show I needed to find an actor who could be my mental version of Eric.

Sophie Jordan, my friend and fellow author (shout-out to alphabetical seating arrangements for signings that led us to each other!), who talked to *everyone* about *738 Days*. I am so incredibly grateful!

Linnea Sinclair, my critique partner and mentor, who reads a draft of every book (proposals, too), patiently responds to all my email freakouts, and helped me figure out my Eric/Dr. Katie issues.

My parents, Stephen and Judy Barnes, who listen weekly to my writing woes and triumphs. Susan Barnes, my sister—and fellow romance novel addict—for being my perpetual sounding board on publishing, life, and which romances we need to read next.

And to you. I love writing romance. And I so appreciate you giving me a chance by picking up this book. Thank you!